RACHEL RYAN'S RESOLUTIONS

Laura Starkey

First published in Great Britain in 2021 by

 embla books

Bonnier Books UK Limited
4th Floor, Victoria House, Bloomsbury Square, London, WC1B 4DA
Owned by Bonnier Books
Sveavägen 56, Stockholm, Sweden

Copyright © Laura Starkey, 2021

All rights reserved.
No part of this publication may be reproduced, stored or transmitted
in any form or by any means, electronic, mechanical, photocopying or
otherwise, without the prior written permission of the publisher.

The right of Laura Starkey to be identified as Author of this work
has been asserted by them in accordance with the
Copyright, Designs and Patents Act 1988

This is a work of fiction. Names, places, events and incidents are either
the products of the author's imagination or used fictitiously. Any
resemblance to actual persons, living or dead, is purely coincidental.

A CIP catalogue record for this book is available from the British Library.

ISBN: 9781471415494

This book is typeset using Atomik ePublisher

Embla Books is an imprint of Bonnier Books UK
www.bonnierbooks.co.uk

RACHEL RYAN'S RESOLUTIONS

To Dan,
Whose faith, encouragement and excellent tea making made all the difference in the writing of this book.

She was filled with a strange, wild, unfamiliar happiness, and knew that this was love. Twice in her life she had mistaken something else for it; it was like seeing somebody in the street who you think is a friend, you whistle and wave and run after him, and he is not only not the friend, but not even very like him. A few minutes later the real friend appears in view, and then you can't imagine how you ever mistook that other person for him.
—Nancy Mitford, *The Pursuit of Love*

University of York

2009

The thorny branches of the bush she was wedged into scratched at Rachel's bare arms. As her oversized sunglasses slid down her clammy nose, she offered up a silent prayer that no one was about to pass by.

Like a character from one of the clichéd cop dramas her mum was obsessed with, Rachel was hiding in a hedge in broad daylight – transfixed by the sight of two people deep in conversation, sitting on a patch of yellowed scrubby grass a few metres away.

It was late July and, although only around ten o'clock in the morning, the day was already warm in the oppressive way that promises an evening downpour. The moisture now pooling at the small of Rachel's back and beneath her armpits, however, was less a consequence of the muggy atmosphere and more a result of her rapidly rising heart rate.

She was *willing* this not to be real. Hoping it might not be true.

It wasn't working.

They were too close together, too intimate. His hand was

resting in hers and their inclined bodies formed a graceful arc, lit from behind by bright sunshine.

He was wearing yesterday's clothes.

Rachel tasted the acrid flavour of impending vomit and wondered if she was going to be sick. *Not here, not now.*

Her stomach contracted, muscle and flesh tightening, curling inwards. *Just breathe*, she told herself.

She scrunched her eyes shut and gulped down lungfuls of air until the twisting sensation in her gut let up a little.

Always a sucker for punishment, Rachel made herself look at them again. He was kissing her now – the other woman.

Even from a distance Rachel could tell this was one of Jack Harper's special signature kisses: languid but delicious, rich with intent. She hated him for this, but for a split second felt her standard longing for him too.

She knew she would never forgive him, and yet, as his arms snaked around someone else's waist, she couldn't help admiring him. His overlong chestnut-brown hair shone in the sunlight, casting an ironic halo of copper-coloured light around his head. He opened his green-gold eyes as the kissing stopped, and his smile – a wide, lazy grin for this skinny girl with a treacle-dark mane – was a baseball bat to Rachel's stomach.

Misery ballooned in her ribcage. Her sadness felt massive – so big it might push vital organs out of place. A sensible voice from somewhere deep inside Rachel insisted that, awful as this was, it still didn't rank as the worst thing that had ever happened to her. But still, how could Jack be doing this? Today of all days? It was crushing.

And his doing it *here* – out in the open, on the lane she so regularly walked down . . . It was as if the location he'd picked sought to minimise his offence. The thoughtlessness of it implied that, to Jack, hooking up with someone other than Rachel was no big deal. There was cruelty in this, she realised, whether he'd intended it or not: it heaped humiliation on top of hurt, spoke of unequal affections. It made her feel stupid for letting herself care so much.

That word, *stupid*, clanged in her head. She should have seen this coming. Jack's Lord Byron Lite act, as she'd once called it, had seen him motor through girlfriends faster than she sped down their reading list of set texts. But her resolve to keep him at arm's length despite his obvious charms had crumbled when he'd told her she wasn't like anyone else, that she was different – that he'd fallen in love with her.

She had believed him.

Hot tears filled Rachel's eyes and she forced her thoughts back to the present, shoving down the hysterical laugh that was bubbling up her throat. This was a *ridiculous* situation.

She needed to get home. She couldn't hide in a hedge forever . . . Not even for another ten minutes, she realised, checking her watch.

Rachel's parents would be arriving soon and they were notorious for being early, particularly on special occasions. And for reasons that only a handful of people knew, including the cheating snake now casually fondling his latest conquest, today was a *very* special occasion.

She didn't want to crash back through her front gate flustered, sweaty and feeling like she'd been freshly disembowelled, only to find them waiting on the doorstep in their Sunday best. She needed to greet them happy, serene and smiling, ready to put the kettle on. The carton of milk she'd popped out to buy weighed heavy in her right hand.

Like the bile that still threatened at the back of her throat, Rachel swallowed her mess of feelings. Now, she decided, was *not* the time to throw them up. If she wasn't going to confront Jack, though, she somehow had to sneak past him and his new friend.

She wondered how long they were going to sit there, the bastards, alternately snogging and making moon eyes at one another. Then the bleak truth occurred to her: Jack and this girl were *utterly* wrapped up in the moment, and the lane was fairly wide... Rachel could probably walk by without them even noticing. The realisation stung, almost as painfully as everything else.

She took a deep breath, extracted herself from her improvised hiding place and walked – quickly, but not so fast that she'd make herself conspicuous – towards the main road.

Rachel had less than half an hour to get home, compose herself and start getting ready for the ceremony.

It was graduation day and her mum and dad were coming to watch her collect her First. They were proud of her. They wanted to celebrate.

London
2019

January 2019

New Year's resolutions

1. Consider exercise an act with actual benefits – both mental and physical – not merely grim punishment for pizzas consumed. Have a proper go at yoga.
2. Also re-download Couch to 5K running app and actually do the programme.
3. Apply for promotion at work at first chance. Move to bigger account and try to get pay rise. Avoid, if possible, further projects concerning dog biscuits, disinfectant, high-quality printer ink cartridges, 'miracle' grass seed, organic vegetables, etc.
4. DO NOT agree to further dates with Laurence. Remember: it's no use having a boyfriend who is good on paper if you do not actually fancy him.
5. Try to remember Mum means well, even during phone calls where she implies I am doomed to

a lonely life of penury because I am thirty with no partner, hardly any savings and no mortgage.
6. HOWEVER, do not (!!!) speak to Mum when suffering PMT. Set phone alerts for likely spells based on period tracker intel.
7. Try to address 'hardly any savings' situation. (If promoted, set aside extra earnings for future house deposit instead of spaffing it all on ASOS.)
8. Try to eat my five-a-day. (Remember horrid rule that potatoes do not count.)
9. Start using proper night cream with retinol.

1

Rachel sat on the cold, hard bus shelter bench awaiting the number 19 from Islington to Finsbury Park. Despite the best efforts of the manspreader next to her, both of her arsecheeks were still fully on the seat she'd claimed before the stop got busy. There was no way she wanted to stand outside; it was only just past six o'clock but already pitch-dark, and the air was a whirl of freezing drizzle. She watched her breath misting and mingling with it, enjoying her small victory.

Four minutes for the bus, according to the electronic display at the top of the shelter. Wincing involuntarily, she wondered if Jessica Williams would be on it this evening.

Rachel pulled her soft navy hat further towards her chilly ears, though her mass of dark-red waves prevented it from making effective contact. It was the second week in January and, as a worthy-looking man in Lycra leggings and fluorescent trainers jogged by, she reflected that her 'New Year, New Me' plans were off to a very slow start.

Unless you counted several panicked sprints towards trains and buses, she had done no exercise whatsoever. She had swerved several phone calls from her mother, eaten a lot of beige food and had yet to buy the retinol cream she was supposed to be applying each night.

Nevertheless, Rachel reasoned, she still had eleven and

a half months in which to keep the promises she'd made to herself. It was important not to be too self-flagellating in January, what with it being a month of general gloom and destitution.

She felt a buzzing from somewhere deep inside the large bucket-shaped handbag that was sitting on her lap. Her fingernails dug into her palms.

Please don't let this be Laurence calling to ask if I fancy an after-work drink. His office was only around the corner from hers, and he kept insisting that they should talk again about their break-up.

Rachel fished for her phone, dodging multiple lipsticks, crumpled receipts and the tangled wire of her headphones. There was no way she was shelling out for AirPods until it finally frayed right through.

Greg calling, the display said, when she finally extracted her phone.

What the hell could he want? She'd only left work ten minutes ago. Surely he had nothing to say that couldn't wait until the morning?

He really had *no* filtering system, Rachel thought: in Greg World, everything was urgent.

She took a breath and tapped the green button, then said, 'Hi.'

'Ray! I got you! EXCELLENT,' Greg gushed, his familiar Australian burr unnecessarily loud, like always.

Rachel couldn't imagine how many times she had politely asked Greg not to refer to her as Ray. It had never made any difference, and now – four years into their professional relationship – she had finally stopped bothering.

'I'm just looking at this copy about the groceries,' he said. 'It's a little bit . . . blah. You know. Not very sexy.'

'Not very . . . *sexy?*'

Rachel was incredulous, but realised she shouldn't be surprised by this assessment. As a copywriter at a digital marketing agency, she'd become used to defending her choice of words – often in the face of criticism from people who didn't know the difference between *your* and *you're*.

'No,' Greg ploughed on. 'This copy does not make me go, YEAH, I have just GOT TO HAVE some cauliflower tonight, I can't live without it, I NEED IT IN MY LIFE.'

Shortly before Christmas, Rachel and Greg had begun work on a suite of new marketing materials for a grocery box company – one of those firms that sold misshapen but 100% organic fruits and vegetables, delivered to your door for three times the price of the ones you could buy at your local Tesco.

As the agency's star client-services man, Greg was hard-working, ambitious and brilliant at schmoozing the right people. His understanding of what copy about cauliflowers could reasonably be expected to communicate, however, seemed typically lacking in subtlety.

'Greg . . . it's a brassica,' Rachel said, groping for a response that felt appropriate. 'Cauliflower is a pretty bog-standard vegetable. It's not a dark, exotic new perfume . . . It's not a lovers' weekend in Paris. I mean, it's not even *kale*. I was kind of going for the "like your mum used to make" angle. Cauliflower is what British people remember having with Sunday lunch when they were kids – or, if they're really unlucky, with their school dinners.'

She made a face then, remembering the bland, overboiled florets that dissolved on contact with her Staffordshire primary school's plastic knives and forks.

'SEE?' Greg cried, exultant. 'THAT'S the kind of writing I know you can do. *Dark! Exotic! Lovers!* THOSE are the kinds of words that are going to inspire people—'

He was now yelling so exuberantly down the phone that the people crammed into the bus shelter could hear his every word.

'Greg,' Rachel said, interrupting his raptures, 'my point is that I'm writing about groceries. The brief from the client was to make the copy informative, engaging and on-brand. They want it to resonate with people, but I'm pretty sure they're not expecting *Fifty Shades of Grey*. This content is about explaining the nutritional benefits of the produce and providing recipe inspiration. We don't need to . . . turn anyone on.'

There was a muffled titter from somewhere to Rachel's left.

Greg blathered on at volume eleven, bright and undeterred.

'Ray, all I'm saying is I think we should look at it again before presenting it to the client. Okay? Maybe SEX IT UP just a little?'

A middle-aged woman on Rachel's right snorted as Greg began to croon Rod Stewart's 'Da Ya Think I'm Sexy?' down the phone.

Ugh, he was a nightmare.

Rachel looked at the bus information board again. The number 19 was still a minute away.

'Fine, *fine*. We can talk about it first thing,' she said, desperate to shut him up.

'Great. Meet me at Java Jo's at nine-ish. We'll get coffee.'

Despite Greg's unparalleled ability to irritate Rachel – and in part thanks to his obliviousness to this talent – she knew they made a good team. He managed to muster enthusiasm for every project they tackled, and it was often infectious – helpful when, as now, they were working with less-than-inspiring subject matter. Greg's natural ebullience assured his popularity with both clients and colleagues, and somehow – despite the regular need for her to squash his more outlandish ideas – he and Rachel had become friends.

As several of her fellow travellers suppressed residual smirks, Rachel poked her head beyond the side of the bus shelter and peered down the road. The number 19 was approaching.

She got to her feet, gathered her handbag and laptop case, and glanced up at the bus as it slid into position beside the shelter.

Jessica *was* there, she saw, for the fourth time this week – though it was only now, as her throat tightened and she felt blood pounding in her ears, that Rachel realised she'd been counting.

Literally larger than life, a phenomenally gorgeous, perfectly lit Jessica – flawlessly filtered and Photoshopped – was staring down at Rachel from the side of the double-decker.

A goddess in a white silk camisole, Jessica wore a half-smile on her plush, pillowy lips – open just wide enough to show off her perfectly even, dazzlingly white teeth. One of her eyebrows was slightly raised, a suggestive forward-slash punctuating the smooth golden skin of her forehead.

Rachel's eyes swept down the image, taking in the long dark hair that reached almost to Jessica's tiny waist, and her ample – possibly augmented – bosom.

In Jessica's French-manicured hand was a bottle, half-full of lurid orange liquid. Beneath her image sat the caption *ANGELJUICE: the detox drink for heavenly bodies*. For a moment Rachel wondered what she was more offended by: the mere sight of Jessica or the fact that she was shilling for a weight-loss company. She rapidly decided it was the latter.

Although standing exposed to the rain – now falling faster in fat, icy drops – Rachel was suddenly sweating. She loosened the scarf around her neck and undid the top button of her coat.

Seconds after she'd scrambled on, the bus pulled away from the stop. Rachel lurched towards a vacant seat and collapsed into it, then rummaged for her phone again. She opened WhatsApp and typed a message to Anna.

Rachel: *Are you and Will still pretending to do Dry January? Because I have a powerful urge to buy wine.*

Seconds later, a message came back:

Anna: *Nah. We cracked last night and had a gin.*

He's coming to ours for dinner btw and I told him to bring Tom too. I'll get them to bring some booze since we're feeding them . . . AGAIN.

Rachel smiled and shoved the phone back in her bag.

This, at least, was something to look forward to: an evening with three of her favourite people, featuring Anna's excellent cooking.

Plus, if she was lucky, there'd be intelligent conversation during which she would not be required to talk dirty about vegetables – or think any further about Jessica and her awful ad campaign.

2

Rachel arrived back at the flat to find Anna in the kitchen making lentil bolognese. There was some sort of garlic flatbread on the worktop, glistening with olive oil and sprinkled with fresh flat-leaf parsley. As the rich aroma of comfort food filled her nostrils, Rachel wondered if she'd ever loved her best friend more than she did right now.

She dumped her handbag and laptop by the back door that led to their little garden, draped her damp coat over a nearby radiator and slumped into one of the four chairs that sat around the battered old dining table. Anna put down her wooden spoon and wiped her hands on her jeans.

'You've seen them, then?' she said.

Rachel groaned in immediate understanding.

So much for banishing all thoughts of the bus ads – but feigning ignorance was useless with Anna, who knew her better than anyone.

'How did you know?'

'Your message. And then something about the way you sat down. Maybe it was the half-angry, half-despondent sigh.'

'I am *not* despondent!' Rachel insisted. 'Mortified on her behalf, more like. I mean, *Angeljuice* . . . A slimming drink for women who've been trained by society to hate themselves. It's beyond cynical. It's disgusting.'

'Er – didn't you try it a couple of years ago?' Anna said, her eyebrows hovering near her platinum-blonde hairline.

'Oh, fine, YES. For, like, two days or something. And that's how I *know* it's disgusting! Not to mention ineffective.'

Anna turned down the gas beneath the shallow, round Le Creuset pan in which she was simmering finely diced vegetables, healthy pulses and herbs. She put the large teal lid on it to keep the mixture warm, then flipped the switch on the kettle.

'Putting aside your totally valid feminist stance . . . are you okay?'

Anna let the question sit for a few moments, making two massive mugs of PG Tips and loading biscuits onto a plate. In lieu of wine, and in light of their virtuous dinner, caffeine and sugar seemed appropriate. Silent, Rachel picked at the remnants of her fortnight-old gel manicure.

'Yeah, I'm okay,' she said finally, as Anna sat down opposite her. 'Of course I am. There's no reason why I *shouldn't* be. And tonight wasn't my first time seeing the posters, anyway . . . That was a few days ago.'

'What?! Why on earth didn't you tell me?'

Rachel opened her mouth to attempt an explanation, but nothing came out.

'Incidentally,' Anna went on into the void, 'not being able to find an excuse for feeling a bit shit doesn't mean the feeling is invalid – or that it doesn't exist. I haven't forgotten this is the woman you used to call Boyfriend Stealer Barbie. You once said there was nobody in the world who made you feel so inadequate – not even your mother.'

Rachel blanched at this, then said, 'Wow. That must have been before Mum perfected her "You won't be fertile forever!" routine.'

Anna laughed, but pursued her point. 'Honestly, I think I'd feel weird about it if I were you. What I don't understand is how she's suddenly started appearing in adverts. How is Jessica Williams a model? I thought she just sat around "influencing" all day, taking photos of her lunch, telling the world where she got her T-shirt from, filming herself applying lipstick . . . That sort of bobbins.'

Anna, who taught English at an 11–18 academy in Haringey, loathed social media in all its forms. She considered it a plague that was rotting the brains of the young, whereas Rachel – a casual user of the most popular platforms – had to stay abreast of digital trends for work.

'Dear, naive Anna,' Rachel replied, her mouth full of tea-soaked chocolate Hobnob. 'Let me explain. Influencers – the big ones, anyway – use their online profiles to get to a place where they can have careers *offline*. They build themselves up via the internet, but they don't want to be contained by it forever. This marketing campaign is part of a bid for real-world fame.'

Privately, and with the professional zone of her brain engaged, Rachel could see that Jessica was a good choice of ambassador for Angeljuice – a brand styling itself as concerned with 'wellness' but clearly more devoted to promoting the super-slim, sexy silhouette its products promised.

With almost a million YouTube subscribers and more than 750,000 Instagram followers, Jessica fit their bill perfectly: she was gorgeous, glossy and able to reach hundreds of thousands of women who wanted to look, dress and live like her.

In addition to the bus ads, Rachel knew Jessica's image was also adorning Tube posters and advertorial magazine spreads – one of which she'd discovered while idly flicking through this week's *Grazia*. She'd long known that Jessica had managed to make a career out of being beautiful, but until recently she'd managed to avoid her. Only in weak moments – occasionally, after one too many gin and tonics – had Rachel scrolled through Jessica's latest posts and indulged herself in feeling chubby and unglamorous.

While Jessica was thin, smooth and apparently ageless, Rachel was unfashionably curvy – complete with cellulitey thighs, a burgeoning collection of fine lines and (depending on the time of the month) a dot-to-dot of spots along her jawline. She was fully aware that regular confrontations with Jessica might test her commitment to feeling fine about herself, but she had no intention of admitting this out loud.

'So you think we'll be seeing more of her, then?' Anna asked. 'More posters, more modelling?'

'I expect so, unless this campaign bombs – which I'm sure it won't.'

'It's so strange. I mean, I guess you thought you'd never see her again.'

'I definitely *hoped* I wouldn't. Actually, I promised myself that if I did I'd cause a massive scene. You know: throw a pint of bitter over her like the wronged woman in an episode of *Coronation Street*.'

'Wow. That I would *love* to see,' Anna laughed. 'Bit

pointless throwing a drink at a picture, though, isn't it? And what about . . . him? Do you ever think about him?'

'Never,' Rachel said decisively enough to mask her relief that Anna hadn't mentioned his name. 'Not any more, and I don't intend to start again now. It's ancient history. I'm over it. And anyway, he was a shallow, heartless fuckwit.'

'Would he get the *Corrie* treatment if you happened to bump into him?' Anna asked, draining her mug of tea and getting up to stir the bolognese pan.

'God, I don't know,' Rachel replied. 'I hope I never find out.'

'While we're on the subject of ex-boyfriends,' Anna said as Rachel began loading the dishwasher with their tea things, 'your mum phoned the landline earlier. Said she's been trying to get hold of you with no joy. Also, she asked how you were getting on with Laurence.'

'Oh, *bollocks*. Sorry. I've been meaning to talk to her.'

'Mmm-hmm.' Anna nodded. 'I had to fudge it and say you two were fine, as far as I knew – but I hate lying, especially when I've not been warned I might have to. Why haven't you told her you and Laurence have split up? It's been, like, three weeks.'

'Ugh, I don't know,' Rachel mumbled, aware that she sounded like a sulky teenager. 'I just couldn't face it somehow. She's always so much happier when I have a boyfriend. She stops griping at me about the future and actually listens to what I say about life right now. Plus, whenever I break up with anyone she immediately assumes that I've either been dumped or made the wrong decision. The idea that I might choose to end a relationship in a calm and mature way because it genuinely isn't working . . . Well, that's completely beyond her. It's infuriating.'

Anna patted Rachel's shoulder as she collected four sets of cutlery from the drawer next to the oven, then began laying it out on the table.

'You need to tell her, though. You know that, yes? Kicking the conversation down the road won't make it any easier.'

'I'll talk to her,' Rachel said. 'I promise. Tomorrow, maybe.'

'Right,' Anna said, in a tone that strongly suggested a lecture was imminent.

Then, as if to offer Rachel a reprieve, the door buzzer sounded. She jumped and ran to answer it with uncharacteristic speed.

Will and Tom were clutching corner shop bags that clinked as they were carried through to the kitchen, then set down on the worktop.

'Wine, as promised,' Will said, swiping a cherry tomato from the salad bowl, then dropping a kiss on Anna's lips.

'Chianti, very nice,' she said as she unpacked the bags. 'Four bottles seems a bit much, though – it's a school night.'

Will shrugged. 'You implied there was a crisis.'

'I did *not*,' Anna hissed, scowling at him.

'Oh, marvellous,' Rachel moaned, throwing her hands up at Anna. 'I take it you've made these two aware that my former romantic nemesis has begun appearing on the side of London buses?'

'Sorry.' Anna grimaced. 'I didn't mean to. I was trying

to work out how widespread the ads were after I saw my first one last night. I asked Will if he'd spotted any, and then I sort of ended up explaining . . .'

'They're *everywhere*, aren't they?' Will said, awestruck. 'All over the Tube as well, did you know?'

Anna fixed him with a glare that suggested she wished he'd turn to stone, then handed him the bottle opener.

'You know where the glasses are.'

Anna and Will were thoroughly, solidly in love, and had been together for nearly four years. Rachel's mum had taken to reminding her, pretty much every time they spoke, that this was a 'significant length of time'. 'It surely means they'll want to live together soon,' she would say. 'And what will you do then?'

Rachel had discovered that 'Find somewhere else to live' was not the correct response to this question, though she was yet to establish precisely what other reaction her mother would deem acceptable.

Anna owned the flat – and its impressive collection of cast-iron cookware – thanks to an inheritance from her grandparents. Rachel was her lodger, so in the event that Anna decided to move Will in, it would be Rachel who'd have to go – though this wasn't a possibility Rachel chose to dwell on.

They'd been close since their first week at university and after graduating had lived together in one rented dive after another until, eventually, Anna had bought their two-bedroomed apartment. It was the ground floor of an old Victorian terrace in Stroud Green.

Theirs was a neat, tidy, tastefully renovated home, and Rachel loved it – but, if she allowed herself to think about moving out, it wasn't the thought of saying goodbye to the roll-top bath or stone kitchen countertops that bothered her. The idea of living alone, or with someone other than Anna, seemed strange and unnatural to Rachel after thirteen years spent beside her best friend. In fact, it was almost too outrageous a prospect to take seriously; like the plot of a bad-taste blockbuster movie, it surely couldn't happen in real life.

For all her mother's doom-laden warnings, Rachel adored Anna and Will as a couple. He was more than a foot taller than her, and yet they always looked to Rachel as if they'd been designed for one another. They fit together properly, in that Will was big and sturdy enough to handle Anna – pixie-like in appearance, but formidably clever and a powerhouse of personality.

To look at her, you'd never guess Anna could face down a classroom full of hormonal teenagers and convince them that poems actually mean things. Five foot nothing in bare feet, she wore her peroxide-pale hair in a 1960s-style crop. This framed a heart-shaped face with a pretty button nose, pink rosebud lips and bright-blue almond-shaped eyes.

Some bloke in a bar had called Anna 'Tinkerbell' once, and Rachel remembered she'd all but eviscerated him. Anna liked to think of herself as 'not small, but concentrated'. Those who knew her well considered this an apt description.

Wordlessly, Tom handed Rachel a wine glass and poured a large measure into it. Rachel had always thought him very different to Will, who – despite his good nature – could generally be expected to put his foot in his mouth.

Nevertheless, they were as close as she and Anna, and also lived together. Will and Tom had known each other since school, and Rachel imagined that Tom – the former state primary kid who'd won an academic scholarship – had probably been a steadying influence on his friend during their teenage years.

Tom wasn't unusually sedate or shy but he always seemed calm and composed in comparison with Will, whose gambolling cheerfulness – along with his broad body, thick beard and seemingly permanent smile – put Rachel in mind of a young, rugby-playing Father Christmas.

Like Will, Tom was tall, but he was leaner. With dirty-blonde hair and grey-blue eyes that were often obscured by Clark Kentish heavy-framed glasses, he looked intelligent and sort of artistic, though Rachel doubted this was deliberate.

She took a long drink, then sighed as the rich ruby liquid warmed her throat.

'Caning it because of the ads, Rach?' Will asked.

'*No*, I couldn't care less about the stupid ads,' Rachel snorted. 'They're propaganda of the patriarchy. However, I do have a meeting scheduled for 9 a.m. tomorrow during which I'll need to convince my colleague that we can't make cauliflowers "sexy".'

'In addition to that,' Anna said as she stirred the pan, 'she's scared to tell her mum she's split up with Laurence.'

Rachel considered refuting this accusation, then decided not to bother. 'Yes, that is also true,' she sighed.

'Surely your mum won't mourn the loss of Loz too deeply?' Tom asked, smiling mischievously at Rachel from his seat on the other side of the dining table.

'*Be nice*,' Rachel said, but grinned back in spite of herself. Will and Tom had frequently been unkind about Laurence behind his back, and Tom had taken pleasure in calling him Loz whenever they met – a nickname he utterly hated. Her friends were right, however: Laurence was terminally dull, and Rachel's attempts to find him interesting and attractive had ended in abject failure.

'Mum just takes it very personally whenever I break up with someone,' she continued. 'She seems to think that, while I remain alone and unmarried, my personal stock plummets with every year that goes by. So, as we begin another year with no big white dress or canapés in sight, I'm sure we can all agree this is quite a difficult time for her.'

Tom threw his head back, laughing from his belly. Rachel felt gratified, then guilty: her mum did find Christmas and its aftermath difficult, as she and her friends all knew – though not for the reasons she'd just outlined.

'Anyway,' Rachel said, pushing the thought to one side, 'Laurence wasn't perfect but he's nowhere near as awful as some of *your* ex-girlfriends.'

'I resent that!' Tom cried, fully aware that she was right.

'Princess Penny,' Will pretend-coughed, carrying two plates of steaming spaghetti and sauce over to the table. 'Even *I* thought she was bougie.'

As the grandson of a knighted supermarket magnate, Will had grown up with the kind of wealth and privilege that Rachel struggled to comprehend – but he had the grace to acknowledge his good fortune, regularly sending himself up as a posh twat while trying very hard not to be one.

'She bought him a subscription to *Tatler*, you know. *Tatler!* Two years on and it's still being delivered to our flat every month.'

Rachel and Anna dissolved into hysterics at the thought of Tom, who'd spent his student days selling the *Socialist Worker*, reading glossy magazine features about lesser members of the royal family.

They only stopped giggling when the urge to eat became irresistible.

Later, Rachel and Tom washed up all the stuff that wouldn't fit into the dishwasher while Will and Anna watched trash TV in the sitting room.

Rachel was sporting a pair of neon-pink rubber gloves, which Tom had wisely handed over without argument. She loathed drying up, and whenever they shared clean-up duty he accepted his fate was to wield a tea towel instead of the scouring sponge.

'Tell me to shut up if you like,' he said as she handed him a clean salad bowl to dry. 'I don't want to upset you, but . . . are you sure you're okay?'

This was another difference between Tom and Will, Rachel thought. She considered them both close friends, but Tom was sensitive to other people's feelings and reactions: subtle and perceptive in a way that Will was not.

As she scrubbed the last smears of tomato sauce from the bolognese pan, rinsed and then handed it to him, she decided to tell him the truth.

'I'm not sure, to be honest. I mean, obviously I'm fed up of my mum going on at me about settling down with someone. But I should probably be nicer to her . . . I should at least answer my phone.'

Tom nodded, perhaps more to show he was listening than to agree that she ought to feel bad.

'And maybe she has a point, anyway. She keeps on about Anna and Will moving in together. They clearly have a future. Whereas who knows where I'm going to be in two years' time, or five? Still on my own writing copy about vegetables for a living if I'm not careful . . . Plus I've been *slightly* perturbed by the bus ads,' she added quickly, before Tom could interject with anything too nice about her employability or chances of finding a life partner. Rachel was suddenly aware that excessive kindness might make her cry, and she didn't want to end up sobbing and snotting all over Tom's sweater.

'Yeah. I imagine they're a bit of a shitter,' he said, stashing clean and dry items in their correct cupboards and drawers. 'The thing to remember, though, is that they're truly awful.'

Rachel scoffed, then turned to face him as the cold tap ran into the sink, flushing away what remained of the scummy washing-up water. 'They are,' she said. 'But she looks incredible in them.'

'Does she?' he said, wrinkling his nose. 'She doesn't do anything for me.'

He poured them the final two glasses of wine from the third – or was it the fourth? – bottle. Either way, Rachel knew she was going to feel fuzzy in the morning.

She looked up to see Tom holding his drink in his fingertips, tilted just so like Jessica's Angeljuice bottle. He was smirking mock-seductively in a bad impression of her pout. They both burst out laughing.

'Seriously, Rach,' he said. 'If, on any level, you are torturing yourself with these images, stop. You have no reason to compare yourself to this woman, or to any other, for that matter. There *is* no comparison. You're one on your own.'

Rachel laughed again as they made their way to the sitting room.

'I guess that's one way of putting it,' she said.

3

Rachel received a text from Greg at 5.58 a.m. the next morning.

She didn't read it at 5.58 a.m., of course; she picked it up at 7.23, having pressed the snooze button on her alarm twice and just as it was dawning on her that she was really quite hung-over, and there was now a 99.9% probability she'd be late for their cauliflower meeting.

She sat up in bed and groaned as she clicked to open the message, which her phone's home screen informed her was eighty-five minutes old. What on earth could Greg have wanted before 6 a.m.? If this was an early-morning missive about vegetables, she feared she might actually strangle him.

The text, when Rachel read it, was short and to the point. Very un-Greg, though typically shouty and insistent.

Greg: *Call me AS SOON as you're up. Need to tell you something IMPORTANT!*

Just as Rachel was asking herself if she could face calling him before she'd had a shower, her mobile began to vibrate in her hand. She considered ignoring it, then reasoned that, for all his melodramatic tendencies, this was the first time Greg had ever tried to contact her so early.

Maybe he had a good excuse. If not, she could tell him to calm the hell down – as well as take the opportunity to confess that she'd never make it to the coffee shop by nine.

'Hello . . . ?' she said. She wondered if he'd be able to tell from her voice that she was still in her pyjamas.

'Oh, thank God,' Greg sighed. 'FINALLY. What the hell have you been doing? Why didn't you call me back?'

'I, er . . . um. Ha. I only just read your message.'

Rachel's brain was too wine-fogged for fabricating excuses. Now that she'd opened her mouth to speak, she discovered it was dry and sticky – as if her tongue had been coated in desiccated coconut.

'You're still *in bed*?!' Greg bellowed, so loud that Rachel flinched and moved the phone away from her ear. 'This is a DISASTER! Get up, get to the office and make sure you *look presentable*. This. Is. Not. A. Drill!'

'Greg, *what* is going on?'

Rachel was heading to the bathroom now. She clamped the phone between her right ear and shoulder, then ran the cold tap until the water was freezing. As she filled a glass, Greg said, 'That better not be the sound of you pissing!'

'Of course it isn't! I'm just getting a drink! Now, kindly tell me what it is that you needed to talk to me about at SIX IN THE SODDING MORNING.'

Rachel generally avoided yelling at Greg, but this morning's hangover had robbed her of patience with his histrionics. The idea that he thought she would urinate within his earshot was also horrifying – though, annoyingly, it underlined the fact that she was in dire need of a wee. She perched on the edge of the bathtub.

'The agency is being taken over,' Greg said, deliberately pausing for effect.

'*What?!*'

Rachel was stunned, which was precisely the effect he'd been hoping for. Her shock echoed off the sage-green metro-tiled walls.

'Apparently it was confirmed last night. I found out very early this morning, from a source who's asked not to be named.'

Rachel rolled her eyes at this, but decided to say nothing. She chugged a mouthful of water, crossed her legs and waited for him to carry on.

'I've suspected this might happen for a while,' he said, and Rachel marvelled that – even at a time like this – he couldn't resist grandstanding. 'I'm not supposed to be telling anyone, but I felt like I had to warn my friends ASAP – you know, to make sure you all come in on time looking professional and ready to slay. This is *not* the day to turn up zombified, stinking of stale booze and clutching a Pret bag full of pastries.'

While she'd had no intention of going to work wearing Eau de Red Wine, Rachel was grateful for Greg's warning. She felt her annoyance with him soften as panic began to swirl in the pit of her stomach.

'Why is all this such a big deal this morning?' she asked, fearful she already knew the answer.

'WOW, you are *slow*!' Greg roared. 'The new owners are coming into the office today! The announcement is going to be made, they'll be introduced, and then they're going to spend the day looking around – working out how our agency is going to mesh with theirs.'

'Mesh?'

'Yes, *mesh*! For God's sake put me on speaker and start brushing your teeth or something. You don't have time to waste.'

Obediently, Rachel switched her phone settings and smeared Colgate onto her battered toothbrush.

'The headlines,' Greg continued, 'are that we're being taken over by Mountaintop Media, based up in Manchester. Apparently they wanted to set up a London office, then decided that acquiring a smallish agency wholesale might make more sense than setting up from scratch. HOWEVER, we may lose some accounts if clients don't like the look of the change. There may be things that Mountaintop can run from Manchester instead of from London, if they're looking to cut costs . . .'

Again Greg stopped on a cliffhanger.

'So you're saying there might be job losses?' Rachel spluttered, minty foam spattering the sink.

'I'll be amazed if there aren't,' he said. 'Which is why we *all* need to make a good impression from the word go. Now get your arse in the shower and get to the office AS SOON AS YOU CAN!'

'Shit – yes. Thanks,' Rachel said, and rang off.

Twenty-five minutes later Rachel had showered, thrown half a can of dry shampoo at her hair and pulled on a slouchy black minidress that ideally should have been ironed. She smeared moisturiser onto her face and resolved to apply some make-up on the Tube, then poured herself into a pair of thick grey tights that, though snug, at least helped to smooth her silhouette.

She longed to sink her feet into the flat cherry-red Doc Martens sitting beneath her bedroom bookcase. Instead, she squeezed them into a pair of chunky-heeled black leather boots she'd bought last winter but barely worn since because walking in them required too much concentration.

She knew they'd slow her progress towards the office but reasoned that her usual slightly student look might not be ideal for today. Relate/Create – R/C for short – was one of those arty workplaces where penchants for piercings, tattoos and quirky clothes had never been troubled by a corporate dress code. While Rachel had always enjoyed going to work in skinny jeans, slogan tops and vintage finds, she now wondered whether the takeover might condemn her to a life of plain black trousers, inoffensive V-necks and smart, sensible shoes.

Get some perspective, she told herself. After all, the dreariness of Rachel's future work wardrobe was hardly the biggest problem she might face after today. More serious by far was the risk that redundancies would follow the takeover announcement; if the new mega-agency she was about to become part of found itself with too many copywriters on the payroll, she could end up unemployed.

Rachel suddenly felt nauseous and wasn't sure whether to blame the thought of losing her job or the after-effects of too much *vino rosso*.

Banging her bedroom door closed, she picked up her

forest-green handbag from the kitchen, dropped her phone inside it and grabbed her laptop case. Doing her best not to panic about what awaited her at work, whether she'd make it there on time, or the very real prospect that she might break her neck in her too-high heels, she exited the flat and dashed in the direction of Finsbury Park station.

Relate/Create was housed in a glass-fronted office complex towards the top of St John Street, just south of Angel. Set back from the road behind a line of trees so tall they dwarfed its five storeys, the building's many large windows and black metal beams looked strikingly modern amid rows of elegant, primarily Georgian townhouses.

The ground floor housed a bar, a cafe and a pizza parlour, while the upper levels were let to businesses of various types and sizes. R/C sat on the first floor, its ninety-eight employees occupying around half the available space.

Rachel passed through the entrance foyer and waved hello to Frank, the security guard currently sitting behind the front desk. She summoned a lift and, as its doors slid shut, examined her reflection in the mirror inside it.

Not too bad, considering she'd done her face on the train. Her pale cheeks were flushed from fast walking, and her wavy auburn hair – tied back in a ponytail – looked deliberately, rather than accidentally, dishevelled. Pure luck.

She wiped away a stray smudge of mascara with her fingertip and looked at the time: 8.57 a.m. She'd made it, but she was starving – not to mention woefully under-caffeinated.

As she entered R/C's open-plan office, Rachel looked for Greg. He was in the far corner of the room, where the client services team was based, chatting to his boss, Karen. Eyeing him from her own desk over in editorial, Rachel eventually managed to catch his attention and let him know she'd arrived. Behind Karen's back, Greg gave her a relieved thumbs up.

The atmosphere was thick with anticipation. Even if Greg hadn't called her, and even in her fuzzy state, Rachel would have realised something was up. Florence, Toby and Isaac – the founders and owners of the agency – were in the main meeting room, visible through its glass wall and door. Seated at the large oval table inside, their heads and shoulders were visible to anyone who walked by. Toby, who was the agency's managing director, seemed to be in full flow, and the people on the other side of the table – presumably the interlopers from Mountaintop Media – were nodding as he spoke.

Rachel could only see their backs, but all three of them looked male and were clad in suit jackets. This didn't bode well, she decided, either for equal opportunities or office culture.

Neil from the tech team – a very clever, if occasionally stroppy, developer – gestured at Rachel from across a bank of desks as she made her way to the kitchen. He nodded his head towards the meeting room and mouthed, 'What's going on?'

Rachel made a face and shrugged like she had no idea. The last thing she wanted to do was get Greg into trouble.

Ducking into the kitchen, she placed an R/C-branded mug beneath the coffee machine spout and pressed the button for an Americano, to which she added a heaped teaspoon of sugar.

When she got back to her desk, her laptop had finished booting up. She settled down to check her emails and spotted that a whole-agency briefing had been scheduled for 9.15 a.m. Thank *God* for Greg and his gobbiness; without his warning she might well have come in late, even if he'd cancelled their cauliflower chat.

In a bid to appear busy, Rachel opened up the fruit-and-vegetable copy she'd been working on the day before. She began looking for opportunities to 'sex it up', as requested – confident she'd conclude there were none.

Within a few minutes, though, figures began to emerge from the meeting room and conversations dwindled into silence.

All pretence of useful work abandoned, everyone in the room looked up.

Toby had made his way to the centre of the office, Florence and Isaac keeping watch from behind.

Donna, R/C's grouchy office manager, shuffled her special orthopaedic chair slightly to the left as Toby hovered in front of her desk. She stared out into the crowd, narrow-eyed, her cerise-pink lips pursed in distaste. Rachel wondered if Donna had recently been force-fed a plate of something foul, or if the cat's-arse face merely signalled her irritation that – just this once – she didn't know what was going on before everybody else.

Toby signalled for attention.

'Morning, all! Good morning! Hi. Hopefully you've seen from your emails by now that I've popped a whole-agency briefing into your calendars,' he said in a voice loud enough to reach all four corners of the office. 'We'll get started in a moment or two, and we *will* need the full hour today – so if you want a glass of water or a comfort break, then now's the time.'

Several people exchanged nervous glances. Some made for the kettle and a few headed towards the toilets. The Mountaintop suits, Rachel noted, were hanging back inside the meeting room, fiddling with laptops and phones. She assumed they'd come out when the time was right.

Rachel stayed seated, now with a clearer view of the glass meeting room. Two of the men from Mountaintop were standing, chatting quietly – one with his back to the room and the other looking out into the office.

The one Rachel could see was maybe in his fifties. His navy suit was simple but perfectly cut, and she had no doubt it was expensively made to measure.

Whoever he was talking to was younger, as far as she could tell. He was taller and trimmer, with warm brown hair just on the right side of the stylishly mussed/messy divide. Even though she couldn't see his face, she felt sure it must be handsome. Good-looking people carried themselves a certain way, in Rachel's experience, and she recognised the telltale stance even at a distance: easy and relaxed, but confident enough to take up space. Beautiful people rarely felt the need to shrink themselves, as she sometimes did.

Toby was using his public speaking voice again, asking everyone to return to their seats.

'Okay. We'll make a start now,' he said. 'Thanks, everyone, for coming along this morning at such short notice. I'm sure you've all worked out that we're together today so I can share some great, and very important, news with you all.'

Rachel glanced beyond Toby towards the meeting room again, her eyes snagging on Mr Probably Good-Looking. He'd now turned slightly towards the crowd, and she willed him to twist his body further around so she'd have a better view.

She wasn't listening to Toby and realised, dimly, that this was not ideal. She should pay attention, but there was a heavy thudding in her ears and a tightness in her chest. For some reason Rachel couldn't fathom – perhaps anxiety, perhaps attraction – she was possessed by a weird determination not to shift her attention until she'd seen this man properly.

Get a grip, she told herself.

Toby was talking timescales now. Rachel forced herself, fleetingly, to look his way and then around the room at her friends and colleagues. There were wide eyes, downturned mouths and furrowed brows. Some faces were blank, as if their owners hadn't yet joined the dots that led from *merger* to *jobseeker's allowance*.

Rachel couldn't concentrate. She was aware of Toby talking but was taking nothing in. Mr Almost Certainly Handsome still hadn't moved.

She was reminded of her early days at university; whole lectures lost to staring across the hall at Jack Harper, always followed by the frantic borrowing and copying of important notes (usually Anna's). It hit her then. The physical longing to see this man was habit. It was muscle memory.

With a jolt, Rachel understood the sharp, fluttering sensation behind her ribcage – the odd muddle of horror and impatience that had seized her almost as soon as she saw him.

He chose this moment to shift his feet, turn his head and stand, straight-backed and smiling, facing out into the crowd. Her neck was sweaty, her head felt light and her stomach was in her shoes. They were in the same room for the first time in ten years, and it was Jack's face Rachel had been straining to see.

4

Her first instinct was to hide. She considered crouching further behind the large computer monitor that sat at the back of her desk, directly above her laptop.

Rachel could feel her face burning. Sweat was beginning to collect between her shoulder blades and she wondered if this was the start of a medical emergency.

No, she thought. *I can't let this person – the only man I have ever loved* and *hated – see me for the first time in ten years, just as I'm seized by what will surely be a deeply unattractive panic attack.*

She tried to take deep breaths, but quietly so that nobody nearby would notice. Maybe if she scrunched herself right down in her seat he wouldn't spot her. Then – once he'd turned away again – she could find her line manager, feign some sort of crisis and head home.

But then what? What would happen on Monday? Would he still be here?

Even if he was back in Manchester by then, their paths were sure to cross sometime. Now they worked for the same firm, it seemed unlikely that Rachel would be able to avoid Jack altogether – even if she managed to put off this initial, excruciating encounter.

Slowly, and berating herself for her cowardice, she slouched out of his line of sight and tried to think. Not for the first time in her life, she cursed her copper-coloured hair. It made her conspicuous in a crowd, to the extent that any sudden movement might accidentally draw his eye. She wasn't ready to face him.

She examined the awful, gnawing feeling that seemed to be eating away at her stomach lining. It was mostly made up of embarrassment, which surely wasn't fair. If anything, he should be shame-faced at seeing her again – not the other way around.

You're not the one who lied and cheated, Rachel told herself. *You're not the person who repeatedly said 'I think you're the one', then started shagging a skinny Kim Kardashian lookalike.*

Nevertheless, Rachel felt as if she was about to be caught out: exposed in her imperfect body, unremarkable job and generally humdrum life. She was livid with Jack, but also with herself: incensed that his mere presence apparently had the power to mortify her.

For a mad moment she even wished she hadn't ended things with Laurence. Meeting Jack as a still-single thirty-year-old was simply too tragic. She wondered if he would think it pitiful that, after all this time, she still lived with Anna.

If only she'd moved on – or up – enough to imply that what had happened between them was old news, now completely beneath her notice. Because at all costs, Rachel realised, he must be prevented from thinking that any of it still mattered. It *didn't* still matter, she told herself: she wouldn't allow it to.

Rachel straightened her spine in her chair, suddenly

determined to be braver. She squared her shoulders and looked, as directly but nonchalantly as she could manage, in the direction of the Mountaintop Media team.

The expensive-suited man was being introduced as the company's managing director. He started speaking, but a quick scan of her workmates' faces told Rachel that a number of them – mostly women – weren't fully tuned in.

She felt rather sorry for him, standing next to Jack; while everyone should be listening to his excited speech about the merger, too many pairs of eyes were dancing left – towards his younger, more glamorous associate.

Right on cue, a *New instant message* notification appeared in the corner of Rachel's laptop screen. It was from Kemi, a junior copywriter with the sort of bone-deep self-confidence Rachel wished she'd had at twenty-three. Or ever, frankly.

Rachel liked Kemi a lot, worked with her regularly and – for safety's sake – often escorted her home after work nights out.

Kemi Percival
Can you believe all this? <brain exploding emoji>
Also: WHO IS THAT GUY on the left??
YUMMMMMMM <aubergine emoji>
Please god, I don't ask for much . . . But can he transfer down here please
And sit at the desk next to mine
. . .

Ugh, she was still typing.

. . .
Preferably naked
Maybe with a red rose between his teeth

. . .
Don't say I'm not romantic.

This was a double whammy from Kemi. As well as struggling to ignore the clear, continuing gorgeousness of her ex, Rachel was now fighting to extinguish the flame of dread that had started flickering in her chest. Until Kemi mentioned it, Rachel hadn't considered the possibility of staff transfers. But why would Jack be here if he weren't somehow going to be involved in running the London office?

She decided to try to be the adult in this conversation.

Rachel Ryan
I guess staff transfers are a possibility <shrug emoji>
Nudity in the office, not so much
Bit risky btw – you never know who from IT is reading this stuff
Anyhow, I'm listening, not ogling
<winking face emoji>
We need to know if jobs are safe, if there might even be options for promotion arising from all this.

Rachel hoped this would move Kemi off her obviously preferred topic. She also hoped she hadn't come across as sniffy and superior.

Kemi Percival
Hahahahaha, WHATEVS
Don't tell me you wouldn't have a go on him too
Tall, smart, seems clever
Just your type

. . .

THOSE EYES, THAT MOUTH . . .

Anyone's type tbh
<tongue hanging out emoji>

Well. That had worked perfectly.

Rachel minimised the IM window and returned her attention to the front of the room. The Mountaintop MD was still talking.

'In the coming weeks we'll be looking at the structure of the teams here and in Manchester,' he said. A low, anxious murmuring began, then stopped when he cleared his throat and started talking again, his voice slightly louder than before.

'There will of course be opportunities arising from our merger, not least the chance to move between our sites, based in two incredible cities. Be open with your line manager in the next few days if you're interested in a transfer, or indeed if there's another move you'd be keen to make. Our aim here is to create dynamic, enthusiastic teams who can do brilliant work they enjoy.

'On the subject of moves . . .' he went on in his rich, friendly baritone.

He turned slightly to his left and Rachel felt her heart stutter in her chest.

'. . . allow me to introduce Jack Harper, one of Mountaintop's senior client services managers. He and a small team from Manchester will be based here from next week, and I know they're all very excited to be joining you.'

Jack nodded, taking his cue to say something. He smiled warmly at his audience before beginning, and Rachel was sure she detected a collective swoon. Surely this couldn't be happening.

'I won't chat for long this morning,' Jack said smoothly. 'I just wanted to say hello to you all, and also how thrilled I am to be coming down to work with you here in London. My team and I all have specialisms that will hopefully complement your expertise, and in some cases really benefit from it. We can't wait to learn from you. Big thanks to those people I've met so far today, all of whom have made me feel so welcome. I'm looking forward to getting to know all of you better in the coming weeks and months.'

We can't wait to learn from you. Bleurgh. Was he always such a suck-up? Rachel felt her nose wrinkle in disgust.

Jack smiled and nodded at Greg as Toby moved forward to start taking questions. Greg gave Jack two thumbs up – a gesture that hit Rachel like a football in the face. Yes, Greg's relentless positivity and lack of boundaries drove her nuts, but he was *her* colleague. *Her* friend. She found herself incensed at the idea that he and Jack might become buddies, though as members of the same department she supposed that was inevitable for them now.

Greg looked over to give Rachel a reassuring wink, clearly unaware of the bilious mess her insides had become. At least that suggested her inner turmoil wasn't written all over her face.

And if she had managed to maintain a mask of neutrality, it turned out this was the moment to keep it in place. Jack, seeing Greg gesture to someone on the other side of the room, followed his gaze and – finally – found Rachel in the crowd.

Their eyes locked, there was immediate recognition in his, and then a rapid softening of his expression. His face settled into a warm, sincere, supremely confident grin that seemed to say, 'Well. Fancy seeing *you* here.'

Unbelievable, Rachel said to herself. *Arrogant, weapons-grade wanker.*

She looked down at her keyboard and began typing, bashing the keys with gratuitous force. She prayed no one would notice the flush creeping up her neck into her cheeks.

The meeting was over. People shuffled back to their desks and began trying to get on with work as normal. Rachel imagined, though, that for most of her colleagues the day would be spent messaging friends about the merger, wondering whether their jobs were safe and setting their LinkedIn profiles to 'open to recruiters'. She made a mental note to switch hers too, once her brain had stopped whirring and she could remember the right password.

The Mountaintop team didn't seem in any rush to leave. As Greg had predicted, it appeared they were planning to stay and observe the workings of the agency, wandering through the office at will, sitting in on meetings and gradually introducing themselves to members of their new London branch.

Rachel worked through everything in her inbox and created a to-do list for the day, determined not to keep scanning the room for Jack. Part of her was desperate to look at him some more, while another prayed for him to spontaneously combust. She felt sure he wouldn't leave without speaking to her, but had no idea when or how they'd come face to face – let alone what they'd say. She felt like one of those innocent grass-grazing animals in a David Attenborough documentary: at risk of being chased down and eaten by a lion at any moment, but unable to predict when doom would come.

Rachel heard footsteps slowing behind her, then felt a presence over her shoulder. Oh *no* . . . Was this it?

'Ray, let's duck into the meeting room and just read over this vegetable stuff again, shall we? The client meeting's at three, so we need to agree on final versions of everything.'

Rachel felt her knotted neck muscles loosen slightly. It was Greg, wanting to chat about cauliflowers again – a prospect she remembered finding rather annoying yesterday, but which now felt like sweet relief.

Once the door of the meeting room was shut, they both exhaled dramatically.

'Serious shit, hey?' Greg said. 'I'm *so* glad you managed to haul your arse in here on time.' There was a judgemental edge to his voice that she didn't balk at because it was entirely deserved.

'Thank you for that. It would have looked horrific if I'd strolled in after the meeting had started with a giant coffee and a pain au chocolat.'

Greg cringed and laughed in agreement. 'What about Mr Gorgeous, though? There's a bonus I wasn't expecting out of this whole thing!'

Brilliant, Rachel thought. Jack mania had seized the whole office and it wasn't even lunchtime.

'I might be a happily married man,' Greg went on, 'but I've always been a sucker for a silver fox.'

'Oh, you mean the MD!' Rachel cried, realising too late that she sounded high-pitched and vaguely hysterical.

Greg smirked at her. 'Absolutely I do,' he replied. 'Jack's pretty but a bit . . . well. Obvious. Though now we know who *you* like the look of.'

He waggled his eyebrows at Rachel suggestively. She bit her lip and decided to keep her mouth shut.

They spent the next hour and a half dissecting the work Rachel had done for It's All Good – the grocery box company – over the past week or two. She successfully spiced up the cauliflower content without turning it into a work of erotic fiction, and also managed to prevent Greg from bastardising the descriptive snippets she'd written about beetroot.

'Beetroots are the MILFs of the vegetable world!' Greg had bellowed halfway through their conversation. 'Once decried as fuddy-duddy things nobody could fancy, now they're fresh, fashionable and LUSCIOUS! We need more on beetroots. *Lots* on beetroots. We need to put them in a PRIME spot on the homepage.'

Having talked Greg down from this insane ledge, by lunchtime Rachel was happy with the final copy they'd be presenting that afternoon. Concentrating on her job had also calmed the incessant jangling of her nerves and she realised, now she was no longer feeling sick, that she was starving.

She'd skipped breakfast and survived, but there was no way she'd be able to cope without lunch.

Craving a gigantic baked potato, a full-sugar Coke and an hour of solitude, Rachel told Greg she'd see him later and slipped away.

Rachel made her way along St John Street and rounded a corner, heading for her favourite no-frills cafe. Cyril's Kitchen had probably been open since before Rachel was born, and it appeared the owner had a strong attachment to its original early-eighties decor.

Old-fashioned, uncool and specialising in deep-fried stodge for committed carnivores, Cyril's was a very poor fit for modern Islington. It was the sort of place that sold builder's tea in oversized mugs, and sausage sandwiches made with doorstep-thick slices of sweet white bread. Almost every item on the menu came with a side of chips, including the full English breakfast.

It reminded Rachel of the greasy spoon down the road from her parents' house in Stoke-on-Trent, and she liked its lack of pretension. At times of emotional-slash-hormonal strain, this was somewhere she could indulge her love of carbs without chiding herself that she should make healthier choices. In this place, there were none.

Cyril himself was behind the counter today, his sizeable pot belly threatening to liberate itself from a too-tight T-shirt that was straining at the seams. He grinned at her as she placed her order.

'Looking lovely as always, sweetheart.'

Rachel suspected he said as much to all his female regulars, but the compliment was cheering nonetheless.

Having paid for her lunch, she settled at a tiny table that was tucked behind the dresser where Cyril stored mismatched crockery, dog-eared paperbacks and week-old tabloid newspapers. You wouldn't know this spot was here if you weren't familiar with the place, and today it felt like a sanctuary. Rachel revelled in being alone for a while.

A few moments later, half-heartedly skimming through a magazine article about 'the *REAL* causes of crow's feet', she heard the chime of the cafe door's bell. Then came muffled conversation – stilted, unnatural chat from Cyril and someone stuffier.

Fuuuuuuuck, that sounded like Laurence's voice. Leaning to her left so she could look beyond the dresser in the direction of the counter, she glimpsed a familiar pinstriped suit and shiny brown brogues. What was he *doing* here?

Rachel wasn't arrogant enough to assume Laurence was pacing the streets in search of her, but this was an odd place for him to be on his own account. While Cyril's was one of Rachel's favourite haunts, Laurence had always refused to set foot in here when they met up for a workday lunch – instead bundling her into Pret A Manger or the local gastropub.

Rachel peeked at him for a second more, then retracted her head for fear he'd spot her. She'd decided not to hide from Jack earlier because, in the brave new world she suddenly lived in, she was going to have to face him sometime. Laurence was a different prospect entirely, and altogether more avoidable.

'Skinny double-shot cappuccino to go, please,' she heard him demand.

Incredible. *Read the room, Laurence: they'll have none of your frothy coffees here. No skimmed milk either.*

Cyril – trying and failing to stifle a snigger – informed Laurence that his hot drink options extended only as far as a cup of Tetley or Nescafé Gold Blend, neither of which were available to take away.

Moments later the bell tinkled again as the cafe door shut.

Rachel's breath left her lungs in a rush of relief. She didn't dislike Laurence, but nor did she want to see him. She felt guilty for breaking things off with him; she worried that she'd hurt him. Even though she had never given him cause to believe they were destined for the altar, he'd been horrified – disbelieving – when Rachel had said she didn't think they had a future together.

As she shovelled forkfuls of buttery, cheese-topped baked potato into her mouth, Rachel reminded herself that she'd had good reasons for finishing with him. Laurence was inoffensive: nice-looking, tallish, a decent enough dresser. He was a pensions actuary and therefore earned good money. Laurence was what Rachel's mum called 'a solid prospect': the steady sort of man who'd never miss a mortgage payment or absent-mindedly put petrol in his diesel car.

But after five months of casual dating, Rachel had

realised that Laurence had begun making plans for them. He'd even started bookmarking properties on the Rightmove app. While she wouldn't have minded living in a million-pound pad, Rachel couldn't see her toothbrush sidling up to his for the next few decades. The fact that he was mapping their lives out had actually made her blood run cold.

The thing was, Rachel had never pined for him when he wasn't around. If they'd gone a week without meeting up, she hadn't suffered for not seeing his face or struggled with the urgent need to touch him.

And while Rachel had been wise enough to know that the stage when you can't keep your hands off each other always ends – either painfully or because it gives way to something deeper – she hadn't been able to help thinking it was one you probably shouldn't skip altogether. That was the bit that reminded you why you were with *this* person, even if they were crap at stacking the dishwasher or kept forgetting to put the bins out.

Rachel tipped her Coke can to her lips, shaking out the last of the fizz. She wondered if Jack was any good around the house. Somehow she couldn't imagine him dealing with dirty plates or lugging black sacks of rubbish outside. He was too celestial-looking for grubby tasks, she thought sourly – not to mention charming and rich enough to have found someone else to do them for him.

It was time to go back to the office. Rachel stuffed her magazine back into her handbag and shrugged her coat on. She wore a vintage houndstooth Crombie – probably a man's in its first life – and she loved it despite its frayed lining and tendency to absorb, rather than repel, rain water.

'Cheers, Cyril,' she said. 'See you soon.'

'See you, darlin'. Keep on smilin'.'

It was what he always said, but today Cyril's standard farewell felt pointed – like he was issuing Rachel with a challenge.

Her near miss with Laurence had rattled her; she still needed to confess the break-up to her mother; her job might be at risk *and* her heartbreaking ex was R/C's new office totty.

She nodded at Cyril as she left, lifting the corners of her mouth into something she was sure looked more like a grimace than a smile. For now, it was the best she could do.

5

It's All Good was based in Blackheath, South London. Rachel and Greg needed to allow at least forty-five minutes to get there for their three o'clock meeting, so the plan was to leave just after two.

Rachel caught up on emails until it was time to go, then packed up her stuff and made her way over to Greg's desk.

'With you in a jiffy,' he said. 'Jack's meeting us in the foyer.'

FUCK.

Shit.

No!

'Jack . . . ?' Rachel choked out. 'As in, er, the new guy?'

'Uh-huh.'

Greg's attention was on an email he'd decided to scan before closing down his laptop. Rachel's face felt hot and her stomach – unhelpfully full of potato – rolled over. She realised she was clutching the edge of Greg's desk for support and urged herself to calm down, fearful the spud would make a comeback.

'Right . . . DONE,' he announced. He shut the lid of his MacBook Air with an unnecessary bang, swept it into its foam sleeve and deposited it in his leather satchel. 'Let's go,' he said, pulling on his coat and giving Rachel a gentle push towards the door. 'What's up with you, by the way?

You look like you've just been served a shit sandwich and told to take a bite.'

They left the office and entered the building's large, sparsely furnished lobby. Next to the security desk, which Frank was still manning, sat Jack. He was perched on a stiff-looking black leather sofa, leafing through today's *The Times* and drinking coffee from a collapsible KeepCup.

Rachel felt a surge of loathing rise up and fill her, wrestling for release. How *dare* he lounge around, languidly sipping his latte? How could he be so utterly unbothered by this unspeakably grim situation?

He stood up and smiled his best smile: a soft grin that radiated warmth and wry humour. Rachel averted her eyes.

'Can I carry anything for you guys? You're pretty laden down . . . Laptop bag?' he asked, pointing to Rachel's bulky case.

Damn him.

'No, thanks,' she mumbled, secretly wishing she could offload the thing.

Greg frowned at her. 'Jack, this is Rachel Ryan – pretty much the best copywriter we have, though she seems determined to hide her light under a bushel. I'm sure you'll get on famously.'

Before she could feel too flattered – or annoyed – by Greg's introduction, Jack was smiling again and opening his mouth to reply.

Rachel looked right at him, eyes widened in alarm. She shook her head slightly, trying to warn him: *Don't say it.*

Too late.

'Rachel and I actually know each other already, from years back,' Jack said. 'We were at university together. I remember her being very clever, though God knows we probably killed a few brain cells with all the cider we used to drink. I'm not at all surprised she's one of your top people.'

Damn him *to hell*.

Greg's light-brown eyes looked rounder than usual. Rachel could almost hear the cogs and wheels of his brain clunking and whirring, processing this new information.

Jack, as Rachel's dad might say, had dropped a massive bollock here. Telling Greg that he and Rachel had had a prior relationship meant Greg would start reading all sorts of (probably true) things into the tension that was beginning to simmer between them. This was why Rachel hadn't mentioned it earlier – but now her decision to say nothing looked weird and suspicious. Greg would assume *she* had something shameful to hide, which was simultaneously inaccurate, unfair and infuriating.

Rachel's eyes met Jack's, square on. She gave him a look that she hoped he knew meant: *Well played, you smug idiot*.

'Well,' Greg said after what felt like an ice age, 'it'll be great for you two to get reacquainted, I suppose!'

'It certainly will,' Jack agreed, treating them to another winning smile.

Rachel was silent, her mouth clamped shut so it wouldn't hang open in horror.

'Shall we?' Jack said, and gestured towards the exit.

They walked the short distance to Angel Tube station. Rachel was grateful that Greg had decided to give Jack a full and detailed explanation of where they were going, who they were about to meet and the work they'd been doing. She plodded along saying nothing, privately praying for a sinkhole to appear in the pavement and swallow Jack whole.

A busy Tube carriage saved Rachel the indignity of small talk on the way to London Bridge, and she decided to give her copy a final read-through after they changed for the train to Blackheath, feigning diligence as she stared down at the A4 sheets she'd brought with her. She felt Greg's curious eyes on her as words swam, meaningless, across each page.

It's All Good's head office was within a large, elegant Victorian terrace round the corner from the station. It had a small outdoor porch stacked with shabby-chic wooden crates, all of them full of (presumably organic, locally grown) produce. Inside, shelves lined the walls of the entrance hall, proudly displaying a variety of vegetarian and vegan recipe books – plus what Rachel assumed must be every celebrity 'wellness' guide published in the past ten years. There were framed supposedly motivational quotations in every room, including the toilet.

While Rachel had been to It's All Good HQ several times before, she couldn't help feeling newly accused every time she stepped across the threshold. *TREASURE YOUR BODY – IT'S THE ONLY PLACE YOU HAVE TO LIVE*, admonished a cream-and-rose-gold poster at reception. Standing next to it, Rachel self-consciously sucked in her marshmallowy stomach.

As she, Greg and Jack waited to be shown into a meeting room, she saw Jack cast his eyes over a cutesy print that read *You gotta nourish if you wanna flourish!* He flashed Rachel a surreptitious smile and raised his eyebrows, inviting her to laugh with him.

She felt the corners of her mouth twitching upwards, then forced them back into neutral. As she rearranged her face, Angus, Josh and Heidi – the joint owners of It's All Good – appeared.

They showed their visitors into a meeting room with a large round table, upon which sat a tray of suspicious-looking drinks. It turned out these were turmeric lattes, made with almond milk. While Rachel decided hers was quite palatable after a few diffident slurps, she was pleased to see Jack practically gagging as he took polite little sips out of his.

'Heidi, Josh, Angus,' Greg said, perhaps aware that the more he spoke, the less he'd be expected to drink, 'this is Jack Harper, a new addition to the client services team at R/C. He's shadowing Rachel and me this afternoon just to get a sense of how we do things.'

Jack stood to shake hands with them all and Rachel noticed that, on her turn, Heidi seemed to grip his fingers for just a moment longer than necessary. He smiled widely at her as he sat down again, and two pink spots appeared on her cheeks.

With some effort, Rachel resisted the urge to roll her eyes. Jack was shameless, and she pitied the women who fawned over him.

'Well, guys,' Heidi said after taking a few seconds to

collect herself, 'this is a brilliant realisation of the brief – thank you. The tone is spot on. There are a few minor changes we'd suggest, just in terms of making sure we're a hundred per cent accurate in what we say about particular products . . . But overall, I'd say we're pretty much good to go live!'

Greg beamed at Rachel from across the table, as if to concede that she'd been right about the beetroot. She'd always appreciated that Greg's priority was getting the right result for clients, regardless of who came up with the ideas that made them happy.

Forty minutes later, and with several copy amendments agreed, the meeting was over. Jack shook hands with the It's All Good team for the second time.

'Thank you for letting me gatecrash this afternoon.' He smiled. 'Though Greg and Rachel clearly didn't need the extra help. It was a pleasure to meet you all, and no doubt I'll be back sometime.'

Heidi stared at him through lowered lashes, her face alight again. *Oh, he's good*, Rachel thought. *No wonder he's in client services: he could sell a cape to Supergirl.*

As the three of them made their way towards the It's All Good front door, they passed another gilt-framed feel-good poster – this time of a depressed-looking salad, limp and lifeless next to a jolly dancing avocado. The caption read: *FEELING BAD? JUST ADD A LITTLE AVO!*

Greg sailed by, oblivious, but Jack saw it and bit back a grin. He looked over his shoulder at Rachel, mirth dancing in his eyes.

She froze her face, refusing to smile. *I know how you work, remember?*

He looked away as he held the door open for her, then walked ahead in step with Greg.

One–nil to me, she thought, staring daggers at his back.

On the train back to central London, all attempts at post-meeting chat had petered out. Rachel, Greg and Jack were glued to their phones, skim-reading emails and checking social media feeds. On the approach to London Bridge they stood to gather their things; time to change for the Tube.

Greg turned to face Jack and Rachel as the train slowed. 'Right. It seems I have a last-minute meeting to get to this afternoon – potential new client on the South Bank. Rachel will see you back to the office from here, Jack. And great work again today, Ray; you smashed it as always. Have a good weekend, guys.'

He threw Rachel a searching look that made it clear he'd noticed something was up, but he was halfway to the train door before she could protest at being left in charge of Jack. She groaned inwardly.

This was hideous: the last thing she wanted was to be alone with her awful, smarm-oozing ex. To boot, there was now no doubt she was going to have to confess at least *some* of the truth to Greg next week.

Greg waved as he disappeared onto the platform. He was soon swept away by a surge of travellers heading for the station exit. There was pushing, shoving and grumbling from the carriage, and Rachel realised she was standing in people's way. She looked down to see Jack watching her expectantly, already off the train.

'Come on, Ray.' He grinned, offering her his hand.

'You can stop the performance now, Jack. I am not your audience.' Rachel held her palms up as if to ward off an evil spirit, then pushed past him.

Something inside her had snapped: her voice was icy and more confident than it had been all afternoon. Now they were alone, the sheer nerve of his friendly cajoling was glaringly in focus – and with Greg gone, so was Rachel's willingness to tolerate it.

She sidestepped him on the platform, then began walking towards the Tube. She didn't bother to make sure he was keeping up.

'Rachel!' He was suddenly next to her. 'Rachel, please.'

'Please *what*?'

She turned to face him, aware her eyes were blazing. She was livid with him for being so smug, so *him* – for being there at all. At the same time, she felt the sting of impending tears and cursed her treacherous eyeballs.

They were standing in the centre of a moving crowd, obstructing other people's progress towards the Underground. Before she could stop him, Jack placed a hand on Rachel's arm and steered her towards the tunnel wall. She felt as though she'd been burned, despite the layers of clothing separating his skin from hers.

'Please listen,' he said, looking less than sure of himself for the first time all day. It was as if Rachel had managed to sneak backstage at the Jack show: this was his face, minus the sheen of self-assurance it usually wore.

Rachel slumped against the concave tiles, signalling that she had no intention of running off again.

'Okay,' he said, pushing his hands through his hair. She knew he was working out what to say next. 'I didn't know. I had no idea. You have to believe I was totally unaware you worked here until today.'

She didn't reply. It seemed too obvious to ask why she should ever believe a single word out of his mouth.

'And then – when I saw you – I just . . . I was shocked. I was *happy*. I was confused . . . I didn't know what to do. So yes, I reverted to type. I guess it seemed easier to turn on the charm than give a big speech about what a dick I was to you all those years ago.'

Rachel's stomach flip-flopped at the thought that he was pleased to see her, and she immediately felt compelled to punish herself for such feebleness. If she were Dobby the house-elf, she'd whack herself in the face with a frying pan right now.

'I was stupid,' Jack went on. 'Cowardly. I should have found a way to talk to you properly this morning, before you were stuck with me coming along to that meeting. I should have been more respectful of your feelings instead of trying to slink out of dealing with them. I can understand why you'd never want to see me again after what happened . . . And now here I am, turning up in your workplace.'

He paused for a few seconds that seemed to stretch on interminably.

'Rachel. I'm sorry.'

He looked right at her, determined to maintain eye contact even though Rachel said nothing.

'Not as sorry as I am,' she finally replied.

He looked for a moment as if he was going to try to take her hand in some grand gesture of contrition, so she shoved it in her coat pocket.

'When I say I'm sorry . . . I don't just mean about now. About today.'

He sounded sad. Sincere. For a split second, Rachel softened.

Then she stood up straighter and picked up her handbag from between her feet. It was time they were getting back.

'Well,' she said, 'at least it sounds as though you mean it this time.' She loaded the words with all the contempt she could muster.

They sat in silence on the Underground from London Bridge back to Angel. The air between them was sour and Rachel found that the longer they sat there saying nothing, the angrier she felt. She imagined plumes of fury emanating from her like poisonous fumes from a fire.

Jack stood behind her on the long escalators back up to street level, then followed her out into the chilly early-evening gloom.

'Rachel, don't you think we should try to clear the air before we head back?' he said gently, catching her by the shoulder before she could walk too far in front.

She whirled round faster than he was expecting. Faster than *she* was expecting.

'*Clear the air?*'

She spat the words out, wanting him to hear air quotes in her tone.

'I see the years haven't tarnished your brass neck. You're an entitled tosser, you know that? Why should I care about clearing the air? If *the air* is somewhat toxic, that's on you, not me. Remember?'

Rachel felt brim-full of rage – as though her fingertips and hair must be crackling with it. She struggled to keep her voice even, to stop herself from saying more. She remembered that only this morning she'd sworn Jack would never be allowed to think what had happened between them still bothered her. She'd shut it out years ago, and it wasn't coming back in.

Rachel swallowed the lump that had formed in her throat as she stared him down. If she let rip at him now, he'd see the strength of feeling he could still stir up – a strength of feeling that shocked and appalled her. Her whole body felt alive with it: heart thumping, blood fizzing with adrenaline, brain struggling to impose logical thought.

'You're right,' Jack said abruptly. 'Again.'

He stepped closer and Rachel tried not to look at him.

'That was a stupid thing to say. You shouldn't have to pretend the air is clear . . . I don't expect you to be nice to me. You don't owe me anything.'

She barked a bitter laugh and hated how it sounded. He flinched a little, as though she'd slapped him.

'I didn't plan to suggest to Greg that we were old friends . . . It just kind of came out. The truth is, when I look back . . .'

He sucked in a deep breath, then tore his eyes from the pavement to her face.

'The truth is, I'm deeply ashamed of myself. Of what I

did to you. You deserved so much better. All I can hope now is that – if I can stop saying all the wrong things for more than five minutes – we might be able to move on. I've changed since the last time we saw each other, and I'm sure you have too. I'm not the bad lad you remember . . . Not quite, anyway.'

A smile flickered briefly on his lips, then died. Rachel's heart beat harder as her memory wound back to kissing them for the first time – knowing deep down, even then, that no good could come of it, and not caring.

She let herself search his face, separated from hers by just a few inches. She stared at him, unabashedly, for the first time all day.

Had he changed? Rachel tried to assess him dispassionately. She looked for features that, by rights, should have aged, degenerated – been rendered less perfect by another decade of life.

Was he shorter than she remembered, or was it just that her (now seriously uncomfortable) boots lent her an extra two inches? Were his lips a little thinner than before? Had she embellished when she'd told herself stories about his eyes: the green-gold hazelly-brown of them, so beguiling that she'd once joked he must be part witch?

The unfortunate truth was that he'd barely changed at all. In fact, he looked amazing. Yes, there were a few more lines around his eyes where the skin creased when he laughed. He also had a little more stubble than he used to wear – probably more than he used to be able to *grow*. But it suited him.

His hair was shorter now, though still a wavy mass of

bronze-tinged brown. He had better clothes: corporate in comparison with what most people at R/C normally wore, but unfussy enough that he still looked more 'senior person in a creative job' than bank manager.

'Come on,' he sighed eventually. 'It's freezing out here and it's past five. Let's get back to the office. We don't have to talk, just walk.'

He was still waiting for Rachel to say something, but she didn't dare try. She felt disgusted, sick with hating him, but also burning with contempt for her failure to loathe him *more*.

They plodded along next to each other in the dark, fingertips almost touching. He was too close; it was agonising. But moving might acknowledge weakness – imply she was overwrought. Better to stay put than seem to run away, she reasoned.

It was at this moment that a bus came to a stop alongside them, bearing an image of Jessica that must have been three metres high. In it, her improbably round breasts were squeezed into a pale-pink tank top, and her lips – thickly glossed to a mirror shine – were parted around what looked like a bar of chocolate.

Rachel read the copy: ANGELBARS: *slimming never tasted sweeter*. It was somehow both stupidly offensive *and* offensively stupid.

She sighed and was surprised to hear the exhalation lapse into a laugh, a tired, sad chuckle that swelled into something crazy. As she giggled, she realised this was partly because, after his performance the other night, she couldn't help imagining Tom trying to imitate Jessica's latest pose.

'What in the world are you laughing at?' Jack asked. He turned away from the bus and fixed his eyes on his feet.

Rachel wiped tears from her lashes and shook off her outburst, glad to see that Jack had been unsettled by the sudden reappearance of the woman he'd cheated on her with. His lips had turned down and he was frowning, frustrated – as if pissed off that fate had seen fit to photobomb his carefully planned 'I'm sorry' scene.

'Seriously,' he said, 'I'm confused. I see nothing funny about any of this.'

Rachel shrugged and shot him a sly smile of her own.

'You wouldn't,' she said, and went back to ignoring him.

6

'It's a clusterfuck,' Rachel declared as she took another sip of gin and tonic. 'A total and utter disaster. The agency's being taken over, everything at work is going to change . . . and then *he* has to turn up into the bargain. You could – not – make – it – up.'

She drained her glass and put it down on the table, then looked around at her friends. Will's soft, usually smiling eyes were anxious and Anna was biting a nail. Tom was frowning, turning a cardboard beermat over and over in his hands.

'I just can't believe it,' Anna said. 'I mean . . . what are the chances?'

'I know. It would probably be funny if it weren't so BLOODY AWFUL.'

Will heaved himself up off the leather sofa he'd sunk into. Recognising that it was probably the most useful contribution he could make to the conversation right now, he said, 'I'll go to the bar.'

'I don't know what I'm going to do,' Rachel sighed. The last of her rage had ebbed away and she felt empty, deflated. Dangerously close to tears.

Slumped down in her seat, she tipped her head back to stare at the ornate ceiling of the pub – an old gin palace on the road into Crouch End. About halfway between the girls' flat and Will and Tom's place, the Hope Tavern was elegant yet unpretentious: the kind of place that served real ale, a wide selection of gins and a good Sunday roast. It had original stained glass in its heavy mahogany doors, dark wood panelling on the walls and roaring real fires in winter.

The four of them ended up here most Fridays, sometimes with additional boyfriends and girlfriends if Rachel and Tom were seeing people. Traditionally, though, their 'start the weekend' meet-up was cheerier than this.

'Maybe I should just leave – look for another job,' Rachel said, squeezing her eyes shut in the hope that, when she opened them again, everything might be back to normal.

'Hmm. That seems extreme, Rach.'

She opened one eye to look at Tom, who was peering at her over the remnants of his pint.

'Why should you quit a job you're good at and which – vegetable bullshit aside – you mostly enjoy? A takeover like this is bound to feel scary, but I doubt you're someone the business will want to lose, even if they're planning to let people go. A restructure could even be good for you. Isn't it worth sticking around to find out?'

Rachel groaned at him good-naturedly.

'Thomas, do you *always* have to be so bloody rational?'

He shrugged and smiled, opening his palms in apology. 'I can't help it. Wisdom is the cross I have to bear.'

Rachel sat up straighter and made a face at him. 'The trouble is, this is not a simple question of what makes sense, career-wise. It's about whether I can stand being in the same office as someone who . . .'

'Broke your heart,' Anna put in: a statement rather than a question.

'I was *going* to say: someone who totally screwed me over and is a massive cheating twat.'

'Oh.'

'I guess only you know how strongly you still feel about him,' Tom said, fiddling with the beermat again. 'I mean, er, about what happened. But I somehow doubt he'll be a shit to you at work. He sounds too clever and far too selfish to risk his own reputation. More likely he'll stay out of your way, especially if you warn him off.'

'Maybe,' Rachel replied, her chin cupped in her hands. 'It might be we don't have that much to do with each other at work anyway . . . We're in different departments, I suppose. And just so we're clear, I do *not* have "strong feelings" for Jack – or about how things ended between us.'

She tried not to wince as his name left her lips.

'In that case,' Tom said, 'what's the harm in giving yourself a few weeks just to see how you handle being around the . . . what was it? "Massive cheating twat"? Then, if you decide it's too uncomfortable, you can start job-hunting.'

Unable to argue with this, Rachel nodded. Will passed her another pink G&T and she popped the gin-soaked raspberry garnish into her mouth, chewing it slowly in order to avoid saying anything.

'It's a bit of a piss-take, this happening at the same time as that busty type's started turning up on buses, isn't it?' Will observed, in a surprise intervention.

Anna gave him a look that said: *YOU'RE CRAP AT THIS, SHUT UP IMMEDIATELY.*

'It kind of is, isn't it?' Rachel murmured, suddenly more inclined to see the funny side than she'd been all day. Anna was still staring murderously at Will in defence of her friend's presumed sensitivities, while Tom looked agog at this sudden decision to wade in.

'I mean, if you were superstitious, you could almost see this as . . . *a sign*,' Will went on, encouraged by Rachel's agreement and finishing his point in dramatic fashion, his tone reminiscent of Mystic Meg.

Anna threw a half-melted ice cube at his head.

'A sign of what?' Tom asked, his eyebrows drawn together. 'Are you saying this is God's way of telling Rachel this arsehole belongs in her life? That they're star-crossed lovers or something?'

At this, Rachel choked slightly on a slurp of gin.

Anna patted her on the back. 'It's not a sign of *anything*,' she said with conviction. 'There are no signs. There is no force ordering the universe: everything's random, even stuff that feels like it can't be.'

'But what about—' Will began.

Anna's thunderous expression killed the question before it was fully formed.

'It's *us* who make stories, find connections, forge links between totally disparate events. We do it to suit our own agendas,' she decreed. She had resorted to using her Teacher Voice, so everyone understood that the matter was now closed.

'*Busty*, though, mate. *Busty?!*' Tom suddenly burst out. 'I haven't heard that word since I was about fifteen. Anna, next time you're at ours I strongly suggest you check under his bed for old issues of *Razzle* magazine.'

Later, as Will and Tom chatted to Nick, the pub's landlord, Anna asked Rachel all the questions she'd held back while the men were within earshot.

'So hit me: Is Jack still a heartbreaker or have the years been unkind? Does he have the receding hairline he so richly deserves?'

Rachel shook her head bitterly. 'Far from it. He looks almost the same. Possibly better, bearing in mind he now wears a suit instead of a student-newspaper hoodie.'

'Damn it. Should have known it was too much to hope that he'd turn into a troll.'

'*Way* too much,' Rachel agreed.

'And did you . . . were you . . . interested? *Affected?*'

Rachel cringed. 'Anna, within a few minutes of him being introduced to the staff I got an IM from a colleague who was already picturing him naked. Even I'm not sure how he does it – but pretty much everyone in the office was "affected".'

'Way to dodge the question, Rach.'

'I'm not dodging! I'm just not sure what you're asking me.'

'I'm asking if you, personally, felt anything. Not necessarily the earth moving, but . . . a spark. An atmosphere. *Chemistry*. Anything that might signal I need to question your sanity, or should start preparing to stage an intervention.'

'Don't be ridiculous. I spent most of the day feeling physically sick at the sight of him or wishing he'd fall into a big hole. Then, when he told me he was sorry and he'd changed and *blah blah blah*, I made it very clear that I've filed him under A for Arsehole. Permanently.'

'Good,' Anna said. 'Just . . . keep your wits about you while you work out what to do next. We wouldn't want him charming his way back into your in-tray. By which I mean, your knickers.'

'*Anna!*' Rachel screeched in outrage, feeling her insides lurch at the thought.

'Okay, fine, I'll stop. I still can't believe it's really happened, though. Do you think it *could* be a sign?'

'What the fuck?! What happened to "There are no signs, the universe is random"?'

'Nothing. I think it's all bobbins, as previously stated. But what do *you* think?'

'Ugh, I don't know,' Rachel moaned, and scrubbed a hand across her forehead. 'If it's a sign of anything, it's that I have terrible taste in men. I binned off Laurence because he wasn't "enough", and now – as if to underline that I'm the Goldilocks of dating – along comes Jack to remind me what happens when I go out with someone who's too much. The search for someone just right continues . . . Probably forever.'

Anna laughed and shook her head. 'Did you check for a ring?'

Rachel sipped her drink, then wrinkled her nose. 'A ring? How d'you mean?'

'Oh my God, Rachel. You didn't think to check for a wedding band? He's, what, thirty-two-ish by now? Yes, he did a gap year, if I remember rightly – so he's older than us. He could easily be married. He might even have kids!'

Realisation hit Rachel with the force of a breeze block. When she'd looked at him this morning, she'd seen *her*

Jack: the one she'd adored, then felt utterly broken by. In reality, though, he could be a completely different person by now.

He could be someone else's Jack, legally bound to them in marriage. He might belong to multiple other people, if he'd become a father. Rachel felt her heart squeeze as she pictured him with children.

He'd insisted that he'd changed, but Rachel had failed to consider what that might mean over and above 'I no longer tell women I love them, then sleep with other people.'

I've been an idiot, she said to herself. *He's probably got some beautiful, intelligent wife back in Manchester – one of those women who produces perfect pudgy babies, gets her figure back within five minutes and then returns to her highly successful career as a neurosurgeon.*

No wonder Jack had tried to avoid dredging up the past when he saw her today. To him, it *was* the past. Old news, long forgotten. Rachel suddenly felt desolate. She desperately wished she'd done something – found someone – to render the events of ten years ago as meaningless for her as they surely were for him.

Could Will be right? Perhaps the universe *was* trying to tell her something.

Then, just as Tom reappeared with another tray of drinks, a horrible thought occurred to her: maybe the cosmos was trying to deliver the same message as her mother.

'More booze,' Tom said, handing Rachel a glass.

'Thanks,' she replied. 'Much needed.'

'I'm sure. And I got these too,' he said, extracting several bags of crisps from his back pockets before sitting down.

'Prawn cocktail! You're the best,' Rachel sighed, snatching up a packet and hugging it in delight.

'Just keep them to yourself,' Tom laughed. 'They're vile – I don't know how you can eat them.'

Anna and Will nodded their agreement. The three of them tore into two packs of cheese and onion, leaving Rachel to devour her own snack without sharing.

'I have something else that might cheer you up,' Tom said once everyone had stopped munching. 'How do you fancy helping me out with some copywriting?'

'Really?' Rachel asked. 'How come? What d'you need?'

'Well, as of today I'm working on a photography exhibition for a PR agency – I got the green light this afternoon. They want me to take the images, but also help curate the thing . . . We're calling it #NoFilter, and the idea is that it'll feature celeb types, body positivity campaigners, mental health experts and so on – all in pictures that haven't been retouched or manipulated. The idea is to explore hidden stories, peep beneath the surface at what's real. Or at least as real as the PR people will let things get . . . The exhibition is really about helping some of their clients seem a bit less, er, two-dimensional.'

'That's interesting,' Rachel said, meaning it. 'But what d'you need me for?'

'Well, the budget's pretty tight but there's scope for me to get some help with the words that will appear next to the portraits. I'd far rather work with you than some random writer, if you're up for it. Basically, you'd be rewording material sent to us so it sounds cleverer, or in some cases meeting the celebs to find out what they'd like to say on the theme of the exhibition.'

'Wow. I mean, I've never done anything like that before . . .'

Exasperated, Anna cut across her. 'She'll do it. She's in.'

Rachel threw her a dark look.

'Oh, come on, you're well capable. It'll be fun. Plus, you need a distraction from the disaster zone that is your *actual* job, after today.'

'That's true,' Rachel said. 'But I'll have to make sure nobody at work objects. I don't want to be accused of moonlighting.'

'On the money I'll be paying you, you won't be,' Tom assured her. 'Look, let's meet up tomorrow and I can explain a bit more. Then, if you decide you're not up for it, I promise I won't be offended.'

'How can I say no? You bought me pink crisps in my hour of need.'

'Yep – I'm a regular hero.'

Anna glanced at Tom, then said, 'Shall I get a final round?'

'For sure.' Rachel nodded. 'Let's drink to The Worst Ever Day At Work, TM.'

'*Your* worst ever,' Anna said. 'But let's not forget the day Rajesh Bains in Year 10 set fire to his GCSE poetry anthology five minutes into my perfectly planned lesson on Robert Browning. Little *rat*.'

Rachel broke into raucous giggles, remembering Anna's story of a hastily scrambled bucket of water, an abandoned lecture on 'My Last Duchess', several soggy teenagers protesting that the incident had waterlogged forbidden iPhones, and her subsequent, irate phone call to Rajesh's parents.

'We'll drink to that too, then: to Rajesh, and his hatred of randy dukes who execute their wives. Best make them doubles.'

7

Rachel woke just before eight on Saturday morning, immediately grateful that she wasn't more hung-over. She felt a little grotty, but experience told her this low-level ickiness was nothing a bacon sandwich and a cup of tea couldn't cure.

Then she remembered why she'd sunk so much gin in the first place. The company takeover. Jack. Her argument with Jack.

Bleurgh.

Rachel curled into a ball and pulled the duvet over her head. Even a Cyril's full English wouldn't be comfort food enough to soothe her now.

She heard the *fzzzz-fzzzz* of her phone vibrating on her bedside table and extended a hand from beneath the bluebell-patterned bedclothes. After a moment's groping, she had it.

A WhatsApp from Tom.

Tom: *Morning! You still up for meeting today to chat about the exhibition? x*

Gah, she'd forgotten about this too – but it seemed churlish to back out now, even though she'd only said yes thanks to a combination of Anna's strong-arming and Tom's strategic snack selection.

Besides, Tom had been typically sage and supportive last night; he'd done Rachel the service of saying things that were genuinely helpful rather than just what she might have wanted to hear. It was definitely her turn to help him for a change.

Rachel: *Yep. When and where? (FYI, am still in bed . . .) x*

Tom: *Of course you are, it's early. Just didn't want to give you the chance to overthink this and back out <winking emoji> Janssens beer bar in Soho? Noon? Dev from the PR agency is coming too – just wants a quick face to face before he releases the budget for copy x*

Rachel, still cocooned in bed, emitted a muffled moan. She always felt like an impostor in Soho – not young, attractive or arty enough to hang out in the same spots as narrow-hipped twenty-somethings wearing cropped tops and ironic trainers.

As for meeting Tom's colleague . . . The last thing Rachel felt capable of this morning was making nice with a complete stranger, let alone a PR type who probably specialised in blowing smoke up the backsides of C-list celebs.

But she wasn't going to let Tom down – not least because he'd already called her out on the temptation to bottle this.

She tapped out a reply.

Rachel: *Me? Overthink? Never. See you there x*

Rachel arrived at Janssens with five minutes to spare. She had on her skinniest jeans, black hiking boots and an oversized eighties-style teal jumper she'd recently snapped up on Depop. Her freshly washed hair was pulled into an unruly bun, high on top of her head.

She glanced at herself in the reflective surface of a craft beer tap. She'd looked pretty good when she left the house, she thought – but after her short walk here from Leicester Square, the tip of her long, straight nose was bright pink with cold. It gave her a rabbity air.

She felt a hand on her shoulder.

'Hey,' Tom said. 'Thanks for coming. You find it okay?'

She smiled and nodded. 'Google Maps is my friend.'

'What can I get you? Go and grab a seat, settle in.'

'I dunno. I'm rubbish with beer . . . What do you recommend?'

'Hmm. Something pale? Or a fruit beer?'

Rachel nodded again. 'Either sounds good. I'll leave it to you. Choose me something nice.'

She found a vacant table, small and round, with leather banquettes on either side and a bud vase of snowdrops in the centre. A couple of metres away stood a fireplace with an ornate carved-wood mirror above it. There were lighted candles at either end of the mantelpiece.

'I like this place,' Rachel said to Tom as he returned from the bar. She took a sip from what could only be described as a goblet of deep-pink beer. 'And that' – she slurped from her glass again – 'is *delicious*.'

'Oh, good, I was hoping you'd say that. About the drink, and the bar.'

It was odd, being here just the two of them. Rachel couldn't remember if she'd been in a pub with Tom by herself before – whether they'd been for a drink like this together, without Anna and Will flanking them.

Just as she was thinking it was comfortable – nice, even – Tom said, 'Dev should be here in a minute.'

His voice was strangely tight, almost nervous. He looked spooked too. Perhaps he was afraid people might mistake them for a couple.

'I told him it was a lady writer I'd found, so he's probably preening,' Tom went on.

Rachel laughed. 'A *lady*?! I'm pretty sure ladies can walk in heels, take pride in their quiet self-confidence and don't say "fuck". Surely my mannish shoe collection, rampant insecurity and potty mouth rule me out.'

Tom was laughing now too.

'Ah, here we go. Dev!' he shouted, gesturing to someone on the other side of the room.

A thirty-something man with fine, symmetrical features and raven-black hair floated over to them. He was clutching a glass of mineral water with a twist of lime and had a silver document wallet tucked under his arm.

Maybe Tom had been right about the preening: Rachel had never seen a man so carefully manicured in her life. Everything about Dev was just so, from his sky-blue lambswool cardigan to his box-fresh Veja sneakers. His warm, dark skin was flawless, and his facial hair so precisely trimmed that Rachel wondered if he'd used a stencil.

'Dev, this is Rachel,' Tom said. 'She's going to help me out with the captions and copy for the show.'

'Darling! Nice to meet you,' Dev replied, shaking her hand. His accent was crisp and cut-glass; he could have played a rake in *Downton Abbey*. 'How much do you know about the exhibition so far?' he asked her.

'Not a lot,' Rachel said. 'Just the central theme and the name. And I understand you represent some of the people who are going to feature?'

'Quite so, I'm with Esteem PR. We're still finalising our list of participants for the show, but we've already confirmed some big names: Sophie French, Alyssia Ahmadi, Joey Nixon, Zack Lanson . . .'

Rachel smiled and did her best to look impressed. She tried to remember what Zack Lanson was well known for, apart from spelling his name with a *K*.

'A number of our clients are keen to start breaking out,' Dev continued. 'Most of the people we look after are known for their social media presences but a select few are ready to open up – connect with fans at a deeper level. And of course this coincides with other, more worldly ambitions they might have, hahaha.'

'Oh, really?' Rachel said. 'Like what?'

'Oh, the usual things . . . Sophie French is keen on acting. Wants to do Shakespeare, apparently! Zack wants to share his, ahem, songwriting with a wider audience.'

'Right.' She caught Tom's eye and grinned.

'If it sounds calculated,' Dev said, theatrically leaning in, 'it is, a little. But we can't justify mounting the show and coughing up for it if there's no business case. That said, we'd like for it to do *some* good: contribute to the conversation about online fakery. We don't want it to be a *totally* hollow exercise – hence getting the body positivity types in.'

'I think I understand.' Rachel nodded, fascinated by Dev's ability to sound cynical one minute and politically correct the next.

Tom said, 'I've explained to Rachel that her role will mainly be taking the celebrities' words – either from emails, or from face-to-face interviews – and shaping them a little. Making everyone sound sincere and thoughtful. Basically, Rach, it's about making sure we have some editorial consistency and keeping the theme alive across the whole exhibition.'

'Sounds great,' she said. 'I'm sure I can do that.'

'What's your background?' Dev asked.

'I'm a copywriter with a digital marketing agency,' Rachel replied. 'We're small, but we've just been taken over by a big firm you've probably heard of: Mountaintop Media.'

'Ah yes, I know of them,' Dev said. 'Well, it sounds like you're well qualified and I get the impression you two will work well together. Tom, I'll leave this with you to look through – it's information on the clients who are a definite yes so far, plus some standard PR snaps so you can see what you're going to be working with – the layers of gloss you'll need to find your way beneath, hahaha.'

He threw back what remained of his water as if it were a shot of some strong spirit, then handed his silver folder to Tom and stood up to go.

'Enjoy the rest of the weekend, both,' he said. 'Divine to meet you, Rachel. Let's touch base again in a couple of weeks when the first shoots are booked in. By then I should have more of an idea of how many non-clients we've got on board. I'll work on booking an exhibition space for July too, and let you know the details when I've got them.'

Dev shook Tom's hand and kissed Rachel on both cheeks before sweeping out of the bar.

'Blimey,' Rachel said, staring after him.

Tom shrug-smiled awkwardly. 'I know. Stupidly handsome, isn't he?' He gestured at his grey marl sweatshirt and soft blue jeans. 'I feel like a hobo now.'

'Oh, rubbish,' Rachel said. 'To be honest, he reminds me a bit of a Ken doll: pristine, but best left in his box. You'd mess him up if you played with him too much.'

Tom sniggered at this, and brightened. He opened the file Dev had placed on the table, which Rachel now saw was embossed with the Esteem PR logo. *Snazzy*.

Inside was the paperwork Dev had promised, and Rachel marvelled at the photographs of his clients as she and Tom began to leaf through them. It appeared that, for most of these people, taking part in a photo shoot without styling, make-up or the promise of retouching would be a new and different experience.

They finished their drinks as they discussed Dev's brief notes on the celebrities.

'Zack Lanson . . .' Tom muttered. 'Fashion and lifestyle vlogger. Famous for virtual tours of his wardrobe. Made a video called *How to Wear a White T-Shirt* that went viral. I mean, *what?* It says here his heroes are the folk artists and singer-songwriters he listened to growing up. Dear God, he has venues booked for his own musical performances in the spring and summer . . .'

'Oh, fair play to him,' Rachel said easily. 'He could be amazing for all we know.'

Tom shook his head and chuckled. 'Call me a doubting Thomas, but I can't see it . . . He'll take a good photo all stripped back, though, and that's what counts. This whole thing is a great opportunity to get my work out there. And the more gigs like this I get, the less time I'll have to spend graphic designing. We had a client this week who wanted his whole website redone in various shades of red. It made me want to cry.'

Rachel laughed and winced in sympathy. 'I'm pleased for you. And now I'm past the point of being able to chicken out, I can see that helping with the copy is going to be fun.'

'Excellent,' Tom said, beaming.

'Another?' Rachel asked, pointing to his empty glass. 'My round. Or is it home time?'

'No more beer for me, I'm afraid.' Tom shook his head and looked at his watch, then the floor. 'I'm meeting someone in Camden at half one, so I'd better think about heading up there soon. I guess I'll see you sometime next week?'

'Ah. Sure.'

At a loss for anything else to do, Rachel retrieved her coat from the corner she'd stuffed it into, put it on and hung her handbag on her shoulder.

'Mind if I take the list of celebs who've said they're in? I'll leave you with the photos and notes – just thought I'd do some extra research of my own.'

'No problem,' Tom said, handing it to her.

'Great. Well. I'll see you soon, then.'

She considered kissing him on the cheek but decided against it, instead raising her right hand in a feeble goodbye wave. Why wouldn't he look her in the eye? And what was that clean, pleasant, lemony smell? Was he wearing *aftershave*?

A short while later, squeezed against the doors of a packed Piccadilly line train, Rachel wondered who Tom was meeting. It must be a woman, she reasoned. Had he met someone new? Someone he was reluctant to introduce to his friends?

That thought bothered her. It wasn't like Tom to be cagey – but he clearly hadn't wanted to discuss this date, whoever it was with.

After five more minutes of poking at her bruised feelings, Rachel concluded that she was hurt. She considered Tom a close friend; she trusted him implicitly. He knew things about her that she'd barely shared with anyone, and it was galling to think that, by contrast, he felt the need to hide things from her.

Stop thinking about it, she instructed herself. *You have far bigger problems right now.*

The only trouble was, she didn't want to think about those either.

8

Anna was gone by the time Rachel got back to the flat. She was off for a movie and dinner with Will and would be back sometime tomorrow, so Rachel had the place to herself.

While she never resented Anna's spending time alone with her boyfriend, Rachel could have done with some company this evening. If she dwelled too much on the events of the past few days, she knew she'd start spiralling. She needed something to do.

Rachel thought about what usually calmed her when she was hovering near a nervo: housework, gardening, attempting something creative in the kitchen. She needed simple activities she could do methodically – the sort that yielded pleasing results and required just enough attention to distract her.

Rachel turned up the volume on a Carole King playlist, plodded to her bedroom and inspected the contents of her laundry hamper. She shoved a dark load in the washer-dryer, then ran warm water and Woolite into the kitchen sink so she could hand-wash the delicates she'd been ignoring since Christmas.

Once she'd hung a selection of damp lingerie and knitwear on Anna's heated airer, she raided the kitchen cupboards. Sugar, eggs, flour . . . chocolate chips and bicarb.

A bottle of vanilla extract that was only slightly out of date. There was also proper butter in the fridge, which meant she was going to make cookies.

An hour or so later, the soothing scent of sweet dough and melting chocolate permeated every room in the flat. Once they'd cooled, Rachel filled one of Anna's floral cake tins with biscuits that, though she said it herself, looked mouth-watering.

She kept two aside, then fastened the lid and made a cup of tea. After digging for Dev's client list in her handbag, she sat down with her laptop and mobile.

Zack Lanson, she soon learned, was the most famous of the group who'd signed up to be part of #NoFilter. Rachel felt her eyes widen as she scrolled through his social feeds and YouTube channel. The white T-shirt video Tom had mentioned earlier had well over a million views.

Alyssia Ahmadi, Rachel discovered, was some kind of wellness warrior. Her Instagram was all cooking with quinoa, daily yoga practice, mindful mantras and designer sportswear. Meanwhile, Joey Nixon was a gaming guru whose reviews of the latest releases could apparently make or break them.

Sophie French seemed to occupy the same cyber space as Jessica Williams: she vlogged and posted about her life and style, partnering with fashion and beauty brands to promote their products. A trawl through Sophie's Insta history revealed she'd even been an Angeljuice ambassador at one stage.

Rachel's thoughts drifted back to the bus ads, and she felt the good mood she'd cultivated start leaking out of her like air from a punctured tyre. Without asking herself what she was doing or why, she typed Jessica's name into Instagram's search bar and opened her profile.

Every beautifully composed, thoughtfully styled photo was like a punch to Rachel's gut. She told herself that flipping through Jessica's summer bikini shots probably qualified as an act of self-harm – but somehow she couldn't resist the urge to look at them.

The emotions Jessica evoked were similar to those Rachel remembered having in adolescence, standing next to her older, more beautiful (and, crucially, non-ginger) sister in family photographs. Rachel's discomfort had usually showed in the developed images; she'd be scowling, looking away from the camera or grinning through gritted teeth. She'd ruined every picture she was in, or at least that was how it had felt. By contrast, Lizzy had always looked relaxed and happy – unconcerned that the click of a camera button might see her weighed, measured and found wanting.

Grown-up Rachel had spent years trying not to compare her appearance or achievements to anyone else's, and she knew that Tom was right: she didn't need to. Rachel was her own person, and broadly happy with herself. Yet Jessica retained a unique power to make her feel dumpy, dull and deficient.

Rachel licked a finger, swept up the cookie crumbs from her plate and devoured them. If this was stress-eating, she decided it wasn't entirely unjustified after the week she'd had. Maybe just one more . . .

As she'd once said to Anna, it wasn't merely the fact

that Jack had cheated on her that hurt. It was also the *way* he'd done it – and who with.

During his pursuit of Rachel, he'd made much of her romantic, singular look: the idea that she was beautiful – handsome, even – rather than conventionally pretty. The strong features Rachel had been teased about in childhood sat differently in her adult face. Without realising it, she'd grown into them in her late teens, and her deep-brown eyes, creamy skin and generous lips – the top one slightly larger than its partner – now combined with her copper waves to give her a dreamy, soulful bearing.

Nevertheless, Rachel had never quite shaken off the idea that she was inelegant and odd-looking. She'd been surprised to discover she appealed to males of the species – particularly the unkempt, poetic types she'd met on her English degree course. But for all Jack's effusive praise of her 'difference', he'd gone and slept with someone lithe, mahogany-haired and tanned: a woman nine out of ten cads would have voted better-looking. It was so depressingly *obvious*, at the same time as feeling like a stunning volte-face.

Rachel's memory wound back to her first meeting with Jack, during Freshers' Week. He'd stood in line next to her at an onboarding event, making wild predictions about which student societies she'd join. 'Women's rugby team? Lego Club? The Princess Diana Society! Hang on . . . Jane Austen Is My Spirit Animal Soc?' She'd finally laughed at that and said, 'Bang to rights.'

They'd become friends, but Rachel had worked hard to keep her wits about her when he turned on the charm.

Even then she'd been expert at checking her own emotions – consigning inconvenient feelings to hidden corners of her heart, from which they'd struggle to resurface.

Ultimately, though, refusing to fall for Jack had become exhausting. It took effort not to let him hold her gaze when he focused his green eyes on her; it was tough to resist the repositioning of a friendly hand slung around her shoulder when it migrated to the small of her back.

Two years on he'd worn her down, drawn her in. It was only once Rachel was completely suckered that he'd decided to burn everything down. It was this, above all, that she had never forgiven him, or herself, for.

And now Jack was back: a changed man, or so he claimed. A *married* man, perhaps . . .

Rachel's hand hovered over her computer keyboard. She'd resisted looking for Jack on the internet for so long that even the thought of searching for his Facebook profile felt illicit. She wondered if this was what a recovering alcoholic might feel like, trying to face down a tumbler of twenty-five-year-old single malt.

Her fingertips shook slightly as she tapped out his name. Writing it felt like admitting he was real again: like bringing him back to life.

He was here, and they had six mutual friends – presumably people they'd been at university with. His page was private, but some of his photos were visible. In his profile picture he wore a navy suit with a crisp white shirt, a cornflower-blue tie and a yellow crocus in the buttonhole. There was a flute of something sparkling in his right hand, and his left arm was wrapped around the slender waist of a woman in a white 1950s-style dress. A wedding dress.

Anna had been right, then. Jack had a wife.

As she stared at the image, transfixed by the sincerity of his smile, Rachel found she wasn't bitter or devastated. To her surprise, it seemed she wasn't anything, really.

She felt oddly numb, as though this were information she couldn't quite compute. It was like being convinced you understood a person, only to find out they had a secret identity – that they weren't who you thought they were at all.

At least one thing made sense: Jack's wife was predictably pretty. She had Nordic-blonde hair cut in a sleek, shining bob. Her eyes were big and blue – almost doll-like – made up with flawless, flicky black liner. Her red-lipsticked mouth was spread wide in a warm, happy smile that matched her new husband's.

This was *fine*, Rachel told herself. More than fine. Perhaps it was even ideal. Jack being married drew a very neat line under their history. Rachel felt relieved, as if she'd just been given a booster vaccination: a shot that would supercharge her immunity to him.

Satisfied, she shut her laptop. Maybe she'd run a bath and start a new book, then order in a pizza for dinner. She padded to the bathroom, poured a capful of her favourite foam into the tub and turned on the taps.

As Rachel surveyed her cluttered bookshelves, hunting for something as unromantic as possible, she chose not to ask herself the obvious question. Why, after what Jack had done and after all this time, should she ever have been concerned about her resistance to him?

Later that evening, halfway through an old Louis Theroux documentary, Rachel's phone rang. *HQ Basecamp calling*, the screen said. It was her parents.

She pressed pause on Netflix, then tapped the green icon to pick up.

'Hello?' she said, and braced herself.

'Don't you "hello" me, young lady, as if you don't KNOW it's your mother on the line. I've been trying to get hold of you for over a week.'

Rachel cringed, genuinely remorseful. 'Sorry, Mum. Really. Work has been crazy since I started back.'

'Has it indeed?' She sounded disdainful, disbelieving. Her Stoke accent got noticeably stronger when she was annoyed.

'We're pitching for loads of new business,' Rachel said. 'I've been staying late a lot, helping out.'

She'd decided not to tell her parents about the takeover or the risk it might pose to her job. There was nothing they could do about it, after all, and it would only worry them – something Rachel always avoided, if possible.

'I see. And I suppose you've been out with Laurence whenever you've had a night off?'

Rachel hated that her mum sounded cheered by the thought of her gadding about with a man she had already dumped. The time to confess had come.

'Actually . . . Well. Laurence and I are sort of . . . not seeing each other any more.'

'Oh, love! What happened?'

Tenderness and concern, Rachel observed. *This won't last long.*

'It wasn't going anywhere, Mum. He's a perfectly nice guy, he's just not the man for me.'

'Are you telling me you've finished with another one? Chucked someone else stable and decent?' Mum's voice was shrill now, and utterly devoid of sympathy. 'I mean, who are you holding out for, Rachel – one of the Hemsworth brothers?'

Rachel boggled, not sure whether to be outraged or amused. 'Obviously not. But I can't stay with someone just because they have a pension plan, Mum. You can't base a relationship on a well-stocked wine rack, or the fact that someone's capable of keeping a grow-your-own basil plant alive. I need to *feel* something for whoever I'm with.'

'Rachel, by the time I was your age I was married with two children,' her mum said.

'*Yes*,' Rachel cut in. 'You were married to a man you were wildly in love with, who hopped on the ferry, left his family in Ireland and followed you home from Dublin after a holiday fling. You're hardly in a position to tell me romance is dead.'

'It wasn't dead thirty-seven years ago! But at best it's on life support these days, what with all this revenge porn and sexting and Grind-It.'

'*Grindr*. And that's an app mostly used by gay men.'

'Don't change the subject, Rachel. Meeting someone nowadays is HARD. Half the blokes out there are weirdos and nutters. And yet every time you get close to one who seems sane and normal, you dump him. I don't understand what your problem is.'

Rachel could feel her temper beginning to fray. 'Right now, my problem is this conversation. Plus the fact that you don't seem to care whether I'm happy, just that I have a man in my life. A sane one, apparently – but even you have to admit that "not an axe murderer" is setting the bar pretty low, Mum.'

'Of *course* I care about you being happy! But will you be happy all by yourself when Anna and Will get married? And when that nice-looking friend of Will's finds someone too, and disappears?'

'Mum, Anna and Will don't even live together yet. There's no way they're getting married anytime soon.' Rachel noticed the speed at which her chest was rising and falling, and tried to take slower, deeper breaths.

'But who's there with you now?' her mum pressed on. 'Nobody, I'm guessing, or you wouldn't have picked up the phone. It's Saturday night, Rachel – you should be out enjoying yourself and you're *not.*'

Rachel groaned. It stung that her mum was right: that, of her closest friends, she was the only one left alone this evening. She wondered again what Tom was up to.

Rachel heard her dad muttering in the background – something that sounded like, 'Jean, for the love of God, rein it in a bit.'

'Rachel,' Mum went on, 'all I'm saying is that lack of fireworks isn't a good reason to finish with someone who cares about you. Dark and dangerous men might feel more exciting, but you can't rely on them. That John Luther's a looker, but you couldn't trust him to do the weekly shop.'

'For heaven's sake, Mum! *Dark and dangerous men?*

Luther? What are we even talking about?' Jack's face floated into Rachel's mind and she batted it away briskly. 'As far as fireworks are concerned, the chemistry between me and Laurence was barely enough to ignite a sparkler. And for the record, I *do* want a boyfriend . . . Maybe even a husband one day. I'm just not prepared to stay with someone when I know it isn't right. It wouldn't have been fair to Laurence to keep seeing him, or any good for me in the long run.'

'Whatever you say, love,' Mum sighed. She sounded more resigned than convinced. 'What are your plans for the rest of the weekend?'

Glad of the change of subject, Rachel cast around for something to say. Her eyes fell on a shoebox in the hallway, just visible from her position on the squashy pink sofa. It contained a pair of running trainers she'd ordered in the sales but had yet to break in.

'I'm planning to go for a run in the morning,' Rachel heard herself say.

'Ah! Trying to lose a few pounds, are you?'

'*No*,' Rachel replied, grudgingly impressed by her mother's ability to take any topic and turn it into a stick to beat her with. 'It's not about losing weight, just about improving my fitness a bit.'

That, and winning the bet she'd made with Will on New Year's Eve. He'd scoffed at the idea that Rachel would ever exercise voluntarily, then promised her a bottle of gin if she made it to the end of the Couch to 5K programme she'd sworn to complete.

'Fair enough. But you have a decent sports bra, don't

you, love? You don't want your boobs batting you in the face every other stride.'

'Oh my God, Mum – yes, I have one,' Rachel said, resisting the urge to point out that it wasn't her fault she'd inherited her curvy build, as well as her hair colour, from her father's side of the family. Modest-breasted Mum had never been above a size eight in her life, apart from during her pregnancies. She was dark-haired, delicately pretty and petite, standing only a tiny bit taller than Anna. 'Can you put Dad on?' Rachel felt bad for dismissing her mother, but she'd had as much veiled criticism as she could bear for one night.

'Course I can.' She sounded crestfallen. 'Love you. Speak to me again soon, won't you?'

'Love you too, Mum,' Rachel said. She meant it, and told herself she wasn't to blame if her mum felt snubbed.

There was a light scuffling as the phone passed from one hand to another.

'Hi there, pet,' said Rachel's dad. As ever, his voice was like balm on a bruise – his soft Dublin accent still strong after almost forty years in the UK. 'How're you doin'? Not fixing to jump off the nearest bridge after that chat with your mother, I hope.'

Rachel laughed. 'No. She gave it her best shot, though.'

'Ah, she means well, you know that. She just worries about you.'

'Honestly, Dad, sometimes I think she worries more about what other people think. You know, when they ask how I am and she has to tell them I'm still not settled down. I know it galls her that Mrs O'Shea from church has three daughters who *all* have husbands.'

'She does hate that Mrs O'Shea,' he concurs. 'But I promise it's you she's thinking about. She wants a happy future for you, and she worries you stand in your own way.'

'I promise you, Dad, Laurence and I were not a good fit. We wouldn't have *had* a happy future. But the right person will come along one day, and I'm sure I'll know him when I see him.'

'All right then, let's leave off that. Anything else exciting happening? Apart from the running?'

'Yes, actually. I'm helping Tom out with some copywriting for a photography exhibition. I'm not being paid much but it should be fun, and I might even get to meet some minor celebs.'

'Grand. That sounds great. And you never know, one of these famous types might fall in love with you. That'd shut your mum up for sure.'

Rachel laughed again, then fought off a yawn. 'I don't know about that, based on what I've seen of the participants . . . One of them plays computer games for a living.'

'What a world,' Dad chuckled. 'I had no idea that was even possible. But you do sound tired, darlin'. Get yourself an early night, why don't you? We'll call you again next week.'

It dawned on Rachel that he was right. Somehow her own exhaustion had escaped her notice – yet her dad had spotted it from 160 miles away. She immediately felt an intense longing for her bed.

'Okay, Dad. I'll see you soon, yes?'

Her vision blurred slightly as she was hit by a powerful wave of missing him. She wished that he were closer, or at least that she could tell him what was really going on. As a little girl, Rachel had believed there was no problem in the world her father couldn't solve – though she'd long since learned there were some broken things even he couldn't fix.

'You will,' he said. 'We've plans to come down with Granny and see a show, so we'll get together then. Sometime in March, I think. Mum will message you about it, I'm sure.'

'Great,' Rachel said. 'I'll let you go, then. Love you, Dad.'

'And you, pet. Always. You look after yourself, and sleep well.'

Against all the odds, Rachel did sleep well. She woke up to see a pale, watery sort of sunlight seeping through her curtains, then pulled them back to reveal a cloudless, ice-blue sky.

A thin layer of frost glittered on the pavement outside her window. There was no sign of rain, which hobbled her standard excuse for staying inside in her pyjamas.

Last night she'd told her parents she was going to start running. Several weeks ago she'd promised *herself* that she would – for the sake of her cardiovascular fitness and a massive bottle of The Botanist.

Before she could talk herself out of it, Rachel pulled on a pair of elderly leggings, a greying sports bra and a bobbled workout top that hadn't been worn in at least four years. Her shiny new trainers would shame this sad ensemble, she thought – but perhaps she'd treat herself to some nicer running gear in a couple of weeks. The promise of a mini-spree in Sweaty Betty might motivate her to stick to her plan.

Headphones in and with her phone and keys stashed in a pocket, Rachel set off. Jo Whiley's voice instructed her to walk briskly for five minutes to warm up, then to alternate running and walking in short bursts. This, it turned out, was far tougher than it sounded.

There were several moments when Rachel feared she might vomit; still others when she contemplated giving up, going back to the flat and making a mound of peanut butter on toast. But despite the screaming of her lungs and the pounding of her heart, she kept going.

As she completed her final sprint, she felt incredible – *invincible* – even though her chest was on fire and her legs were leaden lumps. Perhaps all those people who ranted about endorphins and exercise had a point.

Rachel walked home a sweaty mess, feeling proud and strong and fervently wishing she could bottle the sensation. It might come in handy at work next week, she thought – or, at the very least, during her next conversation with her parents.

9

'So come on, then – spill. Who dumped who?'

Rachel spluttered on a mouthful of cappuccino and swallowed it, too fast, in a bid to avoid spraying.

She didn't know why she was surprised at Greg's abruptness. When she'd walked into work this morning with a worse-than-usual case of the Monday blues, he'd been standing by her desk – loitering with intent. Before she'd even removed her coat, let alone docked her laptop, he'd steered her out of the building by the elbow and then round the corner into Java Jo's.

Now, as the burn in her oesophagus subsided, Rachel considered how best to answer Greg's question. She could try to reject the premise of it – claim outrage and rant that there was no reason for him to suppose she and Jack had ever been an item.

She cast this option aside immediately. While she was used to playing her cards close to her chest, she wasn't a good enough liar to convince anyone with such a blatant fib – especially not someone who knew her as well as Greg did.

She sighed and resigned herself to giving him a slimmed-down version of events.

'I dumped him,' she said, trying to come off as indifferent and realising too late that she sounded more strained and sullen.

'Because . . . ?' Greg demanded. 'I'm sensing this wasn't a "part ways but treasure the wonderful times you had together" break-up. The atmosphere between you last week was so tense I could have sliced it with a cricket stump.'

Rachel looked up in alarm. 'Was it?'

'*Yes*,' Greg said, incredulous. 'When I left you on the train together I felt like a UN peacekeeper abandoning a war zone. I was worried one of you might not make it back to Islington alive.'

'Fuck,' Rachel muttered. Her game face obviously needed work.

Greg eyed her beadily, though not without concern. His mouth was set in a flat, straight line and his eyes – usually bright and playful – were soft with sympathy.

'I finished with him because I found out he'd slept with someone else,' Rachel said. Greg whistled in dismay and shook his head, but she carried on before he could comment. 'I saw them together, I should add – he didn't tell me himself.'

'Ugh,' Greg moaned. 'That is ROUGH. When was this?'

'Right at the end of our final year at university – just as we'd started to make plans for staying together once we left.'

'*Ouch*. No wonder you weren't pleased to see him. When you're hurt like that, it stays with you.'

Rachel felt a rush of affection for Greg – gratitude that he wasn't trying to minimise the pain she'd felt simply because it wasn't recent.

'It does,' Rachel said, suddenly aware that unburdening

herself to someone new felt good. 'I mean, I've moved on – I'm over it. It's not as if I've been living like a nun for the past ten years. But what happened was pretty difficult to forgive and forget. I spotted him with his tongue down another woman's throat on the morning of our graduation. I should have marched over and slapped him, but I didn't. I panicked. I ran away. Then, about two hours later, we had to stand in line together to collect our degree certificates. Our families were supposed to have a posh lunch afterwards, for heaven's sake. It was unbearable.'

Greg's mouth had dropped open, but no words were coming out.

'I had to make up an excuse for my parents – explain why they weren't going to meet the boyfriend I'd spent months telling them about,' Rachel explained. 'It meant a lot to them, being there, and if I'd broken down I'd have ruined it . . . As soon as it was all over, I found Jack and finished with him. Then I moved down here. I hadn't planned to, but my best friend asked if I wanted to come with her and it seemed like a smart way out. I didn't want to be anywhere near *him* so I couldn't stay up north, like I'd thought I would . . . And I couldn't face going back to my parents' house either.'

Stop, now, she told herself, *before you say too much*.

'Ray, this really is the WORST,' Greg said. 'What happened on Friday after I was gone? Please tell me you kicked him in the nuts for old times' sake.'

'Well, we had words,' she said with a hollow laugh. 'I told him I wasn't happy he'd blabbed that we knew each other. He apologised – for that and for everything else.

Said he was ashamed of himself, insisted he'd changed, et cetera, et cetera.'

Rachel appreciated Greg's derisive snort at this.

'You'd have kept all this to yourself, then, if you'd had the choice?' he asked. He sounded almost hurt.

'Probably,' she admitted. 'But that's more about me than you. I just want as few people as possible to know about all this. It's not that I'm trying to protect him,' she went on quickly, palms up in defence of her reserve. 'But I've had some time to think over the weekend, and some good advice. Keeping my job has to be my priority right now. Even if I decide I can't hack working in the same place as Jack, I don't have enough savings to quit before I've got something else lined up. Plus, if people find out Jack and I had a thing and broke up, I'll seem like the loser who punched above her weight and couldn't hang on to her man. Can you imagine the delight Donna would take in spreading *that* story?'

Greg made a face that implied he could envisage her glee all too clearly. The office manager wasn't one for small talk, but her love of gossip was legendary. If a scrap of significant news made its way around the office, it could usually be traced back to her desk; as far as the contagion of scandal was concerned, Donna was always patient zero.

'Even worse,' Rachel continued, 'if I'm mixed up in rumours that Jack's a dirty rotten shagger, I'll look like a sad case: the scorned woman who's still banging on about something that happened a decade ago. I'm better off just trying to pretend Jack doesn't exist, and I'm hoping that won't be too difficult. My guess is Prince Charming will be involved in trying to win big new commercial accounts – the kind of stuff I never get near.'

'You've got it all worked out, haven't you?' Greg said, licking cappuccino foam off his index finger. 'But this is still an epic mess of a situation, IMO. I'd be going postal if one of *my* ex-boyfriends turned up to work here.' He shuddered and made a noise that sounded like *Brrrr*. 'Also, I think there *are* people you could talk to – people you could be honest with – if you wanted to make things easier on yourself. You're highly valued at the agency. Nobody would want to see you leave over this, and I'm certain you're safe from redundancy.'

'Thanks,' Rachel said. 'That's good news. And I'm not going to pretend I'm thrilled about this, but I'll cope – I promise. You're in the circle of trust now, but I'd really rather not add anyone else.'

She pushed her cold, half-drunk cup of coffee to one side, assuming they were done. It was almost 10 a.m. now – surely time for them to put in an appearance at the office.

'While we're telling each other secrets,' Greg said, his voice low, 'I have some news.'

Rachel sat up straighter in her chair; his tone was earnest and his face suddenly serious. He was about to tell her something significant.

'Karen's leaving the agency,' Greg said. 'You know her partner's French – well, they're finally going over there to set up home in Provence. I had to wait until the takeover was finalised for confirmation, but I got the news on Friday night: I'm replacing her. *I'm* going to be the new head of client services.'

Rachel let out a little yelp of excitement. 'That's amazing! Well done. You'll be great, and you SO deserve it.'

Greg was glowing with pride, but the corners of his mouth had turned down. 'I'm thrilled, obviously. But you know this means we won't be working together so closely any more, right?'

'Of course,' Rachel said brightly, as if she'd seen this coming and made her peace with it. In fact, the thought of retiring their double act was a gut punch. She and Greg had worked in near-constant partnership for almost four years, and the truth was she'd loved it – sexy vegetables and all.

Rachel considered the other members of Greg's team. Would she end up working with Theo? Clients supposedly loved him but she struggled to take him seriously. He rode to work on a scooter, spoke fluent Corporate Bollocks and wore raspberry-pink chinos with suede boat shoes all year round. Rachel feared it would take more than *blue-sky thinking* to prevent her from punching him if they spent too much time together.

Partnering Ella might be okay; she could best be described as harmless, though she was so giddy and girlish that Rachel felt like a miserable crone in comparison. She cringed slightly as she recalled that Ella's preferred term for Prosecco was 'loopy juice'.

Rachel stood up, selfish thoughts tumbling away as she moved around the table to give Greg a hug. Her eyes were shiny with unshed tears when they pulled apart.

'I'll miss you,' she said.

'Oh, you won't,' Greg replied, waving a hand. 'You won't have the chance. I'll still be in the office every day. ALSO, you've been promising you'll come to Thursday-night yoga with me for months – so now I'm going to *make* you. And just so we're clear . . .' he added a moment later as they clattered through the door onto the street, 'anyone who thinks you were punching above your weight with Jack is a moron. You're kind, clever, funny and *way* more gorgeous than you realise. It's him who wasn't worthy of you.'

Over the next few days, Rachel's plan to carry on as normal met with more success than she expected. She finalised the content for It's All Good's shiny new website, then caught up with tasks that had been pushed down her agenda by recent events.

Jack spent almost all of his time shut away in meetings with the senior management team, which suited Rachel perfectly. It allowed her almost to believe that the events of the previous week had been a bad dream.

On Monday, Rachel had coolly rebuffed Jack's single attempt at engaging with her. When she and Greg had arrived back at the office after their pow-wow, Jack's apprehensive wave was put down with a stiff 'Good morning' as she stalked past and didn't look back. Since then, their interactions had been limited to polite nods in passing or the occasional holding open of a door.

Greg's promotion had mostly been greeted with smiles and satisfaction. He was well liked, hard-working and, as far as the agency's clients were concerned, a safe pair of hands. Happiness for Greg, however, was tempered by unease about what might be in store for the rest of the staff. One-to-one chats with people whose jobs would be affected by the restructure had started, and not everyone emerged from them calm.

Rachel, more relaxed than many of her colleagues thanks to Greg's reassurance, assumed she was unlikely to be summoned to such a meeting – for which she was abundantly grateful.

'I'm actually okay,' she told Anna over dinner on Wednesday night. 'I mean, it's a weird situation, but so far nothing I can't cope with.'

By Friday lunchtime Rachel was congratulating herself on surviving the first – and surely worst – week of her altered working life. Yes, it had been odd and uncomfortable seeing Jack here and there around the building. As predicted, though, they'd had very little to do with one another – and no doubt Rachel would become increasingly indifferent to his presence as she got used to it. She decided to reward herself with an overpriced 'artisan' sandwich and a stroll around Upper Street's shops.

When she returned to her desk, an email invitation to a 3 p.m. meeting was waiting for her. It was from Isaac, and the subject line simply read *Catch Up*.

Shit. What could one of the agency's co-founders want her for? What if Greg had been wrong and her job *wasn't* safe?

Shakily, Rachel double-clicked to open the message. Instead of a proper meeting agenda, Isaac had written some vague fluff about chatting through plans for the future of the agency and how she might fit in.

She felt her breath stop in her throat as she scanned the list of meeting invitees and saw that, alongside her name, jack.harper@mountaintopmedia.com was listed. *Brilliant*,

Rachel thought. *I may be about to find out I no longer have a job, and the Fates have decided that the ideal witness to my humiliation is HIM.*

She pushed herself up in her seat so she could properly survey the room. She had studiously avoided looking over at Jack's desk all week, but now her gaze was drawn to it. What was this meeting really for? Did he know more about it than she did?

He was on the phone, staring down at a notepad and absently chewing on the end of a biro. Rachel had always enjoyed looking at him when he wasn't aware anyone was watching; his face was different, somehow – open, rather than artfully arranged. *Stop it*, she warned herself.

Before she could shift her focus, he looked up and stared right at her. She hated that his eyes still had the power to shock her. The vivid green in them was clear even at this distance, framed by thick chestnut-coloured lashes and set off perfectly by the rich, biscuity shade of his sweater. The sweater looked warm, butter-soft and expensive. It was cashmere, Rachel supposed, and for a few seconds she allowed herself to wonder how it might feel beneath her fingers.

She turned back to her computer screen, feeling as if a jolt of electricity had just passed through her.

Less than an hour later, Rachel made her way to the small meeting room on the far side of the office. She had a calming cup of herbal tea to take in with her: a medicinal distraction. At the very least, holding it would give her something to do with her hands if, as she feared, she was about to be given bad news.

Isaac was already inside, chugging coffee from a takeaway cup as tall as his head. He was a roundish fifty-something man with wild curly hair that had once been ink-black but now boasted fine streaks of silver. He was in charge of what he called the 'pro-social' division of the business – the part that worked with charitable organisations or government departments to help promote the public good, rather than simply rake in profit.

'Thanks for coming, Rachel,' he said. 'Please don't look so worried. I'm pretty sure what I have to tell you is *good* news. Did you see Jack on your way over here?'

'No,' she replied, stiffening. 'Er – do we need him, though? I mean, I'm assuming this conversation is about my job – what it's going to be, if I still have one.'

'Absolutely,' Isaac said, smiling. 'But this concerns both of you.'

What the hell did *that* mean?

Rachel felt an unspecific creeping dread begin to lap around her ankles, an incoming tide of fear that she couldn't run away from.

'Sorry, sorry,' Jack said as he appeared in the doorway. 'I had a call that ran over.'

Isaac performed a 'don't worry about it' hand-flap, indicated that Jack should sit down and then asked him, 'Is this your first time meeting Rachel?'

Rachel felt her face crumple slightly and knew that Jack had noticed. She braced herself for his 'we were students together' shtick.

Jack cleared his throat loudly, then ran a hand through his hair. 'We met last Friday,' he said, 'but only briefly. I shadowed Greg at a client meeting and Rachel was kind enough to help me keep up.'

'Then allow me to introduce you properly.' Isaac smiled. 'Rachel Ryan, this is Jack Harper. He's going to be in charge of client relationships here on the pro-social side of the business, reporting to me as of next week. Jack, Rachel has been recommended to me as the ideal person to head up editorial strategy for the team. Greg assures me there's no one better. I'm hoping she'll work alongside you – be your opposite number, if you like.'

Rachel was suddenly reeling. Too much was happening at once. Unlike last Friday, Jack was pretending not to know her – apparently out of consideration for her feelings. Meanwhile, Isaac seemed to be offering her a new job . . . But one she'd never have applied for in a million years.

Isaac looked from Rachel to Jack with an expectant expression, and it was only when Jack leaned forward with his arm extended that she realised they were supposed to shake hands. She let him take her fingers and pull them into his. His palm was cool and soft, and she kept her eyes down.

'So what do you think, Rachel?' Isaac said. 'Are you ready to jump out of the commercial copywriting pool? I'm sure it won't shock you to hear that it's likely to shrink over the next few months – though of course that isn't common knowledge yet. This is a brand-new position: a chance for you to own it, really show off what you can do. You'd be working with Jack in much the same way as you've always done with Greg.'

Rachel felt a strangled, horrified little shriek forming in her throat. She swallowed it, then wiped her sweaty palms on her denim-clad knees.

Isaac was offering her the kind of opportunity she'd wanted for months: more meaningful work, a better job title – perhaps even more money. But this was the Salvador Dalí version of the promotion she'd been aiming for: distorted, strange and surreal.

Yet Rachel hadn't missed Isaac's implication that, if she didn't jump for the role he was offering, she might end up pushed out of the agency. Not only were there apparently more writers on the payroll than were needed; she'd look lazy and unambitious if she turned down the chance to do something more challenging than knock out content about cauliflowers.

She glanced at Jack, but couldn't get a read on what he was feeling. His face was a handsome mask: blank and impassive, gorgeous but expressionless. She thought she could detect tension in his shoulders. Perhaps he was frightened she'd freak out, make a scene and scream that she couldn't do it . . . Or maybe he was worried she'd say yes.

Rachel felt her head nodding. Her lips moved and a string of grateful, affirmative words floated from her mouth. At this moment, she realised, she had no *choice* but to say yes to Isaac. Yes to a new, more interesting role, but also to working in partnership with someone who – up until last week – she'd hoped never to see again. She was backed into a corner, and there was only one way out.

'Superb!' Isaac boomed, patting Rachel's shoulder and clapping his hands. 'I'll send a full job description and salary details across to you now, and provided that's all A-okay we'll shift you over to our team first thing next week. There's a little bump in pay to reflect the extra responsibilities you'll be taking on.'

He winked at Rachel, pushed his chair back noisily, then stood up and flashed a toothy grin at Jack. Rachel cringed.

'I can't wait to put you two to work,' Isaac said. 'Something tells me you'll be *perfect* together.'

10

After the meeting, Rachel ran to the ladies. Leaning on the basin, she saw in the mirror that she was flushed and wild-eyed – her pupils swollen to dark pools by the adrenaline rush she was riding.

She locked herself inside a cubicle and sat for what felt like a year on the lid of the toilet, cradling her head in her hands and trying not to hyperventilate. Finally, grateful that nobody else had come into the bathroom during her meltdown, Rachel patted cool water from the tap onto her face, dried under her armpits with a paper towel and went back to her desk.

Jack had been pulled into a long discussion with Isaac, Toby and Greg. Rachel felt him glance at her more than once through the glass wall of the large meeting room and wondered what he was thinking. Surely he couldn't be any happier about this than she was? Or had he known what was coming and chosen to keep his mouth shut?

She told herself she'd come up with something – that there'd be a way she could get out of this without trashing her professional reputation or ripping an unemployment-shaped hole in her already threadbare finances. She just needed time to *think*.

To Rachel's dismay, however, no revelatory idea for sorting out what Greg had aptly termed her 'epic mess' revealed itself over the weekend. Anna, staunch and supportive as ever, plied her with several delicious meals, plenty of wine and countless cups of tea – but between them, they couldn't think of a better way for Rachel to handle things than 'take the new job for now, and try to keep your shit together'.

On Sunday night, Rachel found herself wondering what Will and Tom might have made of Friday's fresh dimension to the catastrophe that was her life. She smiled to herself as she imagined Will waxing lyrical about serendipity in his Professor Trelawney voice, only to have Anna kick his shins under the table.

He'd have been kind, Rachel knew, but unlikely to offer any advice that could reasonably be considered helpful. Tom, on the other hand, might well have suggested something sensible – but as the pair of them were away on a stag do for an old school friend, he hadn't had the chance.

By the time Rachel arrived at work on Monday, the news that she was moving teams had spread. As she made her way to her desk, a handful of people whispered 'Well done', but still more regarded her quizzically. Some, Rachel assumed, must be wondering how she'd scored a step up the career ladder while other people were being shunted sideways or let go. She couldn't blame them.

Rachel felt Donna's hawklike, heavily made-up eyes assessing her as she hung up her coat and got her laptop out. She'd dressed a little more thoughtfully than usual this morning, in a pair of checked 1950s-style cigarette pants and a raspberry-pink silk shirt. Rachel's intention had been to boost her self-confidence rather than look nice for her new colleague. Now it dawned on her that turning up as a more polished version of herself could imply an ulterior motive, if you happened to be looking for one.

She stopped short of asking herself whether Donna's evident suspicions might, on some level, be justified, and kept her head down as she walked into the kitchen.

After making a coffee and picking up a banana from the fruit bowl, Rachel sat down to find she'd already received an instant message from Kemi.

Kemi Percival
I'd undo another button if I were you.
Reveal a bit more of the rack.

Rachel Ryan
What?!

Kemi Percival
I'm assuming the sexy girlboss attire is for Hot Harper's benefit.
In which case, you could def show a bit more skin.

Rachel Ryan
Please, please, NEVER refer to him as that again.
I almost brought back my banana.
ALSO this outfit is for no one's benefit . . . It isn't even new!
I am a modern feminist, I do not dress up for men – especially not at work <strong arm emoji>

Kemi Percival
He IS hot. The name stays <flame emoji>
And we ALL dress up for men as fit as him. I might be a feminist but I'm not blind – and neither are you. Allllll the girls want to know how you pulled this off.

Rachel Ryan
Pulled what off?

Rachel could feel heat rising up her neck. She'd tried to tamp down her annoyance with this conversation, but indignation had begun to burn somewhere behind her ribcage.

Kemi Percival
How you bagged the new job obvs.
I'd give my right arm to spend all my work days hanging with someone that lush . . . <aubergine emoji>
Well, maybe not an arm. Like, a toe or something <shrug emoji>

Rachel Ryan
*So it hasn't occurred to anyone that I might have been promoted because I'm **good at my job**?*

Kemi Percival
Ahhh, don't be like that, Rach, we all know how good you are!!!
We're just jealous you get to work with HH.

> *Donna pointed out what a cushy gig it is.*

Rachel Ryan
> *Ha. I bet she did* <eyeroll emoji>
> *I only found out on Friday – it was a complete surprise.*
> *And I promise you, I didn't ask for this. I swear I'd rather have stuck with Greg.*

Kemi Percival
> *Baaahahahahaha!!!*
> *Pull the other one, it has bells on it* <crying laughing emoji>

Now more frustrated than anyone should be before 9.30 in the morning, Rachel decided not to dignify this with a response.

She clicked the X in the corner of the IM window, took a breath that she hoped would be calming, and started reading her emails.

Rachel and Jack had been summoned to a 10 a.m. 'kick-off' meeting with Isaac and Greg, presumably to discuss whatever work they'd been assigned. As it drew closer Rachel felt anxiety begin to press on her, like a dead weight she couldn't shake off.

She and Jack hadn't spoken properly for over a week. She hadn't sought him out after Friday's meeting, and it seemed he hadn't looked for her either. Rachel knew the mature thing might have been to talk about it, though she couldn't see an upside. If they disagreed about how to handle their situation, it would immediately make everything worse – but the alternative was burying the hatchet, perhaps even an attempt at being friends. She would rather have drowned herself in a vat of Angeljuice.

Rachel felt almost as sorry for Greg as she did for herself. He'd found her first thing this morning, wretched and ready to fall on his sword. He blamed himself – said he'd talked up Rachel's brilliance to everyone who would listen since the takeover, making it clear she was underused and ripe for promotion. He'd even argued that she needed a workmate as bright and talented as herself, never dreaming that Jack might be considered the ideal candidate. Rachel didn't have it in her to remonstrate with him. She knew Greg's intentions had been good, regardless of the consequences.

When she arrived at the meeting room, he and Isaac were already there. Greg's face implied he might as well be in purgatory, and Rachel threw him a resigned sort of smile. She hated that he felt bad about this.

Before she was fully through the door, Jack arrived behind her. Rachel caught a waft of whatever dark, smoky aftershave he was wearing as he followed her inside. It smelled deep and sophisticated, like vintage leather, spices, burning wood . . . It lingered in her nostrils as she took her seat.

'Morning, all!' Isaac beamed, then nudged Greg with his elbow and said, 'What do you make of my dream team?'

Greg looked ruefully at Rachel, then said, 'Great. Very impressive.'

Isaac seemed confused for a moment. Rachel assumed

he'd never heard Greg answer an open-ended question so concisely.

Brushing off his bewilderment, Isaac began to outline Rachel and Jack's first joint project. 'I see you two working almost as a pitching team; you'll focus on one-off projects that could lead to longer-term business, and also on winning new accounts. You'll do the groundwork for the new stuff – set the agenda – before handing over to more junior staff. Greg, as our overall head of client services, will want to stay abreast of what you're doing – but mostly you'll run this yourselves, and ultimately answer to me. The first thing I have for you is interesting – a proper challenge. All right, I'll be honest . . . It's what my rugby-obsessed son might call a hospital pass.'

And there was me thinking things couldn't get any worse, Rachel thought. Jack caught her eye and made a face that suggested he didn't like the sound of this either. She refused to acknowledge she'd noticed it, instead looking down at her notebook.

'The client is British House and Garden Heritage – or rather its director general, Sir Humphrey Caldwell,' Isaac went on. 'They're after a plan that will help increase visitor numbers to their key historical sites, particularly young people. Humphrey is a . . . difficult sort of person. Old-fashioned. Struggles with modern developments such as the internet, women's rights and the fact that we've lost the Empire.'

Sounds delightful, Rachel thought, then clenched her teeth for fear she'd say something similar out loud. She could feel Jack looking at her and sensed he was trying not to laugh at her obvious horror. Urgently, she tried to neutralise her expression.

Isaac, however, seemed unperturbed by his characterisation of Sir Humphrey, and apparently hadn't noticed his colleagues' reactions to it. 'I think the key thing with him,' he went on, 'is probably keeping your head when he's unpleasant – reminding yourself that this is all part of agency life. Humphrey is of a certain generation. From a certain *echelon of society*.' He turned to Jack and said, 'You went to Harrow, didn't you?'

'Yes,' Jack replied, nodding and shrugging his shoulders.

'Good. So did Sir Humphrey. We'll need to find a way to drop that in.'

'Is it relevant?' Rachel asked. 'I mean, is he also going to be informed that I went to St Agatha's Roman Catholic Comp in Stoke-on-Trent?'

Greg suppressed a grin, but Jack didn't bother to hide his. 'I suspect not, though more fool him for not being interested,' he said. 'I get the point: the fact that I'm an "Old Harrovian" has nothing to do with whether we're capable of delivering good work. But the idea that Humphrey will find it interesting gives me a read on him before we even meet. It's useful to know.'

'Precisely,' said Isaac. 'Humphrey has fired the last two agencies who worked for him, so it's fair to say he needs careful handling. We need to ingratiate ourselves with him however we can – and from everything I've heard, Jack is the man for the job. Given their track record, we've negotiated with British House and Garden Heritage that they'll pay a one-off fee for the work you do over the next month or so. That way, if Humphrey throws his toys out of the pram and doesn't want us to actually *deliver* what we recommend, we won't be thousands out of pocket. Having said that,' Isaac continued, 'if we were to end up with BHGH as a longer-term client, it would be a massive win for us. For you two, in particular.'

'Challenge accepted,' Jack said, smiling and apparently undaunted. Rachel stared at him.

'It's not going to be easy,' Greg said, his voice testy. 'It's a tough first assignment. You're going to need to charm the pants off him. Not literally, though . . . Based on my brief meeting with him, I think it's fair to say he's quite homophobic.'

'Dear God,' Rachel said, but Jack grimaced and then smiled again.

'Yet more useful intel. Thank you, Greg.'

'I'll send over everything we have on the client so far,' Isaac said. 'I have some of the stuff their previous agencies have done, plus the client's brief and my notes. That should be enough to get you started with brainstorming ideas. We can chat again in a day or two, and we'll get a desk move sorted as well – seat the two of you with me and the rest of the pro-social team ASAP.'

Greg rushed off to his next meeting, then Isaac got to his feet and made for the door – only to turn back at the threshold with an embarrassed look on his face.

'Just one more thing. Humphrey tends to get my name wrong. He often calls me Abraham, and he's the type of character who'd think I was being impertinent if I corrected him. So if an Abraham is ever mentioned, you know he means me.'

Rachel sighed as Isaac sailed off into the office, ignoring the sound of Jack's muffled laughter.

'This guy sounds like an absolute nightmare,' she said with her head in her hands. 'This *whole thing* is a nightmare.'

'Not at all,' Jack said brightly, and when she looked up he was grinning. 'Between us, we're going to nail it.'

Rachel shot out of her seat, strode past Jack and shut the meeting room door, sealing the two of them in.

'Am I missing something?' she asked. 'What could you *possibly* be smiling about?'

Jack's face fell, but only a fraction. 'Rachel, I know this isn't ideal,' he said, 'but it's the hand we've been dealt. I think we have to play it.'

She scowled at him. 'This isn't a game, Jack – but how very *you* to think of it that way. This is my job, my *life* – which up until recently was going okay.'

He sighed, stood up as if to try to soothe her, then clawed at his carefully dishevelled hair as he decided against it. 'I didn't mean to sound glib. I'm just being realistic,' he said. 'I know that what happened – what I did – was totally, monumentally shit. I've apologised before and I apologise again, unreservedly. But it was ten years ago, Rachel. I'm not the same man.'

Rachel sank back down into her seat. 'I thought I could do this, but I can't,' she said, her voice thin but resolute. 'I can't work with you. Not on winning round Sir Humphrey Horrorbag. Not on anything.'

'What? Are you going to quit? Hand in your notice?'

'Why should I do that?' Rachel cried, incredulous. 'I was here first!'

'Whoa, there, what are we – twelve?'

Rachel felt her face flood with colour.

'We are two people who will never work well together,' she said after taking a deep breath. 'Surely you can see that?'

He sat down opposite her, then raked a hand through his hair again. 'I can see that this is very uncomfortable for you. But the thing is, I *am* here – and this' – he gestured at the space between them – 'is a professional relationship now.'

Rachel threw him a withering look.

'I transferred here because I wanted to help develop the pro-social side of the business,' Jack went on, his voice slightly harder than before. 'And there's absolutely no way I'm stepping back from that. If you're determined not to even *try* working with me, you'll have to ask for your old job back. Or hand in your notice. I think either might seem odd, though, given you said yes to this position last week and only started it an hour ago.'

He lifted his chin a little so the sunlight streaming through the window bounced bright across his cheekbones. *God damn him and his fucking perfect bone structure.*

'I can't just leave,' Rachel said through gritted teeth. 'But you could. You could just stay in the job you already had in Manchester – cancel your move. Then we can forget we ever knew each other.' She sounded surly now, like a moody teenager, and she hated herself for it.

'That's not an option,' Jack said flatly. 'And not just because it's unreasonable for you to ask. I can't be in Manchester any more; I didn't just want this transfer, I *needed* it. Believe it or not, I have as much at stake here as you do.'

Before Rachel had a chance to start decoding what he'd said, he went on: 'I can't change the past, but I'll do whatever it takes to make things easier for you right now. Just tell me what you need.'

His eyes were wide, sincere and fully focused on her face. They looked a shade darker today, almost moss-coloured, against a plain black V-neck. Rachel wondered whether Jack might agree to wear a paper bag on his head during office hours; *that* might help.

'I've never forgiven you,' she said stiffly. 'I'm not sure I can.'

'I never expected you to. I still don't.'

'I don't think you have any idea what it cost me to let you in,' Rachel said in spite of herself, her voice almost a whisper. 'To open up, to tell you things that even *now* I never talk about. We are never going to be friends.'

She felt her eyes begin to prickle and wished she hadn't shown weakness – but if Jack noticed that she was on the edge of tears, he pretended not to.

'I understand,' he said. 'We don't have to be. But given we're at an impasse, perhaps we could try to be colleagues? Just . . . see what happens if we behave like civil teammates between the hours of nine and five. Hate me as much as you like during your evenings and weekends, obviously,' he went on, chancing a tentative smile. 'Buy a Jack doll. Stick pins in it. Do your worst.'

'What makes you think I haven't cast a spell on you

already?' Rachel asked, feeling her lips twist into a half-hearted smirk. She lifted her face to look at him.

'Good point,' Jack said, holding her gaze. 'Perhaps that ship *has* sailed.'

Rachel let out a loud, long breath, feeling the will to fight on leave her. 'You won't quit, and for now I can't quit. So, sure. Let's see how it goes,' she said.

'Thank you.' Jack sighed, and stood up. 'I guess we should be getting back. This meeting room's probably booked.'

Rachel nodded as he reached out a hand to her. She assumed he meant for them to shake again, this time on their flimsy peace accord – but when she took it in hers he held on gently, pulling her to her feet. She stumbled slightly as she rose and ended up too close to him, almost headbutting his chest.

Jack placed his hands on her upper arms to steady her and she caught that fragrance again. Rich. Intriguing. *Sexy*, she had to admit. It smelled like a night out with Don Draper – like tobacco and old-fashioneds in a backstreet New York bar.

'Sorry to interrupt,' said a thin, nasal voice. 'I can see you're *hard at work*. But we're supposed to be in here now.'

It was Donna, with a terrified-looking man in tow. As Rachel skittered backwards, away from Jack and into a chair leg, she thought she recognised him as the wholesaler who supplied the agency's tea, coffee and snacks. No wonder it was Donna's job to negotiate with him on the cost, she thought. She couldn't imagine anyone who'd drive a harder bargain.

'Of course,' Jack said, turning to Donna with a megawatt

smile. 'We'll get out of your way. Rachel, I'll set up a time for us to talk tomorrow, shall I? Give us both a chance to read through the stuff Isaac sends.'

'Fine,' Rachel said, shuffling after him towards the door.

Donna looked her up and down with a smug leer, unable to contain her joy at witnessing what Rachel knew she'd report as a passionate embrace. She made a big show of checking her watch, then said in her signature artificially sweetened tone, 'Close the door, would you? We need to get on.'

Rachel left the room and stood just outside for a moment feeling tired, bruised and sore. Then she stood up straighter and resolved to get on with her day.

Surely, she reasoned as she walked back to her desk, the worst part of it was already over.

11

When Rachel left the office building just before 6 p.m., she found Laurence lurking outside. He was leaning against a lamp post, trying to appear casual but clearly waiting for her.

He looked up and saw Rachel immediately. *Damn it*. If she'd had the time, she'd have crept back inside and asked Frank if she could leave by the side door.

Laurence smiled at Rachel sheepishly and thrust his hands deeper into the pockets of his navy trench coat. She tried to smile back but her lips refused to cooperate, instead contorting themselves into a weary sort of pout.

'What are you doing here, Laurence?' Rachel asked. She didn't want to be unkind, but the last thing she felt like doing right now was rehashing her reasons for finishing with him.

'I was worried about you,' he said. 'I've sent you texts and emails, and I left a voicemail for you last week. I got concerned when you didn't reply to any of it. I thought something might have happened.'

Rachel resisted the urge to say, 'Actually, something *has* happened – not that it's any of your business.'

Instead she mumbled, 'I've just been busy. Work has been pretty intense. And without wanting to be mean, you and I have broken up. I kind of don't *have* to reply to you any more.'

'I never said you did!' Laurence cried, looking affronted. 'I just care about you, muffin. And you know I want to talk things over. I've been asking to meet for a drink for weeks. Honestly, I think you owe me that.'

Rachel cast her eyes skyward and then brought them back to his face, which was set and sulky. 'I really don't see what good it's going to do,' she said. 'And I have asked you *repeatedly* not to call me muffin.'

'Let me say my piece,' Laurence insisted, 'and then, if you never want to hear from me again ... I suppose that's fine. Please.'

Rachel dug the heels of her hands into her eye sockets, not caring if they smudged her mascara. *Fucking hell, Laurence!* It was bad enough that he felt the need to harass her with this 'Ghost of Relationships Past' routine ... But to wheel it out today of *all* days ... She sighed.

'One drink,' she said. Her brain asked her mouth what on earth it was doing.

You're saying yes because you don't want to be cruel, Rachel told herself. Also, she figured that once she'd heard Laurence's speech and still didn't want to be his girlfriend, he'd have to accept they were over.

This would be like ripping off a particularly sticky plaster, Rachel reasoned: unpleasant for a moment, then done with.

They walked together towards Angel, Laurence always slightly ahead of Rachel and occasionally looking back, as if to make sure she hadn't absconded. They turned off the main road and, a few minutes later, stopped outside a wine bar.

'Is here okay?' Laurence asked.

'Fine,' Rachel said.

'What'll you have?'

'Er – red wine, please. Just a small glass. I'll get a table.'

Rachel looked around. The bar was small and stylish, with wood-panelled walls painted a dark shade of some Farrow & Ball blue. There were candles and hurricane lanterns flickering from every shelf, alcove and tabletop. Old black-and-white movie posters and theatre bills adorned the walls, and an enormous vase of yellow roses stood at the end of the marble-topped bar.

Rachel's heart sank. This wasn't the kind of place you just happened upon, nor somewhere you'd bring a woman if your intention was merely to seek closure on the recent demise of your relationship with her. Rachel felt her sympathy for Laurence diminishing in inverse proportion to her rising annoyance.

She took her coat off and sat down at a small square table, deliberately shunning the far fancier booth a short distance away. There was a row of them against the back wall of the room, and they were all small – designed for intimacy. The one Rachel could see into had a fabric canopy and plush velvet-covered benches topped with squishy-looking jewel-bright cushions. She would gladly have sat there with someone she actually liked – but under the current circumstances she thought it best to avoid putting herself anywhere that might remind Laurence of a bed.

Rachel pulled her handbag from underneath the table and dug for her mobile. Laurence was at the bar now, already being served. She opened WhatsApp and wrote a message to Anna:

Rachel: *Do you think I'm being punished for committing some cardinal sin I've forgotten about?*

Two blue ticks. Thank God, Anna had her phone on her.

Anna: *NO. That's your Irish Catholic guilt talking. What's happened now??*

Rachel: *It would seem I'm on an accidental date with Laurence. I'm Withnail: I've come on a date by mistake.*

Anna: *Erm. WHAT??*

Rachel: *He waited for me outside work and convinced me to go for a drink. I felt sorry for him . . . But he's brought me to a romantic wine bar* <woe emoji> *I need you to phone me and get me out of here . . . Give me an excuse to leave. Don't wait any longer than 20 mins* <hands in prayer emoji>

Anna: *Oh my God, he is SUCH a desperado! Got it.*

Anna is typing . . .

Anna: *Make sure you switch your phone ringer on btw. No good if you can't hear me calling.*

Anna is typing . . .

Anna: *I love you, Rach, but honestly . . . We need to have a serious conversation about your taste in boyfriends. TTFN x*

Rachel dropped her phone back into her bag just as Laurence sauntered over as if this were his wine bar, clutching what was obviously not a small glass of wine. Why could this man *never* listen?

'So . . .' he said, then tipped a bottle of some European lager to his lips.

'Yes?' Rachel asked, taking a sip from the massive glass he'd put in front of her. Whatever this was, it was delicious – no doubt purposely so, which took the edge off her enjoyment of it.

'So,' Laurence said, 'I guess I just wanted to understand why you think it's the right move for us to finish. I can't get my head around it, even now I've had a while to mull it over. It doesn't make any sense to me.'

Rachel felt her eyebrows pull together. 'What do you mean, it doesn't make sense?'

'Well,' he said, stretching his long pinstripe-clad legs out beneath their tiny table, 'it seems so *unlikely*. We're a good match, we're of a certain age, I think we want the same things . . . I have a great career and plenty of savings, and I already own my flat. Plus, I've been told I'm fairly easy on the eye.'

He winked theatrically as he said this, then drank from his bottle again. *Ick*.

'Laurence,' Rachel said, doing her best to keep her voice even, 'I'm sorry, but none of those are good reasons to start building a life with someone.'

Laurence frowned, narrowed his eyes a little and said, 'Of course they are. Where's your head? I thought you were more sensible than this, Rach.'

'More sensible than what?'

'Well . . . More sensible than to put yourself back out there when you're approaching midlife. I don't want to be a dick about this, but I think I'm a pretty decent catch. What makes you think you're going to do any better? Bit risky binning me off, I'd say, if you want marriage and children.'

Rachel put her wine glass down as gently as she could. If she kept hold of it, she was definitely going to throw its contents in his face.

'Laurence, I'm afraid you *are* being a dick about this. A massive one. If I hurt you when I finished things, I apologise – I never meant to. But we're not right together. This – *us* – was never going to work.'

'And you think it'll be better to try and pick up some new guy in a bar? Download a bunch of dating apps? Spend half your life playing spot-the-fake-profile-photo and deleting endless unsolicited dick pics?' Laurence's voice was getting louder now. Rachel cringed as the barmaid who'd poured their drinks looked over at him, wide-eyed.

'*Laurence*,' she said, quiet and firm. 'Stop. I think we're done here.' His lips curled into something like a sneer, but before he could spit out a reply she cut him off. 'I'm genuinely sorry, but I don't love you and I know I never will. You need to let this go.'

'Who said anything about love? I'm talking about a solid future, a lifestyle. What's *love* got to do with anything?'

He said the word as if he were jeering at something made-up – a fiction that only callow idiots believed in.

'Oh my God, Laurence. *Everything*,' Rachel said. She stood up, then bent to grope for her coat, laptop and bag. Laurence's legs were idling in the way, and she shoved them so hard he almost tipped off his seat.

'Bloody hell!' he hissed. '*Go*, then. But I give you a month, tops, before you're texting me again. Just let me know when you've realised you want me back. I guess you'll have to hope I'm still available.'

He drank what was left of his lager in one gulp, then shrugged his shoulders in a way that managed to seem both adolescent and aggressive.

Rachel felt sick. She was seething. She also thought she might cry.

How could Laurence – inoffensive, mild-mannered, basil-growing *Laurence* – be saying these things to her? Had he always been this arrogant, this awful? If he had, how had she not seen it?

Rachel didn't want Laurence to have the last word, but had no idea how to claim it for herself. She couldn't think of anything bad enough to call him.

Then her phone started ringing, loud and insistent. It must be Anna. Thank *fuck* for Anna. Rachel thought for a moment about how her best friend would handle this, and suddenly knew what to do.

'Find someone else, Laurence. Move on,' she said in her coolest, most dignified voice. 'I wish you the best.'

Then she turned away, began marching briskly towards the door and answered her mobile.

'Rach? Are you there?'

'Yes, just walking fast. *Tom?*'

'Yeah, it's me, sorry. I'm on Anna's phone. She told me to call you – said something about an emergency exit strategy. She's busy cooking and didn't trust me to stir the pan.' He laughed.

'S'okay,' Rachel said. Her breathing was shallow and her chest felt tight. A high, stinging ache at the back of her throat warned her that a sob was trying to break free.

'Hey,' Tom said, 'what's happened? Where are you?'

'I'm fine,' Rachel insisted, but her voice cracked a little. 'I'm on my way home.'

'You're *not* fine,' he replied, almost in a growl. 'What's happened? Do you want me to come and meet you?'

'No, really – I'm almost at the Tube. I'll be okay, I've just had a shitter of a day . . . Topped off by a run-in with Laurence, who informs naive little me that love isn't real. Also that I was insane to dump him because – and I'm pretty much quoting here – I'll never find anyone better.'

'Fucking hell, what a *tool* that man is,' Tom said. Rachel felt her face twitch, a smile trying to form. He and Laurence had never hit it off. 'Don't give him another thought,' Tom went on. 'He knows nothing about you, nothing about relationships . . . *Nothing* about who might be out there waiting for you. *Loz* knows nothing about anything,' he fumed, 'except perhaps pensions. I suppose he knows a fuckload about pensions.'

Rachel was laughing now. 'So he says.'

'Listen, are you sure you don't want me to come?'

'No, I'm at the station now. I'm going to go down to the platform so I'll be home soon. What's Anna making?'

'Some kind of dhal, I think. It smells amazing – she says it'll be done for when you get back. I'm told there will also be naan bread.'

Rachel could hear him grinning down the phone and she smiled again.

'*Yes*,' she breathed. 'Exactly what I need: carbs, glorious carbs. Right, I'm getting on the train. I'll see you guys in a bit.'

When she got off the Tube at Finsbury Park about twenty minutes later, Rachel found Tom waiting for her at the station exit.

'*Thomas*. You didn't have to do this,' she said, shaking her head at him. But her chest was filling up with some soft, warm feeling she identified as gratitude.

'Well, good evening to you too,' Tom said, rolling his eyes.

He took her laptop bag, passed the long strap over his head and then smiled at her gently. 'And I know I didn't have to; I wanted to. I figured I'd risk a Laurence-style ambush in case you'd rather not walk home alone.'

They strolled in silence for a few minutes until Rachel laughed. 'You know, if you're channelling Laurence, your next move should be to tell me I'm almost past it. Then warn me that I'll die alone and childless if I don't let you knock me up immediately.'

They passed under a street lamp as they made their way up Stroud Green Road. Rachel saw Tom's cheeks were glowing deep pink, as though suffused with emotion.

'I'm okay, you know,' she reassured him, briefly resting her hand on his arm. 'You don't need to be irate on my behalf.'

'Oh, I do,' he said, relaxing a little and grinning at her. 'I'm positively *enraged*. I'm glad you seem to be shrugging it off already, but if I ever see that twat again I'll be forced to rearrange his smug face.'

'God,' Rachel giggled, 'it's a long time since I've had a man swear to defend my honour. It's against my whole belief system, to be honest – but I won't deny that it's weirdly comforting.' On the doorstep Rachel fumbled for her keys, then turned to look at Tom before she let them into the building. 'Thank you for cheering me up,' she said. 'You always seem to know what to say.'

She went to hug him and he opened his arms to her, almost bashful. He patted her back lightly as she leaned against him, but Rachel could feel that his spine was rigid and he'd stiffened his shoulders. *Eek*. This was bad. She'd embarrassed him.

Tom let his hands drop back to his sides and hang there loosely for a few seconds, then stepped back a little and pushed his glasses up his nose. He looked down at his trainers for a moment as if to gather himself, then brought his eyes back to Rachel. His face was calm, composed and kind, like always.

Rachel put her key in the lock and said, 'Sorry. I'll warn you next time I go in for a fondle.'

'I . . . er . . . Right,' Tom said, then coughed and cleared his throat. 'Let's go in, shall we? I'm famished.'

Rachel shut the front door behind them, but paused with the flat key between her finger and thumb.

'Tom?' she said.

'Yeah?'

'I've mortified you already, so I might as well say this. You're a really good friend.'

He was staring at his feet again, softly kicking the side of an Adidas sneaker against the battered hallway skirting board. He pulled his eyes up to hers, attempted a smile that didn't quite reach them, and mumbled, 'Thanks. So are you.'

*

Tom was a good friend. Too good for his *own* good, probably.

If he'd been a slightly worse friend, he'd have held Rachel closer when she'd hugged him tonight. He might have bent his head down over hers so he could breathe in the sweet, coconutty smell of her hair.

A bad friend would have slipped his arms inside that mannish coat she always wore but rarely buttoned up, then spread his hands out on her waist.

A *really* bad friend might have kissed her . . . Kissed her until his mouth was sore, chasing away every last thought of that utter bellend, Laurence – and obliterating all memory of her other arsehole ex.

For fuck's sake STOP, Tom told himself.

He wasn't any of these men. He didn't take advantage of women who were hurt and unhappy. Maybe that made him a mug; it was definitely making him miserable. But still, he had his morals.

Tom sighed heavily as he walked towards home. The air was wet. A chilly mizzle was soaking his face, ears and hair; every exposed inch of him was cold.

He wondered how he'd got into this mess with Rachel, and how, every time he tried to improve things, he managed to make them worse.

Will had made a face at him earlier when he'd said he was going to meet her at the station – shaken his head while Anna's back was turned, as if to say: *Bad move, mate.*

The bastard had been right as well. Tom hadn't intended turning up at Finsbury Park to be a romantic gesture, exactly – but the thought that it might push him further into the Friend Zone hadn't entered his head until Rachel detonated the F-bomb.

God, the way she'd looked at him as they stood outside the door to her flat: her big eyes full of feeling, as dark and wide as he'd ever seen them. Alive, shining like she was about to say something secret and significant . . . He'd felt like there was a fireball trying to burn its way out of his chest. *Give me a reason*, he'd thought – *give me a reason to just sod everything and tell you.*

And then she'd said that thing about what a good friend he was. It was like being shot in the heart. He wanted to scour the scene from his memory, bleach the words off his brain.

Tom had never exactly told Will about his feelings for

Rachel, but somehow they'd reached an understanding that those feelings existed and *weren't* to be talked about. It was as if they'd shared a particularly painful sporting defeat that didn't bear analysis after the final whistle; better just never to mention it.

Tom wondered how Rachel would cope – *if* Rachel would cope – when Anna and Will finally moved in together. *Maybe she could just live with me*, he thought. A simple housemate swap would certainly be a neat solution to the problem.

But the soaring feeling that seized him at this notion was all the proof he needed: it was a terrible idea. Tom would never cope with being in such close proximity to Rachel – every day would be delicious, dreadful torture. It had been bad enough when she brought Laurence, or whoever she was dating, to the pub some Friday nights . . . If he lived with Rachel, Tom knew he'd want to murder any man she ever came home with.

As he rounded the corner onto the street where he and Will lived, Tom asked himself what the hell he was going to do. Mooning and moping wasn't his style, but he'd come close to perfecting it over the past year or so. Asking Rachel to help him out with the exhibition had seemed like a way to add a new dimension to their relationship – to move things on or help her see him in a different light. Now he cursed himself for his hopefulness; the project merely promised more hours and new locations in which he'd have to hide how badly he wanted to touch her.

None of this sat easily in his stomach. Tom was a

fundamentally sensible person, which meant he was almost always honest: the truth was so much less *complicated* than a lie in nearly every situation . . . But not this one, he reminded himself. He'd done the sums plenty of times, and the idea of confessing his feelings to Rachel simply didn't add up.

Despite occasional flickers of something between them (which he couldn't be sure weren't imagined), she'd never given him any reason to suspect that she fancied him. And if he told her the truth without being sure of a return, things could get very weird, very fast. He didn't want to put Will or Anna in an uncomfortable position, or risk destabilising the easy friendship the four of them shared. This was for Rachel's sake as much as his own.

When he pushed his way into the flat it was hot and dark, and the knackered old windows had begun to cloud up with condensation. Will had clearly left the heating on again, the fool.

Tom didn't bother turning on any lights as he shrugged off his jacket, picked up a clean glass from the draining board and then dragged himself to the bathroom. He laughed at his reflection when he caught it in the mirror above the sink; his blondish hair was dark and damp from the rain outside, and where he let it grow longer on top it had fashioned itself into full-on ringlets.

He rested his head against the glass, allowing himself a few seconds of unalloyed self-pity. Tom knew it was better to have Rachel as a friend than risk losing her altogether, but right now he felt the full force of several inconvenient facts.

1. This was really fucking painful;

2. Laurence was off the scene – but if Tom didn't get in there first, she'd eventually start seeing someone else;

3. That might actually kill him; and

4. He probably couldn't go on like this.

There *must* have been a point at which he wasn't hopelessly in love with Rachel, he told himself. Maybe with a bit of effort he could get back there.

The trouble was, he couldn't remember a time before he'd lived to make her laugh – or when he hadn't felt maddened by the urge to kiss her every time she did.

Deep down, he knew he didn't want to.

February

~~New Year's~~ Ongoing resolutions

1. Consider exercise an act with actual benefits – both mental and physical – not merely grim punishment for pizzas consumed. Have a proper go at yoga.
2. ~~Also re-download~~ Complete Couch to 5K ~~running app and actually do the programme.~~
3. ~~Apply for promotion at work at first chance. Move to bigger account and try to get pay rise. Avoid, if possible, further projects concerning dog biscuits, disinfectant, high-quality printer ink cartridges, 'miracle' grass seed, organic vegetables, etc.~~
    - 3a. Try to hang on to job (and temper) despite presence of evil ex-boyfriend.
    - 3b. Ignore everyone who keeps banging on about how fit he is.
    - 3c. Ignore how fit he is.
4. ~~DO NOT agree to further dates with Laurence.~~

~~Remember: it's no use having a boyfriend who is good on paper if you do not actually fancy him.~~

4. Forget that Laurence even EXISTS.
5. Try to remember Mum means well, even during phone calls where she implies I am doomed to a lonely life of penury because I am thirty with no partner, hardly any savings and no mortgage.
6. HOWEVER, do not (!!!) speak to Mum when suffering PMT. Set phone alerts for likely spells based on period tracker intel.
7. Try to address 'hardly any savings' situation. ~~(If promoted, set aside extra earnings for future house deposit instead of spaffing it all on ASOS.)~~ (Do not spend entire pay rise on 'cheer up' treats to distract from heinous ex-boyfriend mess.)
8. Try to eat my five-a-day. (Remember horrid rule that potatoes do not count.)
9. Start using proper night cream with retinol.

12

Rachel had never considered herself a pessimist, but as January dissolved into February she realised that, somehow, she'd adjusted to living as though a piano were permanently suspended above her head.

Like the lead player in a farce, she fully expected that something ridiculous or dreadful could happen at any moment – though she'd given up trying to predict how life might kick her in the balls next. Even if she *had* tried, she'd never have foreseen that the next assault on her sanity would take the form of a day trip to the Cotswolds.

'Sir Humphrey wants to meet you both in person,' Isaac announced on Wednesday afternoon, gesturing at Rachel and Jack as he breezed by. 'He's invited you for tea at his country pile this Friday. It's a very good sign . . . The initial phone call with him must have gone well. It's a bit of a trek, so let's say you'll both work remotely for the day. Just check in with your emails when you can and be back in the office with a full report on Monday.'

He clapped Jack on the back, pulled a trilling iPhone out of his pocket and then strode towards a vacant meeting room, his mobile already clamped to his ear. Rachel stared after him.

'*Where* are we going?' she said, peering at Jack over the top of her computer monitor. Thanks to Isaac's reorganisation of the pro-social corner of the office, she now sat opposite her partner-slash-nemesis. They were separated only by screens, mugs full of pens, and piles of paperwork. Jack's nearness was unsettling in ways Rachel couldn't successfully explain, even to herself – but she was working on becoming blasé about it.

He looked up from his laptop. 'Humphrey's house. He did mention to me when I called to introduce myself that he thought an informal meeting might be nice before we present our plans. I told him we'd have to check our availability with *Abraham*.' He grinned and made air quotes with his fingers.

'Humphrey's *house*?' Rachel cried, ignoring the joke.

Jack's green eyes flashed with amusement, crinkling at the corners as he smiled at her. 'Exactly what is it about the concept of visiting someone's house that you're struggling with?'

Rachel shot him a dark look from behind a stack of notebooks. 'What I mean is, what's wrong with the BHGH office in Chelsea? It's a tad more convenient for us, wouldn't you say? Not to mention more professional – more appropriate.'

Jack arched a thick, chestnut-coloured eyebrow and said, 'I don't think Humphrey cares much about what's convenient for people. Still less about what's appropriate.'

Rachel sighed and scrubbed a hand across her forehead. 'Yeah. I'm getting that . . .'

'His place is right in the centre of the Cotswolds, I think. Nice area. Not too far from Bourton-on-the-Water.'

'*What?*'

Jack was laughing now. 'Rachel, did you bump your head on the way to work this morning? Do you need your ears syringed? You're being strange.' He cupped his hands around his mouth as though he were speaking to someone very far away, then repeated: '*Bourton-on-the-Water.*'

Irritated, Rachel threw a scrunched-up Post-it note at him and then immediately wished she hadn't. To anyone watching – and there was always *someone* watching, she'd noticed – it would look like she was flirting.

'My point,' she said, 'is that Bourton is bloody miles away! I went there once with my family for a weekend. It seems like a long way to go for a chat and a cuppa.'

Jack shrugged, his whole body radiating indifference. 'Clients make ridiculous requests all the time . . . Humphrey's are just more obviously ridiculous than most. Anyway, it'll be nice; it's a day out of the office. A trip to an area of outstanding natural beauty, no less. What's not to like?'

Rachel decided not to answer this question, which felt deliberately provoking. Instead, she set about researching how long it would take them to get there. Jack was smirking in a way that suggested he was perfectly relaxed about the idea of an outing with her, at the same time as highly entertained by her discomfort at the prospect.

'Oh my God, I've just googled . . .' Rachel moaned. 'There isn't even a train station nearby. It's going to be an absolute ass-pain of a journey.'

'It'll be fine,' Jack said. 'I'll drive us. We can work out the details tomorrow.'

He smiled again, then looked down and resumed typing

before she could argue. *Of course* he had a car, Rachel thought. Probably some ridiculous gas-guzzling beast of a four-by-four. Now he'd suggested driving within earshot of several colleagues, though, it was impossible to decline travelling in it. Taking the train to the Cotswolds would doubtless be more expensive and less convenient – and Isaac would never sign off on paying for rail fares if a cheaper alternative was on offer.

Rachel turned back to her computer and mapped the journey from North London to Bourton-on-the-Water, then felt her mouth fall open in horror as she stared at the results. By the fastest route it was a four-hour round trip – and that was if they got lucky and didn't hit much traffic. *Fuck. Ing. Hell.*

I'm really beginning to hate Humphrey, Rachel thought, *and I haven't even met him yet.*

She pushed her headphones into her ears and fired up Spotify, wishing that Tom's latest alt-pop playlist could drown out the awfulness of what she'd just tacitly agreed to.

Four hours, minimum, alone with Jack in a confined space. A whole day together, most of it spent at close range. Endless, excruciating minutes during which she'd have no one to look at or speak to but him.

Since coming to London, Jack had moved into an apartment in Highgate. Rachel had originally argued that it made sense for her to meet him there on Friday morning, since it wasn't far away from where she and Anna lived. In the end, though, his insistence that she save herself the trouble (plus the extra half-hour in bed this promised) proved impossible to resist. She agreed to let him pick her up at 9 a.m. at the flat.

The day was clear and bright, so Rachel decided to wait for Jack outside. Within a few seconds, she realised this was a mistake. It was freezing and she wasn't wrapped up as warmly as usual, having decided that her usual attire of jeans and a chunky jumper might be too homey for high tea with a baronet. Instead she'd opted for a demure dove-grey dress – long-sleeved, high-necked and made of thick fabric, with a flattering skater skirt cut just above the knee. With it she wore black tights and her high-heeled ankle boots, which remained uncomfortable despite repeated attempts to break them in.

Rachel felt put together in a way that she hoped wouldn't seem overdone, and reasoned that at least the blister-inducing footwear wouldn't be a problem. After all, most of her day would be spent in Jack's car. She was trying to stay calm about that.

As she leaned against the aged wall that separated the flat's tiny yard from the street, she heard the front door bang. Will, who'd been locked in the bathroom when she left, was loafing towards her.

'Still here, then? Is he late?' he said, joining Rachel on her perch.

She checked her watch. It was 9.06. 'Hmm. By a few minutes. How come you're not at work already? No company mergers or hostile takeovers to negotiate today?'

'I'm going to Edinburgh for a meeting. Just waiting for a taxi to the airport.' Will patted a canvas overnight bag that she hadn't noticed until now, then placed it on the pavement. Even almost four years into knowing him, Rachel couldn't quite picture Will in his role as a corporate lawyer – firstly because he was so placid, and secondly because, in his personal life, he had a tendency to say daft things where silence might have sufficed.

'God, I need a coffee,' Rachel groaned. 'I should have brought one for the road. And to think, Anna probably has a class full of kids staring at her by now. I don't know how she does it.'

'Me neither,' Will said, misty-eyed and shaking his head as he smiled. 'She's a dynamo. Ah, here's my cab. And . . . fuck *me*. Is that your lift?'

Behind the Uber that had just turned the corner onto the street, some kind of vintage car was cruising. Jack was driving it. *For shit's sake* . . . Why hadn't she seen this coming?

'It would seem so,' Rachel said, feeling strangely embarrassed. Why did everything about Jack have to be so . . . *much*?

Will picked up his bag and waved at the taxi driver. 'That's an MGA Roadster,' he said to Rachel, awestruck and gesturing at Jack's car. 'Gorgeous and very rare. You're going to freeze your tits off in it, I should think, but it's a beauty.'

'Do me a favour, Will – don't be too impressed. We hate this guy, remember?'

'Oh yeah. Got it,' he said, and laughed as he mock-saluted her. Then he pulled her in for a big-brotherish hug and kissed her cheek before opening the door of the taxi. 'See you in a day or two.'

Rachel turned and strode towards Jack, who'd parked a

little way down the street. The car was red and shiny, and it had one of those squashy retractable roofs. Why had she ever supposed he'd drive a Range Rover? This made so much more sense.

Jack leaned across the gearstick and opened the passenger door for her. Inside, the car was all wood and polish, circular dials and soft tea-coloured leather. It was lovely, but she was damned if she'd say so out loud.

Rachel sat down, cursing the low ride of the car. It was conspiring with her high heels and hemline to expose more of her legs than she'd like.

'Morning,' Jack said, smiling. 'Sorry I'm a bit late. I needed to get petrol and thought coffee might be a good idea too.' He gestured to a cardboard holder that was wedged between the seats, inside which sat two tall takeaway cups.

'Oh my God, *yes*,' Rachel said in a rush. 'Definitely.'

'Take either,' Jack said. 'Both generic service station lattes of questionable quality – but the left-hand one has sugar.'

Without hesitating, Rachel picked up the cup with sugar. Today was going to be difficult enough without caring about empty calories.

She took a large, grateful sip, then remembered herself. 'Thanks,' she said. 'This was . . . nice of you.'

Jack smiled and nodded, turned the key in the car's ignition and started driving.

As they waited at a set of lights a few minutes later, he twisted in his seat to look at her and said, 'I'm still waiting for you to say it, Rachel. I can feel it *killing* you, not saying it.'

'What are you expecting, exactly?' Rachel asked. His eyes were dancing and she felt her face split into a smile before she could stop it.

He used to do this all the time: call her out on some snarky thing she was thinking so she'd give in and say it out loud. Back when they were first friends, Rachel had thought that taking the piss out of Jack's vanity, pretensions or the parade of worshipful women he dated was protective. Every jibe was supposed to armour her – remind her of the reasons why he shouldn't be remotely alluring to someone as sensitive as she was.

Once, when he'd asked her why she was so rough on him, she'd half-truthfully explained that his persecution was in pursuit of universal balance. The world was quite kind enough to Jack Harper without Rachel being nice to him as well – and God knew he loved himself more than enough for the both of them.

Now, Rachel sighed at the memory of her own stupidity. Her engagement in their merry war of wit had merely exposed how much she noticed about Jack – galvanised him into flirting with her harder. It had finished with them tangled and breathless, kissing in a corner at a house party. Even at the time, Rachel had been unsure whether she'd won or lost the fight.

'I dunno,' Jack said as the MG picked up speed, a riot of noise rising from its gut as he pressed down on the accelerator. Rachel blinked, brought back to reality. 'I predict something sarcastic,' Jack went on. 'Something cutting. Something like, "Nice car, you flash wanker."'

'Ha!' Rachel laughed, vaguely irritated that he'd called

her reaction to it so accurately. He'd always been sharper than he looked. 'I honestly don't know what you're talking about,' she huffed.

Jack kept his eyes on the road, brows raised in anticipation of the takedown he knew was imminent.

'It *is* a nice car,' Rachel said, 'if you're into that sort of thing, which I'm not. What I actually wonder is this . . .'

He glanced at her briefly and grinned.

'Why can't you just drive a Ford Fiesta like a normal person? At least in *winter*? This is a glorified icebox on wheels. We're going to be frozen fucking solid before we even hit Watford.'

Jack roared with laughter that was almost immediately drowned out by more engine noise, and Rachel felt a little sick.

She didn't know whether to put her queasiness down to the motion of the car or annoyance with herself for sparring with him; sparring with him and enjoying it.

Sir Humphrey Caldwell's house looked like a boutique hotel, or one of the lesser mansions in a Jane Austen adaptation.

It wasn't a Pemberley in size or splendour, but Fawcett Park was large, elegant and beautifully kept: a three-storey late-eighteenth-century manor with enormous sash windows, built of Cotswold stone that had been bleached pale cream by more than two hundred summers.

Rachel felt intimidated by it, which she hated. *Pull yourself together*, she told herself. *You've met plenty of posh people – you practically live with one. There's also one sitting right next to you, driving this ridiculous vehicle.*

'Nice place, isn't it?' Jack said as the car crawled up the long, sweeping drive. Rachel laughed at his understatement – a genuine assessment that she knew was only possible because Jack had grown up in a house like this.

She'd stayed quiet for much of the journey, answering questions when Jack asked them and trying to keep the stilted conversation focused on work. Merely a week after being paired up, and despite her resolution to detest him, she and Jack were already too familiar with one another.

It had been easy to slip into something resembling their old dynamic this morning. *Scarily easy and very stupid*, Rachel told herself – even though it had just been for a few minutes. She needed to put the brakes on. Keep her guard up. *Both*.

Humphrey didn't answer his own front door, which Rachel immediately realised should not have surprised her. The rail-thin, spiky-looking woman who showed her and Jack into a drawing room seemed more likely to be a housekeeper than his wife. She wore a businesslike black skirt suit that emphasised her every angle: elbows, cheekbones, jutting clavicles, shoulder blades.

The woman introduced herself as Mrs Davidson – definitely staff, then, Rachel thought – and invited them to sit by the fire. Rachel must have looked as cold as she felt, huddled deep inside her coat and scarf. Reluctantly, she handed them over when Mrs Davidson offered to hang them for her.

Jack's eyes swept her outfit and she wished she hadn't noticed him looking. Her dress didn't show much skin, but there was no hiding her curves in anything clingy. Rachel's preference for comfortable clothes was only partly responsible for her usual, lazier look; she felt less exposed, less obviously fleshy, when she wore boxy sweaters and flat shoes. Also, random men catcalled at her less.

She looked around the room. The fireplace was of ornate carved stone. The walls were painted pale yellow and the windows were hung with heavy egg-yolk-coloured drapes. Every gilt knick-knack and piece of furniture in here looked precious, antique; the books stacked on a corner table were probably first editions.

Displayed on a walnut sideboard were several (no doubt priceless) nude sculptures. Rachel felt a 'You don't find *those* in the IKEA market hall' joke forming in her mouth and swallowed it.

Humphrey appeared in the room a moment later, shook Jack's hand as though they were old friends and let his eyes linger on Rachel's chest before looking her in the face and briefly grasping her fingertips.

Not a great start.

He was only a little taller than Rachel, and his enormous belly and comparatively tiny, turned-out feet made her think of a walrus.

His shiny black shoes were like wet flippers slapping across the oriental rug as he made his way to a winged armchair. He had iron-grey hair combed over a shining bald spot, and wore charcoal wool trousers with a maroon sweater that looked impossibly itchy.

Once Humphrey had settled comfortably, he turned to Jack and said, 'So, you're a Harrow man? Thank God. Someone who'll speak my language at last.'

Jack nodded. 'Yes, I was there – but longer ago now than I care to remember.'

Humphrey laughed, a brief, brisk boom. 'Ho! Truer for me than for you, my boy! But before we stumble down memory lane . . . who is this lovely young lady you've brought with you today? Your glamorous assistant?'

Oh God. *Assistant?!* Rachel bit back an outraged groan.

'If anything, Sir Humphrey, I am her humble servant,' Jack said, laughing. 'Rachel is our very experienced editorial strategist – you might remember I mentioned her when we spoke on the phone. She and I will be working together to help deliver what British House and Garden Heritage is looking for – a plan to tell your story as effectively as possible to a new generation of visitors.'

Humphrey smiled, seemingly impressed with Jack's chivalry. 'Always good to get a female view on things, I suppose,' he said with a shrug. 'More insight into the mysterious womanly mind!'

Rachel blanched at this blithe yet consummate dismissal of her professional expertise. Entirely dishonestly she managed to mumble: 'Hello, Sir Humphrey. It's nice to meet you.'

As Rachel reminded herself that she would definitely be sacked for throwing one of Humphrey's own *objets d'art* at him, Mrs Davidson reappeared with a silver tray bearing tea things, crustless finger sandwiches and a selection of tiny cakes.

For a split second Rachel panicked that, as the sole female member of this party, she'd be expected to play mother. Mercifully, Mrs Davidson stuck around long enough to furnish everyone with their preferred refreshments before scurrying from the room.

Jack and Humphrey discussed various old schoolmasters and traditions as they nibbled egg-and-cress sandwiches. Rachel ate a crumbly scone smothered in clotted cream and jam, and wished that the tea in the pot weren't a pungent, perfumey Earl Grey.

As she felt the conversation between Jack and Humphrey begin to progress towards a conclusion, Rachel couldn't decide whether to be relieved or horrified that she'd had no part in it. Either way, based on what she'd overheard, Humphrey hadn't revealed anything today that she and Jack didn't already know. This meeting had been about sizing them up, checking that their faces fit – not providing a more detailed brief.

'I see . . .' she heard Humphrey say as she tuned back in to their chat. 'So you've only recently transferred to work with Abraham and . . . what's his name, the limp-wristed Australian?'

Cold fury pooled in the pit of her stomach.

'The only Australian in the office is Greg O'Connor,' Rachel said, her voice clear and cool. 'He's our overall head of client services and a very close colleague of mine. A good friend, in fact.'

Humphrey stared at her for a moment, then turned back to Jack as though she hadn't said anything worth responding to. Rachel was too incensed to focus on what they were discussing.

Then Humphrey rang a bell. An actual *bell*. Mrs Davidson rematerialised with Jack and Rachel's coats and stood by, ready to show them out.

Humphrey seized Jack's hand for another hearty shake, then took Rachel's clenched fist to his lips and kissed the back of it with wet lips. Her toes curled inside her boots. She was certain he'd done it just to make her uncomfortable.

It wasn't until she and Jack were safely sealed inside the MG, emerging from Humphrey's private road onto a winding country lane, that Rachel let herself sigh. In a single, angry exhale, she released a deep breath that she felt she'd been holding for hours.

Jack looked sideways at her, an impish, impatient smile playing on his lips.

'So that was Sir Humphrey Caldwell,' Rachel said, shaking her head. 'What a truly *repellent* human being.'

'Honestly, Jack,' Rachel said after he'd stopped laughing. 'I don't know whether to be impressed or revolted by you right now.'

'Ouch!' he replied. '*Revolted* seems a bit harsh.'

'How can you make nice with a person so totally, irredeemably loathsome?' Rachel groaned. 'He's every bit as awful as Isaac – sorry, *Abraham* – said he'd be. Sexist, leering, puffed up . . . Clearly troubled by the fact that Isaac's Jewish – hence the name confusion, which I'm not at all convinced is an accident, by the way. And then there's the blatant homophobia . . . *So* grim. He needs to be voted off the island.'

'Have you finished?'

Jack grinned at her indulgently and rolled his eyes. Rachel wanted to hit him.

'This is agency life, Rachel,' he said, spreading a placatory palm as he indicated to turn a corner. 'Isaac said it himself when he gave us this account. Plenty of clients are vile in their own ways, but – so long as they pay us and don't actually assault anyone – they pretty much get away with it.'

'Well, Humphrey is the *worst*,' Rachel said. 'I've never been in a professional situation so awkward and unpleasant. I wanted to chuck something at him.'

'I'm glad you didn't. I'm not sure even I could have saved things if you'd drawn blood,' Jack said.

Urgh. Even when he was sending himself up, his complacency infuriated her. Rachel stared pointedly out of the passenger window.

'What did you want me to do?' Jack asked, his voice mild and his eyes full of mischief. 'Should I have challenged him to a duel for ogling your bosom? Given him a lecture on gay rights?'

Rachel felt her whole face ignite at the word *bosom*. 'Do NOT laugh at me,' she said through gritted teeth.

'I'm not laughing,' he said, but his smile was irrepressible. 'This is the game, Rach. This is just how it's played.'

'Firstly, do not call me Rach,' she instructed. 'Consider this your daily reminder that we are not friends. Secondly, I don't need you to tell me how "the game" is played – I've worked for this agency for four years. And thirdly, why is everything a game with you? Do you never take anything seriously?'

Jack sighed, a little agitated now. 'Fine. *Rachel.* But don't you think you're being a bit naive? It's my job to "make nice" with clients, whether I like them or not – it's literally what I get paid for. In this case, I was uniquely qualified to get Humphrey on side; I used his rampant snobbery to our advantage. Is that serious enough for you?'

Rachel scoffed. 'Used it to *your* advantage, perhaps. And you're a patronising arse, by the way.'

Jack threw her a withering look. 'Don't be obtuse – you're smart, it doesn't suit you. We might not be friends, but from Monday to Friday you and I are a team. I thought we'd established that, despite your misgivings. As far as work's concerned, what benefits me benefits you – and that includes sucking up to foul clients whose politics you hate. Also, it's worth noting that neither Greg nor Isaac have felt the need to physically injure Sir Humphrey, but in fact are actively pursuing his business. Ergo, it's our job to win it.'

Rachel scowled at him. *Ergo*, for fuck's sake. *Bollocks to Jack, to Harrow and to Latin.*

'The truth is, you enjoy it,' she said savagely. 'All of it – the chasing, the endless flattery . . . The reeling people in.'

Rachel had gone too far, she knew; this wasn't about work any more. She'd wanted to embarrass him into shutting up. She rapidly realised she'd miscalculated. Jack pushed his jaw out a little, narrowed his eyes at her, let his mouth quirk in amusement. He was eager for the fight.

'I may not be quite the cad I used to be, but I'm still me,' he replied, defiant. His lips curled completely into the smile they'd been promising, and Rachel hated how much she didn't hate it. 'I do this job because I'm good at it,' he added. 'You know as well as anyone that I'm built for persuading people. Coaxing, inveigling . . . Seducing.'

The colour in Rachel's cheeks flared again. *Fuck*. He was doing this on purpose.

There was something arch and challenging in his tone too – almost as if he was daring her to disagree with him. Was he trying to tease her into saying she was impervious, too smart to be sucked in by him a second time?

She needed to get out of this car. How could they *still* be over an hour away from London?

'You know, I'm more like my father than I ever intended to be,' Jack went on, filling the silence that stretched between them. He sounded bitter now. 'He's always been brilliant at establishing relationships, useless at the middle bits and spectacularly bad at endings. Again, I guess you're well qualified to agree that the apple doesn't fall far from the tree.'

Rachel's stomach squirmed.

They lapsed into silence as they drove down the M40. Rachel checked her work emails and, at Jack's request, composed a message to Isaac to let him know that the meeting with Humphrey had gone well. The atmosphere in the car was weird; charged. Jack's grip on the steering wheel was too tight, and the set of his shoulders looked rigid.

As they neared Stroud Green, he cleared his throat and turned to her, eyes intense. 'Listen . . . I'm sorry I said you were naive before. You're not – you're just a nicer person than I am.' He smiled a less smug smile than she was used to. 'You always were.'

Rachel felt a sudden tension in her chest and looked down at her hands, twisting them in her lap. 'Er – thanks?' she said.

'Was that your boyfriend this morning? The really tall guy with the beard?'

It took a second for her to realise Jack's misconception. 'What? No! That's Will. He's Anna's boyfriend.'

'Right.'

Why was he asking? What was it to him? He was *married*, for God's sake – and it was none of his business. Rachel refrained from saying any of this, and deliberately didn't explain that she was single.

They turned a corner, then crawled up Rachel and Anna's street until Jack found a space to pull the car into. It was only around 4 p.m., but the sun had disappeared and the sky was a dull, deep grey.

'Goodnight, then,' Jack said, and looked at her with an intensity that made her insides ache.

The thing that had been missing between Rachel and Laurence was suddenly abundant inside this small, dark space.

Rachel allowed this knowledge to shimmer briefly in her peripheral vision, like a migraine aura. Then she heaved it out of the way, making space for salient facts about the situation: Jack had a wife. Rachel didn't trust him. In many ways, she didn't even *like* him that much.

'See you Monday,' she mumbled without looking at him. She pulled the handle to release the passenger door and clambered out of the MG with as much dignity as its stupid low seats allowed.

Rachel usually enjoyed being right about things, but as she leaned against the front door and tried to compose herself she found no comfort in having known this simple truth all along: getting into a car with Jack had been a very big mistake.

13

It was unusual for Rachel to arrive home from work before Anna, but she was grateful for the silence and emptiness of the flat when she finally made her way inside.

Feeling chilled from the freezing car journey back to London, as well as uncomfortable in her dress and heels, she decided to take a hot shower. She let her hair get soaked, scrubbed her face with some expensive-looking stuff of Anna's and lathered her body with lemon-scented foam. As the bathroom steamed up around her, Rachel was dimly conscious of trying to wash away all traces of her encounter with Sir Humphrey, as well as cleanse her mind of the several impure thoughts she'd had about Jack in the past few minutes.

Out of the spray, Rachel dried herself more vigorously than was really necessary, brushed her teeth and pulled her towel-dried hair up into a knot on top of her head. In her room, she slicked moisturiser onto her face and put on an old pair of jeans, a vest top and a snuggly blue sweater.

By the time Anna got back, Rachel had settled in front of an episode of *Queer Eye* with a massive mug of tea. Anna dropped her work satchel and a bag for life full of exercise books on the floor as she shrugged out of her coat and scarf, then snatched her leopard-print beret off her head. It was the sort of hat Rachel always admired in shops but told herself she could never pull off in day-to-day life. On top of her red hair it would be too 'LOOK AT ME' – implying a confidence in her appearance that Rachel really didn't feel. On Anna, it somehow looked both cute *and* fierce, the boldness of it undercut by her petite prettiness.

'Well? How did it go today?' Anna asked.

Rachel scrunched up her shoulders and made a face that spoke of suffering.

'That good, huh? Will messaged me and said something about a sports car . . . ?' Anna flopped down at the other end of the sofa and raised her eyebrows at Rachel.

'Yeah,' Rachel sighed. 'I don't know why I was surprised, to be honest. It's even a red sports car – it's like he's *trying* to embody the rich-playboy stereotype.'

Anna laughed. 'Have you been back long?' She gestured at Rachel's comfy clothes and fluffy polka-dot slipper socks.

'Long enough to try and shower the cold out of my bones,' Rachel explained. 'It turns out vintage vehicles have really rubbish heaters.'

'Right,' Anna said, then closed her eyes in slow motion as her jaw went slack with shock. 'Oh my God. You've not done anything stupid, have you? Anything you might regret? Anything you might ordinarily, er . . . shower after?'

It took Rachel a few seconds to fully fathom Anna's meaning. 'Oh my God, *no*. Are you mad? What on earth would make you think that?!'

Anna stared at her, apparently still suspicious.

'You can't seriously think I'm so pathetic that within a couple of weeks of him reappearing I'd end up sleeping with him!' Rachel cried.

'You're blushing,' Anna pointed out. 'Your whole head's gone pink. Even your *neck* has gone pink. Which means you've at least thought about it at some point today.'

Rachel groaned and buried her face in a squashy, flax-coloured scatter cushion.

'I don't know what you want from me, Anna,' she said when she re-emerged. 'I hate him for what he did, but I can still *see*. He's really screwed me over by a) turning up again, and b) not becoming a total minger since we left uni.'

Anna rolled her eyes. 'Minging is as minging *does*, in my book.'

Rachel had slumped in her seat and was staring up at the ceiling, avoiding Anna's gaze. After a pause she sighed, twisted her body so she was facing her friend and said, 'You're right. As usual. But just so you know, I have reason to believe Jack's married – so no matter where my mind might wander during weak moments, nothing is going to happen.'

Anna snorted. 'If your only reason for not jumping him is that it would involve one of you being unfaithful, I am not in any way reassured.'

Rachel hid behind her cushion again, annoyed that the deployment of information she'd deliberately held back hadn't had the impact she'd expected. Anna placed her hands on top of the pillow, then gently pushed it out of the way.

'Rach,' she said, her blue eyes wide with worry and her voice devoid of sarcasm. 'I'm not winding you up just for the fun of it, you know. I don't want to see you get hurt. I know Jack has this . . . *thing*. This ability to get under your skin where other men haven't. I only wish I understood it.'

Rachel half-smiled and shook her head. 'I don't think that's it,' she said, her voice low, as if she was confessing. 'I've been thinking a bit about what happened lately, for obvious reasons. It's like . . . I was young when I met him, but felt *old*. I was careful and responsible all the time, and I think I'd got tired of it without even noticing. And suddenly I was away from home, where the only feelings at stake were my own. Jack was exciting . . . When he wanted something – or some*one* – he just went for it. I wondered what it would be like to be that way. He kept trying to get close to me, and eventually I let him because I *wanted* to – because he was gorgeous, because it felt so good to be out of control for a change. The whole thing was a rush – just one with a hideously painful comedown. But I learned my lesson.'

'So you're telling me Jack doesn't have superpowers?'

'Nope. He's just really, *really* good-looking. And I was a walking cliché: the archetypal good girl who found him irresistible. On some level, I suppose I still do.'

'Hmm,' Anna said, frowning. 'When you say you learned your lesson . . . I wonder: do you ever think you might have taken it a bit far? I've never known you to get so swept up in anyone else, since Jack. Do you think there's a chance you avoid "the rush" nowadays? On purpose?'

'What?'

'Well, think about it. Laurence might recently have revealed himself as a total tosser, but he was hardly mad, bad and dangerous to know, was he? I can't imagine he made your knees quiver with chat about how to calculate investment risk. In fact, when was the last time you went out with anyone who didn't like you more than you liked them? When was the last time you really fell for someone?'

Anna's face was bright, lit from within – electrified by the power of what she clearly considered a lightbulb moment.

'Okay, *stop*,' Rachel moaned. 'You sound like one of those cod psychologists off daytime TV. It's a very neat theory, but the idea that I'm going out of my way to date dullards is ludicrous.'

Anna crossed her arms. 'I didn't say *dullards*, and I didn't say you were doing it consciously.'

'I'm not doing it *at all*. Now please can we talk about something else? Literally anything else? Lately I feel like my entire life would fail the Bechdel test. Every conversation I have ends up being about men.'

On some level Rachel meant this – though it was also a convenient way to shut down Anna's attempt to analyse her, which she'd found distinctly uncomfortable.

'D'you know what?' Anna said. 'You're right. Let's not talk about men any more tonight. Let's go out! Let's go to the cinema – we haven't been together in ages. We could just get the bus to Muswell Hill and see the next thing that's showing at the Everyman, even if it's crap. We can eat popcorn and chocolate and get slushies instead of cooking dinner.'

Rachel motioned towards her outfit. 'But I'm in my scruffs. I've taken my make-up off,' she said.

'Dude, you're going to be sitting in the dark. And everyone around you will be looking at the big screen – not at you or your slightly bobbled jumper. Come on. Live a little! Let's do this.'

Not for the first time, Rachel's will to resist collapsed under the weight of Anna's enthusiasm. She heaved herself up off the sofa, pushed her feet into the Doc Marten boots that had been thrown at her and grabbed her coat from the hook by the front door.

They watched a terrible action movie in which the hero repeatedly overlooked a clever female scientist who kept saving his arse, only to hook up with the idiotic waif he'd had to rescue. High on sugary snacks, Rachel and Anna threw popcorn at the screen during the big finale kiss, decried the whole thing as risible nonsense all the way home, and had more raucous fun than they had in a really long time.

The following morning, feeling almost hung-over from the after-effects of an avalanche of junk food, Rachel found herself scrambling to turn down the volume on her mobile phone.

'*Twins!*' her mum was shrieking at her. 'Twins, for goodness' sake! Helen's only been married twelve months and she already has TWO babies. Her mother is going to be *unbearable*,' Jean Ryan went on. 'She'll be on about them morning, noon and night . . . I bumped into her at Costcutter earlier and I've already had chapter and verse on tandem feeding – plus far more information than I needed on the size of Helen's engorged breasts.'

Rachel laughed and said, 'Good morning to you too, Mum. I wonder if Helen knows Mrs O'Shea is going around telling people from church about the state of her mammaries.'

'Rachel Margaret Ryan, do NOT use that word! It's *crass*.'

'You're the one who started talking about them!' Rachel protested. 'I was sitting having a nice peaceful coffee until five minutes ago – but now here I am listening to you rant on about other people's newborns and their milk-swollen boobs.'

She dipped an oatmeal biscuit into her machine-made cappuccino, then bit off a huge chunk before it could collapse into her cup. As she chewed, Rachel readied herself for the inevitable shift in the conversation. News of Mrs O'Shea's latest grandchildren was surely just the opening gambit in a lecture about Rachel's lack of partner and increasingly slim chances of procreating.

'Does it not *bother* you?' her mum asked, as predicted. Her tone hovered somewhere between anxious and irritated.

'Mum, why should it bother me what Helen does? I haven't seen her since we left school. I don't even know what her last name is since she got married. I mean, I wish her well and everything – but I can't say I feel personally affected by her decision to reproduce.'

'Lovey, you know what I mean.'

In her mind's eye, Rachel could see her mother's face: the wounded eyes and disapproving frown that always accompanied sermons on her daughter's single status.

The doublethink Mum was capable of was sort of spectacular, Rachel had to admit. Rachel was supposed to tolerate being criticised, yet also feel guilty for putting her mother in the position where such needling was necessary – as if it were a valuable service Mum was providing at great personal cost, rather than a well-worn routine that simply made her daughter feel shitty.

'Please, *please* can we not do this?' Rachel begged. 'You can't seriously have rung me just to tell me about Helen's babies, then pivot to a lecture about the viability of my remaining eggs. It's Saturday morning. Have some pity! And you haven't actually *said* anything about the babies, by the way – I don't even know if they're boys or girls.'

'Oh, who even cares!' Mum blustered. 'Girls, I think, God help her ... And honestly, Rachel, I wouldn't mention any of this if I felt like you were listening or taking it seriously.'

'Taking *what* seriously?!' Rachel cried. It was only 10 a.m. Surely she'd done nothing to deserve this?

'You can't have children forever, you know – your body just won't be capable,' her mother intoned sagely. 'But you'll find the urge to have a baby just hits you one day, and it'll be powerful – *irresistible*. If you're not already with someone, let me tell you: you'll want to mate with the next man who makes you a decent cuppa.'

Rachel considered the truly terrible cup of tea Jack had made her at work last week: too milky by miles, and strangely sickly – like he'd stirred it with a second-hand spoon, crusty with someone else's sugar. The memory was oddly reassuring.

'As always, Mum, I'm amazed that with skills like these you haven't made a name for yourself as a motivational speaker,' Rachel said. 'I promise you, I'm *fine*. I am neither desperate to be pregnant nor spurning potential partners just to piss you off. And for God's sake, don't start up about

Laurence again because – while it seems the two of you agree on certain things – I had a very unpleasant run-in with him this week. He and I are beyond over.'

'Don't say *piss*,' Mum said. 'And I won't defend Laurence for being rude – but if he wasn't nice to you, it's probably because he's heartbroken.'

Rachel snorted. 'Based on what he said the other night, I'm not sure Laurence *has* a heart. If you X-rayed him, you'd probably find an adding machine where his heart should be. Thanks for being on my side, though, Mum. It means a lot.'

'I *am* on your side! You know that, you daft girl. I love you. I just worry about the future.'

'Right.'

Rachel drummed her fingertips on the kitchen tabletop, praying for this phone call to end – cursing herself for answering it in the first place.

'Have you made any plans for Valentine's Day?' her mum asked, as if this were the ideal topic to move on to. She really was on top form today.

Rachel groaned. 'No, but why would I? I've always hated it, even when I've been with someone. It's a commercial crap-fest – just a load of virtue-signalling from men who, for the rest of the year, can't be arsed to do the washing-up or bleach the toilet bowl.'

'Oh, don't get so angry! I just thought it was worth mentioning. It can be a depressing event if you end up home alone.'

'Mum, there's nothing special about the fourteenth of February. It isn't an *event* – it's a day like any other. If Anna goes out and I have the flat to myself, I'll do what I always do: microwave some leftovers for dinner and watch telly in my pyjamas.'

Her mother sighed and said, 'See? *This* is what concerns me. I give up . . . Do you want to speak to your father?'

'Yes, please.'

'Hi, pet,' Rachel's dad said a moment later. 'Are you okay there?'

'I'm fine,' Rachel breathed, not entirely sure it was true.

'Ach, you know she—'

'Means well,' Rachel finished. 'So you keep telling me.'

Rachel realised that her voice had thickened and her eyes were filling up. 'Let's talk about something else,' she said urgently. 'Let me tell you about work. I've switched teams, I got a bit of a pay rise. And the new client I'm working with looks like a posh walrus.'

He laughed. 'Well, that all sounds great . . . Apart from the walrus-looking fella. That's unfortunate for him.'

Rachel sniffed and made a watery sound a little like a laugh. She told him about her move to the pro-social side of the agency, the British House and Garden Heritage account, working with Isaac and her new and improved job title.

Without even realising she was doing it, she edited Jack out of the story, minimised Humphrey's awfulness and omitted any other details that might give her family cause for concern. Stressing out her parents had been anathema to Rachel for almost half her life and – short of refusing to stay with unsuitable boyfriends – she always did her best to avoid it.

Rather unjustly, Rachel's Sunday-morning run felt no easier than usual after a sedate Saturday night home alone.

Anna had gone over to Will's as soon as she knew he was back from Edinburgh, so Rachel had read a book, eaten cheese on toast and – determinedly ignoring the bottle of wine on the kitchen worktop – tried not to think about Jack, or the tension that had built between them during Friday's car journey.

All weekend she'd been refusing her mind permission to remember the look he'd given her right before she scrambled out of his car. No good could come of dwelling on it – of wondering whether, given another few seconds, he might have tried to kiss her. Nor did she want to consider whether she'd have let him. He was spoken for, and even if he weren't, she'd already been burned by him once. Things were quite awkward enough between them, and tomorrow they had to get back to work as normal.

Now, with Lady Gaga blasting loud through her headphones, Rachel was gladly incapable of thinking about anything but putting one foot in front of the other.

Walk a bit.

Run a bit.

Try not to throw up or die.

This was one of the benefits of running, Rachel had found: it forced her to be in her body instead of in her head. If it weren't for how exhausted the exercise made her, it might almost have felt restful.

She was still painfully slow, and the effects of exertion typically turned her pale skin the colour of slow-cooked red cabbage, but Rachel couldn't deny that her fitness and stamina were improving as she pressed on with Couch to 5K.

Last week, finally convinced she wasn't going to give up before she hit her target, she'd treated herself to a pair of high-waisted olive-green leggings with black power-mesh panels, plus the matching top. Both garments were a feat of engineering: they pushed everything in and up without being uncomfortable, preventing Rachel's squishier bits from wobbling as she ran along.

She'd been going for at least twenty of her allotted thirty minutes, and she was starting to flag. *Come on*, she admonished herself. *Dig a bit deeper. Do – not – stop.*

Finsbury Park was busy this morning. She didn't want to draw attention to herself by coming to a halt. There was safety in movement: a sense that she was anonymous, invisible, as long as she didn't stand still.

Rachel tried not to notice other, fitter runners, nor let them bother her. If she was going to get better at this, she knew she needed to stay in her own lane; remember that she was only competing against her former more sedentary self.

Of course there was the odd moment when Rachel couldn't help sneaking a peek at someone who sped past. Occasionally she'd spot a handsome man among the Proper Runners, enjoying these brief encounters as perks of the programme – a few diverting seconds during what usually felt like a torturous half-hour.

As she rounded a tight corner, Rachel's attention was caught by someone with hair the colour of sea-washed sand. He was very tall, and lean in a way that made her think 'strong' rather than 'skinny'. Even from this distance, and although her view was obscured by his blue T-shirt sleeves, Rachel could tell he had good arms. Not pumped up, gym-honed or big, just . . . *good*. He was holding himself perfectly straight, running from his core, propelling himself forward at a speed Rachel could only dream of. Whoever he was, this guy was fit – in more than one sense of the word, she admitted to herself.

They were moving closer together. They were going to run past one another any moment now. Rachel knew she looked red, dishevelled and clammy. She wished she were one of those girls who could exercise without ending up a drenched, half-dead mess.

At least if this man nodded to acknowledge her as he flew by, Rachel's ensuing blush wouldn't be obvious on her already flaming cheeks. She hoped he hadn't noticed her staring at him.

He was only a few metres away now. And he was . . . waving at her?

Why was he waving at her?

Holy mother, it was *Tom*. Tom was the tall, fit runner. *Tom* was waving at her. Rachel came to a clumsy stop, almost tripping over her own feet.

Tom steadied her, laughing, and pulled her off the path onto a grass verge still crunchy with frost.

'Hey,' he said, breathing heavily, looking down at her and smiling. 'I didn't mean to startle you. I always forget people don't recognise me when I'm not wearing my glasses. Sorry if I've put you off your stride.'

'Haha! My stride?!' Rachel said, her voice a panicky screech.

This was *weird*. She tried to avoid staring up at Tom's face, which was glowing and flushed, his cheekbones highlighted pink.

His lips were parted as he struggled to slow his breathing. Rachel had never really looked at them before, but they were full, plush – almost feminine, with a steep Cupid's bow. His bottom lip dipped slightly in the centre, as if aware of its own ample size and seeking to shrink itself for fear of being noticed.

Disconcerted, Rachel cast her eyes downwards, faking exhaustion so severe she couldn't speak. She immediately wished she hadn't. Tom's navy T-shirt had ridden up above the waistline of his black shorts to reveal a sliver of stomach. Beneath smooth skin a few shades darker than her own, Rachel detected muscle. *Abs.* Further up, the T-shirt was sticking to his chest, implying solid planes and hollows that Rachel had never imagined might be there.

Whoa. Was this the sort of random, inappropriate hormonal surge Rachel's mum had told her about? Was this her ovaries agitating for action? Dazed and dumb, Rachel looked down at her feet, cursing her mother and her dire warnings. Whether their effects were real or psychosomatic, this was embarrassing.

'Ugh, I'm gross, I'm sorry,' Tom said, breaking the silence. He pulled his top away from his torso and let it settle again, no longer plastered to his skin. Rachel felt her breathing begin to ease.

'Oh God, me too,' she said, and she meant it. She was annoyed that Tom was seeing her sweaty and knackered, though her vanity made no sense at all given the various coughs, colds and hangovers he'd seen her suffer over the years.

'How's it going, then?' Tom asked. 'The running, I mean.'

'Oh, not bad. I still feel like I'm going to expire every time I come out, but I think I'm getting better. I'm definitely going to complete the programme – there's a bottle of gin riding on it, after all.'

Tom grinned at her. 'Good for you. Make sure you choose something expensive.'

There was a pause, during which it seemed each of them was waiting for the other to speak.

'I didn't know you ran,' Rachel said eventually. *Eek. Pathetic.*

'Yeah.' He was pulling at his T-shirt again. 'I do 10K a couple of times a week if I can. Clears the head.'

Rachel nodded but stayed silent, afraid she might come out with something else idiotic.

'Well. I'd better get on,' Tom said, pushing his hair off his forehead. His usual waves, damp with perspiration, had spiralled into proper curls – the kind you could fit your finger inside. 'Sorry again if I freaked you out. No doubt I'll see you in the week. I'll be in touch as soon as I have the date of the first photo shoot for the exhibition confirmed, in case you want to come along?'

'Sounds great,' Rachel said. 'Happy running.' She watched him as he jogged away, picked up speed and eventually disappeared. As soon as he was out of sight she winced, wondering what on earth had possessed her to say 'Happy running'.

She shook herself, stuck her headphones back in her

ears and got going again. God, that had been strange. Silly, really – it wasn't as if she didn't *know* Tom was attractive.

But Rachel didn't think of Tom that way. She never had. He was her friend – not some random bloke to be ogled momentarily as he went by. Tom was . . . solid. Permanent. Important.

As her feet pounded the cold pavement, Rachel reassured herself that it was her mother's wild prophesying, rather than the sight of Tom in running gear, that had sent her thoughts spiralling in a direction she'd never have expected.

By the time she got home, she was sure of it.

14

Rachel got to work early on Monday morning, after a disturbed night full of odd dreams. She was awake before seven without need of her alarm, and reasoned that – since rest was determined to elude her – she might as well get up. Getting to the office before Jack was motivation enough, in any case.

When Rachel arrived at work, however, Jack was already at his desk. He was on the phone, listening hard, his eyes cast down and his mouth set in a grim line.

Once Rachel was settled at her desk, she caught his eye and made a cup-tipping motion with her right hand, mouthing 'Coffee?' Jack gave her a grateful thumbs up.

It was 8.40 a.m. by Rachel's watch, and the only other people in the office were Neil from the tech team and Ivan, the agency's IT guy. The kitchen was similarly deserted. Rachel placed one R/C mug and then another beneath the spout of the coffee machine, pressing the *Americano* button twice.

When she returned, Jack was off the phone. She passed him his drink, leaning towards him over the join between their desks so she didn't spill. She caught a waft of his aftershave and held her breath for a moment, determined to ignore it.

Jack's face was inscrutable, but something in the way he

was moving seemed taut and strained. He normally held himself with a sort of graceful confidence Rachel envied, but his usual easy poise seemed to have crumpled. Something was wrong, but there was no way she was going to ask what. She sat down as he murmured his thanks for the coffee, reminding herself that she shouldn't care if he was stressed out, that whatever mess he was in, it might well be of his own making.

Rachel busied herself with reviewing all the British House and Garden Heritage materials she'd amassed so far. Mixed in with Humphrey's brief were notes from Isaac and Greg, plus examples of the work that had been done by other, now discharged, agencies. Her own assortment of ideas – rough sketches, bullet-point lists and blocks of mocked-up text – lurked at the bottom of the thick wad of papers. She still hadn't come up with anything she felt good about, and she and Jack needed to present their plans to Humphrey at the end of next week. Rachel scowled as she reread her own words – as if giving them the evil eye might imbue them with new, more profound meaning.

'Penny for them?' Jack said, and she looked up at him. The clouds had apparently cleared now; his smile was warm and teasing again, and his body back in the fluid, relaxed stance she was used to. She wished she wasn't interested enough to notice.

'Your thoughts,' he clarified, grinning. 'You're looking at that document like you hate it – like you're trying to set it on fire with laser beams from your eyes.'

'I *do* hate it. And rather sadly I wrote the thing.'

Jack grimaced in faux horror, then laughed. 'Maybe I can help to loosen things up a bit. Unblock you, if you're struggling for words . . . You and I are due a catch-up on BHGH anyway. It's not as if Friday was a particularly productive day, workwise.'

'To be honest, I could probably do with bouncing my ideas off someone,' she admitted. 'Finding the right angle on this isn't easy.'

'I'm not surprised. Drumming up new visitors is a tall order when what you're trying to sell them hasn't changed. Humphrey's adamant that nothing needs to be done with the properties themselves, though – or with the artefacts and exhibits they have on show.'

'That's exactly the problem,' Rachel said, nodding. 'All I've really got to work with is smoke and mirrors . . . I'm trying to change people's perceptions rather than sell them something new.' She felt almost vindicated by Jack's understanding of how fiddly this was – of how much rested on her ability to tell familiar stories in a different, more interesting way.

'Have you eaten?' he asked. The change of topic caught Rachel off guard. 'I came straight here this morning,' Jack went on, 'and I'm starving. Do you want to go and get breakfast? We could chat through what you've put together so far – make it a work date.'

Rachel's stomach lurched at the word *date*, then grumbled loudly. Traitorously. Jack smirked at her, daring her to claim she wasn't hungry.

'Okay, I'll come,' she said, wishing she could think of an excuse not to. 'Actually, I know the perfect place.'

They sat at Rachel's preferred table at Cyril's – the one she'd been at on the day she hid from Laurence.

In light of what had happened last week, it now seemed at least possible – perhaps even likely – that Laurence had been here looking for her that afternoon. The idea made Rachel feel a bit queasy, not to mention mad with indignation. Laurence had no right to stalk around North London trying to hunt her down. She was a woman who'd decided to stop seeing him, not a lost briefcase he needed to locate.

'Are you all right?' Jack asked. 'You keep craning to look at the door. It's like you're waiting for the police to burst in and arrest you.'

'I'm fine,' Rachel insisted. 'I'm good.' She sat a little further back in her chair, willing herself to relax. There was no way she was explaining the Laurence disaster to Jack, and after the wine bar incident it seemed unlikely she'd hear from him again in any case.

'Where *are* we, by the way?' Jack said quietly, so that only Rachel could hear. 'It's like a museum in here . . . A tribute to late-twentieth-century greasy spoons. Or did we step through a time portal I didn't notice and travel back to 1982?'

Rachel glowered at him as she shuffled through the pile of documents she'd brought with her, then slid several of them across the table in his direction.

Jack's face had lit up, animated by his thorough enjoyment of teasing her. He hassled his hair with his right hand, then leaned his unshaven chin on his palm in a simper. 'You always did bring me to the nicest places.'

'And you always were a horrible snob,' Rachel said,

crossing her arms and averting her eyes from his face. 'For your information, the food here is amazing – mainly because Cyril cooks everything in proper butter and doesn't believe in cholesterol. And if you still aren't convinced about this place after your sausage sandwich, just think of it as payback: it's the equal and opposite to Friday, and our horrible Old Harrovians' reunion.'

Jack laughed, and Rachel caught herself feeling warmed by the sound of it – satisfied that she'd bested him. *Stop*, she instructed herself.

At that moment Cyril appeared with a tray. He put down two large mugs of tea and a pair of plates, then grinned and winked at Rachel as he shuffled away, his bulbous stomach swaying as he went, swelling over the waistband of his joggers.

The bacon in Rachel's sandwich was fried to perfection – so well done she could have snapped it in two. Ketchup oozed from between the two thick slices of white bread. Cyril knew her well.

Jack looked at his food quizzically, clearly astonished at the sight of a cafe breakfast that didn't involve avocado, perfectly poached eggs or organic sourdough. Nevertheless, within five minutes he'd wolfed it.

'I have to admit it,' he said as Rachel crunched the last of her bacon. 'That was delicious. I can already feel my arteries clogging, but it was worth it.'

'Told you so.' Rachel nodded, picking up her tea and rolling the still-hot mug between her palms. 'But we should talk about the project now we've eaten.' She was keen to keep this 'date' as professional as possible.

'Sure,' Jack said with a shrug. He spent a few minutes looking through the documents she'd given him, then tipped his head sideways and looked at her from beneath knitted brows.

'Go on,' Rachel said. 'Don't spare me.'

'Okay. What you have here is definitely better than what any of the other agencies put together. But it's still a bit . . .'

'Dull. Boring. *I know*.' Rachel groaned and put her mug back on the table.

'I wasn't going to say boring,' Jack said. 'Maybe more . . . teacher-y. There's interesting stuff in there, but it feels too educational. Too worthy.'

'Hmm,' Rachel said, chewing the end of the biro she was holding. 'That's it. I agree with you. I mean, I know we need to make the facts and the history feel relevant . . . Not present them as something people "should" find fascinating on principle. But clearly I need to do better. Looking at them again, there are still bits of these mock-ups that read like a GCSE textbook.'

'Yeah.'

'Hmm,' Rachel murmured again. 'I wonder . . . Ironically, I reckon I might need to think *more* like a teacher here.'

'How d'you mean?'

'Well. Anna spends half her life trying to convince kids that works of great literature – even if they're hundreds of years old – still have something to say to us, here and now. I've seen her plan enough lessons to know the trick is putting the right twist on whatever text they have to study.'

'I'm listening,' Jack said, and he was. Rachel had his full

attention; it was nerve-wracking, exhilarating, like being trapped in the beam of a searchlight.

'So what if . . .' Rachel was thinking on the spot now, but she felt like she was chasing an idea worth pursuing. 'What if instead of focusing on the houses and the stuff inside them, we thought about who *owned* them or worked in them? Humanised it all a bit?'

Jack nodded at her, his green eyes bright with interest.

'Most of these places are hundreds of years old,' she continued, fizzing with excitement. 'Each one has to have had at least *one* resident with a story worth telling. Right?'

'Sure. You'd certainly think so.'

'So, we find those stories. And we use them as a hook – we create content about the love affairs people had, the gambling debts they ran up, the insane art collections they amassed . . . We bring historical facts into focus through the drama.'

'That sounds like a strategy to me.' Jack grinned.

'You think?' Rachel grinned back. Her smile was broad, sincere and unguarded; delight at having hit upon the right approach made her forget, for a moment, who she was bestowing it upon.

'There's actually loads we could do with this,' Jack said, suddenly energised, dragging a hand through his hair again. Rachel wondered if it was unconscious, or an affectation designed to make other people think about tangling their own fingers in it. Either way, she wished it didn't work. 'We could encourage social sharing,' he went on. 'Get people using hashtags to mark which stories resonate with them. If we can convince Humphrey to spend the money, we could do some *amazing* interactive stuff through a BHGH app: maybe even augmented-reality content where you could put your own face in a portrait, an important item of clothing or whatever.'

'That could be cool.' Rachel nodded. 'I think there's something here. I'll pick a couple of the bigger properties and see how the approach might work – check it has legs. Maybe we could catch up again tomorrow when I've mocked up some new materials?'

'Perfect.'

Jack placed his hands flat on the tabletop, then pushed himself up out of his chair, still smiling. 'Guess we should get on, now we know what we're doing.' They both bundled coats, scarves and gloves back on before waving their thanks to Cyril and heading out into the cold.

As they walked the short distance back to the office, Rachel felt elation and unease fighting for supremacy inside her. The thrill of beginning what she knew would be good work was muddled with disquiet at how well she and Jack had pulled together: how easily they'd come up with a plan worth pitching.

She'd never wanted to be paired with him – everything in her had resisted the idea that they could be a team. Yet this had been natural. Effortless.

Even worse, it had felt good.

'I'm really not sure about this, Greg,' Rachel said as she stepped across the threshold of Viva Vinyasa yoga studio on Thursday night. 'I have no coordination, no flexibility and no balance. I'm going to topple over and kill someone.'

Greg, lurking behind her in the doorway, gave her a gentle shove and said, 'Don't be idiotic. The mats are well spaced and you'd never kill anyone even if you did land on them. Maybe just cause extensive bruising.' He pushed her again, harder this time. 'I promised you katsu curry and cocktails after this, but my side of the deal only stands if yours does. *Go.*'

Reluctant but resigned, Rachel trudged forward and found a mat in the furthest corner of the room. There were only two others nearby, which she reasoned reduced the chances of her accidentally battering a fellow yogi. Greg took the mat to her left, adopting a serene cross-legged pose that Rachel thought she should probably try to imitate. She let the studio's plinky-plunky music wash over her as she shut her eyes, instructing herself to relax.

Moments later the yoga teacher appeared as if from nowhere. 'Namaste,' she said, in precisely the kind of breathy, ethereal voice Rachel had expected. 'Welcome to our friends and to our newcomers tonight. I'm Jasmine. I'll be with you this evening as we breathe through a flow of poses to stretch, unwind and strengthen your muscles and minds. My wish,' she continued in her airy sing-song, 'is that we'll leave here tonight a little sweaty, perhaps, but . . . serene. Settled in our very deepest selves.'

Sweaty but serene? Rachel tried not to laugh.

'This woman talks like a cult leader,' she hissed at Greg. 'I bet she's actually from Barnsley or somewhere, and her real name is Sharon. Beneath her accent lies a northern lass desperate for escape.'

Greg stuck his tongue out at her. 'Shut up, you cynic.

Jasmine's an excellent teacher. And as far as I know, she's from Henley-on-Thames.'

'We'll begin with some deep breathing, as always,' Jasmine crooned. 'Then we will gliiiiiide into mountain pose.'

Everyone in the room began arranging their bodies into elegant shapes. Greg seemed to know what he was doing, so Rachel parked her sarcasm in favour of trying to copy him. The last thing she wanted was to draw attention to herself and her cluelessness.

As Rachel tried to keep up, the effort required to do the right things at the right times drove all other thoughts from her mind. It was a little like when she was running: holding her body in positions that challenged it rendered her unable to ruminate on anything else. For this she was grateful.

Over the past few days Rachel and Jack had continued working on the new strategy for British House and Garden Heritage, in preparation for next week's presentation. Rachel knew their stuff was good, but the pleasure she'd taken in creating it unnerved her. Some part of her knew their old closeness had helped rather than hindered them.

When they were brainstorming, their chemistry was undeniable – ideas sparked like tiny electric shocks between them, occasionally flashing bright enough that Rachel worried other people might notice.

Outside those conversations, though, Rachel remained angry with Jack – and afraid of what might happen if she let her resentment go. Years of dismissing him as all style and no substance had ended abruptly, with the uncomfortable realisation that, while he obviously lacked humility, Jack didn't want for intelligence. Working with him so closely over the past few weeks had reminded Rachel that he was creative and clever, as well as stupidly charming.

Lying on her back on her yoga mat, her limbs dewy with perspiration, Rachel heard Jasmine say, 'And now come back to yourselves, back into this room. Let your consciousness drift up, *lift* into the here and the now. Allow any worries still lingering in your mind to dissipate, fade away, like ripples on a pond. *Be well*,' she concluded, impressively.

A chime sounded, signalling the end of the session. People began to sit up, gathering their things and nodding to Jasmine as they departed. Rachel looked at Greg, who wore a smooth, vacant expression that made her want to laugh.

'Don't tell me you didn't enjoy that,' he said under his breath. 'I could see you got into it. You were pretty good too, for a first-timer.'

Rachel pulled her socks on, then hauled herself to her feet. There was no changing room at Viva Vinyasa, which was a small, independent space run by Jasmine and her partner. Rachel and Greg had agreed to go for dinner in their yoga gear, so she shrugged on an oversized slogan sweatshirt, retied her ponytail and put on her boots and coat.

'Ready?' she asked.

'Oh, come on,' Greg said, buttoning up his coat and winding a long crimson scarf around his neck. 'Admit it: you had fun.'

'I've exercised muscles I'd forgotten I even had, *and* had

to hold in about a hundred snarky comments. I feel like it's done me some good, though.'

'Well, that's a start,' Greg said. 'Shall we eat?'

'Definitely.'

Greg led her on a short walk into Clerkenwell, stopping when they arrived at a restaurant with a green neon sign that promised noodles, sushi and bento.

Inside, they ordered cherry blossom spritzers and – on Greg's strong recommendation – two katsu curries (tofu for him, chicken for her), plus a portion of gyoza dumplings. Once their waitress had delivered their drinks, along with a small dish of salted edamame, Rachel said, 'So, how have you been? How is it being Mr Important? I miss you. It's weird not working with you every day.'

Greg arched an eyebrow. 'From where I've been standing, it seems like you're coping pretty well without me. Maybe even enjoying the change.'

'What's that supposed to mean?' Rachel asked, pausing with a bean halfway between the bowl and her mouth.

'It means that when you first told me what had happened between you and Jack, I'd have put money on you quitting your job or killing him within a couple of weeks . . . At the very least, I expected you to look miserable all day, every day. And you don't.'

'Oh.'

'*Oh*, indeed. Obviously no one else in the office knows you used to be together, but I'll be honest: I don't think reports of a romantic connection between you would exactly be front-page news. It's pretty clear there's *something* there. My question is: what?'

'We're teammates,' Rachel said, shifting in her seat and staring hard at the melting ice in her cocktail. 'That's it. I'm just trying to make the best of it.'

'Psshhhhh. You're clearly still attracted to him.'

Rachel looked up sharply, contemplated denial and then dismissed the idea, sagging back against her chair.

'Fine. Maybe I am. But that's irrelevant. I can recognise he's nice to look at without doing anything about it. Without even liking him, necessarily. And *he* doesn't need to know.'

'Hmm,' Greg said. 'Maybe not. But I think he'd be interested in the information.'

'No way. Definitely not.' Rachel shook her head emphatically.

Greg chuckled. 'Ray, for a highly intelligent woman you're incredibly bad at reading people. Bordering on dim-witted.'

'Honestly, *you're* the one who's reading this situation wrong. I'm certain of it. I have good reason to be.'

Greg shook his head, untroubled by her defence. 'Whatever you think you know, put it to one side and look at the situation with your own eyes. You're ignoring what everyone else can see, plain as day.'

'What do you mean, "everyone"?'

'I mean me, obviously. And possibly Donna – she seems to be taking an interest.'

Rachel groaned. 'This is ridiculous. I don't even know what we're talking about, and yet I feel like I'm going to have the scarlet letter pinned to my jumper when I come into work tomorrow.'

'Let me break it down for you, darl. Nobody apart from me knows about your history with Jack, but your colleagues are not blind. People are starting to notice he's into you.'

'Rubbish,' Rachel said, with a short laugh that she hoped would signal contempt for the idea. Her heart seemed to be beating too hard and too far up her torso. Her pulse was throbbing in her throat.

'*Ray*,' Greg sighed. 'He's desperate to get your attention. Maybe it's just to see if he can catch you a second time, or maybe he's genuinely smitten. But he looks at you like he can't decide whether to ruffle your hair or eat you.'

Rachel shivered as her stomach performed a somersault.

'As for you,' Greg went on, pointing at her with a forkful of vegan gyoza, 'you look at him like you can't decide whether to run for the hills or serve yourself up in a snack box.'

'*GREG*,' Rachel moaned, burying her face in her hands. '*Stop*.'

'What I'm trying to say is, I get it: you're confused. Your formerly frosty feelings towards Jack have melted somewhat in the face of his hotness. Just be careful. I've always thought dipping your pen in the office ink is a bad move – and that's in situations where someone *hasn't* already revealed themselves to be a cheating bastard.'

'Nobody is going to be dipping anything *anywhere*,' Rachel said, embarrassed and off balance. 'And honestly, I think you should be giving me props for my professionalism here. It's been quite an effort just being civil to Jack most of the time. Now can we please change the subject?'

As if in answer to her plea, the waitress reappeared with the rest of their food and set it down in front of them. 'Another round of drinks?' she asked.

'As soon as you can possibly bring them,' Rachel said. 'Thanks.'

'More booze on a school night?' Greg grinned, raising an eyebrow at her.

'It has green stuff in it,' Rachel scowled. 'And fruit. You're always telling me I should enjoy more plant-based foods.'

He smiled at her again, then suddenly burst out: 'Oh my GOD, I almost forgot to tell you about Valentine's Day!'

'What about it?'

'Well, apparently Mountaintop Media make a big thing of it every year. And now we're part of the fold, R/C will be doing the same.'

'Gross,' Rachel said. 'What's going to be happening? If there are plans for a kissing booth or a man auction, I'm going to have to call in sick.'

'No, no,' Greg said, 'nothing like that. It's all about balloons, apparently.'

'*Balloons?*'

'Yes. Colleagues are encouraged to order balloons for one another anonymously – in theory, for the sake of expressing professional admiration, rather than a latent desire to hump each other. You pay two pounds for each balloon you want to send, write the card that goes with it, and all the money raised goes to charity on behalf of the agency. Then, on V-Day morning, volunteers come in early to decorate the office. All the balloons are tied to their recipients' chairs – each one with its own little note from the sender – so that when people get to work they have a fun surprise.'

'Wow. So it's a schmaltzy popularity contest, like something from an American teen movie. It's making me feel ill and it hasn't even happened yet. It's a miracle my food is staying down.'

'Mock all you like, but people are going to *love* it. And it gets better: who d'you think Toby has put in charge of this whole thing?'

'Oh God . . . *No*,' Rachel sighed as she reviewed the most likely candidates and arrived at the obvious, ominous conclusion.

'YES!' Greg grinned, delighting in Rachel's dread. 'Donna will be taking payments, keeping track of who's ordered what and making sure all the balloons make it to their rightful owners. I wouldn't put it past her to steam open all the envelopes before the cards are attached to them, while she's at it.'

'Ugh. Nor would I,' Rachel said. 'This is madness: she's already far too interested in other people's lives. Letting her do this is like licensing her to be Chief Office Gossip. Toby might as well have given her a plaque for her desk.'

Greg laughed. 'Yep. But there it is.'

'I'm not looking forward to this,' Rachel said. 'I've always hated Valentine's Day, but at least in years gone by I was safe from it in the workplace.'

'What are you more afraid of?' Greg asked. 'Getting a balloon from Jack or *not* getting a balloon from Jack?'

Rachel mashed at her drink's limp mint garnish with her straw before meeting his eyes.

'Honestly?' she said. 'I'm afraid of caring either way.'

15

'Happy Valentine's Day!' Greg yelled at Rachel as she strode across the office on Thursday morning. She grimaced and threw a sarcastic thumbs up in his direction, ignoring his sniggers as she fought her way towards her own desk, wading through the sea of pink and red that obscured her route.

R/C's open-plan workspace was a hellscape of tacky romantic paraphernalia. In addition to the hundreds of balloons tied to the backs of her colleagues' plastic swivel chairs, vases of flowers sat on desks, large glass jars of chocolate hearts were strategically placed near every workstation and glittery, bright-pink bunting that spelled out *LIVE, LAUGH, LOVE* had been suspended from several ceiling-height bookcases. *Bleuch*.

It appeared that around half the people here today had also followed Donna's mandate to 'get into the spirit of things' by wearing red, pink or otherwise festive clothing. Rachel spotted Kemi leaning against Ivan's desk, reading the card that had been attached to a balloon he'd been sent. She was wearing a red denim miniskirt and a bright white T-shirt with a gigantic heart emblazoned across the boobs. She'd even adorned some of her braids with red beads.

Rachel was pleased that, along with her black skinny

jeans, she'd put on a blue-and-yellow star-print shirt this morning. It would have pained her to comply with one of Donna's ridiculous diktats accidentally.

Feeling almost traumatised by the office decor, Rachel arrived at her desk and dumped her stuff. Opposite her, Jack was barely visible inside a cloud of balloons. His desk and chair were festooned with them, some tied to his seat and others – presumably those that wouldn't fit alongside the rest – placed around his computer monitor, weighted down with heavy plastic hearts.

'*Urgh*,' she sighed, searching for his face among what seemed like a hundred inflated orbs. 'It's not exactly subtle, is it?'

Jack batted a pink balloon aside and grinned at her. 'We did this every year in Manchester. I think it's rather sweet.'

'You would,' Rachel grumbled. 'You're always voted prom king.'

Something like jealousy squirmed inside her as she surveyed the evidence of his Office Heart-Throb status. No doubt the majority of these balloons were from Kemi's gang of Jack fans. He looked as if he neither knew nor cared who'd sent them – and also, infuriatingly, as though he wasn't in the least surprised to have received many more Valentines than anybody else in the room.

'Do you think it's safe to approach the kitchen?' Rachel asked. 'Or will I be required to recite a sonnet before I'm allowed across the threshold?'

Jack's smile widened. '*Could* you recite a sonnet if someone . . . I don't know – say, me – decided to bar your way?'

She glanced at him, managing to look disdainful despite the playful glimmer in his green eyes. 'Of course I could.'

'You remember more from our Shakespeare module than I do, then,' he said with a shrug, referring to a ten-week stint they'd spent studying poetry, plays and performance in their second year of university.

'That's hardly surprising,' Rachel huffed, remembering how reliant he'd been on her research when they were writing their final essays. She stood up, brushing off the memory of his head bent close to hers, poring over *The Tempest* at a lamplit table in the library. 'Do you want anything to drink?'

Jack shook his head, his mouth twitching, teasing her with another smirk. 'Surely you're not going to pretend you can't see those three balloons tied to the back of your chair?'

'Of course I can see them. I'm doing my best to ignore them.'

'I'm afraid we can't have that,' Jack said, shaking his head. 'As your resident man from Mountaintop, I insist that you try a bit harder to participate in today's carefully planned fun.'

Rachel curled her fingertips, making air quotes at him. '"Carefully planned fun". The clue is in the name. Forced jollity is never actually enjoyable – it's a law of nature, like gravity. What goes up must come down, and organised merriment is awful.'

Jack laughed and shook his head again. 'Who pissed on your Coco Pops this morning? And *don't* change the subject. Don't make me stand in the kitchen doorway and demand to be paid for passage in poetry, Ryan. Open the bloody cards.'

Calling her by her surname was a clear manipulation – he was crossing a line and they both knew it. It had always been his way of signalling endearment, oddly laced with a reaffirmation of distance; evidence that she was just another mate, but also proof that she was different from the short-lived 'girlfriends' whose surnames he never learned. He hadn't dared to try it again until now.

At the same time as Rachel's eyebrows shot up in shock, she felt herself thrill at the sheer cheek of him.

'Oh, *fine*,' she sighed, sitting down dramatically.

The first balloon – a cerise-pink one – was clearly from Greg. The card that came with it read:

Roses are red, hedges are green, you're DEEPLY sarcastic but still Copy Queen. PS: Yoga again next Thursday – no excuses.

She smiled at it and propped it up against a pile of paperwork.

Rachel's second balloon was red, with a card that was obviously from Kemi.

Thx for all your support over the past few years with work (also for always getting me home when I'm hammered, ha!). Put a word in for me if you're still determined not to go for it yourself... YKWIM ;-) xxx

Rachel made a face, then slid the card across her desk until it disappeared beneath a notepad.

Balloon number three was a pale rosy pink. Rachel felt Jack watching her as she fumbled to open the note that was stuck to it. The message was written in graceful, looping handwriting she recognised immediately.

I'm better when I'm (working) with you. Thanks. J x

Colour crept up her neck and into her face. She had no idea what to say – no clue what this even *meant*.

'Coffee,' she blurted, shooting up out of her seat. 'I still need a coffee. Are you sure you don't want coffee? Tea?'

'I'm fine, thanks,' Jack said, a small smile settling on his lips.

Rachel turned away, afraid to look at it, and scurried in the direction of the kitchen.

A couple of hours later, Rachel was lost in the life of Lady Sarah Latymer, once resident at the flagship British House and Garden Heritage property, Hartwell Abbey.

Lady Sarah had been the darling of the late-nineteenth-century literary set; a patron of novelists, poets, playwrights and artists. She'd had passionate affairs with both male and female writers, controversially championed universal suffrage and home rule for Ireland, and had given over most of the abbey for use as a convalescent home for injured soldiers during the First World War.

Her husband, Lord George Latymer, was dull as ditchwater by comparison but, aware of their client's flagrant misogyny, Rachel took care to include him in the narrative she was currently weaving around Hartwell: the story she wanted to tell about Sarah's life through the building she lived in, the clothes she wore and the letters, images and objects that had survived her.

The sample content on Hartwell Abbey was a core part of the proposal Rachel and Jack had been working on ever since last week's breakfast at Cyril's Kitchen. They'd be meeting with Humphrey tomorrow to present their vision for BHGH's new digital strategy, and it would be the first test of her skills since Greg had recommended her for promotion – as well as the first time she and Jack would be jointly responsible for a pitch.

Rachel knew that, if all went well, she and Jack would cement senior management's view of them as a talented, well-matched team – but despite her ambivalence about providing proof that their pairing could work, she couldn't bring herself to root for failure. As a half-Irish state-school-educated woman, she wanted to wipe the sneer off Humphrey's florid face by showing him a plan so compelling he couldn't spurn it. She and Jack were due to review one another's contributions to their presentation one last time this afternoon, then run a final version past Isaac, Greg and Toby.

As Rachel read through her copy, deleting the odd word and replacing others with clearer alternatives, she heard Donna's reedy voice ring out from the other side of the room. 'Rachel Ryan? *Seriously?* Well, if you're absolutely sure. She's over there.'

A young man bearing an obscenely oversized flower

arrangement was following the direction of Donna's pointed finger. When his eyes found Rachel, he started moving her way.

'What the actual *fuck* . . . ?' she murmured under her breath.

Jack didn't hear her, but emitted a whistle as the vast bouquet sailed towards their workstation. His lips had parted in astonishment at the sheer heft of the thing, and his eyes were wide and full of questions.

'Sign here, please,' the delivery guy said to Rachel as he deposited the flowers at the foot of her desk. The arrangement was way too big to fit on top among all her work stuff. Rachel scribbled her signature on the proffered tablet and wished that everyone would stop staring at her. Donna was eyeing her with frank disbelief.

Close up, Rachel could see that there must be a hundred red and cream roses here. They were elegant and lovely with richly coloured velvet-soft petals. The dozens of stems were tightly packed into a circular container a little like a hatbox, which bore the florist's name and King's Road address in neat gilt letters. A thick cream envelope was nestled amongst the blooms, and Rachel's fingers trembled slightly as she reached for it. She couldn't think of anyone who'd send her such a lavish, expensive gift on a day she didn't even *like*. That mystery aside, the sheer spectacle of all this was mortifying.

She tore open the card and read it, shock and disbelief giving way to furious anger within seconds.

The roses were from Laurence.

Giacomo's, tonight at 7.30. I'll have champagne on ice. You know it makes sense. L x

Jack cleared his throat loudly as Rachel looked up from her flowers. He was rolling his shoulder blades back as though to release some tension between them. If the rage that had seized her was written on Rachel's features, Jack apparently couldn't read it.

'And there was me thinking *I* was popular,' he muttered, perhaps less playfully than he'd intended. There was an edge to his voice that sounded almost resentful.

Jack isn't happy that someone else has sent me flowers. Rachel recognised her enjoyment of this immediately, choosing to acknowledge it but not analyse the reasons why her bouquet should bother him.

Right now, it simply felt satisfying that – probably for the first time – Jack was realising *he* might not be her dream date. Rachel let the idea settle around her like a cool mist, soothing her ire. She stayed silent, staring in awe at the roses, contemplating the bizarre truth: in being such an arrogant, flashy idiot, Laurence may just have done her a favour.

'Er . . . *Wow*,' Jack said. 'I didn't know you were attached.' The words came out formal and forced, almost petulant.

'Well. Why would you?' Rachel replied, all innocence. 'I never said.'

It wasn't exactly a *lie*, she told herself. More like economy with the truth: a careful dance around the facts. Besides, she didn't owe Jack anything – he hadn't mentioned his wife in the whole time they'd been working together. He had zero right to any knowledge of her personal life.

Rachel pulled her mobile out of her handbag and snapped a photo of her massive bouquet, as if she were about to post it on Instagram. She took care to smile into her phone as she pretended to type out a gushing caption.

In reality, she was texting Laurence.

Rachel: *Hey. The flowers are lovely. But you really, REALLY shouldn't have, and not just because I hate Valentine's Day. I think we said all we needed to say last time we met, so it's a no re tonight. I'm sorry if that's not what you want to hear. Please, take someone else out for dinner and fizz. I hope it goes well if you do. R.*

That should do it, she thought. Polite and kind, but firm. Unambiguous.

Three dots skipped across the bottom of the screen as Laurence typed his response.

Laurence: *Like I said: 7.30 tonight. I'll be standing by with the Moet. You know you'd rather drink bubbles with me than eat an M&S ready meal for one. Be there or be . . . single? L xxxxx*

Rachel felt ferocious – more capable of violence than at any other point in her thirty years on the planet. What the hell made Laurence think she'd be home alone and miserable tonight? That she needed this attempt at a chivalrous intervention? For all he knew she was off out with someone nice – someone who wouldn't win gold, silver *and* bronze at the Backhanded Compliment Olympics.

The fact that Laurence was sort of right about her plans for the evening was totally irrelevant, she told herself.

Rachel took care not to let the anger burning in her belly make its way up to her face. She smiled gently at Laurence's message, decided it was pointless to reply and plopped her phone back into her bag.

'Big plans tonight, then?' Jack asked her, without looking up from his computer screen. He didn't want to meet her eyes, it seemed – and his evasiveness amused her.

'Oh yeah,' Rachel replied, 'absolutely.'

Again, not a lie, as such. Rewatching *To All the Boys I've Loved Before* on Netflix had been on her to-do list for weeks. She was genuinely looking forward to it.

For the rest of the afternoon, Jack was quiet. Chastened. Perhaps even a little sulky. Rachel couldn't help taking pleasure in his prickliness – revelling in the knowledge that his ego had been bruised.

Not only did his discomfort feel like divine retribution for all the time she'd spent pining over him during their uni days, it also sharpened the outline of their relationship, which had become increasingly fuzzy since that Friday trip to Bourton.

Rachel had already realised that while Jack thought she had a boyfriend she felt safer – though from what, exactly, she wasn't sure. Maybe from his flashes of flirtatiousness, which, in truth, his own marital status really ought to prevent. Maybe from her own feelings: her growing awareness that she was no safer from fancying him than Kemi's gaggle of 'Hot Harper' obsessives.

They met to chat through their presentation, trying to ensure they'd anticipated all the awkward questions Humphrey might ask and then taking Isaac, Toby and Greg through the slides. Jack didn't mention the flowers again, or the plans he thought she had. She deliberately didn't ask him what he was doing, though she assumed he'd be having dinner with his pretty wife. In which case, she wondered why he seemed so morose.

At 5.30 p.m. precisely, Rachel shut the lid of her laptop, unplugged it and packed it away. She'd worked hard enough that she didn't need to stay late, but she was also keen for Jack to observe her exit from the office – even if, under the weight of a hundred roses, this was less graceful than she'd have liked.

His 'Have a good night' was half-hearted, and Rachel tried not to interrogate why that made her so happy. Only when she was walking from her bus stop back to the flat did she feel her good mood begin to wobble. She was staggering, struggling to manoeuvre her gigantic box of blooms – the sight of which was making other pedestrians point and stare. To many, she knew, she was a Valentine's Day success: one of the lucky women who'd received gifts symbolic of deep, sincere devotion.

The truth was that Rachel had almost dumped Laurence's bouquet in a skip halfway between the R/C office and the nearest northbound bus shelter. In the moment, though, she couldn't bring herself to do it. It wasn't the flowers who'd insulted her. *They* didn't deserve to die unloved, carelessly thrown away amid old vinyl flooring, broken light fittings, empty beer cans and the mouldering remains of kebabs.

Laurence himself was another matter, of course. If Rachel could have cast *him* into a pit packed full of rubbish and dubious days-old meat, she'd have done it in a heartbeat. It was curious, she thought, that he could claim to adore her at the same time as making it so abundantly clear he believed she was a charity case. How else could she interpret his certainty that, without him, she'd wind up alone? She'd *rather* be alone than with Laurence: that much she knew for sure.

Rachel dropped the hatbox onto the doorstep of her building, searched for her keys and pulled them from the bottom of her handbag. As she pushed her way inside, dragged the flowers down the hall and opened the door to the flat, she tried to ignore the voice inside her head that was saying: *Surely you'd prefer secret option number three, though? Being with someone great?*

The voice seemed to grow louder and stronger in the silence of the empty flat. Anna had plans with Will tonight, and she was obviously already gone. There was a faint whiff of her heady date-night perfume in the air.

Rachel sighed, shucking off her coat and scarf and setting her laptop bag down on the kitchen floor. She wandered over to the fridge to assess her dinner options. Two-day-old mac and cheese would do, she decided – and there were enough leaves left to make a decent side salad, even if the avocado and cherry tomatoes lurking in the crisper had seen better days.

In the door of the fridge was a mini-can of G&T – train-picnic leftovers from a couple of months ago, when she and Anna had taken a very windy day trip to Brighton. Without pausing to muse that slurping gin from a tin was definitely somewhere towards 'pathetic' on the spectrum of solo V-Day behaviours, she opened it.

It was only when she turned away from the fridge, having resolved to wait a while before microwaving her supper, that she saw it: a package on the table, wrapped in brown paper, her name on the outside in huge Sharpie'd letters.

What now? she wondered.

After several enthusiastic pulls on her can, Rachel sat down and began to strip the sellotape off the join between folds of parcel wrap. Once the package was open, she laughed aloud. Inside was a DVD of *The Blair Witch Project* – the only horror film she'd ever watched, and which only one person in the world knew had given her nightmares for a fortnight. With it was a packet of what looked like dog mess. Its label informed her that it was in fact *Premium Chocolate Poop*. Written on the back of the packet was: *Because I think you're The Shit.*

There was a card too, which she opened eagerly. It was disgusting: an A5 glitter-covered pastel monstrosity with a cuddly bear clutching a sign that said *Happy Valentine's Day*. The words *Valentine's Day* had been crossed through, however, and the word THURSDAY written in black marker across the bear's snuggly stomach.

Rachel giggled as she opened the card to read the message inside. There were more crossings-out – a sentimental cookie-cutter message struck through in favour of something more personal.

Because it's just another unromantic day, and I know how much you hate it. (Also because I'm hilarious.) T x

Later that evening, Rachel messaged Tom.

Rachel: *So Valentine's Day blows, as ever. But it turns out dog poo is surprisingly tasty* <poop emoji> *Thanks x*

She added a photo of her half-eaten packet of chocolate. A moment later his reply arrived.

Tom: *Glad to hear it* <smile emoji> *You ok?*

Rachel: *Yeah, despite another grand gesture from Laurence . . .* <gross face emoji>

Tom: *WTF???!!!*

Rachel: *I'll explain next time I see you . . . Headlines are: he sent an embarrassingly huge bunch of flowers to me at work, but at least didn't turn up himself.*

Tom: *Seriously, that guy's creepier than the Blair Witch.*
Are you free this Saturday morning, by the way?

I've managed to book space for the first exhibition shoot – it's with our friend the white T-shirt influencer. He's up for a face to face chat too.

Rachel: *Deffo, wouldn't miss it! Send me the address.*
Also nothing is creepier than Blair Witch, which I am obviously NOT watching.

Tom: *Haha, I reckon Loser Loz comes close. I'll watch with you again sometime if you like, it's important to face one's fears etc.* <laughing emoji>
See you soon . . . Tomorrow I guess?
Night x

Rachel: *Night night. And thanks again xxx*

Rachel went to bed feeling far happier than she'd expected to a few hours earlier, and only partly because she'd gorged on sugar.

She might not have a boyfriend this Valentine's Day, but she had a boy *friend*; one who'd thought about her, wanted to make her smile and had found a way to show he cared without making her cringe.

It was weird but true, Rachel thought, that a packet of fake faeces could seem more thoughtful than a hundred gorgeous roses. Yet there it was.

16

The BHGH office was near Chelsea Embankment: six miles and half a world away from Stroud Green's shops, takeaways, crowds and constant traffic. The organisation's London HQ was a four-storey red-brick terrace within sight of the Thames – elegant and striking against a cloudless, turquoise sky.

As Rachel made her way towards it on Friday morning, she spotted Jack leaning against a tree reading something on his phone. He was wearing a suit for the first time since the day the Mountaintop takeover had been announced, and even from this distance it was a *lot*.

He was a living, breathing Burberry advert: classically handsome, slender, almost aristocratic-looking . . . But just tousled enough to look stylish rather than staid.

He stood up straight to greet her, brushing the back of his navy overcoat clean.

'Morning.' He smiled. 'Isaac's just messaged. He and Greg are in a cab, apparently – they should be here soon.'

'Cool.'

Rachel didn't know what to say or where to direct her gaze; it was a little like trying not to stare directly into the sun.

'You look lovely, by the way,' Jack said.

Rachel shifted her weight from one foot to the other,

resisting the urge to say 'So do you.' In the end, unable to come up with anything better, she murmured, 'Oh.'

Jack rolled his eyes at her obvious confusion. 'You are literally the only woman I've ever known who reacts to compliments with such surprise. Your mystery man clearly needs to up his game – perhaps pay you a few more in between bouquets.'

Rachel made a noise that sounded like *Fffffft*. She felt like laughing. In light of recent events, the idea of Laurence saying anything genuinely nice to her was ridiculous. Pushing the urge to giggle away and refusing to be drawn on the identity of her Valentine, she said, 'Er, maybe. Thanks, anyway.'

In truth, she'd put on a high-necked voluminous midi dress this morning so as to shield her body from close inspection by Humphrey. Her hair was loose, though, falling past her shoulders in soft red-gold waves that even she could see looked like something out of a Pre-Raphaelite painting.

She'd left it unstyled for the sake of not wasting a good hair day and because the weather seemed settled – unlikely, for once, to render her head an explosion of tangles and frizz. Only now did she remember that Jack had always found her hair wildly romantic when it wasn't scraped back in a sloppy bun. She felt him looking at her again and tucked it behind her ears.

He shook his head at her fondly and asked, 'You feeling good about this morning?'

'As far as our work is concerned, I feel great . . . Though I can't say I'm looking forward to actually presenting it.'

'We'll be fine,' Jack said with an airy wave of his arm. 'Humphrey will see things our way; he'll love the plans we've put together.'

'Oh, to possess the supreme and unwavering confidence of an Old Harrovian,' Rachel retorted, only half-joking.

Before Jack could reply, a black cab pulled up beside them. The kerbside door opened and Greg and Isaac spilled out of it onto the pavement, an urgent mass of smartly dressed arms and legs.

'Morning, guys, sorry we're a little late,' Greg said, pulling Rachel in for a quick hug as Isaac paid their fare. 'You're going to be brilliant,' he whispered into her ear. 'I have every faith you'll impress the snooty old bastard.'

Rachel smiled as Greg turned to Jack, nodded his head and greeted him – a polite but comparatively cool acknowledgement, Rachel noted. She felt warmed by Greg's loyalty, and her smile widened a fraction.

'Are we ready, then, Dream Team?' Isaac gushed, his boyish cheeks apple-red and round, shining with open excitement. 'It's time to go and win this account!'

'It is,' Jack agreed, checking his watch. 'Five minutes until showtime. We'd better head inside.'

Isaac pushed open the heavy, glazed front door of the building with Greg close behind. Jack made way for Rachel and she followed them, her feet heavy as breeze blocks – clearly reluctant to walk towards another encounter with Humphrey.

Delicately, as if to steady her nerves or steer her in the right direction, Jack placed a hand at the base of her spine.

Rachel froze, shocked – not sure whether she wanted to lean into the touch or jerk away in horror.

Before she could decide on an appropriate reaction, he'd moved; Isaac had turned around and was hissing something at them frantically, clearly needing to make his point before they were within earshot of anyone who worked for BHGH.

Rachel stepped further forward, straining to hear him and struggling to push her heart down from her mouth, back into her chest where it belonged.

'Don't forget,' Isaac was saying, grim-faced. 'I answer to *Abraham* here. So try to avoid calling me by my actual name this morning, if at all possible.'

Sir Humphrey Caldwell looked more walrus-esque than ever this morning, in a jacket that was so tight under the armpits it made his short, chubby arms seem to flail when he moved them, independent of the rest of him. *Flippers*, Rachel thought, and stifled a smirk. She assumed this suit must have been made especially for him on Savile Row – some years and many indulgent dinners ago.

He took her hand when she tried to shake his, turned it over and kissed it wetly, then allowed his eyes to meander downwards from her face to take in the rest of her. She fought the urge to cry, 'Eyes UP, you old perv!', instead sitting down and discreetly mopping her moist knuckles against the fabric of her dress.

Rachel had expected Humphrey to be flanked by one or two other BHGH bigwigs – one of whom might even be a woman. He was alone, though; clearly the decision to appoint a new digital agency rested only with him. She realised this shouldn't have surprised her.

The room they were in was large but sparsely decorated, and cold. The walls were painted a bog-standard magnolia and the floor was carpeted in some dark synthetic stuff. There was no furniture except for a large antique-looking table and the six matching chairs that surrounded it. A single, lonely picture stared down from one wall: a portrait of the Queen from sometime in the 1970s.

It was a waste of gorgeous space, Rachel thought; the light in here was beautiful, flooding in through a huge sash window bordered by traditional wooden shutters and looking out over the street towards the river. It was the perfect room for an intimate wedding ceremony, she mused – then realised that her mother's endless marriage chat must be getting to her.

After a few moments of pleasantries, and while Jack was setting up his laptop to project, a young woman with long blonde hair, caramel-coloured skin and long, designer-jean-clad legs brought in tea, coffee, milk and sugar.

'There's a good gal, Cressy – thank you.' Humphrey leered. The woman, who Rachel thought must have been twenty-two at the outside, retreated from the room without reacting. 'Cressida is one of our volunteers,' Humphrey said. 'What d'you call them these days? *Interns*. Graduated from St Andrew's last summer, according to her grandfather – old friend of mine. Just getting some experience in the charity sector before going on to have a glamorous career as a Kensington housewife, I should think. HA!'

Isaac and Jack chuckled courteously, Greg pretend-coughed to cover his disgust and Rachel stared so hard at her coffee cup she feared her eyes might bore holes through the china.

'*There,*' Jack muttered, after plugging a final twisted lead into the nest of wires and sockets in the centre of the table. He sank down into the chair next to Rachel, evidently relieved.

She wished their seats weren't so close together; there must have been no more than three inches between them. She also wished he didn't smell so good, or feel so warm next to her bare, goose-pimpled forearm.

'Shall we begin?' Humphrey said, addressing Jack. It seemed to have passed him by that Rachel's name was also on the opening slide of their PowerPoint deck.

'Absolutely, Sir Humphrey,' Jack replied. It had become clear during their few weeks' acquaintance with Humphrey that he liked to be addressed as 'Sir' whenever his name was used, which Rachel thought was absurd – indicative of a need to elevate himself above the plebeians he so evidently despised. She'd resolved early on to avoid addressing him directly if possible, fearful that the temptation to refer to him as plain old 'Oi, you' would prove irresistible.

Jack launched into their preamble, setting the scene for the new strategy he and Rachel had devised. His style was engaging and familiar, but deferential – respectful of the client/agency relationship in just the right way for a stickler like Humphrey.

Rachel took over from him to explain the rationale for the storytelling approach they'd taken. As planned, she showed off the content she'd mocked up for Hartwell Abbey; she'd had it designed and animated so that she could model how a visitor might click through an interactive app. Humphrey nodded soberly, and Rachel wondered how much of what she'd said he actually understood.

Jack picked the presentation up again as it neared its end, pointing out the particular appeal of their strategy to younger people and the potential for a linked programme of events that could build partnerships with schools and colleges.

Humphrey, genial and smiling, clapped his hands together the moment Jack finished speaking. Aside from questions about the likely cost of developing some of their more high-tech ideas, there was nothing he felt the need to discuss further.

'Well, you've done it,' he said, leaning across the mahogany tabletop to shake Jack's hand. 'I knew a man of your calibre would come up with the goods. Inspiring stuff, just excellent.'

Rachel, apparently irrelevant to the proceedings, pressed her lips together and balled her hands into fists.

'Truly an exceptional idea,' Humphrey went on, addressing only Jack, 'to *humanise* the houses – certainly I can see that the masses need direction to appreciate these fine old places. Not everyone has *our* innate appreciation for tradition, art and architecture, of course.'

Rachel stared at a crack in the ceiling, fixing her eyes on it so she wouldn't roll them. She'd expected to be in the back seat when it came to driving today's pitch, but this felt like being cast out of a moving vehicle partway up the M6.

Isaac and Greg were silent, though Greg's face wore an expression that Rachel decoded as 'aghast with a sprinkling of appalled'. Jack was nodding and smiling as if nothing were amiss, and Rachel felt a fleeting urge to stab him in the thigh with her biro.

Humphrey was still gushing. 'How lucky we are to have found you at last,' he said. 'The *right chap* for the job. I think we can safely say that we'd like to go ahead with some version of this, subject to agreeing schedules, budgets and so forth. Abraham, bravo for bringing him in.'

Isaac started, remembering after a few seconds that Humphrey meant him. He grinned to cover his delayed reaction and said, 'We're certainly happy to have him as part of our London team, Sir Humphrey, and I'm thrilled we're going to be continuing our work with you.'

Greg shot Rachel a wide-eyed, remorseful look. She knew he was galled by Humphrey's ignorance, but understood that as client services director he couldn't see the benefit in arguing. After all, they'd just won their pitch.

She shut her eyes as a familiar heat behind them warned her that angry tears were forming. Clearly her annoyance wanted expression – and crying was apparently its preferred medium, since ranting at her client and colleagues wasn't an option.

'I must protest, if I may.' Rachel started as a hand settled on her left shoulder. Jack's voice was careful and affable, his charm dialled up as high as it would go. 'We're forgetting Rachel in all our excitement. The focus on people rather than objects was her idea, originally – *stories, not stuff*, as she puts it. It's her we should be praising for the fundamentals of this new plan, which I couldn't have come up with alone.'

Rachel felt her mouth fall open and Isaac dropped his fountain pen on the floor with a dull thud. Greg's eyebrows quirked up, powered by some combination of disbelief and approval.

Humphrey harrumphed and hawed, then said, 'Of course. Mustn't overlook the lovely lady. Marvellous work, my dear.'

It was hardly an in-depth review, but it was some acknowledgement of Rachel's efforts and she was glad he'd been forced to make it.

Jack's hand fell away from her and she turned to him with a small smile. He nodded slightly – a gesture that said *We're on the same side*. Their eyes met, candid and careless, for the first time all morning, and something cracked inside her, a shell suddenly threatening to shatter completely.

Jack turned back to Humphrey and Rachel started breathing again. There was more hand-shaking, promises that a timeline, staff plans and costings would be worked up and sent over, and then the R/C team was outside again, gathered on the pavement debating the best way to get back to Islington.

'Drinks later,' Isaac announced as they folded themselves into an Uber. 'Absolutely no excuses. This is a huge win for us – a glass of something fizzy is mandatory after work tonight.'

Greg had somehow commandeered the front seat of the cab, while Rachel and Jack were relegated to the back.

Isaac was wedged between them, beaming like a child on his way to a seaside holiday.

Jack held up his hands, acquiescing easily. 'You'll get no resistance from me. Rachel, you'll come, won't you? Greg?'

'Er . . .' Rachel began, ready to protest that her Friday night was already spoken for. But Greg was nodding and smiling, and she wavered; she should join her colleagues for one celebratory tipple, surely?

She resolved to text and tell her friends she'd be late to the Hope, praying that Anna wouldn't make any assumptions – especially not ones that strayed too close to the truth.

Jack glanced over the top of Isaac's curly head at Rachel. His eyes were soft again, green and deep and ridiculously lovely, and she couldn't bear to look at them.

She tore her gaze away and stared out of the taxi window, watching Belgravia flash by as if everything was normal. As if her insides weren't melting.

At five o'clock Isaac ordered the whole pro-social team to down tools, insisting that everyone traipse around the corner to the Albion Inn for drinks and nibbles. Toby, thrilled with the day's success, was coming along too. He'd already sent a celebratory email to the whole office, congratulating Rachel and Jack on winning their pitch and extending the invitation to enjoy some free fizz as soon as the working day was over.

The pub was already busy when they arrived, but Isaac had had the foresight to pre-book a large table earlier in the day. Rachel went with a handful of her colleagues to claim it while the others made a beeline for the bar.

She sat down in the centre of a polished wood bench peppered with well-worn squashy cushions and felt Jack squeeze around the table to sit next to her. *Shit*. She'd hoped he'd go and help carry the drinks so she could blend in with the client and copy juniors, shielding herself from him by sitting in between a few of them.

Before he could speak to her Rachel seized the opportunity to turn away, joining in a conversation about the terrible film she and Anna had recently watched. Apparently they weren't alone in having hated it.

She was more than halfway down a flute of cava before she finally had to acknowledge that Jack was right beside her. He nudged her gently and said, 'Is everything okay? Have I done something?'

Rachel took a fortifying slurp of her drink and shook her head. 'No. Everything's fine. As fine as it *can* be, I guess, given the inherent weirdness of this whole situation.' Booze had already loosened her tongue. 'If anything,' she sighed, 'I should probably say thank you. For having my back this morning, I mean – for not letting me be window dressing when I'd actually done half the work.'

'More than half, I'd say,' Jack said. 'And don't mention it.'

He grabbed an almost-full bottle of cava from one of the silver ice buckets on the table and topped up their glasses.

'We did well this morning,' he said. 'And my suspicion is that Humphrey's going to quibble over costs, which probably means the likes of you and me are too expensive to stay on this account day-to-day. Here's to passing him on to some juniors.'

'God, I'll drink to that,' Rachel replied. Jack lifted his

glass and she clinked hers against it, relieved at the prospect of moving on to other projects.

'So,' Jack said, his face folding in a wolfish grin, 'are we friends again yet?'

'*No. Maybe . . . Stop looking at me!*'

She buried her face in her hands and he chuckled.

'I don't *know*,' Rachel said after a minute, peering through her fingertips, then finally lowering them. 'I'm pretty sure I still hate you.' She said this without conviction.

Jack dipped his head towards her, unbothered. 'You always did a bit, even when we were together. So, in all honesty, I'm not sure how relevant that is.'

Rachel looked around them, alarmed at the thought that their teammates might have overheard this reference to the past – but also shaken that he'd brought it up at all.

'It's fine, nobody's listening,' he said, smiling again, laughing at her panic.

She made a face at him, narrowing her eyes. Even if no one was listening, some people were *looking*. A new crowd of R/C staff had arrived at the pub, Kemi and Greg among them.

Kemi was deep in conversation with Ella, who had a whole bottle of Prosecco in one hand. Both of them were glancing every so often at 'Hot Harper' with undisguised thirst. Greg was trapped at the bar chatting to Theo, but his gaze was focused over the office bore's shoulder, locked on Rachel and Jack. Rachel lifted a hand to greet him, and he raised a sardonic eyebrow in answer.

Rachel shuffled on her backside, trying to put some space between herself and Jack for the sake of common decency – and to help calm her surging blood pressure. He'd thrown his suit jacket over the back of a chair, removed his tie and rolled up his shirtsleeves: a look that, much to Rachel's dismay, was working for him.

As she fidgeted, the cushion she was sitting on slid too quickly against the smooth wood beneath it, tumbled towards the floor and tried to take her with it.

She yelped and Jack grabbed her before she could slip too far, catching her hand in his, pulling her towards him and holding her steady. His palm curled around her fingers and stayed there too long, clinging on as she righted herself. It was delicious and excruciating. She wanted it to end right now, and absolutely never.

After what felt like hours Rachel reconnected her brain with her body, pulled her hand free and took a deep breath of air that smelled, unavoidably, of Jack. She scrambled away from him as if he'd stung her, almost upending several drinks as she got to her feet.

With Jack staring at her as if she were mad, she managed to choke out 'Sorry, loo' before pushing past him and dashing in the direction of the ladies. She had to get out of here. No good could come of staying and drinking more alcohol.

When she emerged from the toilets, she'd resolved to collect her things and be on her way. She crossed her fingers and prayed that she could creep out of the pub without Jack noticing – that he'd moved away from their seats to chat to someone in a corner, or on the other side of the bar . . . Or in a completely different building, several miles away.

No such luck. Jack was still sitting with Rachel's stuff and had even put her handbag on the bench next to him in an attempt to save her place. Theo, resplendent in his raspberry-pink trousers, was no longer lecturing Greg but had closed in on Jack, undeterred by the bag and talking non-stop despite receiving little encouragement to do so.

'Ah! Rachel! You're back!' Jack said, his voice shrill, his eyes beseeching. Rachel choked back a laugh. He had never more clearly needed rescuing, and after the way he'd stood up for her this morning she didn't have it in her to abandon him. Today, at least, Jack didn't deserve to be thrown under the Theo bus – doomed to a whole night of conversation that consisted entirely of buzzwords.

'Sorry, Theo,' Rachel said. 'D'you mind if I nab my seat back? It's just all my stuff is here and I don't want to lose track of it.'

'Oh . . . Yah. Sure.' Theo nodded, not moving.

'Also,' Rachel said, momentarily inspired, 'I heard Donna say she needed to speak to you a minute ago when I was going by – something about your last expenses claim. I think Greg told her you'd come over here.'

Theo shrunk in his seat, staring around him like a small rodent suddenly aware of a nearby snake.

'Thanks, Rachel,' he muttered. 'I'll, er . . . I'll go and find her.'

Once she was back in her seat, Jack handed Rachel a new drink and asked, 'Was that true?'

'Nah,' she said. 'Fastest way to get rid of him, though – nobody wants a lecture from Donna on a Friday night. Twenty quid says he's scooted halfway home by now.'

'You're evil,' Jack said. 'I'm impressed. What is his *deal*, by the way? I only understood about thirty per cent of his waffle, and at one point I think he said, "Sometimes you have to punch a puppy to pivot your thinking." I was quite alarmed.'

Rachel laughed. 'Standard. I'm told his clients love him, though my gut feeling is they're too scared to risk looking thick by admitting they have no idea what he's on about.'

When Rachel had exhausted her knowledge of Theo's best corporate catchphrases and they'd finally stopped giggling at 'Let's face our fears and just open the kimono', Jack asked: 'So how come you're still here? It's past ten. I assumed you'd have one drink and then shoot off to meet your man.'

'Oh,' she said, surprised it was so late. Then, 'Business trip. I'm seeing him tomorrow.' The lie skipped out of her mouth before she could stop it.

'Ah. Love's young dream!' Jack warbled. 'And here's me, a sad singleton with no weekend plans beyond Netflix and a Chinese takeaway.'

Rachel whipped her head left to look at him. 'What's that?' *This doesn't make any sense.*

'Yes. You are looking at a man in the throes of a very unpleasant, very expensive divorce.'

'Wow. I'm sorry to hear that.' *Very sorry. Definitely. Sort of.*

'Thanks,' Jack said, scratching the side of his stubble-shadowed face. 'I deserve it, though. I guess you could call it karma. The dumper becomes the dumpee, the player gets played, blah blah blah.'

'Wow,' Rachel said again.

So the lovely woman in the white dress had finished with him. Had *cheated* on him? Had broken his heart? This did not compute.

Yet it also made sense, in a 'through the looking glass' kind of way. Jack had transferred down here to lick his wounds, to get away from his messed-up marriage, Rachel supposed. This explained his behaviour that morning when they'd been at the office early: the sad set of his shoulders and his general air of defeat. Maybe he'd been on the phone to his wife, or a lawyer . . .

And *this* was why Jack had been determined to stay at R/C after the takeover, in spite of the awkward discovery that he'd have to be around another, different ex in order to keep his new job.

'Did you . . . Do you have any children?' Rachel asked.

'No. That was one of our issues. I wanted them, she didn't.'

Rachel nodded, mute, not wanting to say 'Wow' for the third time in five minutes. Her head was fizz-foggy and this was too much to take in.

She couldn't avoid the impression that this news threw some of Jack's recent behaviour into sharp relief, and she needed to work out how she felt about that. Rachel was more thankful than ever for her recently acquired fake boyfriend – not to mention the no man's land he'd laid down between her and the real, live man sitting two inches away.

Rachel felt her phone vibrating inside her handbag, shoved between her feet under the table. She ducked down and fished it out to see several messages from Anna, culminating in:

Anna: *Heading home from the Hope. We all missed you <sad face emoji> ! See you back at the flat??? x*

Rachel tapped out a reply.

Rachel: *Yep. Sorry, big celebrations here . . . Leaving shortly x*

Anna is typing . . .

Anna: *You're coming home alone, right?* <see no evil emoji>

Rachel: *FFS, OF COURSE I AM.*

Rachel looked up from her mobile to find Jack watching her. 'Time to head off?'

'Yeah, I should probably get going,' she said, aware that he'd assumed the messages were from her boyfriend.

'I'll walk you out – head back to my little bachelor pad.'

Rachel got her stuff together, not sure what to do with his self-deprecation.

They said goodbye to several colleagues still dotted around the pub and propping up the bar, some of whom were now quite worse for wear. Kemi and Ella had both been served large glasses of tap water by Toby, who was watching them fearfully – willing them to drink some non-alcoholic fluid before he had to find them taxis.

Greg squeezed Rachel's arm, kissed her cheek and said, 'Tell me he's just putting you in a cab.'

She squeezed back. 'He's just putting me in a cab. There's nothing happening here, I promise.'

'See you Monday, everyone,' Jack announced above the

general chatter, waving as he and Rachel made their way to the pub door.

Brilliant, Rachel thought. She really could have done without him advertising the fact that they were leaving together. It didn't look good, even though it was totally innocent.

They waited on the pavement for just a few moments before Rachel's Uber appeared.

'I'll see you on Monday, then,' Jack said. 'Have a great weekend, and thanks for tonight. It's the best fun I've had with anyone since moving here.'

He inclined his head towards Rachel's, grazing her cheek with his lips. They were soft and cool, chilly as the winter air, but her skin blazed at the touch. Heat radiated from the spot where his mouth had been, spreading down, up and out until her entire body felt hazy and warm.

It would have been easy to lock her hands behind his neck and tip her head back, to let herself be kissed. In this moment she was sure that Jack wanted her to, and her certainty terrified her.

'Bye,' she said, stepping away from him, breathless and not a little unsteady.

Rachel climbed into the taxi without letting herself look back, fearful that – for all her assurances to Anna, regardless of her good intentions and despite his past misdeeds – she'd pull Jack in after her.

17

By ten o'clock on Saturday morning Rachel had made her way to Shoreditch, procured an overpriced coffee and picked up a selection of bite-sized breakfast pastries. The sweet, buttery aroma drifting through the gaps in their cardboard container was so good her stomach grumbled, audibly tormented by the promise of food. Resisting the urge to sink her head into the box and inhale its contents, she looked down at her phone to consult Google Maps again.

The address Tom had given her for today's photo shoot was supposedly close now. She needed to concentrate on where she was going or she and her delicious-smelling croissants would sail straight past it.

A minute or so later Rachel was standing next to the bricked-up arch of an old railway bridge. *This* couldn't be it, surely? But allegedly she'd reached her destination, and she was definitely on the right street. She noticed there was a slender black wooden door in the right-hand side of the wall. Next to it, above a bell push, was a neat brass plaque with *A24* written on it.

Rachel checked Tom's message again. Yep – that was the number he'd given her. This had to be the place.

Tentatively, she pressed the shiny round doorbell and heard a high, brisk *brrrrrrring* from within. There was a creak and the door opened inwards, its bottom catching on a thick coir-and-rubber mat that sat just behind it.

Tom's spectacled face appeared, smiling, and he beckoned her inside. He took the box she was carrying and set it on the zinc worktop of a tiny kitchen area tucked into the near left-hand corner of what Rachel could now see was a cavernous space.

Despite the irregular texture and greyish tinge of the Victorian bricks that curved high over their heads, it felt new in here; the air smelled like fresh paint, carpet underlay and cleaning products.

The opposite wall – which at one stage must have been the other open side of the railway arch – featured a tall strip of window that stretched, gleaming, across its full width. Soft, moody light streamed in from the drab sky outside, illuminating what was clearly the studio area: a patch of floor that Rachel guessed was roughly three square metres, around which a collection of photographic equipment was arranged.

'Bloody hell,' Rachel said. 'This is quite a place.'

'Isn't it?' Tom beamed. 'I managed to get it cheap, there was a cancellation . . . You're early, though – Zack with a *K* isn't due until elevenish. I'm just experimenting a bit with the light in here so I can decide what to do with him. In fact, you can help me with that.'

'Sure,' Rachel said. 'I thought you might need a hand setting up. I brought food too.'

'I saw that, you're a legend. I'm starving.' Tom dug around in the box, pulling out a tiny pain au chocolat and devouring it in one bite. Rachel found a mini raisin whirl and ate it only slightly more gracefully, then gulped what was left of her coffee before depositing the cup in a recycling bin beneath the kitchen counter.

'Also,' Rachel said through a mouthful of almond croissant, 'I thought it might make sense to have a catch-up on Zack before the shoot, and obviously I missed you last night.'

'Yeah.' Tom nodded, poised with a square of flaky jam-filled pastry between his finger and thumb. 'The pub was weird without you.'

'Sorry. Work thing. It was kind of unavoidable. Jack and I won a big pitch and the MD laid on free drinks to celebrate at the local. We couldn't not go.'

'We?' Tom said, his forehead creasing slightly. '*We* as in you and Jack, your cheating ex-boyfriend turned workmate? So, what . . . You're buddies now?'

Rachel turned away from him to riffle through the kitchenette's cupboards in search of a glass. She found one, then filled it from the cold tap.

'We're not *buddies*,' she said when she was facing him again. 'But we're getting on okay, I guess. *You* were the voice of reason who said I should give working with Jack a try, at least until I found another job. We could hardly function as a team if I spent every spare minute imagining his slow and painful death, could we? So I've pressed pause on the murder-plotting for now . . . Bloodlust is never a good look on redheads, anyway.'

'I don't think *blood*lust is really the issue,' Tom muttered, then cleared his throat and pointed at the stainless-steel fridge. 'Whatever. There's milk in there, and loads of coffee pods and tea stuff in the drawer. Help yourself while we're here.'

'Will do.' Rachel nodded, wondering whether last night's encounter with Jack was still hanging on her, fusty and lingering like stale cigarette smoke. She realised she felt embarrassed. Tom was shrewd and rational, and he'd consider it the height of stupidity to get close to someone who'd already proved they couldn't be trusted. Rachel didn't want to dent Tom's good opinion of her, nor think too much about whether he might be right.

'So, Zack . . .' she said, hopeful that focusing on the task at hand might soften the sudden spikiness of the atmosphere.

'Mr *How to Wear a White T-Shirt*,' Tom said, eyebrows raised. He gestured at his torso. 'Do you think he'll tell me I'm doing it wrong?'

Rachel sipped her water and shook her head. 'You're not,' she said, taking in his plain white top, blue Levi's and the vintage Fair Isle cardigan that was hanging off his shoulders. 'At least, *I* don't think you are.'

His T-shirt pulled tighter against his stomach as he shoved his hands into his jeans pockets and smiled, and Rachel flashed back to inadvertently eyeing up his abs on the morning she'd seen him in the park. *Awkward*.

She wished she could delete that image from her brain's SD card; she really shouldn't have it. It felt like the copy of *Forever* by Judy Blume that was passed around her Year 9 class until Sister Philomena confiscated it. Inappropriate. Contraband.

'Did you know,' she said to cover her unease, 'that Zack's main musical influence is the California scene of the late sixties? Joni Mitchell, Jackson Browne, Crosby, Stills and Nash . . . I was raised on that stuff. I wonder if he's any good . . . *Also*, he's been romantically linked with several of the other influencers on our list; I believe there was a very messy break-up with Alyssia Ahmadi.'

Tom's eyes were round. 'Where are you getting all this?' he asked, amused.

'Here and there,' Rachel said, shrugging. 'There's loads of stuff about him online, obviously. He even has a Wikipedia page.'

'Wow. Okay, so I guess it's best to avoid romantic relationships when you chat to him – but maybe use the music thing as a hook to get him talking about honesty and truth as ideas. Loop him around to the theme of the exhibition via something we know he's into.'

'Got it.'

'In terms of the image we're after, the focus is on getting him to smile. Almost every Zack picture in existence has him pouting or brooding. He's quite jolly in his YouTube vids, but it seems he channels Heathcliff for photos.'

'Right. Maybe I'll see if I can find a playlist he'd like – help him relax. There's an Alexa over there that should connect to my phone.'

'Great idea. Now, hop onto the stool in front of the camera, would you?'

'Er – what?'

'I need to test the light. See what I'm working with.'

'Oh. Okay.'

Rachel shuffled into the centre of the studio area, treading softly on the roll of background paper that Tom had pulled into place. It was a pale, blueish off-white, and she hoped her well-worn boots wouldn't leave prints on it.

She scrambled up to perch on the stool, which was slightly too tall for her.

'Hang on,' Tom said, 'let me lower that a bit. We don't want you falling off it; where there's blame, there's a claim.'

He helped her down, then fiddled with the underside of the seat until it had come down by a few inches. Satisfied, he held Rachel's hand as she climbed back up.

'Okaaaaay,' Tom breathed, moving back a few paces to assess the set-up. He stared at her thoughtfully, pushing his hair off his forehead.

This was *strange*. It felt intense . . . And exposing. Rachel was surrounded by lights and reflectors, everything trained on her face. She fought the urge to pull her sweater over her head and hide, instead trying to remain as still as possible. Tom looked like he was considering something complicated; she didn't want to put him off.

He came closer again and she instructed herself not to move, though the urge to run away was now stronger than ever. Tom reached up to faff with a huge boxy thing just behind her. As he arched his body around hers she could smell washing powder – presumably the stuff he used to keep that white T-shirt bright.

He retreated and stood directly in front of her. 'May I?'

Rachel nodded, though she had no idea what she was agreeing to.

Tom placed two fingertips on the underside of her jaw and tilted her head up, tipping it to the left. Rachel felt her lips come apart to suck in a sharp breath that betrayed her surprise at being touched, but she stayed still.

'Sorry,' Tom whispered. 'I know it's weird.'

'S'fine,' Rachel whispered back. It was definitely weird. But weirdly, also fine.

'Can I take this hairband out? It'll help me see how the light hits different textures.'

'Uh-huh,' Rachel answered, trying not to shift her head.

Tom fiddled with the elastic until her hair came loose, then pushed his fingers into the waves at the nape of her neck, gently fanning them so they fell down her back.

'Oops – didn't mean to tickle you,' he said softly, feeling her start at the contact. He fell back, putting himself a respectful distance away.

Tom fumbled in his pocket and pulled out something that looked like a calculator. It had a small white ball on top.

'Light meter,' he said, answering Rachel's unspoken question. He extended his arm and let the thing hover a few millimetres from the right-hand side of her face, then pressed a button and waited.

Tom moved the meter until it was suspended above Rachel's head, then fiddled again with the controls. After several more checks, he seemed happy.

'Cool,' he said, grinning at her. 'Don't move a muscle.'

He strode away, ducking behind a large square camera, then picked up a long, thin black wire with what looked like a silver trigger on its end. He held the metallic thing in his hand as he looked through the viewfinder.

'Smile, Rach,' Tom said, then fired the camera. It emitted a loud, rather pleasing *snap*.

'You blinked,' he laughed. 'And before that you just looked terrified. You know this is a camera and not a grenade launcher, right? Relax your shoulders a bit if you can . . . You look great, by the way.'

Rachel puffed out her cheeks, blowing away a rush of air that signalled she didn't believe him.

'Trust me,' he said. 'Now, come on, I need you to smile properly. Think joyful thoughts . . . No, no, not like you're straining to go to the loo.'

'Fuck *off*, I'm trying!'

'That's better.' *Snap*.

'Right. Now think about something properly hilarious. I dunno . . . Laurence being rugby-tackled by Will. Or having the crap kicked out of him by Anna . . . I'm not sure which would be scarier, to be honest.'

Rachel laughed, imagining her two friends tag-teaming: Will knocking Laurence over and Anna whacking him around the face with her leopard-print beret. *Snap*.

'Beautiful,' Tom said, then shook his head as she rolled her eyes at him. 'Rach, listen. I—'

Brrrrrrrring. BRRRRRRRRINNNNNG.

'Ah. Zack must be here.'

Tom turned and made for the door as Rachel slid off the stool.

She shook her head and pressed her hands against her cheeks to quell the sudden, intense warmth in them. Then she pulled her hair back up into a high, messy ponytail before following him.

Zack Lanson was shorter than Rachel had expected, but he was every inch the influencer. He was wearing a Belstaff leather jacket that probably cost as much as her monthly rent, plus a long fine-knit scarf so soft and luxurious she'd happily curl up and sleep in it.

Rachel found herself transfixed by Zack's eyebrows. They were a rich dark brown and more perfectly arched than any she'd ever seen – except perhaps Jessica's in those stupid Angeljuice ads. He must have them threaded, she concluded. Perhaps she should ask him where.

'Hi, thanks for being here,' Tom said, shaking hands with Zack and the younger man he'd brought with him. 'I'm Tom and this is Rachel, the copywriter for the exhibition. She'll chat with you about your thoughts on the theme and I'll be taking your photo.'

'Lovely. Nice to meet you both,' Zack said in his trademark cockney wide-boy accent. 'This is Nate, my assistant.'

From where Rachel was standing it looked as though Nate, a solidly built black guy barely out of his teens, chiefly assisted with carrying Zack's stuff. He was weighed down with garment bags, a large glass bottle of what Rachel hoped was water and a massive metallic vanity case.

Rachel took the water out of Nate's hand before the bottle could fall and smash, then helped him to drape Zack's clothes over the arm of the small mustard sofa that sat in the kitchen area.

'Thanks,' Nate said, flashing Rachel a smile.

'No problem.'

'So, what do you want me in first, Tommy?' Zack asked. 'A suit, perhaps? I've brought my YSL skinny tuxedo, I look the *dog's* in that.'

'It's just Tom. And actually, what you're wearing is probably perfect – the famous white tee plus your jacket.

We'll mainly be doing just head-and-shoulders shots anyway, and we're after a kind of "off-duty" look . . . I'm sure you're all clued up on the exhibition concept after speaking with Dev.'

'Oh yeah, absolutely,' Zack said, not sounding clued up at all. 'I remember now – we're keeping it real for this one. Seriously, though . . . Are we talking no hair and make-up *whatsoever*? Not even a bit of CC cream, no highlighter? I don't wanna look all pale and tired, my followers expect me to be fresh. And what about contouring?'

Tom looked alarmed, as though he wasn't sure what most of these words even meant.

'Think about the kind of shot you'd see on a 1960s album cover,' Rachel interjected. 'Or imagine a really gorgeous, natural photo of a good-looking artist – say, Springsteen. That's what we're aiming for.'

Tom closed his eyes in relief, nodding and giving her a thumbs up behind Zack's back. He motioned for her to carry on talking.

'The idea is we want to show a different side to you,' Rachel continued, 'create an image that's artistic, a little raw, kind of vintage in style. Less polished than usual, but beautifully lit and composed, so still *really* flattering.'

'Got you,' Zack said, brightening. 'Shame I didn't bring my guitar, now I think about it – would have been the perfect prop. Nate, mate – could you take all this stuff back to the flat? Maybe pick up the Hummingbird?'

Nate's face crumpled at the prospect of more fetching and carrying. Rachel didn't blame him.

'Honestly, there's no need,' Tom said. 'I promise we can get the vibe we're after without it.'

'We want to capture the music in *you*,' Rachel said, trying not to cringe or catch Tom's eye in case she laughed. 'I don't blame you for wanting to show off the Gibson, though. Is it the cherry-coloured one you have?'

Rachel guided Zack towards the studio area, chatting with him about instruments, songwriting and a folk music documentary they'd both seen. She handed Tom her phone as they passed him, preloaded with a playlist she was confident Zack would like. Tom got it going while Rachel settled Zack inside the ring of lights and reflectors, and Nate clattered around the kitchen working the coffee machine.

As Tom adjusted the equipment and the voice of James Taylor meandered around the room, Rachel chatted with Zack, noting down everything that might be suitable for his mini-bio and soon feeling like she had plenty to work with.

Before long, Tom had established a comfortable dynamic with his subject, taking flurries of photos, tweaking some aspect of their set-up or composition and then shooting more. Zack was clearly more confident than Rachel had been in front of the camera, shifting his body and tilting his face on cue in the way a fashion model might.

Tom had to work hard, joking and chatting to keep Zack engaged and prevent his face falling into its standard brooding stare. Gradually, though, Zack's expression started to relax, his face becoming more real somehow as Tom gave him room to unwind.

Rachel watched Tom work, fascinated by a side of him she'd never seen before. Occasionally she'd creep up to glance at the photo monitor, startled every time by the beauty of the images he'd captured. She made a mental note to thank Anna for pushing her into doing this; it was fun and interesting, and she couldn't imagine someone else here in her place.

As the shoot neared its end, Zack had an idea that no one could deny was worth exploring. He wanted to try taking some photos in the suit he'd brought with him, but wear it scruffier than usual – rough it up and subvert the style his fans were used to seeing.

As Zack retreated behind a screen to change and Nate lugged a heavy-looking YSL bag across the room, Tom pulled his mobile out of his coat pocket and put the phone to his ear, presumably to listen to a voicemail. Rachel could tell immediately that something was wrong.

Sinking into a plastic chair, he dropped his face into the palm of his left hand as he clutched the phone in his right.

'What's happened?' Rachel asked under her breath, crouching down and clinging to the arm of the seat. 'Tom?'

He groaned. 'It's my brother.'

'Your *what*?'

As far as Rachel knew, Tom was an only child – but she told herself now wasn't the time to badger him into explaining the sudden appearance of a sibling.

'Is he okay?'

'No. Well, yeah . . . But he's twatted in some pub not too far away. Which wouldn't be a problem if it weren't for the fact he's only fifteen.'

'*Fifteen?* So the age gap between you is . . . No, forget it – that's not important right now. Was he calling you for help?'

'It's not him, it's his mates. They're terrified he's going to get them all arrested, and they don't dare call his mum. None of them are even supposed to be in London.' He clawed at his dark-blonde head. 'Urrrgh, fuck it, I'm going to have to go and get him.'

'No,' Rachel insisted, 'it's so unfair for you to have to abandon the shoot when it's going so well. And it's only the first one – what will Dev think? Listen . . .' she went on, not entirely sure where she was going with this, yet certain it couldn't be anywhere good. 'I have enough notes on Zack to pull my copy together. Let me go and fetch your brother. Although you'll need to give me his name and some sort of description.'

Taking responsibility for a hammered teenage boy was somewhere between camping and giving up cheese on Rachel's list of Things I Have No Desire To Do, but Tom's face was desperate and it made her insides hurt. He shut his eyes and sighed as he processed what she'd said.

'Really?'

'Really. How long ago did his friends leave that message?'

'Only about ten minutes, thank God.'

'Right. Give me your phone so I can get your brother's number. I'll find them.'

'Are you sure about this?' Tom asked. 'It sounds like he's in a proper state.'

'Thomas, I have about a thousand Irish cousins and I've spent *many* summers hanging around the street corners, parks and pubs of County Dublin. I promise you, your brother won't be the first battered schoolboy I've kept out of harm's way.'

Tom nodded at her gratefully.

Rachel grabbed her handbag and pulled her coat on, then stopped. 'Er – who am I looking for again?'

'Oscar Evans. Answers to Ozzy. Looks kind of like me, I guess, but shorter.'

'Right. Leave it with me. If it looks like Zack's still here when I get back, I'll find somewhere else to take him.'

'You're brilliant, Rach,' Tom said. 'I can't thank you enough.'

She smiled at him, then reached up and gave his arm a squeeze. She slipped out of the door just as Zack, dazzling in his slim-cut designer suit, stepped back in front of the camera.

18

Oscar Evans was exactly as described: shorter and rounder than Tom, but with familiar facial features that denoted they must be brothers. Also, he was hideously drunk.

Rachel found him with three slightly less incapacitated friends, slumped against the outside wall of a pub on Bethnal Green Road. After establishing that they were capable of getting themselves home, Rachel put the other boys on a bus to Liverpool Street station and instructed them to get on the first train back to Colchester. This, she'd been informed, was where they all lived.

She said they could call her again if they needed anything, but also left them in no doubt that she wasn't some soft touch. If any further rescues were needed today, she warned, it would be the police or their parents picking them up off the pavement. Rachel got the impression the boys took her at her word, and felt confident they wouldn't drink any more.

Oscar himself was in no fit state for public transport, so after getting him to sip some bottled water she threw her arm around his waist and helped him plod slowly back in the direction of the studio. What should have been a ten-minute walk took more like twenty, but eventually the railway arches were back in view. When she got close enough, Rachel saw that the door to A24 was propped open.

Concluding that Zack and Nate must be gone, she hauled Oscar inside. Tom rushed over to them, pulled his brother's arm from around Rachel's shoulders and manhandled him into a seated position on the kitchenette's yellow-gold sofa.

'Thank you so much,' Tom said, folding Rachel into the tightest hug they'd ever shared. She leaned into it, enjoying the sensation of being held upright by someone else after the exertion of getting Oscar back here.

'Fuckin' hell, get a room . . .' came a groggy voice from the corner.

Tom whirled around, advancing on Oscar in a single angry stride.

'Watch it,' he warned. 'You are in a *world* of shit with me, but that's nothing compared with the bollocking you'll get from Christine if I phone her and tell her what's happened.'

Oscar quailed and looked as though he might throw up. 'Don't. Please.'

'Here's what's going to happen. You are going to sit there quietly and drink some more water while I put this equipment away. Then you're going to come back to my flat and stay there – at least until you're in your right mind and I've worked out what to do with you.'

Oscar was no longer listening. He was now half-asleep and smirking, his head leaned back against the couch he'd been deposited on.

'I'll help you get him home,' Rachel said. 'You finish packing up, I'll call an Uber.'

'Rach, you've already done enough. Honestly, don't let me – *this* – take up any more of your Saturday.'

'Stop arguing,' she said. 'The car's already on its way.'

Tom sighed and shook his head, but continued sliding lights and lenses back into their foam-packed cases.

Moments after he'd collapsed the final tripod and slipped his laptop into his bag, Rachel said, 'Taxi's here.'

Between them they loaded Tom's equipment into the boot of the Prius that had pulled up, then went back inside the arch for Oscar. Tom dragged him to his feet. 'Stay quiet and act normal,' he ordered, 'or the driver won't let you in the car.'

'Psshhhhh, no such thing as normal,' Oscar slurred. 'Fascist conspiracy.'

Rachel tried not to laugh as Tom made a face and hissed, 'Not a word.'

They helped Oscar shuffle towards the taxi and then clamber inside.

'What's up with him?' the driver asked, pointing, the second the car doors were closed.

'Jet lag,' Rachel said swiftly. 'He's just very, very tired.'

Oscar began sniggering as the driver rolled his eyes and put the car in first gear. 'You're paying for a full valet if he chunders.'

'He won't,' said Tom grimly, then looked at Oscar. 'It's not far and he'll hold it in unless he wants his mum to get the bill.'

Oscar went pale and remained silent the rest of the way back to Stroud Green.

By the time the taxi stopped a few metres away from Tom and Will's building, Oscar looked thoroughly nauseated.

His skin was damp with the unhealthy sheen of the soon-to-be sick.

'He's going to throw up,' Rachel said as they heaved him out of the Uber.

''M fine,' Oscar mumbled unconvincingly.

'Maybe it's just being in the car,' Tom said, putting his key in the front door and shoving it open. 'He'll be better once we get him inside.'

Rachel guided Oscar down the corridor and let him lean on her as Tom unlocked the flat door.

'You're well fit, y'know,' Oscar said, as if this were a crucial truth that had just become clear to him. He stared at her with doe-eyed, inebriated adoration.

Rachel laughed. Tom pulled Oscar away from her, tugging him into the flat by his coat sleeve.

'You never said you had a fit girlfriend,' Oscar slurred. 'Why didn't you tell me you had a fit girlfriend?'

Exasperated, Tom briefly let go of his brother to tear at his own hair. Rachel observed it was becoming curlier and more unruly as his annoyance with Oscar increased.

'Rachel *isn't* my girlfriend, Oz,' he said, with a touch more feeling than Rachel thought was necessary. 'Men and women can be friends, you know. They can be in each other's lives without needing to sleep together.'

Gee, thanks, Rachel thought, then reproved herself for being so ridiculous. Tom was only telling the truth, after all: there'd never been anything romantic between them.

Oscar swayed towards Rachel, staring up at her with eyes that she noticed were the same shape as Tom's, but brown instead of blue.

'Go out with me instead,' Oscar said, taking both her hands in his and gesturing at his brother. 'He's an idiot anyway. And he's old.'

'Oh, for fuck's *sake*,' Tom grumbled, reaching for Oscar to move him away.

Oscar tightened his grip on Rachel's fingers. He looked greener than ever.

'OSCAR!' Tom bellowed, his temper finally fraying.

'You can't split us up,' Oscar insisted, throwing his body towards Rachel's. 'She's lovely. I think I might love her.'

Tom hooked an arm around Oscar's middle. 'You're going to knock her over. And you don't love her, you've only known her an hour.'

'You're just jealous!' Oscar shouted triumphantly, still holding on to Rachel's hands. 'Back off, you had your chance!'

'I'm sorry about this, Rach,' Tom said, looking wretched. He moved backwards, still clinging to Oscar's waist and trying to pull him away from her.

'Nooooo!' Oscar wailed, resisting.

Even as she saw Oscar clutch a hand to his stomach, Rachel couldn't help giggling at the ridiculous spectacle of it all. She was still laughing as his jaw went slack and he lurched towards her, his stomach convulsing in an almighty heave that she realised, too late, would have very unpleasant consequences.

A fountain of projectile vomit erupted in Rachel's direction, spraying her from her shoulders down to her waist. Before she or Tom could register what had happened, Oscar staggered forward and threw up again – this time spattering Rachel from thigh to shin with vivid reddish puke.

Oscar sank to the floor and put his head between his knees as Tom surveyed the carnage.

'Oh my God. Oh my *God* . . . Is that blood? Is he *bleeding*?'

'No,' Rachel said. Beneath the acrid upchuck smell emanating from her sweater was an intensely sweet aroma she recognised.

'I'm pretty sure that colour's blackcurrant cordial. I think this is snakey-B vomit.'

'Thank God,' Tom said, relief giving way to horror as he looked more closely at Rachel, taking in the full extent of her soaking. 'Oh fuck. Look at you.'

'Yeah. Bit grim,' Rachel said, feeling very grossed out and queasy herself but trying not to show it. 'It's probably a good thing he's been sick, though . . . His colour's already coming back.'

It was true. Oscar looked pathetic, curled up in a ball on the stained sitting room rug – but his cheeks had lost the waxy, washed-out look they'd had before.

'Sorry,' he moaned from the floor, sounding almost coherent.

'Get him to bed,' Rachel said, pointing. 'Honestly, I'm okay for a minute.'

Tom sighed in resignation and crouched down to Oscar. 'Come on, you absolute arsepain. I'll be back ASAP, Rach.'

He hoisted Oscar up by his armpits, then helped him walk to the bathroom.

Rachel heard the sound of running water and low voices rumbling from the other side of the door. Delicately, she peeled off her damp sweater, inordinately grateful it was a button-down, and dropped it on the floor – careful to pick a spot that would need a mop in any case. Then she stood as still as possible to try to keep Oscar's vomit contained, very aware that her neck, shoulders and chest were exposed in just her bra and cotton cami.

A moment later the bathroom door creaked open. Tom helped Oscar to the spare bedroom-slash-office. Through the open door, Rachel saw him lay his brother on an ancient IKEA futon. When he came back to the open-plan kitchen and living area, Tom was carrying Oscar's dirty clothes.

'I'll wash and dry yours too,' he said. 'If you want me to, that is. I can lend you something until your stuff's sorted . . . And I'm guessing you'll want a shower.'

'That would be great, I'm totally disgusting,' Rachel said. 'I think there's snakebite sick in my hair.'

'Urghh, I don't know what to say. I'm so *unbelievably* sorry. I hope Oscar has the world-class hangover he deserves after this.'

'He won't,' Rachel laughed. 'Kids never do. But it's okay. It's not your fault.'

'Let me find you some stuff to wear while I get your clothes clean,' Tom said, heading towards his bedroom. He came back with a pair of blue joggers and a familiar grey marl sweatshirt – one she'd always liked, with a faded image of a snow-capped mountain and the word *MONTANA* printed above it in crumbling red and white letters.

'There are clean towels in the cupboard behind the bathroom door,' Tom said as he handed the stuff to Rachel.

'Help yourself to anything else you need. We'll stick the washing machine on after. And sorry again . . . A *million* apologies.'

'Thanks,' Rachel said. 'But please stop apologising. Best you check on your brother while I'm getting cleaned up – make sure he's sleeping on his side and not his back. Just in case.'

'I will.' Tom nodded, then raised his eyes to meet hers. 'You're being ridiculously cool about this.'

'It's fine,' she said, looking back from the bathroom doorway. 'What's a little vomit between friends?'

'Rach?' Tom called before she could close the door. 'One more thing.'

She bobbed her head and waited.

'It's just . . . You could never be disgusting. Even covered in teenager's puke, you're lovely. Oscar was right about that. I wanted you to hear it from someone sober.'

Rachel smiled and waved the compliment away, retreating into the bathroom.

With immense relief, she stripped off and started the shower running, trying not to think about how bizarre it was that she was naked in Will and Tom's flat.

Rachel emerged from the bathroom clean, if oddly attired. Tom's too-long navy joggers pulled tight across her hips when she moved; they were cut for a tall, slim man, not a woman with no thigh gap. Conversely, her top half – braless – was drowning in his soft, oversized Montana sweatshirt.

She'd used something with a citrussy, mannish fragrance to wash her hair and body, and the scent now clung to her skin. The sweatshirt smelled fresh – clean and soapy – but maybe a little like the citrus stuff too. Breathing in Essence of Tom each time she moved was odd but not unpleasant, Rachel decided.

She made her way into the kitchen area and placed her soiled clothes, which unfortunately included her underwear, into the washing machine.

'Can I start this now?' she asked.

Tom looked up from the patch of rug he was ineffectually scrubbing.

'Yeah. Let me, though, the machine's ancient and the settings are awkward. I wouldn't want you to boil-wash your stuff by accident.'

'Under the circumstances, a hot wash might be best.' Rachel smiled.

Tom came to stand behind her, then twisted a dial on the front of the machine and slammed the door. It whirred into life immediately.

'How's Oscar?' Rachel asked.

'Passed out, but looking less peaky by the minute. My suspicion is he'll wake up ravenous, feel far less foul than he deserves to and have no memory of declaring his undying love for you. Apologies for that, by the way – he was clearly overwhelmed.'

'Ha! Not a problem, really. It was quite nice in a way . . . More sincere than Laurence's roses, in any case.'

'Hmm, I don't know how much of an accolade *that* is. But I'll be sure to mention it to Oscar during the Serious Talk we'll be having later.'

Rachel moved towards the sofa and armchairs at the

other end of the room, stepping over a spray bottle of Vanish and several wet patches of floor.

'I think your rug's DNR, Thomas,' she said. 'Literally – it looks like it's bleeding out.'

'You're probably right,' Tom said from the kitchen. 'I guess if it's today's only casualty, that's not too shabby.'

A few minutes later he joined her on the sofa, placing a tray with glasses of squash and sandwiches on the coffee table.

'Amazing,' Rachel said, picking up a granary creation that appeared to contain chicken and sliced tomato. 'Ooooh, that's good.'

They ate and drank in silence, but when the last sandwich had gone Rachel turned to Tom and asked: 'So. Are you going to tell me?'

He shifted uncomfortably, colour momentarily draining from his face. Then he asked, 'About Oscar?'

Rachel nodded.

'Ah. We've only recently been in touch, and I wanted to get to know him a bit before introducing him to anyone . . . Who knows, maybe he'll even meet my mum at some point.'

'Er. Okay?' Rachel's face betrayed her confusion.

'Oscar is Christine's son. Christine is the woman my dad ran off with when he left my mum and me. She was one of the secretaries at his firm and twenty years younger than him. I was fourteen.'

None of this was news to Rachel, exactly. She knew Tom's parents were divorced and that their split had been bitter – but there'd never been any mention of his dad having more children.

She nodded, signalling she was ready to hear more.

'As I think you know, I barely saw my dad after the split. He and Mum hated the sight of one another, and when he and Christine moved to Essex everything sort of fell apart. I was lucky if I got a birthday card. I grew to hate him almost as much as Mum did for choosing someone else over us. After a while I stopped trying to keep up any contact.'

'I don't blame you,' Rachel said, livid on teenage Tom's behalf.

He shrugged. 'I found out towards the end of last summer that shortly after they ran off together, Christine and my dad had a baby. Oscar. It seems Mum couldn't bear to tell me Dad had binned us off and started another family straightaway . . . I was hurt enough. I suppose she was worried I'd feel replaced. And after that, I guess there was never a good time to tell the truth.'

'Bloody hell,' Rachel breathed. 'I mean, your poor mum. But . . . what a thing to keep from you.'

'Yeah. I've been pretty angry with her. In her defence, though, she always thought my dad would tell me himself. Of course he *left* Christine within a couple of years for another woman – disappeared again – so that never happened. And there was no love lost between Christine and my mum, so I don't think the idea of trying to forge a relationship between Oscar and me ever occurred to them. It was easier for them to ignore one another.'

'That's awful.' Rachel twisted in her seat, struggling to comprehend what she was hearing.

'Yeah,' Tom agreed. 'Anyway. As you've probably worked out by now, Oscar is a bit of a handful. He started poking around Christine's attic one afternoon – the story is he'd taken to smoking up there – and discovered a wallet of old photos inside a leftover box of our dad's. There was a little boy in some of the pictures, and he realised it wasn't him—'

'Because your eyes are blue, and his are brown,' Rachel interrupted.

'Exactly. So he interrogated his mum, and within a couple of weeks – even though she told him not to – he'd tracked me down online.'

'Wow. I guess you can't fault his nerve.'

Tom laughed and shook his head. 'Definitely not. And he's a good kid – he's just a bit mixed up. When Christine found out he'd been visiting me in London, she freaked. I didn't know he'd been going behind her back, and I told Oz we needed to sort things out properly before we could carry on spending time together – that I couldn't come between him and his mum. Clearly, my sensible speech hasn't worked.'

'No,' Rachel agreed. 'But at least you tried. What are you going to do now? I mean, aside from give him two Nurofen and a round of dry toast when he wakes up.'

'I'm going to have to call Christine and tell her he turned up here today. She'll be even madder with him than I am.' Tom winced.

'Maybe there's a way you can tell her *most* of the truth but avoid getting him into too much hot water,' Rachel said.

Tom frowned.

'Just . . . don't be too hard on him,' she went on. 'I was a younger sibling. It's a tough gig, even without all this extra complication thrown in. And this is a wonderful thing, or it will be: you and Oscar are lucky to have found each other.'

Tom squeezed Rachel's hand, then sprang away as the washing machine gave an almighty *CLICK*.

Rachel jumped too.

'Laundry's done,' Tom laughed. 'Is all your stuff okay to be tumble-dried? Do you want a cuppa while it goes round?'

'Yes and yes,' Rachel said. 'I'll shift the washing while you put the kettle on.'

'Cool. Changing the subject entirely,' Tom said as he put teabags into two mugs, 'I think the shoot went brilliantly this morning. The photos look great, and I liked Zack – even though I was snarky about him to start with.'

'Me too.'

'He's left us two tickets for his first gig. It's at some tiny music venue in Highgate next month. D'you fancy it?'

'Er, *yes*,' Rachel said, as if Tom was being very stupid. 'How could we not go? He might be this generation's Bob Dylan.'

Tom snorted. 'Let's not get too excited – I have a feeling there's a reason the tickets are free. I'll text you the details.'

They moved back to the sofa and drank their tea, chatting over Tom's plans for the next exhibition shoot. He got up to check the contents of the tumble dryer when it beeped, then said: 'All done. I guess you're good to go.'

'Oh. Okay, thanks,' Rachel said, realising that she was actually in no rush to leave. Oscar would wake up soon, though, and Tom needed to talk to Christine. It would be easier for everyone else if she went home now – and in any case, she had no reason to stay.

Tom stood aside as Rachel pulled her clothes out of the drum, perhaps aware that it would be weird for him to handle her smalls.

'I'll just go and change,' she said.

In the bathroom, Rachel checked her reflection and immediately wished she hadn't. Her hair was frizzy from using men's shampoo, and her post-shower, make-up-free face looked washed out and tired. She couldn't blame Tom for being so quick to deny they were an item when Oscar had suggested it; right now, she wouldn't want to go out with her either.

Fully dressed, Rachel folded Tom's shorts and sweatshirt before heading back to the living room.

'Right. Guess I'll see you next week sometime?' she asked.

'For sure,' Tom said. 'By the way . . . Will doesn't know anything about any of this yet. Do you mind keeping it to yourself for a while?'

'Of course not. Can you message me later, though? Let me know how Oscar is. How *you* are?'

'I promise.'

Rachel handed Tom his clothes and put her coat on, deeply relieved it had been spared Death by Snakebite.

Tom saw her to the flat door, then pulled her into a hug. 'Thank you again, for everything.'

'My pleasure,' Rachel said into his chest. 'Well . . . mostly. Say goodbye to your brother for me, won't you?'

'Yeah,' Tom laughed, stepping back slightly. 'A very formal, platonic goodbye so he doesn't get his hopes up.'

He smiled lopsidedly at her and for a split second her stomach twisted. Weird. Maybe she needed more food.

'Rach,' he said as she opened the door. 'Keep this. Even I can see your jumper's shrunk in our rubbish dryer. It's only fair, and it looks better on you, anyway.'

He handed her the Montana sweatshirt and Rachel knew that she should argue. She loved it, though, and couldn't bring herself to protest. She accepted the soft grey square, hugging it to her chest for a second before dropping it into her bag.

'Bye, then,' Rachel said, feeling strangely emotional as she pulled the door closed behind her. This really had been an odd day.

*

That evening, Tom's list of Things To Feel Bad About was as follows:
1. Using the photo shoot set-up as a pretext for touching Rachel's face. (Bad.)
2. Using the photo shoot set-up as a pretext for touching her hair. (Somehow worse.)
3. Almost confessing how he felt about her, then losing his nerve. (Pathetic.)
4. Putting Rachel in the position where his idiot half-brother could projectile-vomit all over her. (Unforgivable.)

5. A variety of daydreams involving Rachel in his shower, which were only intensified by the sight of her wearing his clothes.
6. The destruction of the sitting room rug, now languishing in a skip at the local dump.
7. Getting Oscar grounded for a month, even though he'd held off telling Christine the full details of her son's Adventures In Alcohol Poisoning.
8. Seeing red and implying that Christine couldn't handle Oscar when she tried to blame Tom for his behaviour.
9. Making a non-date with Rachel that he very much wished was a proper date, which would involve her listening to awful music under (sort of) false pretences.
10. Not feeling nearly guilty enough about 1, 2, 5 and 9.

March

~~New Year's~~ Ongoing resolutions

1. Consider exercise an act with actual benefits – both mental and physical – not merely grim punishment for pizzas consumed. ~~Have a proper go at~~ Continue letting Greg drag me to yoga.
2. ~~Also re-download Complete Couch to 5K running app and actually do the programme.~~ Keep running at least twice per week – *always* being careful not to perv on anyone improper.
3. ~~Apply for promotion at work at first chance. Move to bigger account and try to get pay rise. Avoid, if possible, further projects concerning dog biscuits, disinfectant, high-quality printer ink cartridges, 'miracle' grass seed, organic vegetables, etc.~~
    3a. Try to hang on to job (and temper) despite ~~presence of evil ex-boyfriend~~ hideousness of certain clients.

3b. Ignore everyone who keeps banging on about how fit ~~he~~ Jack is.

3c. Ignore how fit he is.

3d. Ignore the fact he keeps trying to be friendly/nice/possibly quite flirtatious.

3e. Ignore the fact he is getting divorced.

~~4. DO NOT agree to further dates with Laurence. Remember: it's no use having a boyfriend who is good on paper if you do not actually fancy him.~~

4. Forget that Laurence even EXISTS (despite usefulness of overblown 'romantic' gestures for creating illusion of deeply devoted boyfriend).

5. Try to remember Mum means well, even during phone calls where she ~~implies I am doomed to a lonely life of penury because I am thirty with no partner, hardly any savings and no mortgage~~ insists on talking about the babies/breasts of people I went to school with.

6. HOWEVER, do not (!!!) speak to Mum when suffering PMT. Set phone alerts for likely spells based on period tracker intel.

7. Try to address 'hardly any savings' situation. ~~(If promoted, set aside extra earnings for future house deposit instead of spaffing it all on ASOS.)~~ (Do not spend entire pay rise on ~~'cheer up' treats to distract from heinous ex-boyfriend mess.)~~ hot new outfits for work – see 3c.)

8. Try to eat my five-a-day. (Remember horrid rule that potatoes do not count.)

9. Start using proper night cream with retinol. SERIOUSLY.
10. Do the best possible job helping Tom with exhibition. Be supportive and discreet re Oscar.

19

Rachel and Jack's success with Sir Humphrey saw them drafted in to help oversee a flurry of small pitches in the following few weeks. Their names began to be used in tandem, as though they were twin halves of some 2-for-1 deal: 'See what Rachel and Jack think'; 'Ask Jack and Rachel for their take on it'; 'Jack and Rachel might be able to help.'

Kemi and her friends openly resented this, and Rachel fielded countless impudent questions about the nature of their relationship from women whose interest in 'Hot Harper' was far from professional. This was irritating, but Rachel couldn't help feeling warmed by her proximity to Jack's star – excited by her colleagues' envy, although it was mostly misplaced.

When Greg suggested she might be enjoying the speculation surrounding their closeness, however, she strenuously denied it – even threatening to cancel post-yoga cocktails if he wouldn't stop sniping. Greg complied, but his silence on the subject still spoke volumes – as did his regularly raised eyebrows.

Rachel knew that a handful of her co-workers still considered the mystery of her Valentine's Day flowers unsolved. On the other hand, she was aware that, while Jack had assumed the bouquet was from her secret suitor, plenty of other people thought he'd sent it to her himself.

As far as Greg knew, the identity of the giver remained unknown, even to Rachel – a misconception she was happy for him to hold on to.

By mid-March the cheering trumpets of daffodils had taken over London's parks and window boxes, and Rachel had finally finished Couch to 5K. She didn't feel as though she'd lost any weight, but that had never been the point. While her clothes weren't any looser there was a pleasing new firmness to her thighs, and sprinting to avoid missing the bus had become noticeably easier. Most importantly she felt proud of herself for not quitting – for pushing through the pain and believing she could do it, despite her lifelong loathing of exercise. She and Anna celebrated her achievement with several large gin and tonics from the huge bottle of The Botanist that Will had given her on the weekend of her final training run.

When Rachel returned to the R/C office after lunch one Tuesday afternoon, she found Jack waiting for her – one eyebrow cocked and his gaze trained on a £1 bunch of bright-yellow blooms she'd picked up for her desk.

'For me? You shouldn't have,' he said, grinning in the way that never failed to make Rachel feel like an invisible rope was tied to her stomach: one he could tug on gently or reel all the way in at will.

She shot him a death stare. 'Haha.'

Determined to ignore him, she removed a trio of biros from a glass Kilner jar in the corner of her desk, then ripped off the paper tie around the daffodils' stems. Aware that Jack's eyes were still on her, she dropped them into the jar and took it to the kitchen for water.

'If you wanted a floral arrangement for your desk, surely you could have just put in an order with your other half?' he said when she got back. Rachel made murder eyes at him again, but a now familiar feeling of satisfaction stirred in her stomach. Refusing to engage with him on this, Rachel had realised, felt like a superpower.

It had occurred to her that she was playing with her own feelings as well as Jack's ego by persisting with the ruse that she was attached – and yet she couldn't seem to stop. Every time he tried to goad her into talking about her 'boyfriend', the thrill of declining to be drawn on the topic got stronger.

'Isaac wants to see us this afternoon,' Jack informed her. 'There's more new pitch work. Something bigger this time, I think, quite challenging from the sound of things.'

'That's good,' Rachel said. 'It'll be nice to get stuck in to something harder again.'

Jack smirked. 'Please go on. I love it when you talk dirty about digital content strategy.'

She flushed, annoyed but amused in spite of herself. 'Do shut up, or I'll be forced to staple your sensitive parts to your swivel chair.'

'Ewwww,' breathed a voice behind her. Rachel winced, turning to see who'd spoken – though she already knew.

'Walking past you two should come with a "not suitable for work" warning,' Donna said. She swept past Jack's desk towards the kitchen, giving Rachel a look that was one part disgusted, one part jealous and two parts self-satisfied.

'I've no idea why, but that woman really hates me,' Rachel sighed.

'She hates everyone,' Jack said with a shrug. 'But mostly other women, I think – particularly if they have the nerve to be pretty *and* clever.'

Rachel stared down at her keyboard, not wanting to acknowledge the compliment. She opened up an email that didn't require an urgent reply and began typing a response at speed, her fingertips hammering the keys as though someone's survival depended on a swift but comprehensive answer to the question of whether the terms *log in* and *login* were interchangeable. (It didn't, and they weren't.)

That afternoon Rachel sat in the small R/C meeting room, cradling a cup of tea in her hands as Isaac waxed lyrical about the importance of the pitch he was about to assign them.

'This is a national charity with *incredible* reach – a household name even more recognisable than BHGH. And it's in the medical-slash-mental health space,' he went on. 'If we get this and do a good job, it will open up doors for us that I've been trying to knock on for years. You guys are undoubtedly the team for the job, but – as with BHGH – I think your client-side contact is a bit of a thorny character.'

Rachel groaned aloud at the thought of dealing with another sneering sexist, then tried to mask the noise by taking a huge gulp of tea. It went down the wrong way immediately, and Jack smacked her between the shoulder blades as she coughed and spluttered beneath Isaac's unbroken chatter.

'Oh, come on, Isaac – do tell,' Jack said. 'Rachel and I can't cope with the suspense.'

Rachel made a face that she knew he'd understand meant *Have a day off, kiss-arse*. In response, Jack smiled at her serenely as Isaac resumed his speech.

'We are talking about Lighthouse UK,' he announced impressively.

Jack sat up straighter in his chair and nodded, his green eyes bright and approving.

Rachel felt herself twitch – felt some memory spark in a dark corner of her mind. *Lighthouse UK* . . .

She ought to know about this organisation – she'd definitely heard of it – so she dipped her head and crossed her arms as though she was well informed and listening attentively.

Lighthouse UK . . . It was definitely ringing a bell.

As the ringing became louder, it twisted into a discordant, grating clamour that only she could hear. Keeping time with it, Rachel's breathing became heavier and faster, echoing in her ears. Her heart was pummelling her ribcage so hard she thought it might crack a bone. She was panicking. *Why* was she panicking?

Isaac was still talking, and as Rachel tuned back in to the conversation she suddenly understood.

'NHS hospitals . . .' Isaac was saying. 'Terminally ill children . . . Grief counselling . . . Bereaved brothers and sisters.'

Rachel felt her body flash hot, then cold, then hot again. She felt as if she were watching all this in a mirror – or as if she were trapped at the bottom of a deep pool, seeing events unfold in a blur while her lungs filled up with water.

'You all right there, Rachel?' Isaac asked. 'You look like you've seen a ghost.'

Jack was staring at the carpet, focusing on a very specific spot between his shoes.

'I . . . erm. Yes. Sorry. I think maybe my lunch hasn't agreed with me. I'll be fine, though. Carry on.'

'Cantina van?' Isaac asked, grimacing in sympathy. 'I'm sure I had a bad beef taco from there once.'

Rachel nodded, despite the fact that she'd been nowhere near the mobile Mexican takeaway since her experience with an enchilada several months ago.

She took a breath that she hoped no one noticed was shaky, then passed a hand over her forehead to tuck a stray lock of hair behind her ear. Her fingertips came away clammy.

'I was just saying this pitch is for Olivia Mason, the CEO. She's very clever but also incredibly controlling. I know you had to dig deep to come up with ideas that would deliver what Sir Humphrey wanted, given how little he was prepared to compromise on the day-to-day running of things. With Olivia, it's going to be the opposite: a matter of taking her ideas and presenting them back to her . . . Embellished, probably, but intact. She feels she knows what Lighthouse's new digital platform should look like,' he continued, 'and she won't take kindly to her ideas being second-guessed.'

Jack was nodding as though this were no problem, but Rachel's head snapped up in surprise. Annoyance briefly cut through the swell of alarm inside her. 'But this is a whole new website build, right? I'm sure Olivia's as smart as you say, but what qualifies her to come up with a complex plan that includes the site map, writing content, linking up their online and offline comms . . . ?'

Isaac tipped his head to one side and frowned. Rachel couldn't tell whether he was irritated with her for being difficult or if the notion that this might be a problem hadn't previously occurred to him.

He sighed. 'What I'm saying is, unless she's asking for something undeliverable or which will actually create problems for Lighthouse, I'd strongly advise avoiding any sort of confrontation. Give her what she wants and I'm confident we'll get this. *Then* we'll be in a whole new league when it comes to the clients we can approach.' Isaac's spherical face was suddenly sharper, hungrier. 'Big medical research charities, government-backed initiatives, organisations with influence overseas . . . We need this. I *want* this. So we have to get it right – by Olivia's standards, if not our own.'

Rachel tried to relax her forehead, knowing she needed to smooth away the line that had almost certainly appeared between her eyebrows. There was no point in arguing; she'd never known him so serious or resolute. This was obviously the side of Isaac that had seen him sail through Cambridge, co-found an agency before the age of forty and then engineer a deal to sell it for several million pounds just twelve years later.

'I know this isn't normally how we do things,' he went on, calmer now. 'But I think that with a bit of finessing, the plans Lighthouse have in mind will work just fine.

Your creative muscles can rest a little, Rachel, and we'll make sure they're put to better use on whatever we give you next.'

'We understand completely, Isaac,' Jack said, 'and I'm sure it's going to be a great project to work on.' He looked to Rachel for agreement, but she found herself unable to speak. Even if the client weren't some micromanaging megalomaniac, this was one of the last accounts she'd ever want to work on. She felt sick – as though she could pull an Oscar Evans-style spectacular at any second.

'Bless you, Rachel, you really do look ill,' Isaac said. 'Maybe get yourself home, get to bed. And don't come in tomorrow if you're still rough.'

When Jack's eyes met Rachel's, they were anxious. She wondered whether he was worried for her or simply concerned she'd muck up a massive work opportunity. Then an ugly thought seized her and wouldn't let go. She stared at him until he looked away.

'I have another meeting,' Isaac said, oblivious to the sudden tension in the air. He got to his feet and patted Rachel on the shoulder as he ambled out of the room. 'Feel better.'

She stood up too, faster than she'd meant to – as if she were going to fly at Jack and punch him.

'There are people waiting to come in,' he warned, pointing behind Rachel to the cluster of designers standing on the other side of the glass wall.

'Somewhere else, then,' she hissed. 'I need to talk to you. Now.'

Jack followed Rachel into the open-plan office, past the team who'd been waiting for their meeting to begin. He leaned against the glass wall with a searching look on his face, as if he wasn't quite sure where this was going. She wondered whether the expression was genuine, and the fire in her belly burned brighter.

She grabbed his forearm and yanked him upright, then pushed him forward by the small of his back, propelling him towards the doors on the opposite side of the room. He let her direct him, and beneath her rage she recognised the way her stomach flipped at the warmth in her palms – the kick of excitement that came with feeling body heat radiating from his torso and through his clothes. *Pathetic*.

Rachel bundled Jack through the building foyer. She shoved him past Frank the security guard, who stared as they went by – looking for a moment as though he was tempted to intervene on Jack's behalf, then obviously thinking better of it.

Once they were outside, Rachel dragged Jack round a corner and into the alley where an assortment of waste bins and recycling containers lived. It wasn't picturesque but it was fairly private, and it would have to do.

'Did you know about this? Did you *do* this?' she demanded, and he shrank back against a dumpster, shocked by the force of her fury.

'Do what?'

'Wheedle your way onto this account for the sake of the kudos, knowing you'd have to take me with you – knowing that I'd find it painful, and simply not caring?'

Jack's mouth dropped open, forming a perfect O in his annoyingly perfect face.

'Or was getting me involved part of the plan?' Rachel went on, her voice bitter and near breaking. 'Bring someone with personal experience on board – a sad little sister who's still secretly messed up. Get her to relive the worst days of her life, just to make sure every word on the new website for bereaved families *rings* with authenticity.'

Jack buried his face in his hands, then shoved them through his hair as he brought his head back up to look at her.

'Are you serious?' he asked.

'Serious as cancer,' she said, her face twisting and her eyes beginning to fill.

'Rach . . . Ryan. *Please.*'

Jack risked placing his hands on her shoulders, holding her still and staring into her eyes.

'Do I want to work on this project? Yes, now the opportunity is there. But Isaac decides who leads on accounts, not me. And your . . . your first-hand knowledge of charities like Lighthouse didn't even enter my head until I saw your face in there.'

'*That* I can believe. God knows you're not renowned for your sensitivity on the subject of my sister dying.'

He let his hands fall away from her and hid his face in them again, scrubbing at his eyes.

'The way I reacted when you told me about losing your sister was . . . terrible,' he said. 'Truly. But I couldn't understand how you'd kept it from me for three whole years. It was like you'd dropped a bomb – the prospect of meeting your parents was terrifying enough . . . and then you told me how much pressure was on you to make graduation special for them because your sister never got to do it. Because you lost her before she even *started* at uni. So I freaked out, got drunk and ruined everything. I gave in and slept with someone who'd been pestering me for months because I was angry, because I felt like you'd been lying to me – if only by omission.'

'I saw you the morning after, remember?' Rachel scoffed. 'You looked pretty happy being *pestered* from where I was standing – which was in a fucking *hedge*, by the way. And I lied, as you put it, to everyone at uni except Anna. You were only the second person in the world I chose to tell about the worst thing that's ever happened to me.'

Hot, angry tears made tracks down Rachel's face. She wiped them away, not bothering to try to preserve the integrity of her eye make-up.

'If I could take it all back and change it, I would,' Jack said. 'In a heartbeat.'

He reached for her hand and she tried to pull away, but his palm closed around her fingers like a vice. He refused to let go.

'I'm devastated that you still think so badly of me. I swear to you, I didn't engineer this. But I have to ask . . . If Isaac is oblivious to your family situation, I'm assuming nobody else here knows either?'

Rachel shook her head.

'Not even Greg?'

'No one. I mean, it's not something you bring up by the coffee machine, is it? "My sister died when I was fifteen, my parents were destroyed and nothing was ever the same again."'

She flipped her body 180 degrees so she was standing next to him, her back against the bin.

'It's not that I'm in denial,' she said, her voice cracking. 'It's not like I think refusing to talk about it means she'll reappear, like I'll wake up and find it was all a terrible dream. But I was almost *defined* by losing Lizzy from the second she was gone. At home I had to be careful, calm and sensible. The last thing my mum and dad needed was to worry about *me* going off the rails. At school people felt sorry for me, or uncomfortable around me, or they ignored me – *or* they insisted I must want to talk about it. I wasn't the ginger girl any more, I was the girl with the dead sister. And maybe this makes me an awful, selfish person, but I hated that. I didn't want to be that girl at uni. I didn't want to go back to being that person after graduation. And I don't want to be her now either.'

Jack nodded. 'I don't think that makes you selfish. And you could never be awful.'

Rachel sighed, feeling like she was slowly deflating. 'Maybe I should just tell Isaac I can't do this – explain that he'll need to break up his dream duo for this job.'

'He won't,' Jack said. He was still holding on to Rachel's hand. She realised that as her resistance to his grip had slackened, he'd laced his fingers through hers. 'We're a team,' he told her. 'If you feel like you can't work on Lighthouse, I completely understand – but I don't want to do it without you. If you want me to, I'll talk to Isaac and ask him to put us on something else.'

'You will?'

'Just say the word.'

'But . . . how would you justify that? What would you tell him?'

'Some version of the truth, probably,' Jack admitted. 'I think I'd have to. Awful as it is, I think the only way to avoid talking about your own loss is to do the project: focus on other people's situations instead.'

Rachel sighed again. She couldn't deny there was a certain logic to this.

'And what about you?' she asked. 'I mean, asking to switch assignments won't do you any favours in terms of your position here. This is a huge account and we both know you can bring it in – it would cement your celebrity status for good.'

Jack ignored her sarcasm. 'I'm good at what I do. There'll be plenty more chances for me to get this agency coveted, lucrative clients.'

Rachel pulled her hand out of his and crossed her arms. He was infuriatingly confident.

'On the other hand . . .' Jack said, '*if* we go ahead with Lighthouse, I'll be with you, supporting you – and I'll know the truth. And at least it sounds as if the content side of things won't require too much soul-searching. It seems pretty clear Olivia Mason already knows what's best when it comes to writing material for her new website.'

'True.'

Rachel stood up straighter and pulled her shoulders back a little. Jack was right: refusing to work on this account was guaranteed to raise questions about her past, not to mention her emotional stability. What kind of person was still *this* churned up about a bereavement – even a close one – after almost sixteen years? A loss they never breathed a word about, even to good friends? She decided to put those questions away for examination at some future, unspecified time.

Then there was the risk that she'd mark herself out as difficult or unprofessional by refusing to do the work she'd been given. All things considered, it might be better to put her head down and get on with this. It would be a difficult few weeks, but ploughing on was probably preferable to publicly dredging up past pain.

'Okay,' Rachel said, subdued but certain.

'Okay?'

'Yeah. I don't think I have much choice here, do I? Sticking with the account seems like the lesser of two evils.'

'It's going to be fine,' Jack said bracingly. 'And it'll be over within a few weeks, just like the BHGH pitch. Once we get this done, we'll be on to the next big thing – other people will be manning the account – and we never have to talk about any of this again if you don't want to.'

Rachel nodded. Jack reached for her hand again, squeezing it and then letting go as they turned to walk back into the building.

'Will you be all right?' he asked as she headed towards the ladies.

'I think so,' she said. 'And . . . I'm sorry I had a go at you before.'

She leaned on the door to the women's toilets and looked at the floor.

'Forget it,' Jack said before she could go in. 'But . . . do you think we could actually try being friends now? It seems like you might need one, and you never did give me a straight answer to that question.'

Rachel looked back at him, drained and weary, wondering how long it would take to fix her puffy, mascara-streaked face.

'I think you already know it,' she said, turning away from Jack as she entered the bathroom. 'You always bloody did.'

20

That evening Rachel arrived home from work to find Anna clattering around the kitchen in a tiny pink dress. It was brilliant cerise with a structured bodice, covered in a feather-light tulle that flared from her waist to fall in layer upon layer of soft, delicate waves.

On anyone else it would have been garish, but Anna's short hair and the black studded belt she was wearing offset its sugary sweetness. She had a pair of black strappy sandals on her feet, their heels so high that Rachel felt dizzy just looking at them.

She dropped her bags on the kitchen table and stared. 'If I'd thought you'd be this dressed up for dinner I'd have at least thrown on some lip gloss before I came home.'

'*Funny*,' Anna said, smiling. 'I'm out with Will tonight. It's our four-year anniversary, remember?'

'Ahhh. Yes, you did mention it. You look ace. But, er – what are you doing?'

Anna was still opening cupboards and drawers indiscriminately, picking up magazines, books and envelopes, then huffing and putting them back down again.

'Looking for my phone,' she said. '*Bloody* thing. I'm late. Will should be here any second.'

'I'll find it,' Rachel told her. 'You finish getting ready. You'll break your neck racing around in those shoes.'

Anna retreated to her bedroom, re-emerging a few minutes later wearing a tiny black leather jacket and carrying a clutch bag.

'Here,' Rachel said, handing over Anna's battered old iPhone. 'It was in the fruit bowl . . . ?'

Anna was known for putting her phone down in odd places, then blithely walking away. Rachel had been baffled but not surprised to find it nestled next to a bunch of browning bananas.

'Huh. Thanks,' said Anna. 'Are you sure I look okay?'

'Nope, not okay – stunning. Where are you off to?'

'I've no idea, but Will said to dress up – so I hope for his sake it isn't pizza and a pint at the pub.'

Rachel laughed. 'I'm sure it won't be. Will you be back tonight?'

'Yeah. An overnight bag doesn't really go with this outfit, and I have an early meeting tomorrow. The head wants to go over our plans for engaging Year 11 with extra revision sessions – plans that currently consist of "arrange a few tutorials, then hope the kids show up". Unless she's willing to offer cash incentives in exchange for attendance, I'm not sure what else she expects us to do.' Anna rolled her eyes.

'Ugh, don't think about it tonight. Have a brilliant time. I won't wait up.' Rachel winked.

'Thanks.' Anna gave her a quick, fierce hug just as the doorbell rang. 'See you later,' she called over her shoulder, shouting to make herself heard over the click-clacking of her heels on the hardwood floor.

Annoyed with herself for not remembering she'd have to

cook tonight, Rachel opened the fridge and began assessing her dinner options. They could best be described as limited.

In the end Rachel decided to go for a run on the well-lit roads of Stroud Green, then immediately offset the calories she'd burned with a takeaway. She had a halloumi and falafel feast Deliveroo'd to the flat and ate it flopped on the sofa, watching a comfortingly awful straight-to-Netflix film as she sipped her still lemonade. It was tart but just the right side of bitter, with fresh mint leaves swirling on its surface.

Sometime later she heard the scrape of a key in the flat door and heaved herself up into a sitting position. She realised she'd nodded off on the sofa, and the left side of her neck was tight and stiff. She kneaded it vigorously as she tried to acclimatise to being awake again.

Rachel looked at the clock on the stereo. 10.56 p.m. This was an early finish for a special dinner date, even by Anna's school-night standards. *Eek* ... She hoped nothing weird had happened.

Anna wandered into the sitting room and eyed what was left of Rachel's meal, still in an array of foil containers on the coffee table. 'Dude, you really need to learn how to cook.'

Rachel wrinkled her nose and shrugged. 'I forgot you were out tonight, so it was takeaway or a trip to Tesco. You're home early, though. Did you have a good night? Where did you go?'

'Le Gavroche,' Anna said, her eyes sparkling and her cheeks glowing so red they clashed with her dress. 'I've never been anywhere so posh. It was *amazing* ... I'm totally stuffed, though. Every time I thought I couldn't manage another bite, the waiter reappeared with something else smothered in cream.'

She sank down onto the couch cushion next to Rachel's, patting her stomach through the bright-pink corset that constricted it.

'Wow,' Rachel said, impressed. 'Definitely not your standard pub scran, then. Will must have been planning this for months – I think it's really hard to get a table there.'

Anna nodded, her face still scarlet. Her eyes were blazing and liquid; she had the sort of look people get on thrill rides at theme parks, or (Rachel assumed) when they're about to launch into a bungee jump or skydive. It was an expression that bridged the gap between excitement and fear. Rachel also noticed that Anna was squeezing her left hand with her right, her knuckles turning white under the pressure.

'Anna . . . is something wrong?'

'No, no, no, nothing's *wrong*,' she said, oddly shrill. She looked down at her hands. 'Everything's fine. Wonderful, even. But there is something I need to tell you. Something important.'

'Okaaaaay?'

Rachel stretched out the second syllable of the word, intending for it to sound playful and puzzled – trying to undercut Anna's deep-and-meaningful tone. Even as she heard herself say it, something inside her sank. Anna was serious; something important had happened, and no amount of arsing around could make light of it.

Add it up, Rachel told herself. *You don't need a PhD in maths to work this out.*

Anna and Will had been together for longer than Rachel could imagine being with anyone. They adored one another, utterly and unambiguously. And he'd taken her to a Michelin-starred restaurant for their anniversary . . .

'You guys have decided to move in together,' Rachel said. It wasn't a question. She didn't need to ask.

Inside her own head, Rachel's voice sounded flat and colourless. She was going to have to do better than this. She couldn't make Anna feel bad for moving on with her life, regardless of what that meant for her personally.

Anna made a face that Rachel couldn't read. She rubbed her temples, and as she lifted her left arm Rachel caught a flash of something shiny and substantial. Something adorning her left hand.

'Oh my God . . .' Rachel said. 'Will *proposed*? He's asked you to *marry him*?!'

She prayed that Anna would mistake her shock for excitement.

'He did! I just can't believe it . . . It was a total surprise. Honestly . . . I didn't know he had it in him!'

Anna was doing her best not to gush, and failing – though Rachel didn't blame her. She caught her best friend's fingers and stilled her animated gesturing so she could study the ring up close. It was lovely: a large, clear diamond cut in a square and set on a fine band that Rachel guessed was probably platinum. It was solid and unfussy – elegant and beautiful, but somehow strong in its simplicity. Perfectly, unmistakably Anna.

Rachel's eyes were full of tears that she knew wouldn't be contained, and as they began to fall she smiled and laughed. It was important that they seem like tears of unqualified joy, rather than the happy/sad cocktail she was actually feeling.

'It's gorgeous,' Rachel said, gently bending Anna's fingers so her engagement ring sparkled in the dim light of the sitting room's Liberty-print standard lamp. She pulled her into a tight hug, resting her tear-streaked face on Anna's shoulder. 'I'm totally thrilled for you both.'

This was true, but Rachel also felt like she was falling – as though she'd stepped off a cliff edge and was loose in the air, flailing out of control and hurtling towards the ground. At some point, she knew, she'd crash into it.

'You'll be my maid of honour?' Anna asked, pulling away to look Rachel in the eye. 'I promise I won't make you wear anything awful or force you to help make papier mâché place settings.'

'Of course I will. And of course you won't.' Rachel smiled, gripping the edge of the sofa and, inside her pyjamas, clenching her stomach muscles to try to halt the churning of her falafel-filled belly. 'Now . . . Shall we celebrate your big news with a cup of tea and a biscuit before bed?'

'Yes, please,' Anna said, 'but hold the Hobnobs . . . After tonight I may never eat again.'

21

By Friday evening, Rachel was utterly drained.

She'd spent almost her whole working week smothering the grief that threatened to seize her each time bereaved brothers and sisters were mentioned. The effort was exhausting.

Olivia Mason had sent over a folder full of research findings, plus her preferred list of articles for the new Lighthouse website – guides to the thoughts and feelings that cancer patients' families might have, plus advice on how to handle their emotions.

In spite of Isaac's warnings, Rachel had dug through the data and added several subjects to the roll – important things she felt Olivia had missed, but which she knew might matter to the people who applied for the charity's help.

Outside the office, it was taking every ounce of Rachel's remaining energy to appear happy and excited for Anna and Will. She *was*, of course, but she was also anxious and sad. Anna and Will were planning to get married over the August bank holiday weekend on his grandfather's estate in Gloucestershire. For all their urging that she didn't need to rush, Rachel intended to be out of the flat by then – she just had no idea where she'd go.

At 6.15 p.m. Rachel trudged to the ladies to change her top, apply a little perfume and touch up her make-up.

Tonight was the night of Zack Lanson's gig, and she was meeting Tom at Highgate Tube at seven.

'Nice top,' Jack said when she reappeared. He pointed at the forest-green wrap Rachel had put on with her indigo skinnies.

It *was* a nice top – a Marilyn Monroe-style shirt made of soft matte silk that crossed in a deep V over her chest and then tied at the side, pulling her in at the waist. She'd chosen it deliberately; she always felt good in it, and it was foxy without being too obvious.

'Thanks.' Rachel nodded. 'It's one of my favourites.' She checked her emails one last time and then shut the lid of her laptop, leaning down to place it in the lockable cupboard beneath her desk so she didn't have to lug it with her to the gig.

'You off somewhere nice this evening? Out with your man, I suppose?' Jack asked as she turned the key in the door. Rachel deliberately waited a few seconds before standing up to reply.

'Just to a music thing,' she said. 'I've no idea whether the guy playing will be any good, though – the tickets were freebies through work.'

'*His* work, presumably?'

Rachel noted Jack's refusal to ask her (pretend) boyfriend's name.

'Yeah.'

'And what does he do?'

Rachel paused. This was starting to feel a little treacherous. It was one thing to delight in Jack's misunderstanding of her relationship status, but quite another to start embroidering his mistake with half-truths and contorted facts. Her Valentine's Day flowers had been from Laurence, and tonight she was out with Tom – two different men that, with no plan or forethought, she was now melding into a single fake partner.

'He's a graphic designer with a sideline in photography,' Rachel said, deciding without difficulty that this sounded far cooler than 'pensions actuary'.

Jack nodded, his eyes narrowing in annoyance. He sat up straighter, as though he were about to ask another question.

No, no, no, Rachel thought. She'd never been a good liar, and the more detailed her fantasy love life became the more likely she was to trip herself up, tangled in the web of her own fibs.

She looked at her watch. 'I'd better get going. I'm meeting him at seven.'

'Right. Have fun, then,' Jack said.

He looked back at his computer screen, but Rachel observed with some satisfaction that he kept half an eye on her as she walked towards the door. She pretended not to notice, letting it swing shut with a bang.

When Rachel reached ground level at Highgate she was hot and bothered, her coat stuffed under her arm and her cheeks rosy from the stifling warmth of the Underground. Tom was standing by the exit, looking as cool and calm as always. He was wearing jeans and a navy down jacket, unzipped to reveal the soft cable knit underneath.

'Hey!' he said, smiling wide when he saw her.

'Hey yourself.' She smiled back. 'You've not been here too long, have you?'

'Nah.' Tom shook his head. 'We'd better get going, though, if we want to make it to the bar before Zack comes out. I have a feeling drinks might prove a necessity this evening, assuming you haven't brought earplugs.'

Rachel slapped his arm as they fell into step and began walking up the street. 'O ye of little faith,' she said, and he laughed.

Within a few minutes they'd reached the venue for the gig: an arts centre in a vast Victorian villa. There was a crowd of young people outside, mostly girls in skimpy outfits but also the odd boy in spray-on jeans and designer trainers. Several were waving banners sporting slogans such as *MARRY ME ZACK!*, *I want ur babies* and *luv u + ur plain white tee*.

'*Wow*,' Rachel said as she and Tom headed up the steps to the entrance. 'We've found the right place, then.'

They queued for the bar, bought two bottles of beer and then found their way to their seats. Zack was performing in the theatre space, and on stage a single spotlight illuminated the three-legged stool that was waiting for him.

Rachel cringed. With no other musicians or backing singers in sight, Zack's vocals and guitar skills would be totally exposed. If he was good the effect could be intimate; magical, even. But if he wasn't . . .

The lights in the room went out and a hush fell upon the audience. The on-stage spotlight gradually brightened to reveal Zack, perched on the stool and casting delicate shadows as he gently picked at his Gibson guitar strings.

Yes, he was wearing a trilby hat indoors, and his sheer white shirt was unbuttoned almost to his navel, displaying a triangle of shiny, tanned flesh. But he wasn't a bad player, Rachel decided. Maybe Tom would have to eat his words . . .

I met a girl and I asked for her naaaaame,
Knew straightaway my life would never be the saaaaame . . .

His voice wasn't *terrible*, Rachel thought . . .
We sat under a tree and we shared a can of Fanta,
And then she binned me off, like I didn't even maaaaatter . . .

. . . but holy mother of God, his lyrics were appalling. Rachel felt Tom's shoulders shaking and swallowed a giggle. She didn't dare look at his face – that would finish her. She elbowed him as Zack continued to warble.

How could a girl so hot, with those gorgeous angel eyes,
Turn out to be a heartless bitch, her body cold as ice . . .

Tom snorted and Rachel tittered. She sipped from her beer bottle and tried not to focus on the words of the song. This was increasingly difficult as Zack grew in confidence, his voice soaring higher and louder above his strumming.

*Of course it's no big secret that we had amazing sex
But then you went and left me, and my heart was
ripped and wrecked . . .*

'Did he just rhyme *sex* with *wrecked*?' Tom whispered. Rachel doubled over, silent-laughing so hard she thought she might pass out.

She took some deep breaths and drank some more beer, and Tom did the same. By the time the song neared its end they were clutching one another helplessly. Just as Rachel thought she'd composed herself, Zack's voice swelled again. Wailing and woeful, he belted out what he clearly believed were the final killer lines of his opening ballad:

*I wish I'd known back then what I know for sure
right now,
Underneath the Gucci, you're a TOTAL FUCKING
COW.*

Tom was wiping tears from his eyes when he and Rachel finally looked at one another. Rachel was certain the eyeliner she'd so recently perfected was now trickling down her cheeks in black rivulets. They clapped along with the rest of the audience, most of whom were at least ten years younger than them and none of whom appeared in any way perturbed by Zack's dubious songwriting.

'Have we died and gone to hell, do you think?' Tom asked, his voice low. 'What have we done to deserve another *hour* of this?'

'You're kidding; this is the best fun I've had in ages,'

Rachel laughed under her breath. 'If I was in hell, I'd still be at work.'

Tom raised his eyebrows, but before Rachel could say anything else the noise in the theatre petered out and Zack spoke into the microphone.

'Thanks. Thanks for being here at my debut gig, where I'll be sharing some of the songs I've written since finding fame. That was "Glacier Girl", about a woman who really hurt me. This next one means a lot to me too – it's called "Stiletto Heel On My Heart".'

Tom bit his bottom lip and Rachel felt her eyes widen. Zack plucked the Hummingbird's strings again, filling the theatre with a sweet and tender melody, which he proceeded to bury beneath an avalanche of inane lyrics.

By the time Zack began his final song – 'Tinder Tragedy' – Rachel and Tom had their giggles under control, despite having drunk several more beers each. Once Zack had taken his bow and they'd made their way out of the arts centre, Tom threw a wry smile at Rachel and said, 'I hate to say I told you so.'

'Oh, fine,' she laughed. 'You were right. He's less Neil Young, more Neil from your Year 9 English class. Bless him, though, he can play, his voice is pretty good . . . and I do love a man who can sing. He just needs some new lyrics.'

'I don't know. I think the real low point was when Nate came out and started banging that tambourine during "Beam Me Up, Hottie".'

'Oh *God*,' Rachel guffawed. 'Poor Zack. He really

thinks he's going to make it as a singer-songwriter, doesn't he?'

Tom shrugged, his eyes sparkling. 'He probably *will* – and fair play to him if he does. He's not doing anyone any harm singing songs about shoes, soft drinks and sexy aliens, is he?'

'STOP!' Rachel giggled, as they both beamed.

'D'you fancy another drink?'

'Sure,' Rachel said. 'Where to?'

'There's a pub that does the most amazing hot wings up that hill, if you're game for the walk?'

'Oooooh, yes,' she agreed. 'I haven't had anything since lunch. I could definitely eat some chicken.'

When they made it to the pub, Rachel insisted that Tom find a table while she paid for their drinks and snacks. Once she had two pints, a pot of nuts and a wooden spoon with their food order number, she began roaming the room in search of him.

She spotted him in a corner, seated at a tiny table with a tall, skinny blonde girl standing over him. The girl had her hand on the table, just millimetres from his. What was going on?

Tom saw Rachel coming and waved, and the blonde girl retreated – soon swallowed up by the mass of bodies gathered around a huge table near the window.

'Am I interrupting something? Salting your game?' Rachel asked, intending to sound impish but coming off annoyed.

'Nooooo,' Tom said, shuddering slightly.

'She *was* coming on to you, though,' Rachel said. 'And I only left you alone for five minutes!'

She told herself she shouldn't be surprised by someone approaching Tom while he was alone in a bar; he was a good-looking guy with (as Rachel had discovered) a surprisingly muscular stomach. It still felt weird watching some stranger sidling up to him, though.

'Seriously, she's not my type at all,' Tom muttered, his face colouring. 'And on the subject of types, I want to hear more about your enjoyment of men who can sing. Sensitive muso is a bit of an obvious kink for a writer, don't you think?' He wiggled his eyebrows dramatically.

Rachel poked him. 'Whatevs. It's not like I've ever actually dated someone who fits that description. I mean, can you imagine *Laurence* singing?'

Tom laughed, scooping several pistachios out of the bowl between them, then freeing the nuts from their shells. 'Maybe a funeral dirge, or some sort of fascist marching song.'

'Haha!' Rachel laughed, shaking her head and grimacing. 'God, what was I *thinking* going out with him?'

'I did try and tell you he was awful,' Tom said, arching one dark-blonde eyebrow. Then his eyes clouded over and his mouth turned down a little. 'But . . . if you want the truth, I think you thought he was solid. Safe. That he wouldn't inspire any feelings you couldn't control.'

'Thomas Evans, you're *insightful* when you've had a few beers. Annoyingly insightful. But in any case, it turns out I was wrong about not feeling anything intense for Laurence. I feel *very* intensely that I'd like to kick him in the nads next time I see him.'

'Agreed.' Tom nodded. 'While we're talking about hard-to-control feelings . . . how are you getting on at work? With the ex hanging around, I mean?'

'Work is . . . well . . . hideous,' Rachel sighed. 'I'm stuck on a pitch for a bereavement charity that specialises in helping families who've lost a child. It's all a bit close to home, and nobody at work knows about Lizzy. I've never talked about it to anyone there, not even Greg.'

Tom winced. '*Jack* knows, though, I assume?'

He said the name with a pinched look on his face, as though it tasted bad.

'Yeah.' Rachel nodded. 'He's . . . sort of helping me get through it.'

Tom's mouth went flat – his lips pressed together so tightly they almost disappeared. 'I thought you said the two of you weren't buddies – that you were merely tolerating him for the sake of looking professional. This sounds like more than that to me.'

Rachel rested her chin on a balled-up fist. 'It's . . . complicated,' she said, as a young waiter carrying a huge basket of sauce-smothered chicken wings emerged from the throng of drinkers opposite their table.

'Enjoy!' he said, setting it down before scurrying back to the bar.

'What did Anna say when you told her about the pitch?' Tom asked.

Ugh. Why couldn't the man just eat some food instead of throwing out more questions?

He tried again, his eyes level with Rachel's, insisting

on an answer. 'What did Anna make of the fact you're keeping the truth from the rest of your colleagues?'

Defiantly, Rachel chewed on a spicy wing, then took a sip of ice-cold beer to soothe the burn. 'I didn't tell her about it,' she admitted eventually. 'Any of it.'

'What? Why?'

'I was assigned the project on the same day she and Will got engaged. There was no way I could steal her thunder – ruin one of the happiest moments of her life by bringing up my dead sister.'

Tom shut his eyes, as if in pain. '*Fuck*.'

'Yeah. And now she's so thrilled all the time – even when she isn't talking about the wedding I know she's *thinking* about it. I keep catching her staring at her ring, wiggling her fingers so it catches the light. There's never going to be a good time to raise this. Jack reckons that, once we get the account, we'll be moved on again,' she continued. 'He says that within a few weeks all this will be done, at which point I can stop thinking about the past. I think he's right.'

Tom's eyebrows met above the bridge of his nose, which he was also pinching.

'Well. As long as *Jack* thinks this all makes sense.'

'Hey,' Rachel said. 'Don't be like that. It *does* make sense. This way I don't have to worry Anna – and I don't have to explain to a load of people that I'm not actually an only child, I'm a bereaved one.'

'I'm sure it suits Jack perfectly that he's the only one in your office who knows about Lizzy,' Tom said bitterly. His grey-blue eyes were flashing in a way Rachel had never seen before. 'I've no doubt he's very pleased to be comforting you through every difficult moment on this project – happy he's the only one you can confide in. And I'm absolutely sure I know *why*, even if you can't see it.'

'What do you mean?' Rachel asked, irked by the implication that she was naive.

'I mean I hope you're reading him right,' Tom said. 'I hope you're sure he's acting for your benefit. I hope you understand what's *motivating* him. He strikes me as someone who's excellent at turning any situation to his advantage – using it to further an agenda best known only to himself.'

'You've never even met him!' Rachel cried. 'And I'm not an idiot – I know how he operates. I'm not going to fall for him a second time.'

She'd meant to say 'fall for *it* a second time'. She paled as she realised her mistake.

'Hmm,' Tom mumbled, averting his gaze and smashing a pistachio shell into tiny shards. 'Sounds like you have it all in hand.'

Rachel snapped a chicken bone in two and threw it aside. She stared at him miserably.

'I don't think we should talk about this any more,' she said. 'But please – trust me when I say that I'm keeping a safe distance between myself and Jack. Nothing's happening.'

Tom rubbed his eyes, suddenly looking tired, then tugged on a thick wave of hair as if he were trying to yank some unpleasant thought from his brain. 'You don't need to justify yourself to me, Rachel. You're my friend, I care about you and I'd hate to see you hurt – but let's be honest, it's none of my business who you date.'

He sounded stoical, almost cold, and for some reason his words felt like a punch in the stomach.

'No, I guess it's not,' she said, her voice small and sorry for itself. 'This is depressing. I don't want to fight. We need to talk about something else.'

She munched on another chicken wing, trying to work out what to say.

'If you were a Zack Lanson song, which one would you be?' she finally asked, and Tom's lips twitched – the corners tilting up far enough that she knew they'd soon be okay again.

'Tough one,' he said a moment later, 'but maybe "Hold My Hand, Crush My Heart". Either that or "What Do You See in Him"?'

Rachel laughed, ignoring the barb – allowing him the final word because he was funny.

'I'm definitely "False Filter",' Rachel said. 'How could I not love a song about the evils of Instagram?'

They both laughed, easy with one another again.

'How are things with Oscar, by the way?' Rachel asked after they'd finished their food.

'Not too bad,' Tom said. 'As predicted, he was in deep with Christine after Snakebitegate – but she saw sense once she finished accusing me of leading him astray . . . Realised that it was actually pretty lucky we were around to help him.'

'Too bloody right,' Rachel agreed.

Much later, lying awake in bed, Rachel wondered how a fun evening's banter had descended into something that felt perilously close to a row – an argument she couldn't help worrying she and Tom had put off temporarily, rather than properly concluded.

She also asked herself how she'd ended up defending one man she should hate to another whose judgement she'd always trusted . . . Someone who'd never been anything but a strong, supportive friend to her – even if his honesty was occasionally tough to take.

Tom would never like nor trust Jack; that much was clear. Meanwhile, Jack certainly wasn't keen on the version of Tom he'd imagined as Rachel's boyfriend. She thanked her lucky stars that, despite the numerous ways it had already screwed her this year, the universe hadn't seen fit to put the two of them in a room together.

April

~~New Year's~~ Ongoing resolutions

1. Consider exercise an act with actual benefits – both mental and physical – not merely grim punishment for pizzas consumed. ~~Have a proper go at~~ Continue letting Greg drag me to yoga, provided he refrains from making snide comments re Jack/me and Jack.
2. ~~Also re-download Complete Couch to 5K running app and actually do the programme.~~ Keep running at least twice per week – *always* being careful not to perv on anyone improper.
3. ~~Apply for promotion at work at first chance. Move to bigger account and try to get pay rise. Avoid, if possible, further projects concerning dog biscuits, disinfectant, high-quality printer ink cartridges, 'miracle' grass seed, organic vegetables, etc.~~
    3a. Try to hang on to job (and temper) despite ~~presence of evil ex-boyfriend hideousness~~ control-freakery of certain clients.

3b. Ignore everyone who keeps banging on about how fit ~~he~~ Jack is.

3c. Ignore how fit he is.

3d. Ignore the fact he keeps trying to be friendly/nice/~~possibly quite~~ flirtatious.

3e. Ignore the fact he is getting divorced.

~~4. DO NOT agree to further dates with Laurence. Remember: it's no use having a boyfriend who is good on paper if you do not actually fancy him.~~

4. Forget that Laurence even EXISTS (despite usefulness of overblown 'romantic' gestures for creating illusion of deeply devoted boyfriend. Try not to spin any more tales re 'boyfriend', though – don't want story to get too complicated . . .).

5. Try to remember Mum means well, even during phone calls where she ~~implies I am doomed to a lonely life of penury because I am thirty with no partner, hardly any savings and no mortgage~~ insists on talking about the babies/breasts of people I went to school with.

6. HOWEVER, do not (!!!) speak to Mum when suffering PMT. Set phone alerts for likely spells based on period tracker intel.

7. Try to address 'hardly any savings' situation. ~~(If promoted, set aside extra earnings for future house deposit instead of spaffing it all on ASOS.)~~ (Do not spend entire pay rise on ~~'cheer up' treats to distract from heinous ex-boyfriend mess.)~~ hot new outfits for work – see 3c.)

8. Try to eat my five-a-day. (Remember horrid rule that potatoes do not count.)
9. Start using proper night cream with retinol. SERIOUSLY.
10. Do the best possible job helping Tom with exhibition. Be supportive and discreet re Oscar. Avoid arguing with Tom about Jack.
11. Be a good friend (and bridesmaid) to Anna. Help with wedding organisation and keep selfish, sad worries about how much I'll miss her to myself.

22

Olivia Mason was almost half an hour early for the Lighthouse UK pitch meeting. It was 9.48 a.m. on the first Tuesday in April and she wasn't due until 10.15 – but she was already sitting in one of the armchairs next to Donna's desk, her hands folded neatly in her lap as she looked around the room.

'*Damn*,' Jack said. 'I bet she's done this deliberately. I hate being caught on the hop. I'll go and get the laptop set up in the meeting room. You go and chat her up for a few minutes while I sort it.'

'*Me?* You want *me* to go over there and talk to her?'

He looked at her like she was an idiot. 'Yes, Rachel. Isaac's on a call, so one of us has to go and pretend it's absolutely fine that Olivia's turned up way ahead of schedule. This is a *test*. It's an attempt to see how easy we are to fluster, how ready we are to jump to it and present her with our plans.'

She gaped at him, still not understanding.

Jack sighed. 'Whoever isn't cosying up to her and making coffee needs to handle the technical stuff: getting the right cables into the correct sockets so our presentation displays properly on the big screen . . . And while I'm generally better at both cosying *and* computers, even a man of my talents can't be in two places at once. You're challenged by anything electronic, Ryan, so I'm afraid it falls to you to be winsome and witty with the client for a few minutes. I know you can do it.'

He nodded his head in Olivia's direction as if to say: *Off you go, then.*

Rachel huffed at him, decided that introducing herself to Olivia was probably the lesser of two evils, then turned on her heel and marched away.

She wasn't looking forward to meeting Olivia or talking to her for an hour about bereaved families, and the sight of the woman herself did nothing to quell Rachel's nerves. The Lighthouse UK CEO was dressed in a mint-green skirt suit – the kind that Rachel remembered her school headmistress wearing in the late 1990s. Beneath it was a crisp white cotton shirt, buttoned all the way up to her pointed chin. She had salt-and-pepper hair cut in a sharp bob that fell just to her jawline – a strong, defined slope that put Rachel in mind of someone she'd met before. She had no idea who.

Olivia wasn't unattractive, but she looked as though she gave no consideration whatsoever to whether she looked nice – as if such musings might be beneath her. Her aim, Rachel guessed, was to appear tidy – competent and respectable rather than appealing. If she hadn't been so thrown by Olivia's general air of austerity, Rachel would have liked that about her.

Her thin lips didn't so much as twitch at Rachel's approach. *God*, this was going to be painful . . .

'Hi, Olivia – thank you for coming to us this morning. It's lovely to meet you,' Rachel said. Somehow it all came out sounding like a question: as if she wasn't sure who Olivia was, let alone whether she was happy to be making her acquaintance.

'Likewise,' Olivia said, her voice clipped and her mouth jerking almost imperceptibly in what Rachel assumed must pass for a smile.

Olivia extended a hand for Rachel to shake – cool, slender fingers with a sandpapery palm.

'Can I get you anything to drink?' Rachel asked her. 'Tea? Coffee? Water?'

'Nothing, thank you,' Olivia replied, settling back into her armchair again. Rachel perched on the neighbouring seat, oppressed by the silence Olivia seemed determined to maintain.

'Have you had far to come this morning?' *Ugh – fail.*

'No.'

Rachel suppressed a sigh. She should have tried an open-ended question.

They sat side by side for minutes that seemed to stretch into months. Rachel kept looking over towards the meeting room, shuffling in her seat to try to work out whether Jack was ready for them. What the hell was taking so long?

Then he was striding across the room, his face bright and confident, smiling so warmly at Olivia that Rachel felt sure her chilly veneer would melt.

'Olivia! I'm so sorry we've kept you waiting,' Jack said, as if it was their fault and not hers that she'd been twiddling her thumbs for twenty minutes. He was great at this, Rachel thought, for about the thousandth time since January. If she hadn't already known that Jack was annoyed by

Olivia's early arrival, she'd definitely have believed his apology was sincere.

Olivia stood up and shook his hand, as she had done Rachel's, and gave him the same anaemic smile. 'Jack. Nice to see you.'

'Let me show you to the meeting room,' Jack said. 'Rachel, would you mind giving Isaac the nod that we're about to begin? And perhaps letting Greg know? I'm sure that as our overall head of client services he'd like to meet you, Olivia – though of course it would be me or someone else here on the pro-social side of the business handling your account, should we be so lucky.'

Rachel didn't appreciate being sent off on this errand. Jack wasn't her boss; he didn't tell her what to do. She glared at him but did as he'd asked for the sake of appearances, watching him lead Olivia in the opposite direction. As she loitered by Isaac's desk, she noticed Jack and Olivia were suddenly chatting quite comfortably. 'How the bloody hell did he manage *that*?' she muttered.

Isaac was beside her before she could make sense of it, waving his arms at Greg as they headed towards the meeting room. Greg rolled his eyes in understanding at the situation and started walking over.

'Sorry, what was that, Rachel?' Isaac asked, turning his face a little.

'Nothing,' she said. 'Let's get in there and get this done.'

While Olivia's face betrayed no reaction during Rachel and Jack's presentation, the Lighthouse UK pitch went well. Rachel felt like she was an actress playing the part of a disinterested professional: someone who was capable of treating this as just another project, rather than a woman with first-hand experience of losing a family member too young.

She knew the stage choreography – which chair she should sit in to make sure co-presenting with Jack went seamlessly. She arranged her face just so, softening her mouth and eyes so she looked calm and obliging.

Rachel knew her lines, and how she needed to say them in order to convince Olivia that R/C could deliver her vision for the new Lighthouse website, enhancing the platform she'd imagined without deviating too far from her ideas.

In a way, Rachel realised, this was really nothing new. She'd been pretending for years that she wasn't exactly the kind of person Lighthouse sought to help – lying by omission whenever she was asked if she had any brothers and sisters.

It wasn't exactly untruthful to say no, was it? And it was easier – *so much* easier – not to open the door in her head that led to Lizzy. Better not to think about the things she'd felt, done and said during her sister's long illness, and the nagging sense that she'd got so many things wrong. Better not to dwell on the knowledge that she'd never be able to fix it all now.

Olivia struck out the extra editorial ideas Rachel had included in the content plan – literally put lines through them on the paper copy of the presentation that lay on the table in front of her. She might not know it, Rachel thought, but she was crossing out people's pain; scribbling over their messiest, least convenient emotions as if she didn't believe they were real. As if they didn't *matter*. Frustration flared in Rachel's chest – a flame threatening to lick up her throat and out of her mouth.

Rachel knew the advice guides she'd suggested would have been useful – vital reading, even – for some of the people Lighthouse was supposed to support. What was more, the charity's own research confirmed the need for them. Rachel wanted to snatch Olivia's Montblanc pen out of her thin, parched fingers; to stop its progress across the printout she was carelessly defacing.

At the very least Rachel wanted to argue – but she was afraid to make a scene. Somehow Olivia's coolness guaranteed that gainsaying her would seem dramatic. Rachel would look like she was ranting even if she stuck to discussing the data and kept her personal feelings locked up. She sealed her lips, pressing them into a tight, straight line.

Jack didn't react at all to Olivia's brusque dismissal of the points Rachel had tacked on to the strategy. He'd told her when they test-ran the pitch that he didn't expect they'd make it onto the final site map – so she shouldn't have been surprised that he didn't defend them. He caught Rachel's eye and nodded his head at her, so slightly that nobody else would notice. It wasn't an *I told you so* look – more an acknowledgement that she'd tried, and commiseration that she'd failed. A gesture that meant *Now we move on*.

Isaac and Greg congratulated the two of them on a job well done after Olivia had left. Greg hadn't stuck around for the whole meeting, and joked that as an Aussie he couldn't cope with the sub-zero temperature in the room. 'You didn't need me,' he said, 'and that woman is *cold*. It's like she has her own personal weather system: if I'd stuck around for the whole hour I'd have needed two weeks on Bondi Beach just to warm back up.'

Olivia had said she'd be in touch once she'd made a final decision on which agency to instruct. Isaac and Jack were confident, but Rachel mostly felt indifferent – relieved that the pitch was done and glad that, even if it went their way, her part in the Lighthouse project was now over.

'Lunch?' Jack said as Isaac walked away from them, already on his phone.

'It's only half past eleven,' Rachel answered. 'Bit early, isn't it?'

'Not if you're hungry. Which, as you know, I always am.'

This was true. Jack could eat for England, yet stayed slender – almost skinny – in the way top fashion designers seemed to like. He wasn't *manly* at all, when Rachel thought about it: not solid or muscular or outlandishly tall – particularly in comparison with Will or Tom. Jack's appeal was in how he held himself: how he moved and dressed. And in his face, which was all eyes and cheekbones and perfectly proportioned lips.

'Come on, Ryan,' he said. 'Let me take you out to brunch, if that's what you'd prefer to call it. Let's go back to that charming place with the eighties decor and heart attack sandwiches. You did well with Olivia this morning, and I know it was hard. Allow me to buy you a mug of builder's tea in celebration.'

'Fine,' Rachel said, knowing it was a bad idea but powerless to resist the promise of a crispy, ketchup-smothered bacon butty. 'I'll get my coat.'

By the end of the afternoon, the tight ball of anxiety that had been sitting in Rachel's stomach had begun to unwind. Brunch with Jack had been good fun. *Too much* fun. They'd talked about work but also books, politics, films they'd seen and people they'd known at university. Trying to keep her distance from him felt more and more like swimming upstream: exhausting, and ultimately pointless. Being swept away in some manner was probably inevitable, she knew; the only question now was whether or not she'd drown.

He'd asked about her faux beau again: How had they met? How long had they been together? Panicked, Rachel had mumbled that they started out as friends four years ago, only becoming something else more recently. She felt strange and uneasy about misrepresenting her relationship with Tom – because it was him, now, that she thought of when Jack tried to wheedle information out of her. Tom wouldn't like being drawn into a lie, and she couldn't bear to think of him finding out she'd been fibbing about what they were to each other. The very idea made her toes curl up inside her boots.

At around 4.30 Jack announced he was going to Pret to pick up a proper coffee. 'Want me to bring you one back?'

'Oh, yes – that would be great. Cappuccino?'

'Done.'

He shrugged his jacket on and wandered away as Rachel

heard her laptop chime, announcing the arrival of new emails.

Several messages had downloaded to her inbox – a few CCs on projects she was consulting on, an all-staff message from Donna that Rachel suspected would be a (justified) rant about the state of the communal fridges . . . But there was also an email from Isaac, with the subject line *Lighthouse – we did it!*

She didn't open it. Her attention had been caught by a message from Laurence.Myles@clarencefairbankfutures.com.

No, no, NO. What could he want *now*?

Rachel dragged the message to her trash folder without opening it. She crossed her arms over her chest.

It was a long while since she'd heard from Laurence. Maybe he'd simmered down and realised what an arsehole he'd been. Perhaps he was sorry. Maybe this was an apology email . . . In which case, it wouldn't hurt her to read it.

Rachel opened the trash folder and then the message, which was simply titled *Hi*.

Her jaw dropped. This was *not* an apology email – in fact it was the furthest thing from an apology email Rachel could imagine.

This was a gloating missive about some new woman Laurence was seeing; a smug announcement that Rachel had missed her chance with him, as he'd predicted that night in the wine bar.

Given that the email made clear he'd only been seeing his new girlfriend for a few weeks, Rachel couldn't help feeling Laurence's tone might be prematurely triumphant.

> Last time we met I told you I wouldn't be on the market for long – so in the interest of being straight with you, as of halfway through last month I am taken. Cassandra is *amazing*. She's an accountant at one of our sister firms – super-bright, well educated and successful. Gorgeous too: tall and blonde . . . My usual type. You were a bit of an anomaly, to be honest.

An *anomaly*?! Rachel let out an angry breath. What an *uber*-twat this man was. How had she ever let him anywhere near her?

She read on.

> Cass seems like she might be the jealous sort, so I'm telling you this in order to avoid any incidents. My suspicion is she won't take kindly to competition, so don't be tempted to call or text me. Cass and I are spending a lot of time together, and she'd almost certainly find out if you started sniffing around.

This was too much. Rachel hadn't initiated any contact with Laurence since *December*. The man was delusional. And the phrase 'sniffing around' made her so mad she could punch her laptop screen.

Laurence's parting shot was as inflammatory as the rest of his message:

> In spite of how badly you hurt me, I wish you a happy future. I hope you won't be lonely for too long.
> Rgds, L.

Rachel had to hand it to him: Laurence took passive aggression to a brand-new low. This email could probably be studied by psychology students; it was a masterclass in how to be highly offensive while claiming to *be* offended. It was the literary equivalent of stabbing someone in the back and then complaining that their blood had stained your knife. It was unbelievable.

Rachel clicked *Reply*. She was raging, and she wanted to have her say – not least because (as if to conclusively prove his idiocy) he had abbreviated the word *regards*. What a *tosser*.

'Laurence,' she wrote.

I don't know what you've been smoking but it has clearly caused hallucinations. You appear to believe I'm desperate to go out with you, when in actual fact I finished with you LAST YEAR because <u>I didn't want to see you any more</u>. Given your new lady friend is apparently a possessive psycho, perhaps it's *you* who should stop contacting *me*.
Rachel.

Her finger hovered over her mouse, which was positioned right next to the *Send* button.

God, it was tempting to click it. But what would that really achieve? Rachel took a deep breath and drew her hand back towards the edge of her desk. She knew that even acknowledging receipt of this email would, in Laurence's mind, reopen their dialogue; it might make things worse rather than better. Laurence was certainly arrogant enough to convince himself that any response to his diatribe must imply she still cared – even a response that pointed out he was demented and demanded he never bother her again.

She deleted what she'd written, watching every word disappear from the screen with faint disappointment. Then she moved Laurence's email to her junk folder, put her head in her hands and took a few yoga-style breaths to try to calm down. She was livid, but she knew she'd done the right thing.

'Are you all right there? Have you seen Isaac's email?'

Jack put a takeaway cappuccino down next to Rachel's left elbow, then lingered. *Too close*. And he had that Don Draper-y fragrance on again. She tried not to breathe it in.

She looked up at him. 'No. I saw it come in but I haven't read it yet. How have *you* read it already?'

He waved an oversized, expensive-looking rectangle at her. 'Rachel Ryan, the smartphone. Have you met? I was bored in the coffee queue.'

She rolled her eyes, then opened Isaac's message.

'Fuck, fuck, *fuck*,' she breathed.

'I thought you might say that. Or something along those lines.'

'She wants us to stay on the account? You said this would work just like BHGH – like with Horrible Humphrey. *You* said we'd end up staffing this with juniors and overseeing from a distance. This sounds like she wants us on the project all the time – three or four days a week!'

Rachel was aware that the pitch of her voice was

rising; every word she uttered sounded more frantic than the last.

'Calm down,' Jack murmured. 'It's okay. It's not as bad as it seems. Yes, she wants us on the build phase of the project – and for more time than I could have anticipated. But once the new platform is up and running and we've populated it with content, the day-to-day stuff can be handed over.'

He crouched down next to her desk so he could look at her properly – talk to her with their eyes level, the way you'd speak to a small child in distress. It annoyed her.

'It'll just be a few months, Rachel, and Olivia asked for you personally. She might not want your editorial ideas, but she wants your talent; she knows you're the best writer we have.'

'Can I say no?'

'Maybe. I don't know. It definitely wouldn't be easy. If you refuse to be involved, Olivia might pull the account – she's very used to getting what she wants. Losing us Lighthouse wouldn't do you any favours with Isaac, let alone Toby or the people up in Manchester.'

'Wow, thanks.'

'I'm just being honest. Like I said before, I can talk to Isaac about this if you'd like me to – but the situation now isn't much different than it was then. If anything, the stakes are higher because we've won the pitch.'

'You're right,' Rachel sighed.

She slumped in her seat and he placed a hand on her shoulder. She wished he wouldn't touch her like this, even though it felt good; people could see, and it only threw fuel on the gossip fire.

'I'll be with you all the way,' he said, standing up and moving around to his side of their adjoining workspace.

'Yeah. I know.' Rachel nodded, not sure how helpful he would be. 'Thanks for the coffee.'

Come to the boys' flat from work, Anna's WhatsApp message instructed. *They're cooking for us, apparently.*

Rachel: *WTF? Do we trust them to cook for us?*

Anna is typing . . .

Anna: *<shrug emoji> It'll probably be student food – pasta bake or something. Even Will can't mess that up.*

Rachel: *I wouldn't be so sure . . . But hey, who doesn't love a pasta bake? I'm in.*
What time should I head over?

Anna: *Will's been working from home today so I'm already here. Anytime x*

Rachel checked her watch. It was almost six already.

'I'm going to head off,' she said in Jack's direction.

He looked up from his computer. 'Oh, right. I hadn't realised the time. I'm in no rush to get home, for obvious reasons . . . Are you doing anything tonight?'

It was a loaded question. If she said no, he'd suggest a drink. Dinner, perhaps. And then what?

'Just going to have some food with friends,' she said.

'And your boyfriend, I suppose?' Jack asked. *Man*, he was persistent.

Rachel's enjoyment of his interest in her faked relationship was diminishing with every needling question. Keeping up the charade was starting to feel like work, and she was angry with herself too. Pretending to have a boyfriend was undeniably pathetic; she didn't need a partner to validate her existence, and she'd never seen herself as the sort of woman who'd make one up.

'Yeah,' she said, shrugging. 'We're all kind of mates together.'

'I saw you, you know,' Jack said, catching her eyes with his and trying to hold them.

'Saw me what?' Rachel asked. She looked away from him deliberately and shoved her laptop into her bag.

'I saw you with him.'

Her stomach fell away.

Jack had a weird look on his face – as if he was happy he'd thrown her off balance, but also like it was costing him something to admit he'd spotted her out with another man.

Rachel swallowed. 'Oh. Where? When?'

And *what* had Jack seen, she wondered. It wasn't as if she and Tom – or anyone – were wandering around London hand in hand, staring into each other's eyes and smooching under street lamps.

'Walking up North Hill in Highgate,' he said. 'I live near there. You looked like you were ranting about something; he was laughing at everything you said.'

She nodded, feigning nonchalance. 'Sounds about right.'

That must have been the night of Zack's gig. No doubt Jack had seen her and Tom on the way to the pub, still laughing about his angsty lyrics.

'Blonde, isn't he? With self-consciously geeky glasses.'

'Blondish,' Rachel said, bristling. 'And I *like* his glasses – they're cute.' As she said it, she realised it was true.

'He doesn't look like your type,' Jack said, frowning. 'And he's ridiculously tall.'

'Ha! What would you know about my type?' Rachel laughed.

'Well,' he said, fixing her with his green eyes and grinning, 'it used to be me.'

'It *also* used to be that guy from Westlife,' she said. 'The one with the piercing stare who is, in fact, gay. I don't think my teenage taste in men means very much.'

'You don't.'

It wasn't a question; it felt more like a challenge. Jack had raised one chestnutty eyebrow and his lips were curled up at the corners. He was enjoying this game, and Rachel needed to end it.

'I really don't,' she said, putting her arms into her coat sleeves. 'And I don't want to be late. I'll see you in the morning.'

'Night, then,' Jack said, and he smiled so wide she could see his whole mouthful of perfect, straight white teeth.

Half an hour later, Rachel was standing outside Will and

Tom's building. She pressed the buzzer, hoping Will would be the one to answer the door. She felt almost grubby after talking to Jack about Tom; like she wasn't sure she could look him in the face.

The front door opened and Anna peered around it, a green biro in her mouth and her glasses pushed up on top of her head. She must be marking kids' exercise books.

She smiled and beckoned Rachel inside, then said, 'They've mugged us off, Rach – they've ordered Domino's, lazy bastards.'

'I heard that,' Will said as they entered the sitting room.

'You were meant to,' Anna answered, sticking her tongue out at him.

Rachel was laughing. 'What happened to making us dinner? I was promised pasta bake. I expected to come in here and find you guys chopping vegetables, or at least opening a jar of Uncle Ben's.'

'Cooking doesn't get tougher than this!' Tom shouted from the kitchen, brandishing a four-pack of beers and a bottle opener.

She laughed again. 'At least tell me you ordered some of that cheesy garlic bread . . . ?'

'We did,' Tom said. 'Of *course* we did. Want a drink?'

'Sure.'

Too many carbs and two bottles of Asahi later, Rachel and Anna were getting ready to head home. Will was due in Dublin the following morning and would be leaving for the airport in the small hours. Anna had said she was buggered if she was staying over tonight only to be awoken by his 3 a.m. alarm.

'You good to go, Rach?' she asked.

'Yeah. I might just pop to the bathroom, though.'

The last time she'd been in here was on the day Oscar threw up all over her. At the time she'd been preoccupied with getting blackcurrant-coloured vomit out of her hair, but now she was feeling nosier. She was struck by how sparse the room was in comparison with the bathroom at their place. There were no pink razors in the shower caddy, no exfoliating body brushes, no half-finished bottles of body lotion or abandoned anti-ageing eye creams. Will and Tom didn't have any slowly perishing pot plants or mascara-stained flannels, like she and Anna did.

Then she spotted a posh-looking rose-scented body scrub on the window ledge. It clearly didn't belong to either Will or Tom, and Rachel knew it couldn't be Anna's. She loathed floral fragrances and always chose green or mannish scents.

So whose *was* it? Could Tom be seeing someone who'd stayed over and left it here?

Rachel thought back to the day when she'd met him and Dev in Soho. Tom had gone off on some kind of date after, and never told her who with.

She unscrewed the lid of the heavy, expensive glass jar and breathed in the aroma. It was sweet but not syrupy; fresh, light and lovely. Rachel felt a sudden surge of dislike for whoever owned it, then forced her annoyance down like bad-tasting medicine.

She put the container back on the ledge. She was being weird. Inappropriate, even. Screwing the lid back on the jar, Rachel told herself that if Tom was involved with someone, she was bound to be nice. And if he wasn't ready to talk to his friends about her yet, he didn't have to.

'Bloody hell, Rach, you've been ages!' Anna yelled through the bathroom door. 'Are you okay? Have you fallen down the loo?'

'Sorry!' Rachel called back. 'I'm coming now.'

She washed her hands noisily, avoiding her own eyes in the mirror above the sink, then went back to her friends.

23

'What do we think about calla lilies?' Anna asked as she stir-fried a wok full of vegetables the following Monday night. 'I was originally thinking dahlias and roses, but I wonder if calla lilies might be more elegant. I guess it all depends on the dress I choose, but I need to get a florist sorted . . . Rach? Rach, are you listening?'

Rachel looked up from the book she was reading – a taut crime thriller foisted on her by her mum – and arranged her face. In truth, she wasn't sure what calla lilies looked like and didn't much care. But Anna's excitement about wedding planning was something a good friend – a less selfish friend – would share.

Smiling despite the waterlogged feeling in her chest, Rachel said, 'Dahlias get my vote, but they've always been my favourite. Can you not book a florist now and confirm the details later?'

'Maybe,' Anna mused. 'I keep wondering about hydrangeas too . . . Pale pink, perhaps, or white.'

Rachel merely nodded, and after a few minutes' silence Anna asked, 'How's everything at work? How are things with Jack?'

'Fine,' Rachel lied. 'All very professional.'

In reality, the situation was rapidly spinning beyond her control. Rachel only had so much energy, and staying cheerful about Anna's upcoming nuptials – not to mention keeping her emotions in check as she worked on the Lighthouse account – was exhausting. Rachel couldn't fight on all fronts, and pushing Jack away required resolution. Industry. It always had, and right now she didn't have the stamina for it.

Falling into friendship with him had been easy – effortless – because she didn't have to *do* anything. Rachel and Jack ate lunch together, stayed late at the office and shared Jaffa Cakes during meetings. It was like being back at uni except that the spectre of Rachel's fake boyfriend put a different perspective on things, shifting the balance of power in her favour.

My Deed Detector's bleeping, Kemi said via IM one morning. When Rachel didn't respond, she clarified: *Are you and HH doing it?* – ever dismissive of the possibility that someone from IT might be monitoring her messages.

Rachel Ryan
  NO. We're just friends. Colleagues.

Kemi Percival
  <eyeroll emoji>
  He looks at you the way I look at my Nanna's jollof rice.
  Put the poor man out of his misery. He's way too hot to leave idle and unshagged.

Rachel Ryan
  Nothing's going on between me and Jack.

I don't know what more I can say, Kem.

Kemi Percival
You could say, Yes, Kemi, I'll have a really good go on him and report back in detail <tongue out emoji>

Rachel Ryan
FFS. No.
I have work to do.

On Thursday evening, Greg tackled her about what was happening with the two of them. Since the last time Rachel had told him to stop bringing it up, he'd said very little – instead restricting himself to the pulling of pert, significant faces. Tonight, however, over post-yoga donburi bowls and bubble tea, he was determined to push for answers.

'Things seem to have kicked up a gear, Ray,' he said. 'I can feel the sexual tension from the other side of the office. I can practically *see* it, like a heat haze.'

'You're imagining things, Greg,' she replied, fully aware that he wasn't.

'I am *not*. And I overheard a conversation by the coffee machine the other day, during which someone claimed you'd been seen pashing him by the recycling bins.'

'*What?*'

'You heard. Is it true?'

'Obviously it's not true.'

Evidently, someone had seen Rachel take Jack into Dustbin Alley for the purpose of berating him about the Lighthouse account. Whoever had noticed them had either seriously misinterpreted the situation or twisted what they'd seen into some Mills & Boon-style tryst.

Greg persisted, ignoring the incredulous expression on her face.

'Have you slept with him? Recently, I mean.'

'For heaven's *sake*,' Rachel hissed. 'What do you think?'

'Honestly? I don't know what to think. That's why I'm asking.'

'I. Have. Not. Slept. With. Him,' she said, too loud and grinding her teeth. 'Not *recently*, anyway.'

A prim-looking tourist at the next table sat up in shock, as if she'd just overheard the start of some satanic ritual.

'Are you planning to sleep with him?'

'Oh my God, can we *not*?'

'I'm only pushing you on this because I care – because of everything you told me about Jack back in January. I just hope you know what you're doing.'

'I'm thirty years old, Greg. And I know I look like I belong in period costume, but I'm not the naive ingénue you seem to think I am. Of course I know what I'm doing.'

'Forgive me, darl, but didn't your last boyfriend plan out some sort of Stepford Wife future for you, without you even noticing? Frankly, I'm not convinced you're all that great at interpreting blokes' intentions.'

Greg was joking with her, but his words still stung. Rachel felt glad she hadn't told him about Laurence's *post*-break-up behaviour. Her failure to see his meltdown coming was hardly an endorsement of her judgement.

'I'm doing just fine, thank you,' she said, then sucked

what remained of her passion fruit tea up her straw. Petulant, she plonked the empty plastic cup down on the table – as if *it* were somehow responsible for her snit.

'Sure you are,' Greg said, folding his arms and smiling at her sardonically.

'For your information,' Rachel said, her temper flaring, 'I'm actually seeing someone.'

Bollocks. What had she said *that* for?

'Really?' Greg asked, his tawny eyes wide with surprise. 'Who? Since when?'

Shit, shit, shiiiiiiiiit.

'Nobody you know, and not for very long. But he's nice. He's *good*. And Jack knows.'

Rachel could feel herself starting to sweat. Why was she doing this? Letting Jack think she was attached was one thing, but actually telling Greg a bare-faced lie? That was something else.

'Well. Based on how he's acting, I'm not sure Jack really cares,' Greg said, his brows knitting. 'He's going to make a play for you sooner or later, so you'd better decide on an answer to that question you evaded before: Are you planning to sleep with him?'

Rachel winced, but didn't answer.

'Personally, I'm not much for the "all's fair in love and war" approach,' Greg continued. 'I think it kind of sucks to pursue someone you know isn't free. I'm more a "do as you would be done by" kind of guy.'

'Hmm,' Rachel muttered, still reeling from her own recklessness. 'I'll bear that in mind.'

'Do,' Greg said, seeming satisfied. 'Now. Shall we order

some of that Japanese cheesecake for dessert? I'll split one with you.'

'Okay.' She nodded. 'But only if we can talk about something else. I can't believe I'm saying this, but . . . I think I miss those conversations we used to have about vegetables.'

Someone – Rachel suspected Greg – had decided that a work night out was necessary. It was planned for Friday night, the day after his cross-examination of her at the noodle bar, and she was seriously tempted to swerve it.

The last time she and Jack had been in a pub together, he'd told her he was getting divorced and almost given her heart failure by kissing her goodnight. She didn't want to think about how things might go now that he was openly flirting with her. For all her protestations, Greg was right: Jack *was* chasing her, and he was less discreet about it by the day. Worse, there was a powerful part of her that wanted to be caught.

'Don't even think about piking out,' Greg said when Rachel bumped into him in the kitchen. 'You're coming. This is a whole-agency event. There are people coming down from Manchester to celebrate the start of the new financial year – the first with us as part of Mountaintop. It's supposed to be an opportunity for bonding, hence the sexy location and hefty bar budget. Not turning up will be a very bad look.'

Rachel groaned. 'I hate this kind of thing, you know I do. And I have a dentist appointment right after work . . .'

'So go. Have your teeth cleaned and come back into town,' Greg said briskly. 'Unless you end up having emergency root canal – and I'll want to see a *receipt* for that – I'll expect you in the bar by eight o'clock.'

Almost to her annoyance, Rachel's check-up and session with the hygienist went smoothly. By 6.15 she was on her way back to the flat to get changed – resigned to spending the night in a state of high stress, and resolved not to put away too much booze.

She squeezed into a black stretchy minidress and pulled on a pair of sheer black tights with a polka-dot pattern. It was an unusually bold look for her. *Too* bold, perhaps?

Not if she kept her hair and make-up simple, Rachel decided – and she would, because she didn't have time to faff with them. She unwound her hair from the messy bun she'd shoved it into this morning, tipped her head upside down and blasted it with texturising spray.

When she was right side up again, Rachel realised Anna was lurking in her bedroom doorway.

'You look hot – like you've just been for a roll in the heather with Poldark,' she said, admiring her friend's headful of disorderly waves. 'It's working for you.'

'I'd honestly rather throw on a hoodie and come to the Hope,' Rachel moaned. 'Is this dress too short?'

Anna eyed her, appraising her outfit. 'It's cheeky, but you look good. And it has sleeves, which balances out the legginess. Stop worrying. Go. Have *fun*,' she admonished.

She didn't even think to suggest that Rachel steer clear of

Jack: a mark of how little she knew about their increasingly messy relationship.

Rachel rummaged in her make-up bag, mainly for the sake of avoiding Anna's eyes. There was so much she wasn't telling her just lately – so many things they weren't sharing. It felt wrong.

Rachel patted a little cream blush and highlighter onto her cheeks, then smeared clear gloss onto her lips.

'You look lovely,' Anna said. 'Where is it you're going again?'

'Some secret speakeasy near London Fields,' Rachel told her. 'Apparently there's this totally innocuous door on a bog-standard street, and behind it is a twenties-style bar. First you have to find it, then you have to say the right password to get in.'

'Wow,' Anna said. 'That's elaborate. Kind of cool, though.' She was smiling.

'I imagine Greg had something to do with the choice of venue,' Rachel said, unable to resist rolling her eyes. 'Not only is it *very* trendy, it's about five minutes' walk from his house.'

'Well, I think it sounds fun. Park your snark and enjoy it. You can tell me all about it in the morning.'

'Sure.' Rachel nodded, all but certain that she wouldn't.

It was only when Rachel got off the bus in Hackney that she realised she should have paid more attention to Greg's directions. She was on the right street, but too many of the buildings looked the same. How was she supposed to know which one was the front for a Prohibition-style bar?

When she passed by a storefront with bright-red window frames, she remembered: Greg had said to find the black door to the right of the barber's. Rachel looked through the glass: this must be it. The walls were covered with photos of well-coiffed bearded hipsters and blokes with *Peaky Blinders* haircuts.

Next door to the salon was a building that looked, to the casual observer, like a house – but the door was black and there was a shiny chrome intercom panel beside it. Rachel pushed the button firmly, letting it go when she'd heard it buzz.

'Password, please?' someone said.

Oh *hell*.

'Hello? Is there someone there?' came the intercom voice again.

'Argh, sorry!' Rachel cried. 'My boss told me the password but it's totally slipped my mind.'

'I can't let you in without the password, I'm afraid.'

Rachel sighed and looked up at the sky. It was dark, but she could see it was full of angry grey clouds. Any second now it was going to start raining.

'Seriously?' she said. 'I'm with the work group that's booked out the whole venue for this evening. How would I even *know* about that if I wasn't part of the same company?'

'I can't let you in without the password,' the disembodied voice repeated. 'You'll need to call one of your colleagues and ask for it.' The intercom connection cut off.

'For the love of *God*,' Rachel wailed. She put her handbag on the pavement, then bent down to fumble for her phone.

She rang Greg and got his voicemail, then tried Kemi with identical results.

Clearly everyone was having too much raucous fun to hear a mobile ring. Rachel felt fine raindrops stippling the exposed skin of her hands and face. *Perfect.*

Just as she'd concluded it was time to give up and go home, Rachel felt a presence behind her. She knew, without even looking, that it was Jack.

'Let me guess,' he said, as she turned to face him. 'You forgot the password.'

Rachel nodded, then mumbled something about pretentious nonsense.

Jack stepped forward, putting a hand on her waist to move her a little to his left. Her stomach flew up into her throat, and he smirked at her – as if he'd seen it move.

He pressed the button on the buzzer panel.

'Password, please?'

'Mint julep,' Jack said.

'Push the door.' There was a dull click, and Jack opened it with a shove. 'After you,' he said, motioning for Rachel to head inside.

The lighting in the bar was warm and moody, and mostly came from wall lights and old standard lamps. Many of them had red shades, which added to the shabby-chic, deliberately sleazy look of the place. The furniture was tasteful but mismatched, and there were old cream tiles and exposed plaster on the walls. The air smelled aged and leathery, but still clean – antique rather than musty.

The glassware Rachel could see was all vintage in style. Most of her colleagues seemed to be holding heavy-bottomed cut-glass tumblers full of dark, amber liquid, or gold-rimmed champagne saucers brimming with pale, pastel-coloured froth.

'Drink?' Jack asked.

'Yeah.' Rachel nodded. 'I'll come with you to the bar and see what there is.'

It wasn't ideal that they'd arrived together, she reflected. Even though they'd only met on the doorstep, it must look as if she and Jack had been together all evening. Kemi caught Rachel's eye and made a kissing face.

'What do you fancy?' Jack asked.

'Hmm,' Rachel said, scanning the chalkboard above the bar. There must have been fifty different cocktails listed there, many of which she'd never heard of before. 'Ooooh, I'll have a French 75, please.'

'Lemon, sugar, champagne and gin,' Jack read, looking up at the menu. 'What could possibly go wrong?'

'I don't think it's *my* alcohol intake we need to worry about,' Rachel said, nodding at Kemi after Jack had placed their order. She was giggling, winking at them from the other side of the room through hands that she'd cupped into a heart shape.

'D'you think she's trying to tell us something?' Jack asked, leaning in so Rachel could hear him over the general hubbub. Beneath her colleagues' conversations and laughter there was the sound of glasses clinking, the clang of cocktail shakers in motion and soft jazz spilling from well-concealed speakers. This was the sort of bar Jack belonged in, Rachel decided; old-fashioned, classy and expensive, but somehow suggestive of smut.

'*I said*, do you think she's trying to tell us something?'

'Nothing I don't already know,' Rachel said, suddenly rash. She hadn't even had a drink yet, and she was letting herself spar with him.

There was something about this place. If Rachel was coquettish tonight, maybe she could blame the dim, sexy lighting.

A bow-tied barman handed them their drinks, and they moved away from the serving area to make space for the people behind them.

'Is that so?' Jack's eyes were dancing dangerously. 'I like you in this bar, Ryan. And in that dress.'

He leered at her melodramatically and she whacked him on the arm.

'*Stop it*. People already think we're having some sort of affair.'

'Let them,' he said with a shrug. 'It makes no difference to me. But I suppose you have your boyfriend to consider.'

'Exactly.' Rachel nodded, pleased that he sounded put out and already feeling wobbly after a few glugs of her cocktail. 'Now, make yourself useful and introduce me to some Manchester people.'

As the night wore on, the agency's most senior staff began to head home. This, combined with the copious quantity of free cocktails they'd provided, meant many of those left behind misplaced the inhibitions they'd held on to while their bosses were around. There was still money behind the bar, and one way or another it was going to be spent.

As closing time approached, Rachel – far from sober

but of comparatively sound mind – took stock of the state of her colleagues.

Greg was arguing with Theo, who didn't want to accept he was too drunk to drive his scooter home to Fulham. Ella's new boyfriend had come by to collect her some time ago, but Kemi – who'd been her partner in Prosecco-guzzling for most of the night – was slumped in a corner looking sleepy.

'I should help her get home,' Rachel said to Jack, who'd been hovering beside her for most of the night. 'She doesn't live far from me.'

'I'll give you a hand,' he said. 'We can share a cab.'

Between them, they hauled Kemi up and out into the street. She was chatty but mostly incomprehensible, which Rachel was grateful for; the handful of coherent comments Kemi *did* manage were about Rachel, Jack and their 'sitting in a tree' status.

Jack laughed every time Kemi insisted they must be 'doing it', but listening to lurid speculation about her own sex life made Rachel want to die.

Greg had shaken his head at her when he'd seen them pulling Kemi towards the door – not in disapproval, exactly, but perhaps in disappointment. Combined with the alcohol sloshing around in her stomach, it had made Rachel feel a bit sick.

'Do you know her address?' Jack asked.

'Yeah. I've done this before.'

After a fifteen-minute cab ride, they pulled up outside a three-storey building. Set back from the road, it had at least twelve stone steps leading up to the front door.

'What are you doing?' Jack asked Rachel as she unbuckled her seatbelt.

She made a face at him. 'Kemi's never going to get up those stairs by herself,' she pointed out. '*And* she lives on the second floor of the building.'

Jack sighed, then scrambled out of the front passenger seat and walked around the car to open Rachel's door.

'Want me to wait?' the taxi driver asked.

'Not for me,' Rachel said. 'I only live five minutes away. Jack?'

'I'll walk you home,' he said, then shook his head at the driver and handed him a twenty-pound note. Kemi, who nobody had thought was listening, burst into triumphant laughter.

Once they'd deposited Kemi safely in her bedroom, Rachel and Jack strolled in the direction of Stroud Green Road.

'I'll never hear the end of this,' Rachel sighed. 'Kemi was already convinced that there's something happening between us. After tonight she's going to be unbearable.'

Jack just laughed.

'It isn't *funny*,' Rachel said. 'Nothing that people are saying is true, but it makes me look terrible.'

'How so?'

'Well, for a start,' she replied, straightening her spine, 'I have a boyfriend. But also, a woman who has a workplace romance always ends up with the rough end of any rumours that go round. It's always *her* who's supposed to have seduced *him*.' Rachel wrinkled her nose in distaste. 'And if the man is someone senior,' she continued, 'it's usually assumed that she's shagging him for the sake of getting on. When have you ever heard of a bloke being accused of sleeping with a co-worker to help kickstart his career?'

'Never,' Jack admitted. They were standing side by side outside Rachel and Anna's building now, their backs against the wall that separated the front yard from the street. 'You're wrong, though.'

'About what?'

'You were wrong when you said that none of the gossip is true.'

His voice was low and urgent. Sparks skittered down Rachel's spine.

Self-reproach mingled with anticipation as Jack turned his body 180 degrees to face her, planting his hands either side of her on the wall, boxing her in. She could feel him breathing. His air smelled like mint leaves and bourbon.

'People are saying there's something between us, and there is,' he went on. 'People are saying I want you, and I do.'

Rachel shook her head, refusing to look at him. '*People* don't have all the information. They don't know we were together at uni. They don't know what a bastard you were. They don't know that I—'

'—have a boyfriend,' Jack finished, sounding bored. 'That makes them . . . ill-informed. It doesn't make them wrong.'

He skimmed a fingertip over the skin on the back of her hand, tracing up from her knuckle and then dipping it inside the sleeve of her jacket. He circled her wrist, then turned her hand over and placed his palm on top of it. It felt something like being electrocuted.

He lowered his face towards hers. Just as she thought he was going to kiss her – just as her mouth opened a fraction in readiness – he stopped.

He was *grinning*.

He stood up a little straighter so that, for their lips to touch, she'd have to reach for him.

No. No *way* was she going to kiss him.

'Such a pity you're attached,' he breathed, his mouth so close to hers she could practically taste it.

She pulled her hand out from beneath his, tipped her head to one side and said, with far more composure than she felt, 'Not for me, it isn't.'

Jack was still smiling, but he'd stepped back completely now. His hands were in his pockets.

'We make sense together, Ryan. We both know it. We always did.'

'You do realise this is all a terrible cliché, don't you?' Rachel asked, common sense fighting for supremacy over the champagne buzz still warming her blood. She groped for something sarcastic to say. 'People like you always want back the love they gave away!' she cried eventually. 'And people like me want to believe you when you say you've changed.'

This second point, she had to admit, she wasn't so thrilled about.

Jack's forehead scrunched up, but he was still smirking. 'Are you *quoting* at me? I've heard that before. Is that poetry?'

'*Yes*, it's poetry,' Rachel said, drawing herself up to her full height. 'It's Taylor bloody Swift, you philistine.'

She stomped past him, letting the front gate slam shut and instantly hoping that it hadn't woken Anna or any of their neighbours. Jack was laughing softly.

'Goodnight, Ryan,' he chuckled. 'I'll see you on Monday. I guess you'll let me know when you decide whether or not you *believe I've changed*.'

24

The final Saturday of April saw Rachel on the Tube to Soho, on her way to meet Tom. He and Dev were keen to show her around the small gallery they'd booked for the #NoFilter exhibition, which was due to open in a couple of months' time.

When she emerged from Leicester Square station into the crowds and commotion of the West End, the day was bright, the breeze was gentle and the pavement free from puddles. It finally felt like spring.

For the first time in months Rachel had left the house without a proper coat, throwing a thrift-shop blazer over her skinny jeans and sweatshirt. She felt light – liberated, somehow – and she was looking forward to seeing Tom.

It wasn't lost on her that he was the person she'd been most honest with over the past few months. While Rachel's truth-telling had been largely accidental, the consequence was that she felt more comfortable with Tom than almost anyone else at the moment. It was a relief to be around him, somehow – like she could press pause on trying to impersonate someone whose life was going swimmingly.

The only thing Tom *didn't* know was that he'd been mistaken for her besotted boyfriend – and, frankly, this was information Rachel felt he could do without.

As she walked up Charing Cross Road, through throngs of tourists clustered outside theatres and chain restaurants, Rachel glanced up and noticed she'd just outpaced the number 24 bus. She span to look back at the shiny red double-decker – with a new photo of Jessica Williams emblazoned on its side.

Several people tutted, bashing into her or barging by as she stopped to stare at the glossy image.

Rachel's sightings of Jessica had diminished in frequency since the January detox campaign, and their power to demoralise her had dwindled as more immediate problems claimed her attention. Now, though, Rachel found herself riveted. This was a genius bit of marketing, she had to admit.

Gone were the flimsy-yet-wholesome clothes from Jessica's previous ads for Angeljuice and its brand of cereal bars. Now she sported a shiny scarlet bodysuit – long-sleeved, but with a V-neck so wide and deep it was incredible her nipples weren't on show.

Jessica's lips – poutier and puffier than ever – were painted a vivid, blazing crimson, and a pair of pointed red horns peeped out above her curtain of lustrous pitch-black hair.

HELLFIRE FAT BURNER, shouted the picture's big, bold caption. Then, in smaller letters: *Look* devilishly *slim this summer. Try the hot new supplement from the makers of Angeljuice.* Pinched between Jessica's forefinger and thumb was a bright-red pill.

Rachel gaped at the ad. Was Jessica seriously promoting weight-loss capsules to her hundreds of thousands of fans? This was different from advertising supposedly healthy snacks or endorsing 'cleansing' drinks. It made Rachel feel a little sick.

Decade-old remnants of jealousy reignited alongside Rachel's outrage, then seemed to burn away. As usual, Jessica looked incredible – but Rachel's distaste for diet culture was stronger than her envy of an old rival's sex appeal.

She shook her head at the bus, turned away and kept walking. She didn't bother to look up again as it picked up speed and went past her.

The venue for #NoFilter was on Greek Street: a tall, thin building squeezed between a French restaurant and a posh optician's. The outside was painted blinding white, and the brilliant, 'blank canvas' effect continued inside. The place was stylishly fitted with original stripped-wood floors and carefully considered lighting. Large sash windows overlooked the bustling street below, allowing sunshine to bathe the high-ceilinged rooms in brightness.

'It's *gorgeous*,' Rachel said, beaming at Tom and Dev after they'd led her up to the top floor.

'Newly refurbished,' Dev said, smoothing a hand over his glossy black quiff. 'We'll spread the exhibition over all five floors of the building, ordering the images and words so that as people walk through there's a sense of story. You two will be in charge of that, obviously.'

Rachel smiled at him and nodded. Dev looked as polished today as he had when they'd first met in January, though he'd shaved off his beard since the last time she'd seen him. His skin, she could now see, was radiant – perfectly smooth and poreless, like a baby's. She wondered what moisturiser he used, then resolved to go to Boots on the way home and buy the retinol cream she'd been promising herself since New Year.

'Dev managed to convince the owners of this place that having a show of starry photos would guarantee ongoing celebrity interest,' Tom said, winking.

Dev was smiling. 'Indeed. Though the discount I negotiated will probably be swallowed twice over by the budget for press night . . .'

'Press night?' Rachel asked.

'A glorified launch party for the show,' Dev explained. 'We invite a range of people with an interest in the exhibition, plus as many journalists as we can get, to come and see it before it opens to the public. Everyone drinks champagne, nibbles on canapés and says how *marvellous* it is. Which, of course, it will be, hahaha. If we're lucky, #NoFilter gets mentioned as the hottest ticket in town in *Hello!* magazine, as well as coverage in *Grazia* and all the weekend papers.'

'Wow,' Rachel said, a little taken aback.

'You'll be there, of course,' Dev went on. 'Everyone who worked on the show will come along on press night, as well as all of our models.'

'Speaking of whom . . .' Tom put in, pulling an iPad out of his backpack. 'Let me show you the latest snaps.'

He perched on the top step of the staircase that led from the high point of the gallery to the floor below, then patted the space next to him, beckoning for Rachel to sit. She squeezed into it, ending up pressed far closer to Tom than she was used to. He smelled lemony and clean. It was the scent that still lingered on the sweatshirt he'd given her.

Tom flipped through a selection of images featuring an almost unrecognisable Alyssia Ahmadi. She was grinning artlessly into the camera – a far cry from her usual smile, which was the smug grin Rachel associated with macrobiotic types who insisted positive thinking was the key to success, while blithely letting their wealthy parents pay the mortgage.

Tom had photographed Joey Nixon outside, which in itself was noteworthy. His followers rarely saw him without headphones or a console control pad in his hand. In the exhibition images he was surrounded by nature: trees just coming into blossom, a moody-looking River Thames and – in one photo – a black Labrador that had shaken off its owner, bounded into shot and licked Joey's face.

Rachel felt like she might burst with admiration. 'These are amazing, Tom,' she said. 'It's like they're different people, but in a good way.'

'Want to see some of the shots I've done of the normals too?' he asked, grinning.

'Ugh,' Dev groaned. He was at their backs, looking over their shoulders. 'I've been bracing myself for these. Some of the mental health advocates look like vagabonds – overgrown beards, ill-fitting tunic tops and hideously dehydrated skin. I'm slightly worried they'll ruin the whole aesthetic of the show. Are you absolutely *sure* we can't airbrush them?'

'Of course we can't,' Tom laughed, scrolling through

shots of doctors, campaigners and politicians. None of them were as beautiful as the influencers, but he'd managed to catch every face looking open, honest and good.

'I love these too,' Rachel said. 'How is it that we've known each other four years, Thomas, and it's only *now* I'm realising you might be a genius?'

He shrugged and smiled at her. 'I guess I hide it well.'

'All right, you two,' Dev said from behind them. 'I could live without the love-in. These are solid, Tom. They'll fit in fine with the client shots.'

Tom heaved himself back up to standing, then reached for Rachel's hand to help her do the same. 'I'll send you low-res copies of the final shots we select for the show, Rach. You can use them while you're working on the text. Just shout if there's anything else you need.'

Rachel replied, 'Cool,' then followed Tom as he began making his way down the gallery's four flights of stairs.

'Well done, both,' Dev said as they approached the front door. 'Things are shaping up nicely. Before I forget, Tom: there are one or two influencers I'm still trying to get on board. If we have last-minute additions, we might have to accommodate them as part of photo shoots we've already booked.'

'Not a problem,' Tom said. 'Just keep me posted.'

'Will do. Right, I'm off. Wedding planning,' Dev moaned. 'I ask you: how can it be that there are six hundred people coming to celebrate my marriage?'

Rachel's mouth dropped open. 'I don't think I even *know* six hundred people.'

'Knowing them isn't the point,' Dev said. '*Inviting* them

is. A good chunk of them I've probably never even met – like Aditi's old piano teacher from when she was eleven, plus her husband. And they'll jolly well *come* too. At least I'm not the one paying for the samosas.'

He shook his head as Rachel and Tom laughed, then bustled away.

'What are you up to now?' Tom asked. 'Fancy lunch and a fruit beer? That bar you liked is only round the corner and their *pommes frites* are spectacular. I can fill you in on all things Oscar-related.'

'Honestly, I'd love to,' Rachel said, and meant it. 'But I've been drafted in for wedding duty this afternoon too. Anna's asked me to meet her in Muswell Hill. I think we're looking at dresses.'

'Ah. Cool. Well, have fun,' Tom said. 'By the way – the next big influencer photo shoot isn't for a while, but I wondered if you might want to come along? It's the session with Sophie French, and she seems very keen on being reinvented.'

'Definitely! Let me know when it is and I'll make sure I don't double-book myself.'

'Will do. Enjoy this afternoon. And Rach . . . ?'

'Yeah?'

He was looking at her gently – with an expression that was kind and concerned, but somehow managed not to seem patronising.

'It's going to be okay, you know, all this wedding stuff. *You're* going to be okay. I promise.'

Rachel nodded at him, not trusting herself to say anything back in case her voice cracked.

She wanted to believe him – wanted him to be right, like he almost always was. She just didn't see how it was possible.

May

~~New Year's~~ Ongoing resolutions

1. Consider exercise an act with actual benefits – both mental and physical – not merely grim punishment for pizzas consumed. ~~Have a proper go at~~ Continue letting Greg drag me to yoga. ~~provided he refrains from making snide comments re Jack/me and Jack~~. Give up trying to control subject matter discussed over dinner.
2. ~~Also re-download Complete Couch to 5K running app and actually do the programme.~~ Keep running at least twice per week – *always* being careful not to perv on anyone improper.
3. ~~Apply for promotion at work at first chance. Move to bigger account and try to get pay rise. Avoid, if possible, further projects concerning dog biscuits, disinfectant, high-quality printer ink cartridges, 'miracle' grass seed, organic vegetables, etc.~~
    3a. Try to hang on to job (and temper) despite

~~presence of evil ex-boyfriend hideousness~~ control-freakery of certain clients.

3b. Ignore everyone who keeps banging on about how fit ~~he~~ Jack is.

3c. Ignore how fit he is.

3d. Ignore the fact he ~~keeps trying to be friendly/nice/possibly quite flirtatious~~ is openly trying to shag me.

3e. Ignore the fact he is getting divorced.

~~4. DO NOT agree to further dates with Laurence. Remember: it's no use having a boyfriend who is good on paper if you do not actually fancy him.~~

4. Forget that Laurence even EXISTS ~~(despite usefulness of overblown 'romantic' gestures for creating illusion of deeply devoted boyfriend~~. Try not to spin any more tales re 'boyfriend' ~~though — don't want story to get too complicated . . .)~~ – situation is already quite complicated enough.

5. Try to remember Mum means well, even during phone calls where she ~~implies I am doomed to a lonely life of penury because I am thirty with no partner, hardly any savings and no mortgage~~ insists on talking about the babies/breasts of people I went to school with.

6. HOWEVER, do not (!!!) speak to Mum when suffering PMT. Set phone alerts for likely spells based on period tracker intel.

7. Try to address 'hardly any savings' situation. ~~(If promoted, set aside extra earnings for future house deposit instead of spaffing it all on ASOS.)~~

(Do not spend entire pay rise on ~~'cheer up' treats to distract from heinous ex-boyfriend mess.~~ hot new outfits for work – see 3c.)
8. Try to eat my five-a-day. (Remember horrid rule that potatoes do not count.)
9. ~~Start using proper night cream with retinol. SERIOUSLY.~~ Regularly apply retinol cream purchased from Boots in pursuit of perfect, Dev-style skin.
10. Do the best possible job helping Tom with exhibition. Be supportive and discreet re Oscar. Avoid arguing with Tom about Jack.
11. Be a good friend (and bridesmaid) to Anna. Help with wedding organisation and keep selfish, sad worries about how much I'll miss her to myself.

25

It was unusual for Rachel to take a half-day off work, but today she was going to start the weekend early. Anna wanted to meet her at some random shop in Wood Green, near school, and she had a free period every Friday afternoon. Coincidentally, this was the only time when the 'by appointment' store she'd found could open for them.

'We can make an event of it,' Anna had said. 'Look at the dresses, spend some quality time together and then get to the Hope nice and early.'

Rachel hadn't had the heart to argue, though she was apprehensive. What sort of place would Anna be dragging her to *this* time? So far they'd been to look at wedding gowns in swanky boutiques, high-end department stores and specialist dressmakers' studios. They'd drunk a fair amount of free Prosecco, but nothing they'd found had been right. Not a single dress Anna tried on had felt like *her*, somehow.

'I look like an ornate toilet roll holder,' she'd said of a voluminous French lace gown in a bridal shop in Kensington – much to the chagrin of the owner.

'More like a pint-sized Disney princess . . .' Rachel had replied in a vain attempt at diplomacy. Anna had glowered at her. '. . . Which is obviously *not* the look you're going for.'

Anna was already waiting outside the shop when Rachel

arrived. It was a small place, but neat, tidy and stylish. The storefront was painted dark grey and there were two beautifully dressed mannequins in the window.

One was in a midnight-blue evening dress, and the other wore a diaphanous chiffon gown in pale turquoise. It had long sleeves with flamboyant feather trim that had been dyed bright cyan. Both garments, Rachel thought, were probably 1960s originals – dresses made decades before she and Anna were even born. The sign above the door announced, in shiny bronze letters, that the shop's name was Tempo.

'It's a vintage boutique!' Rachel cried, smiling.

'Yes.' Anna nodded. 'Specialising in formalwear, particularly designer pieces: vintage Dior, Balenciaga, Hermès, Pucci, Ossie Clark . . .'

Rachel sighed, clutching at her chest as though her heart might burst with excitement. 'How did you find this place?'

'Well, it's fairly new,' Anna said. 'And honestly, I just happened to walk past it one afternoon last week. It hadn't occurred to me to try looking for a vintage dress to get married in, but . . .'

'It's a *great* idea,' Rachel said. 'I have a very good feeling about this.'

'Me too.' Anna smiled, and rang the doorbell.

They were let in by a woman with deep amber skin and shoulder-length Afro hair. Some of her curls were highlighted shades of caramel, honey and gold, and her big, wide eyes were dark brown. Rachel guessed she was no older than twenty-five.

'You must be Anna,' she said, grinning. 'I'm Zahra. We spoke on the phone.'

'Yes!' Anna said, shaking Zahra's hand. 'And this is Rachel. She'll be my maid of honour.'

'Just the two of you, is it?' Zahra asked. 'We don't need to wait for anyone else?'

Anna shook her head. Rachel cringed. They'd had this conversation in every wedding dress shop they'd visited – though at least Zahra had the sense not to ask, point blank, 'Isn't your mum coming?'

Anna's mother lived in Spain, and they didn't speak. They'd had barely any contact since Anna was about thirteen – the age at which she'd realised it hurt more to try to have a relationship with her mum than to pretend she didn't exist.

Nicola Taylor had given birth to her daughter at twenty and rapidly decided that motherhood was too tough a road to walk alone. She moved back into her parents' house in Dagenham, then out again not twelve months later, leaving her baby girl behind.

Anna always said her gran and grandpa were the only parents she'd ever known, and – as far as Rachel was concerned – they'd been outstanding ones. Their granddaughter was the best, most brilliant person she'd ever met.

When they passed away, they'd left Anna everything they had – including the ex-council house she'd grown up in, which Anna had sold so she could buy the Stroud Green flat. Even six years on, it still made Rachel feel sick to think that Anna's mother hadn't bothered to help plan her own parents' funerals – nor even attended her father's. What she *had* done was mount a legal challenge to the will that left their worldly goods to her daughter. Thankfully, it had ended in failure.

'Yep – just us,' Anna said brightly, smiling at Zahra and clutching Rachel's arm. Rachel found her hand and held it for a moment.

Zahra nodded and Rachel caught a glimpse of her left ear, which was adorned with an array of tiny, twinkling piercings. The woman was stunning – and probably wearing her own stock, Rachel thought. She had on an ochre maxi dress with a psychedelic leaf print in shades of orange, black and lime green, likely a find from the seventies. It looked perfect, like it had been made for her.

'Nice, isn't it?' Zahra asked, and Rachel realised she must have been staring.

'It's awesome.'

'It was like a sack when I found it.' Zahra smiled. 'I do alterations and reimagining of vintage stuff, as well as just trading in the pieces I source – so if we find something you love but it isn't a great fit, that's no problem.'

She turned to Anna. 'Based on our chat and what you told me about your style and size, I've put aside a few things I think you might like. Why don't I go and get the rack, then pop the kettle on while you take a look?'

Anna grinned when Zahra reappeared, wheeling a clothing rail along with her. It was hung with garments in varying shades of white, blush, cream and oyster. All of them were different, and none looked like anything Anna had tried on during previous attempts at wedding gown shopping.

She and Rachel riffled through a selection of dresses while Zahra made tea. One was flapper-style and entirely made of chiffon. Another, probably from the 1930s, was made of vanilla-coloured silk; it had a high-necked sunburst front, a low, scooped back and subtle gold trim.

Anna looked beautiful in everything, though some of the dresses were several inches too long for her. Zahra, however, claimed she'd saved the best for last. 'Now I've met you,' she said, 'I'm even *more* convinced this one's going to look amazing.'

Anna took the dress she was handed into the changing area, then emerged a few minutes later with a blazing, jubilant look on her face. She was a vision, and she knew it. Rachel felt her eyes well up and Zahra clapped.

Anna was wearing a 1960s cocktail dress that fell to her knee. It was made of thick cream satin and covered in tiny clear-glass beads that shimmered as she moved. The bodice, cut square above Anna's bust, sat separately from the skirt; elevated above the waist, it was embroidered with small peach flowers. Beaded tassels hung from its glittering hem.

'This is the one,' Anna sighed.

'It *so* is,' Rachel agreed. Anna, with her pixie cut, petite figure and doll-like face, was wearing the hell out of this dress – *it* wasn't wearing her.

'And here's the best bit,' Zahra said, triumphant. She pulled a box off the shelf next to her, opened it and freed an elegant bolero jacket from several folds of tissue paper. She handed it to Anna.

'I made this to match the dress so it could be worn

during the daytime, always hoping the right bride would come along.'

'It's *perfect*,' Anna said, and slipped it on. It sat snug on her shoulders and had slender three-quarter-length sleeves with pale peach edging. She looked iconic – like a model. Like a shorter, more grown-up Twiggy.

'This dress is your sartorial soulmate, Anna,' Rachel declared. 'You *have* to buy it. Give Zahra all your money before someone else can come along and say they want it. Give her all your worldly goods. Give her Will, if she wants him.'

'All I'll need today is a deposit, if you decide to go ahead,' Zahra laughed. 'In which case, we could also make a couple of appointments for fittings – just so I can adjust the dress and jacket to your measurements exactly. If you like, I can also help you source shoes and accessories to go with them . . . Maybe even a bridesmaid's dress?'

'Yes, yes and yes,' Anna said, elated. 'Yes to *everything*. Here's my debit card.'

Half an hour later, on the bus back towards Finsbury Park, Anna rested her head on Rachel's shoulder. She was quiet but smiling – thoughtful but contented.

'Thanks for being there for me,' she said softly. Rachel knew precisely what she meant.

'Always,' Rachel replied. 'Forever. I wouldn't have missed that fashion show for the world.'

They arrived at the Hope just after five and settled at a table in a sunny spot by the window. Rachel bought a bottle of chilled Provence rosé and poured out two glasses.

'God, that's lovely,' Anna said, taking a sip. 'Let's crack into the crisps.'

Rachel tore open the two bags she'd placed on the table – one cheese and onion and one prawn cocktail. Anna made a disgusted face at the pink packet, then dragged the blue one towards her.

They sipped and crunched in silence for a while until Anna turned to Rachel and said, 'Right. There's something we need to discuss.'

Oh *God*, what was this going to be about? Was Anna going to ask her to move out of the flat early? Rachel was barely coping with the idea of leaving as it was.

'It's your birthday in two weeks,' Anna went on. 'And you haven't exactly had the easiest year so far. I thought it'd be nice to make a fuss of you – have a proper party.' She said this in her lightest voice, but Rachel could detect the unease swimming beneath it; misplaced guilt trying to surface.

'Anna, it's not your fault Jack turned up at the agency – nor that I got lumbered with him as a work partner. Shit happens.'

'It does,' Anna agreed. 'And . . . things evolve. Life moves on, in loads of ways. But that isn't always easy; it takes time to see the good in change sometimes.'

Rachel swallowed. She knew where this was heading, and she didn't want to go there. Firstly, she didn't want to make Anna feel bad for getting engaged, and secondly – while marriage might be great for Anna and Will – Rachel really couldn't see any way in which this was 'good' for her.

'Anna, I'm okay. Really. You don't need to be worried

about me, and you *don't* need to organise a big birthday bash to cheer me up.' This second point, at least, she really meant.

'The thing is,' Anna mumbled, taking another slurp of wine as if to steel herself for what she had to say next, 'I've already done it.'

'What?'

'I've already sorted it. The party.'

Rachel tried and failed to prevent a groan from escaping her lips.

'It's okay,' Anna said soothingly. 'It's not like I've hired a big venue, invited your gran and booked a caterer to make finger sandwiches . . . It's just a small gathering of people in a really cool bar. Tom knows the guy who owns it, and he owed him a favour.'

'*Tom* knew about this?' Damn, he was good at keeping things to himself.

Anna was nodding. 'Yes, he helped me sort it all out. We haven't told Will, though – he's terrible at secrets, he'd have spilled it within days.'

'Hmm,' Rachel said, arching one auburn eyebrow. 'I don't know if that's entirely fair . . . He caught you off guard when he proposed.'

'That's literally the *only* time he's managed to hold anything in,' Anna huffed. 'And it's entirely beside the point. The *point* is, you are having a birthday party – and you can't moan about it now or get edgy about not wanting to be the centre of attention because it's all arranged. All you have to do is turn up. You *need* this. It's for your own good, Rachel.'

Rachel resisted pointing out that 'it's for your own good' was the sort of thing you might say to someone about to undergo a colonoscopy. She leaned back in her chair and let out a long, resigned breath.

'Fine,' she said. 'And . . . thanks? I think?'

Anna poured more wine into their glasses, grinning with undisguised relief.

'It's going to be great,' she said. 'It's at this cool piano bar where you can do karaoke with a live band!'

'Whoa, okay – that does sound fun,' Rachel conceded.

'And I've invited everyone already so they all had plenty of notice,' Anna went on. 'I sent out the emails weeks ago.'

'You did?'

'Yep.' Anna raised her glass, as if congratulating herself. 'It's not a huge crowd – us four, plus a few of the uni lot who are local, plus a few of your work friends.'

Rachel felt the stem of her wine glass slip between her fingertips. She managed to set it down on the table before it fell.

'My work friends?'

'Mmm-hmm. Greg and his husband. Kemi, Ella and Theo. Isaac couldn't come.'

'*Theo's* coming? I'm not sure he even likes me. I don't know nearly enough Business Bullshit to have a whole conversation with him.'

Anna shrugged. 'Kemi said you were pals.'

Rachel rolled her eyes, then noticed Anna was chewing the inside of her cheek.

'Is there more?'

'Well,' Anna said, taking another sip of wine. 'It seems Kemi also let the party plan slip to Jack. She assumed I'd be inviting him because – according to her – you two are thick as thieves at the office. She says he's definitely going to make it. I can try and uninvite him if you like, but I guess it might be awkward . . .'

'No, no, it's fine,' Rachel said, her voice reedy and thin.

This was a disaster. A car crash. A *catastrophe*. What the hell was she going to do?

Jack and Greg were about to be thrown together with Tom – who they both thought was her boyfriend – in a boozy karaoke bar. It was the sort of judgement day that, as a lapsed Catholic, she should really have seen coming. *Of course* if she told lies about one person to another, their paths would eventually cross.

But how could she confess to Greg – let alone Jack – that she and Tom had never been anything more than good friends? The thought of admitting her dishonesty made her feel nauseous and sad.

Meanwhile, Anna would be crushed if Rachel asked her to cancel the party . . .

Before Rachel could come up with a strategy that might get her out of the mess she was suddenly in, Will and Tom turned up.

'I've told her about the birthday party, Tom,' Anna said. 'I think she needs another drink.'

Tom looked from Anna to Rachel, then said drily, 'As I predicted, she looks thrilled. I'll go to the bar.'

Anna laughed and Rachel attempted a less horrified facial expression.

Will threw his work bag underneath the table, kissed Anna's forehead and then sank into the chair next to hers.

'Party?' he said, bewildered. 'No one's said anything to me about a party.'

Rachel spent the rest of the evening trying not to panic – and determined not to *look* like she was panicking. By any sane standard, Anna and Tom had done a nice thing for her; she didn't want to hurt their feelings.

She was quieter than usual, but Anna more than made up for Rachel's reticence. She exclaimed about Zahra's beauty and the awesomeness of her shop, refused to answer any questions about her wedding dress and then regaled them with tales of the past week's classroom disasters.

Tom glanced at Rachel once or twice with thinly veiled concern, but she shook her head at him when he threw her a questioning look while Anna and Will were distracted.

As the night wore on – and as she sank several more glasses of wine – Rachel relaxed a little. Yes, she was up shit creek without a paddle, but no amount of worrying would solve her problems tonight. *Instead*, said a sensible voice from somewhere in her mind, *you're going to have to try and sort it out tomorrow. Probably while nursing a hangover.* Rachel told it to shut up.

Anna was ranting about *Romeo and Juliet* – or, more specifically, about 'Baz flippin' Luhrmann's *Romeo + Juliet*'.

'Despite repeated warnings about it being only an *adaptation* of the play,' she was saying, her eyes narrowed and her voice full of righteous anger, 'I've LITERALLY LOST COUNT of the number of times Romeo's Hawaiian shirt has been brought up in essays – ninety per cent of which also mention guns. Jamie De Luca handed in a piece of work this morning that referred to Mercutio "getting capped" by Tybalt. Would it have killed him to write . . . well. "*Killed*"?'

Rachel's eyes were streaming, and Will and Tom were shaking with laughter.

'Having fun, are we? Well. Ha-fucking-ha.'

All four friends looked up in surprise at the aggressive interruption.

'Oh, *no* . . .' Tom muttered. Anna's blue eyes were huge, like two turquoise saucers in her face.

'*Laurence?*' Rachel said. 'Laurence. What are you doing here?'

'I'm here to have it out with you,' Laurence said, standing over her and swaying.

Tipsy as she was, Rachel could see that he was drunk – and not the nice sort of drunk that buys a round for the whole bar and then leads a chorus of 'Champagne Supernova'. Laurence was *mean* drunk, and he was here to cause a scene.

'Have what out with me?' Rachel hissed, exasperated.

'You talked to Cass about me, didn't you?'

'*Who?*'

'Cass! My girlfriend! *Ex*-girlfriend now, thanks to you!'

'I have no idea what you're talking about, Laurence. I don't know who she is. I couldn't pick her out of a line-up, and I promise you I've never spoken to her.'

'Of course you have! Why else would she dump me?'

Rachel heard someone break into helpless laughter, then

realised it was her. *She* was laughing, hysterical at the sheer absurdity of the situation.

'Because of this, Laurence!' Rachel made an all-encompassing gesture with her arms. 'Because you do stuff like *this*.'

Still unsteady on his feet, Laurence advanced a step closer towards Rachel, who was still sitting down. Within seconds, Tom had put himself between them.

'Enough now. No more. Go home, calm down and sleep this off. And maybe consider making an appointment with a therapist first thing in the morning.'

Laurence sneered at him. 'I wondered how long it would take *you* to get your paws on her. Always waiting in the wings, weren't you? Are you the reason why she finished with me?'

Tom leaned forward, towering over Laurence by several inches. 'I. Said. Enough.'

He looked almost menacing, and Laurence shrank back.

Rachel stood up and put a hand on Tom's arm. 'It's okay,' she said. 'I've got this.'

She squared up to Laurence, daring him to shout her down when her very best friends were behind her.

'I finished with you because of *you*,' she insisted, firm but not shouting. 'Because you're an overbearing, insensitive, arrogant, entitled bully.'

Laurence opened his mouth, ready to retort.

'*I'm not finished!*' Rachel seethed at him. 'You've bothered and harassed me for months, after I told you I didn't want to see you any more. You continued to contact me by phone and email long after our relationship was over, even though I asked you not to. You sent flowers. You turned up *at my work*. And now you've followed me to my favourite pub to throw around insane accusations – to suggest that I might have deliberately sabotaged your relationship with some woman whose name I couldn't even remember! None of this is okay. And actually, it's only now that I'm realising just how NOT FUCKING OKAY it is. It's crazy – and Tom's right. It stops, right now.'

Tom was still at her elbow, and Rachel stepped back towards him, thankful for his support. Laurence's eyes were angry slits in his scowling face.

Will, who until now had stayed silent, stood up and folded his arms. His hulking frame dwarfed Laurence's; he was a man-mountain, built like the proverbial barn door. Will's arms, Rachel thought, were probably almost as broad as Laurence's *thighs*. He could floor him with a single well-aimed shove.

'Couple of things,' Will said, in the same friendly tone he'd have used if he were asking someone whether they knew the latest Arsenal score. 'Number one: your behaviour sounds an awful lot like stalking. Now, I'm not a criminal lawyer, Laurence, but it seems to me that the police would take a pretty dim view of all this – as might your employer, or any future employer, should Rachel decide to prosecute. And we' – he indicated himself, Anna and Tom – 'are going to make sure she dials 999 immediately if she ever sees or hears from you again. Number two: despite my build, I am a very mild-mannered man. But if anything's going to inspire me to throw a punch, it's seeing another bloke try to intimidate a woman – especially one I love.

Rather foolishly, you've gone one step further too: you've disturbed Friday Night At The Hope, which you know *full well* is sacrosanct.'

'*And* you interrupted my *Romeo and Juliet* story, you wanker!' Anna yelled, poking her head out from behind Will's arm. Rachel bit back a laugh.

Laurence's shoulders had sagged and he'd begun slinking away – as if he wanted to leave but was frightened to turn his back in case someone lunged for him.

'*Go*, Laurence,' Rachel said. 'Go for good. Don't ever contact me again, or I will report you.'

He tried to glare at her, but the alarm in his eyes won out. He looked like he was trying to think of some way to salvage his dignity. In the end, he just spun around and walked away – and Rachel knew that, finally, she was rid of him.

'Oi, you!' she heard a voice bellow. It was Nick, the pub landlord, and he was pointing at Laurence. 'You don't come in here again. YOU'RE BARRED. Now GET OUT OF MY PUB!'

After Laurence had slipped out of the door, Nick murmured, 'I've always wanted to say that.'

Rachel, Anna, Tom and Will were all sitting down again now, laughing with relief, not quite able to believe what had just happened.

'Shall I get another round?' Tom asked.

'Definitely,' Anna said. 'I found that whole drama very sobering. We need to counterbalance its effects immediately.'

'You've got to give it to him, though . . .' Will said, draining the last of his pint.

'Give *what* to him?' Anna demanded before he could finish.

'Well. I always said he was boring, but crashing in here pissed and apoplectic definitely wasn't *dull*, was it? I mean, he seemed like a stodgy, straight-laced actuary but it turns out he's a borderline sociopath. Who could have seen that coming?'

Anna shoved him and laughed again. Will stood up to help Tom with the drinks.

Rachel smiled wanly, and answered Will's question in her head. Maybe I could have seen it coming. Maybe I *should* have.

'I hope you didn't mind my intervening back there,' Tom said to Rachel as the four of them stood outside the pub after closing time. 'I didn't mean to tread on your toes – he just looked really aggro.'

'Honestly, it's fine,' Rachel said. 'I was grateful. For *all* of you.'

Anna and Will were chatting with some friend of his from the local rugby team, and she and Tom had drifted to one side, alone together.

'What a psycho, though,' Tom sighed. 'I never did like him.'

'At this point I'm not entirely sure *I* ever did. I think maybe nice, harmless Laurence was some sort of mirage. A figment of my imagination. I'm sorry he had a go at you, by the way.'

'What? *Oh*. That thing he said about me "waiting in the wings"? Don't worry about it.'

Tom shrugged and kept his eyes down. That made what Rachel knew she needed to say next a little easier.

This was her chance – probably her best chance, she realised – to tell the truth about her screw-up to the one person who might be able to help her. She was going to take it.

'Tom . . . Laurence isn't the only person recently to make that assumption about us.'

His head jerked up. 'How d'you mean?'

'Jack saw us out together in Highgate on the night we went to see Zack play. He thought you were my boyfriend.'

'Okay . . . ?' Tom was looking at her, puzzled, his eyebrows drawn down.

'And I let him. I let him think that. He *still* thinks that. Which wouldn't be a problem if it weren't for—'

'Your birthday. Right.'

Tom had buried both hands in his hair, and was massaging his skull as though he thought it might stop his brain from exploding.

'Rach . . . I mean . . . *Why?* Was it about making him jealous?'

'Maybe. Partly, I think,' she said, flooding with shame. 'But it was also handy for keeping him at a distance – putting myself out of bounds.'

'And how's that working out for you?' Tom asked, acidly.

'Er. I think it's fair to say that the fence I've put up between us is . . . rickety,' Rachel answered. 'He seems less and less bothered about . . . trying to climb over it.'

'What a guy,' Tom sighed. 'Pursuing a woman who

seems like she's in a perfectly happy relationship. Always a good sign.'

He sounded harsh. Bitter. Unlike himself.

'Happy relationship?' Rachel asked, risking a raised eyebrow.

'You *were* happy that night,' Tom said. 'We both were until we started bickering about the person we're bickering about right now.'

'Touché,' Rachel admitted.

'And I'm assuming you haven't told him I'm a shit boyfriend – I mean, presumably that wouldn't serve your carefully considered agenda.'

'Of course I wouldn't say that. You're lovely, which is exactly what I've told him – and which he absolutely hates.'

Tom shook his head at her, but his lips had loosened, no longer frozen in an angry line.

'So what's your plan, then?' he asked. 'How are you going to get out of this? Do you need me to dump you?'

'What?' Rachel cried.

'If I dump you, you won't need to admit to anyone that we aren't together.'

'True. I hadn't even thought of that . . . But then you couldn't come out for my birthday, which would be rubbish – you don't turn up for the birthday party of someone you've just chucked. And . . . I want you there. It'd be shit without you. If you're not with me, who'll help to get Anna and Will off the karaoke stage when they want to sing the full nine-minute version of "Bat Out of Hell"?'

'Fine, fine, I won't dump you,' Tom said, unable to resist laughing at the promise of Anna and Will's performance – a party piece he and Rachel had seen several times before.

'However, this leaves us with only two options.'

'Which are?' Rachel asked.

'You confess the truth to Jack, or you and I have to *pretend* to be an item on the night of your birthday party.'

'You'd do that?' Rachel's eyes were huge. Hopeful.

'Apparently,' Tom grumbled. 'Even though it's stupid, juvenile and bound to backfire.'

'Really?'

'Yes. I mean, you've obviously lost the plot, but I can't bear to think of you telling anyone – let alone *him* – that you've faked having a boyfriend, made it all up. He'd use your humiliation as a springboard for his next sexual advance.'

In the privacy of her own head, Rachel agreed with him.

'You're not made-up,' she argued, pushing the thought of Jack to one side and waving a finger at Tom. 'You're right there.'

Tom rolled his eyes at her pedantry. 'I will be your not-invented-but-fake boyfriend on your birthday. For one night only. But, Rach, this is a standalone performance. I won't come out of retirement after this – so no more lies.'

'I promise,' she said as Anna waved at her to hurry up and start the short walk home. 'As soon as my birthday party's over, I'll find a way to end the charade. And, Tom? Thank you.'

He nodded at her wearily, his arms limp and hanging at his sides. 'Don't mention it.'

He threw her a weak, joyless smile before he shouted goodbye to Anna and Will, then turned and headed home.

26

On Saturday evening a fortnight later, Rachel and Anna were walking through Clerkenwell towards the venue for Rachel's birthday party. They'd both dressed up for the occasion, Anna in a leather miniskirt and Rachel in heels, black skinny jeans and a vintage chiffon blouse the colour of Parma violets.

'That shade makes your hair look *insanely* red,' Anna had said approvingly before they left the flat, insisting that Rachel amp up the drama by donning a darker shade of lipstick than she'd usually wear.

Rachel had complied, and Anna was right – she looked good. She should be *feeling* good too, but the absurdity of what she and Tom were about to do wouldn't leave her alone; it was buzzing around her head like a wasp, determined to sting her before it deigned to fly away.

Also, she hadn't yet confessed to Anna that this evening was the stage for a fauxmance of the kind you'd usually see in a made-for-TV movie. But they were almost at the piano bar, and she was going to have to warn her friend what was coming before they went in.

'You've told Jack WHAT?' Anna demanded after Rachel's first attempt at an explanation. She was aghast, and she had less than five minutes to adjust to the news that *tonight, Matthew, Tom was going to be . . . Rachel's boyfriend!*

It wasn't only cowardice that had led Rachel to leave her admission to the last minute. She knew that Anna wouldn't approve of the ruse, and the less time she had to get indignant and teachery about it, the better.

'In my defence, I didn't *tell* Jack anything. At least, not to begin with,' Rachel said. 'He made an assumption I chose not to correct, and . . . well. Perhaps it ended up going a bit far.'

'A bit far?!' Anna thundered. 'That's one way of putting it. For God's sake, what a MESS . . . And I presume this is all for the sake of driving Jack wild with jealousy?'

'Not exactly,' Rachel said, choosing this moment to examine, then pick at, the rough edge of a fingernail. 'Though it does appear to have had that effect. It was as much about trying not to feel so *pathetic* around him – trying to send a signal that he couldn't just pick me back up and play with me whenever he felt like it.'

Anna let out an angry breath that Rachel was surprised didn't ignite the fence they were standing next to. 'After everything – the cheating and the endless tears and the bottomless rage – you couldn't send him that message *another* way?' she asked, incredulous. She shook her head briefly, as though she were embarrassed on Rachel's behalf. 'Did it even *work*?'

Rachel felt like the wind had been knocked out of her. 'Not exactly.'

Anna was wearing a pained expression, as though she could smell something unpleasant.

'And Tom is in on this?' she asked. 'He's agreed to this *ridiculous pretence*?'

Rachel nodded weakly but kept quiet – fearful that saying the wrong thing might fan the flames of Anna's rising, righteous anger.

'I suppose you didn't think at all about Tom's feelings,' Anna said, starting to walk again. 'About how this might affect *him*.'

'Well . . . I suppose it's annoying for him,' Rachel mumbled, not quite sure what Anna was expecting from her and stumbling to keep up as she strode around the corner. The piano bar was now in sight. 'And I know it's wrong of me to have involved him in a lie.'

Anna squeezed her eyes shut and took a deep breath. '*Un-fucking-believable*.' Rachel noted that her friend's shoulders had travelled several centimetres north towards her earlobes. Also that she was swearing, which years spent in the classroom had largely cured her of – no matter what the provocation.

Anna sighed, then seemed to collect herself. 'We don't have time to talk about this now; your birthday guests – or should I say *audience*? – await.'

Rachel flinched at her sarcasm.

'The one thing I will say is this,' Anna went on. 'In all the years I've known you, I've never thought of you as manipulative. Guarded, definitely. Scared to let people in. Economical with the truth at times, for the sake of self-preservation. But this is *game-playing*, Rach: messing with other people's emotions for your own ends. And it seems not to have occurred to you that someone might get hurt.'

With that, she marched forward, pushed open the huge

wooden door to the bar and went in, holding it open behind her.

Reeling, Rachel followed.

That could have gone worse, she told herself – though she wasn't entirely sure how.

Will handed Rachel an amaretto sour, and after eating the sticky cherry garnish off the side she told herself to sip it slowly. *Resist the temptation to neck it.*

The cold tang of the drink was delicious on her tongue: a welcome distraction from the weirdness of the situation. Almost everyone who'd been invited to her birthday celebration was here now, and she'd already dealt with Kemi's astonishment at being introduced to her 'boyfriend'.

'I'd have believed you weren't shagging Harper if you'd told me you had a hottie at home,' she'd said, dumbfounded. 'And he is *super*-hot. Maybe even more so than Jack, if you're into the sexy scientist look.'

Rachel had bristled at this. 'Tom's a graphic designer, Kemi. Not everyone who wears glasses is a scientist.'

'Whatever. He's still a total snack,' she'd said, shrugging. Rachel, unreasonably annoyed by the exchange, had been glad when Ella appeared and Kemi flew screaming across the room to greet her.

The combination of bourbon and amaretto in her drink had already begun to tamp down Rachel's anxiety. What was initially a rolling boil of worry in her stomach had reduced to a simmer. She suspected she'd be able to ignore it altogether by the time this glass – or maybe the next one – was empty.

A moment later Tom was back from the bathroom. With some difficulty he squeezed himself onto the velvet-covered bench that Rachel, Anna and Will were already sitting on, separating her from the others. Greg and his husband Carlos were sharing their booth – one of several that had been reserved for Rachel and her friends.

Tom could have sat next to Greg, in the obviously available space on the other side of the table. When she looked at him to query why he was squashing her, he widened his eyes in a meaningful stare. 'We're supposed to be an item, aren't we?' he whispered when no one was looking. 'And wasn't this *your* idea?'

It felt odd being this close to Tom when it wasn't strictly necessary. They were crushed together from shoulder to knee, their legs touching under the table and their arms colliding each time one of them moved. It wasn't uncomfortable or unpleasant, but it was definitely unsettling.

He smelled so much like himself: of citrus, soap powder and something else enticing that she couldn't put her finger on. It was the same fragrance she'd noticed that day in the beer bar, when he'd gone off on his mysterious date. All of Rachel's senses were overloaded, short-circuiting. The nearness of someone large and male, the noise of the bar and the sharp sweetness of her drink were all conspiring to muddle her thinking.

Carlos's voice cut through the general clamour and brought Rachel back to the moment. 'It's lovely to meet you, finally,' he said. 'Greg's told me so much about you.'

'Oh God,' she laughed, 'don't believe a word he says.'

'I'm told you two are great friends,' Carlos chuckled, his low voice and Spanish accent somehow making the word *friends* sound softer and warmer.

Carlos was taller and more conventionally handsome than Greg, with high cheekbones, abundant white-streaked hair and eyes the colour of chocolate truffles – but he lacked the easy, open confidence that came naturally to his husband.

'Well, *that's* true,' Rachel said, smiling. She looked at him and Greg side by side and decided they were well matched. A look of perfect understanding passed between them and Rachel felt briefly envious: painfully aware of her isolation. Greg was sure to quiz her about her own relationship the moment his chance arose – and for a few short seconds she sincerely wished it weren't faked.

Impatient to get some singing underway, Anna and Will went to find out when the band would begin playing. Tom and Carlos made their way to the bar for more drinks and – as Rachel had anticipated – Greg immediately rounded on her.

'So, tell me about Clark Kent,' he said. 'I want to know *everything* – or as much as you can spill in the time it takes for him to buy you another cocktail.'

'Who?' Rachel asked, nonplussed. Greg looked at her like she was the most tiresome person on the planet.

'Your tall drink of water over there,' he groaned, gesturing at Tom. 'He's *lovely*, but he clearly plays it down. He'd stop traffic with those eyes if he started wearing contacts.'

Rachel nodded, dumb, and felt herself flush. Then she told herself it was stupid to be coy. If she felt embarrassed, it should be because she'd allowed a tiny lie to become a huge one and – as of tonight – had dragged poor Tom into helping her maintain it.

'Stacked too,' Greg pronounced, always happy to hold a conversation mostly with himself. 'Nice arms, and I bet he has abs *for days* underneath that T-shirt.'

Rachel flashed back to bumping into Tom in the park, seeing him peel a layer of damp fabric away from the stomach muscles it had stuck to. Her cheeks were burning.

'Oh my God, you're *smitten*,' Greg said, amused by Rachel's silence. She felt terrible – sickened by her own dishonesty.

Before Greg could say anything else that made her want to curl up and die, Tom reappeared. He sat down on Greg's other side and within seconds they were chatting like old friends. Rachel felt her shoulders sag in relief. He was playing his part brilliantly.

'Music's going to start in ten,' Anna said, plonking herself back down at the table. 'So people can start requesting songs anytime now. Will and I already have about five numbers on the list.'

Rachel smiled and raised her glass in salute, and Anna mirrored the gesture – but her answering grin didn't make it as far as her eyes.

Tom looked at Rachel and mouthed the word '*Five?*', then set his face in a horrified grimace.

Rachel laughed, and he laughed with her. Perhaps this was all going to be fine.

Jack arrived at the bar just after nine – fashionably late and armed with a large gold gift bag.

'Happy birthday,' he said, leaning in to kiss Rachel on the cheek. 'Sorry I'm a bit late. You look gorgeous.'

'Thanks,' she said, taking the present from him and willing her heart to stop hammering. 'You really shouldn't have, though.' Inside the bag was a bunch of beautiful pale-pink roses and a bottle of champagne.

Anna and Will were halfway through a lusty, tuneless rendition of 'I Got You Babe'. Greg was watching them, boggle-eyed at the massacre of a beloved Cher song, and Carlos was talking to Tom.

'Drink?' Jack asked Rachel, inclining his head towards the bar and throwing his dark-grey jacket over the back of a nearby chair.

'A glass of fizz, please,' Rachel said. She watched him move through the mass of drinkers in the main bar, marvelling as several people – men and women – tried to catch his eye in the seconds it took him to cross the floor.

Then Tom was beside her, his hand on her shoulder. 'So. That's him.'

'Yeah.' Rachel nodded.

Jack had somehow managed to jump the bar queue; he was being served already. He didn't even do it *deliberately*, she thought – things like this just seemed to happen for him, and he let them.

'I get it,' Tom said. She turned to look at him, eyebrows up. 'I mean, he's obviously handsome. And he has some charisma, which a surprising amount of beautiful people lack. He looks like he belongs in an ad for an heirloom watch brand.'

Rachel wasn't sure what to say. Tom wasn't being nasty – in fact everything he'd said about Jack was complimentary. It just didn't sound that way.

'You're absolutely *sure* you want to let him think we're together?' Tom asked, pushing his glasses up his nose a little and looking down at Rachel for an answer. She felt a bit like a first-year student who'd just been asked a tricky question by the not much older but significantly better-read tutor she wanted to impress. Her stomach turned over.

'Yes,' she said. 'I'm sorry. We have to – I mean, as long as you're still willing. I promise that after tonight I'll spin some story that sorts this out. You won't have to lie for me a second time.'

'Okay, then,' Tom replied, looking at her steadily. His grey-blue eyes seemed to blaze in the semi-darkness of the bar. Then he took her right hand and held it in his left, weaving his fingers through hers as Jack made his way back to them.

Jack handed Rachel a glass of cava, then extended his hand to Tom.

'Nice to meet you,' he said. 'I'm Jack.'

It was almost as if he expected some sort of reaction; like he thought Tom would wince or turn suddenly pale when he realised who he was meeting. Tom looked blank, as if he'd never even heard of him.

Rachel felt like laughing, and was also morbidly satisfied to note that Jack stood a good three inches shorter than

Tom – who took full advantage of the height difference when he leaned forward to greet him.

'Tom,' he said. 'Nice to meet you too. You're a colleague of Rachel's.'

It was a statement rather than a question, and it didn't entertain the possibility that there could be – or ever *had* been – anything more between Rachel and Jack.

Rachel was impressed. Tom, whose default setting was affable, sunny and smiling, was suddenly ice-cold. His poker face was outstanding.

Annoyance flashed on Jack's face, so briefly that Rachel would have missed it if she'd blinked. He smoothed out his features, then took several deep pulls on his bottle of beer.

After a few more minutes of stilted, awkward conversation, Rachel, Tom and Jack drifted over towards the stage. Someone was hitting all the high notes in a heartfelt rendition of 'Somebody to Love' by Queen, and when she got close enough to make out his face, Rachel was astonished to discover it was Theo.

Kemi, Ella and Ella's boyfriend whooped and cheered as Theo finished, triumphantly belting out the final 'tooooooooooooo looooooooove' and bowing as he made way for the next performer.

Greg was up now, singing 'Your Song'. What he lacked in melody he made up for with feeling, swaggering up and down the stage and imbuing every word he sang with high emotion.

Kemi and Ella had found Jack, pulling him into a conversation he looked desperate to escape. He looked over at Rachel pleadingly, clearly appealing for assistance. She shrugged at him and tried not to laugh. Tom was holding her hand again.

Rachel felt eyes on her and looked up to realise they were Anna's. There was a crease between her pale-blonde eyebrows. She glanced at Tom, then back to Rachel, then at their entwined fingers. She turned to talk to Will.

He'd apparently taken the news of Rachel and Tom's fake date far better than Anna had, electing not to ask questions but instead concentrate on enjoying the evening. If Anna had hoped Will might talk his friend out of what she'd called 'this ridiculous pretence', she was sure to be disappointed. According to Tom, the sum total of his reaction had been, 'Bit weird, but okay.'

As Greg left the stage, the karaoke compère began reviewing his list of would-be performers.

Tom tucked Rachel's hair behind her left ear, then whispered into it: 'Don't freak out, but you're next.'

'*What?!*'

'Rach, we have to stop *them* from singing again, at least until we've had a few more drinks.' He indicated Anna and Will. 'Come on, we both know nobody in here deserves to suffer through their version of "I Know Him So Well". Consider this your civic duty. Also, you're the birthday girl: you need to have your moment in the spotlight.'

Rachel was smiling nervously, still unconvinced.

'Okaaaaay, do we have Rachel ready to sing?' the compère asked through the microphone, his eyes sweeping the room.

'If you don't, *they will*,' Tom breathed in her ear. Then he twisted around a few degrees to look at her, his face stony and serious – as if they were in an action film and she was the only person who could defuse the bomb.

'Oh, fine!' she laughed. *Sod it. How bad could it be?*

Rachel waved her arm above her head to make her presence known, then pushed to the front of the crowd and climbed up to take the stage.

The band struck up and she recognised the song immediately: 'Valerie', as performed by Amy Winehouse. Being up there was less scary than she'd expected. The lights that illuminated the band and stage shone so bright in her eyes that she could barely see the people watching her. It was freeing, and before long she was fully absorbed in her own performance – strutting and shimmying as she sang, reacting to the cheers of the audience.

Then it was over, and Tom was helping her down off the raised platform.

'That was *ace*,' he said, gathering Rachel into a bear hug. She wasn't sure whether the embrace was real or for show, but she leaned into it anyway.

Some while and several drinks later, Rachel found herself chatting to Will. Anna was telling Greg and Carlos a story that kept cracking them both up, and Tom had disappeared – maybe to the bar.

'Having a good night, Rach?' Will asked, slinging an arm around her shoulder.

'Definitely,' she said. 'But sorry if this whole . . . *thing* is a bit weird.'

Will scrunched up his nose, dismissing the idea. 'It all looks pretty natural from where I'm standing.'

'That's good, I guess . . . ?'

'Yeah. Ooooh, look, your *other* man's up to sing.'

Will was right: Jack had stepped onto the stage and was adjusting the microphone. The sound of keyboards and percussion filled the room, and Rachel recognised the opening bars of 'Common People' by Pulp.

'Oh *no*,' Will said. 'Terrible song choice.'

'Why?' Rachel asked, perplexed. 'This is a great tune.'

'Bloody hell, Rachel. Surely I don't need to explain to *you* of all people that someone who went to Harrow has no business singing about renting a flat above a shop. Anna would call this "cultural appropriation", and – do *not* tell her I said this – she's right. I wouldn't dare sing this song as if it meant something to me. I'd be murdered.'

Rachel laughed, but as Will's words sank in she felt the truth of them. As far as she could remember, Jack hadn't even needed to take out a student loan – he'd lived off an allowance from his parents the whole time they were at York.

This was definitely a bit rich, she thought, as he belted out the lines about working-class hardship in his RP accent.

He was really going for it, though. As she looked around, Rachel noted that there were plenty of women who seemed entranced – and in no way politically affronted – by his performance. The irony of it was clearly lost on them, but Rachel wasn't sorry Will had brought it home to her.

Jack bowed and then sauntered off stage, heading straight for them. Rachel's stomach swooped – as if she were standing on a high ledge, about to jump off.

Before he could say anything, Will pointed. 'Ah. Tom's up – this'll be worth hearing.'

Rachel looked up at him in surprise. 'Will it?'

Will nodded and grinned. 'The man's a dark horse. Irritatingly good at almost everything.'

Tom shook hands with the compère, who slapped him on the back as if he were an old pal he hadn't seen in years. Rachel remembered what Anna had said about him knowing the people who owned this place. Then, to Rachel's surprise, the band's keyboard player vacated his stool so Tom could sit on it.

'What the . . . ?' she started. But before she could finish, the beginning notes of a song she knew rang out of a nearby speaker: a mellow, familiar piano riff. And *Tom* was playing it.

And then there were words: 'It's nine o'clock on a Saturday . . .'

'Ugh. *Billy Joel?* "Piano Man"?' Jack snorted. 'I suppose tonight's cheese course is served.'

Rachel felt a sudden urge to hit him, but limited herself to hissing, 'Shut *up*.'

Will was smiling serenely. 'This isn't cheesy, it's classic. And this is a *piano bar*, mate – he's going to bring the house down.'

Tom's voice was right on the melody and full of character. His singing wasn't showy, but every word he uttered was authentic – *believable*. Rachel's skin started to prickle, goosebumps breaking out on every exposed inch of flesh.

By the time Tom got to the chorus it seemed that everyone in the bar, including the staff, was singing along. Rachel joined in too – though she discovered that the line about a drink called loneliness couldn't get past the lump that had formed in her throat.

Will had been right. When Tom sang the final words of the song, the whole place erupted – people were clapping, stamping and shouting for more. Tom motioned for the keyboard player to take his seat again, then placed the microphone back on its stand at the front of the stage and stepped back into the crowd.

'I'm going to go and see where Anna's got to,' Will said.

Rachel gave him a thumbs up, then realised that Jack must have slunk off partway through Tom's performance. *Huh*. She hadn't noticed.

Tom was walking towards her, and she shuffled forward through the mass of bodies to meet him. As soon as she was close enough, she threw her arms around his neck. It was pure and instinctive, and she hadn't thought it through. As their bodies collided, Rachel registered that she was a little drunk, as well as suddenly emotional.

'That was . . . I don't even *know* what that was. It was amazing,' she said, staring up at him. 'How did I not know you could sing? And since *when* can you play the piano?'

'I had lessons as a kid,' he said, pushing a dark-blonde wave off his forehead. 'And you don't know everything about me, Rach.' He raised one eyebrow and made an exaggerated Bond-villain face. 'I have my secrets.'

Rachel gave a short laugh, then registered the presence of Tom's hands on either side of her waist. Their noses were only centimetres apart.

She knew she should find some way to move, open up

a gap – spin around playfully and pull him towards their friends, perhaps. Holding hands so they could pretend to be a couple felt fairly innocent, but this full-frontal closeness did not.

She could feel his chest rising and falling, pressed up against hers. His breathing seemed shallow and too quick – maybe from the exertion of playing and singing. Rachel realised her pulse was racing too, but she had nothing like Tom's excuse.

What *was* this? What was she *doing*? She didn't know. They were still looking at each other.

Then, in a matter of seconds – maybe less than a second – something shifted between them. Rachel marvelled at the thousand shades of blue and grey in Tom's eyes: sea, sky, storm clouds. Cornflowers, turquoise, stone.

Greg had been right: they were beautiful. She felt like she'd never seen them properly before – never looked at them in the right light.

'So . . .' Tom whispered. 'Do you think we have everyone convinced?'

'I reckon so.' Rachel nodded. But neither of them moved.

Tom dipped his head and something inside her lit up like a flare. She tilted her face, arching her neck back and throwing her weight onto her tiptoes. He spread his hands on her back, pulling her further in.

Tom touched his lips to Rachel's. Lightly. *Too* lightly. This was the merest pressure: the sort of force you might use for brushing a feather off bare skin, or lathering shampoo into a baby's downy hair.

She kissed him back harder, without hesitation, pushing

her hands into his sandy hair and opening her mouth. He drew away almost immediately, moving his hands to her upper arms so he could steady her.

He was right to. Her head was swimming.

The look on Tom's face was incomprehensible. Was he shocked? Embarrassed? Angry?

Without thinking about what she was doing or why, Rachel moved forward, closing the distance he'd just opened up between them.

Tom kept his head up, several inches out of the way of hers. He wouldn't look at her, let alone kiss her – but he let her bury her face in his T-shirt as she held on to him. *God*, he was tall . . . And he really did smell good.

Rachel's legs felt less solid than they were supposed to, and she let herself collapse against him a little. He absorbed the extra weight without comment, not even shifting his feet.

When she opened her eyes, she was surprised to find they were still in the piano bar. Nothing and no one had changed and – while she wasn't sure why she'd expected anything different – that somehow seemed surprising.

'Feeling a bit wobbly?' Tom murmured.

'Yes, actually,' Rachel said, nodding her head. It was still resting against his chest.

'I daresay endless birthday fizz and industrial quantities of amaretto have got something to do with that,' he said into her hair. He was smiling, though; she could hear it in his voice. Rachel didn't argue, but she wasn't sure tipsiness alone could explain why her legs felt like they'd liquefied.

'Maybe we should get you home,' Tom said. 'It looks like people are starting to head off anyway, and this place will be closing soon. I'll go and find Anna. Let's sit you here for a minute.' He twisted around, then helped her onto a nearby chair – so subtly and gently that nobody watching would have noticed she wasn't totally stable.

Then there was a large, cold glass of water next to her and Tom was on the other side of the room, extracting Anna and Will from their conversation with Theo. They looked grateful.

Greg and Carlos, she saw, already had jackets on, and Kemi was scrabbling under a table for her zebra-print coat. *Good*, she thought. Rachel was ready to go home, but it was never a good look to get so lashed that you had to leave your own party before it was really over.

Suddenly, and without warning, Jack pulled up a chair beside her – so close their knees were touching. He was also ready to leave, his jacket back on but unbuttoned over the fine-knit V-neck jumper he was wearing.

'Thanks for inviting me,' he said. 'This was fun – though Anna doesn't seem to have missed me much.'

'Thanks for coming,' Rachel replied, ignoring his reference to Anna's frostiness. 'And for my birthday present too. That was lovely of you.'

She waited for him to say goodbye, then stand up and go. He didn't. Instead he let out a huge sigh, as if he'd just lost a fight with himself.

'Tom seems decent enough,' he said.

'*Decent?*' Rachel snorted. 'He's so much more than decent. He's wonderful, and . . .' She didn't complete the sentence out loud, but in her head she said, '. . . and he doesn't deserve to be used like this.'

'Yes, yes,' Jack muttered, waving his hand as if to bat the thought of Tom away. 'He's madly in love with you. Any fool could see that. He looks at you like you're the sun coming up. But I'm not giving up on you. There's something between us, and he doesn't get to win without a fight.'

Rachel realised her mouth had fallen open. Jack smiled, confident that this brazen statement of intent was responsible for her shock. Then he kissed her – technically on the cheek, but far closer to her mouth than anyone reasonable would have deemed appropriate.

He got to his feet, then said, 'I'll see you on Monday.'

Rachel stared after him. He was gone before Anna, Will and Tom reappeared.

27

Rachel woke up early, parched and feeling a little sick. Within seconds she realised she had a very special hangover on her hands: a morning after the night before that would require careful, deliberate management.

Too much water, drunk too fast, might lead to vomiting – and if she began being sick, who knew when she'd stop. On the other hand, if Rachel drank too *little* water, the throbbing at her temples would worsen.

Paracetamol, she knew from experience, must be approached with caution. Painkillers sometimes irritated her stomach, so she decided to put them off until her queasy gut had accepted a peace offering of toast.

Rachel glanced at her phone's home screen for the time: 7.53 a.m.

She shuddered. This was a foul time to be up on a Sunday, especially after going to sleep so late; it must have been after one when she got home.

It was only when she sat up in bed that Rachel realised she couldn't remember how she'd got there in the first place. Her last recollection was of being in a black cab and telling Anna, Will and Tom how much she loved them.

Tom.

FUCK.

She'd *kissed* him. Or he'd kissed her . . . He'd started it, technically – she was going to cling to that.

And Jack had been there, and he'd been jealous. He'd actually been a bit of a wanker, if she was remembering right. He'd said something too: something about her and Tom that seemed important.

She couldn't remember it now, but perhaps she would when her insides started functioning properly again.

She needed that toast. She needed something to drink.

Rachel stood up – definitely a little shaky on her feet – and stumbled across the room to retrieve her dressing gown.

God only knew how she'd ended up wearing pyjamas. A quick check revealed she still had her bra on beneath her floral button-down top. This suggested Anna had been involved in getting her out of her clothes and into her nightwear.

Memories – some fuzzy and others all too clear – began bursting across Rachel's consciousness, exploding one after another like tiny fireworks. She pulled her star-print towelling robe around her shoulders, then leaned her head against her closed bedroom door and took a deep breath. Reluctantly, she let her mind's eye zoom back in on the thing she knew for sure was true, but which she'd been trying to keep out of focus.

In her head, she could see herself doing it: standing on tiptoes so she could properly reach Tom's lips – necessary even in heels. Throwing her arms around him without a second of consideration. Sort of – oh God – *launching herself* at him, only for him to pull back in total amazement.

Yes, he'd put his mouth on hers first – but he'd jerked

away as if she'd tasered him the moment she began to respond. That much Rachel definitely remembered.

The reality of her situation began to dawn on her. Multiple pieces of the puzzle seemed to float in the air, then begin arranging themselves in slow motion. Watching the awful picture emerge was like waiting for the inevitable *SMASH!* after knocking over a glass; it seemed to take forever, but it was always going to happen. Rachel turned to lean her back against the bedroom door. She shut her eyes, confronting the ugly conclusion she'd now come to.

That soft kiss on her lips was the final act from Tom's 'Be the Perfect Fake Boyfriend' playbook. It was just part of his frankly *incredible* performance. She'd thrown herself at him because the line between truth and lies had become blurred in her head – much to Tom's horror, it seemed.

Rachel contemplated blaming it all on the fact that she'd been drinking. That was certainly the spin she'd have to put on things when she spoke to Tom – though, at this point, she didn't know how she'd even be able to look at him without melting into a puddle of shame.

She traced her top lip with her index finger, trying to put herself back in the moment – trying to make sense of what had happened. A shiver rushed down her spine. It was like she'd tasted something strange but lovely and couldn't accurately describe it, even to herself. At least, not without trying it again . . .

STOP, Rachel told herself, just as her stomach rolled over, finally threatening mutiny. She straightened up, deciding to obey her body's demand for carbs.

She plodded to the bathroom, used the loo and brushed

her teeth, then looked in the mirror and scrubbed away the remnants of last night's make-up. There were bruisy shadows under her eyes. She looked terrible.

As Rachel walked into the kitchen, she yelped and clutched her throat in shock.

Tom was there, sitting at the table with his head bent over a spy novel. There was a mug of black coffee in front of him.

'Shit,' he said. 'Sorry. I didn't mean to scare you.'

'For fuck's *sake*,' Rachel moaned, then sank into a chair. 'What the hell are you doing here?'

'Well, good morning to you too,' he said, his mouth hitching up in a wry smile. 'I'm here because after we let the taxi drive off it started to rain. I didn't fancy walking home in it, and Anna said it was okay for me to kip on the sofa.'

A cursory glance at Tom confirmed he was wearing the same jeans and navy T-shirt he'd had on last night. He looked slightly mussed, Rachel thought, but nowhere near as dishevelled as she'd be after a night of sofa surfing. From some cheeky corner of her brain came the message that unkempt early-morning Tom was kind of hot. Annoyed, she moved it to her mind's trash folder.

'Coffee?' Tom asked, standing up. He gestured at the half-full cafetière on the worktop. Where the hell had he even *found* that? She'd never seen it before.

'Can't face it,' Rachel said. 'I'm ruined.'

She could hear him laughing as he rooted around in the fridge.

'Here,' he said, placing a can of cold Coca-Cola in front of her. 'Drink this. And maybe have a couple of these.'

He fished in the front pocket of his battered chestnut-coloured satchel, which was hanging from the back of his chair. Then he threw a dog-eared box of painkillers onto the kitchen table.

After a few slurps of Coke, Rachel rested her head on the shiny wood of the tabletop, breathing in the sweet, almond scent of the polish Anna must have used on it yesterday. She heard the sound of a cupboard opening, the rustle of plastic packaging, the click and twist of the toaster dial and the depression of its four bread trays.

'Peanut butter? Marmite? Jam?' Tom asked. 'Or is this a "tiny scraping of butter in case everything comes back" situation?'

'The last one,' Rachel mumbled, without looking up.

Perhaps she drifted off, because it seemed only seconds later that a plate of lightly buttered toast was being put down in front of her. Delicately, she took a bite. Then another. She washed down each mouthful with Coke.

She didn't feel *better* by the time she'd finished, but her stomach was calmer and it was no longer a painful effort to hold her eyes open. She picked up Tom's packet of Panadol and swallowed two pills with the last of her drink.

After closing the box she pushed it across the table to Tom, who'd been quiet all this time – regularly turning pages in his book while munching on two slices of crunchy wholemeal, thickly coated with peanut butter.

Now the bodily effects of her hangover were receding, Rachel was left with plain, undiluted mortification. Embarrassment bloomed in her chest, intense and abundant; she wished she could disappear. She imagined herself shrinking away to nothing, like the Wicked Witch of the West when confronted with a bucket of water.

Rachel wanted to look at Tom, but didn't dare. She couldn't examine his features or test her reactions to them – not least because she didn't want to be caught in the act. It was bad enough that she'd tried to plant an unwelcome snog on him; the last thing she needed was for him to think she was still mooning after him the next day. She averted her eyes from his bottom lip, which he was nibbling softly – presumably in reaction to some exciting passage in the John Le Carré he was reading.

In over four years, and excepting nights when they'd been watching films, this was probably the longest they'd gone in one another's company without talking. The silence between them felt heavy and uncomfortable, now Rachel was awake enough to think about it. This was a strained, awkward sort of quiet that wasn't natural for her and Tom, and both of them knew it.

Just as Rachel had made up her mind to apologise for jumping him, Tom put his book down on the table – facing down so he wouldn't lose his page.

'Rach,' he said, softly. 'About last night . . .'

Rachel buried her face in her hands, unable to look at him.

'I want to apologise,' Tom said.

She peered at him though interlaced fingers. *What?* His eyes were as regretful as his voice.

He carried on: 'I played my part a little too well, I think. Took the performance too far. I should never even have thought about kissing you. That was . . . not okay. Not okay at all.'

Rachel gaped at him. He was blaming *himself* for the fact that she'd tried to put her tongue in his mouth? Some ember inside her glowed at the memory, and she stamped on it.

This was typical Tom: gallant, thoughtful and kind. Rather than letting her apologise for trying to cop off with him, he was shouldering all the blame for the meeting of their mouths. To spare Rachel's blushes, *he* was apologising to *her* – when surely they both knew it should be the other way around.

'It's . . . It's fine,' she said. 'Really.'

'It isn't,' Tom insisted. 'You're my friend, you're important to me and you'd had far too much to drink for anyone to be kissing you – either for real, or as part of some act. I think I got carried away winding up Jack – who, by the way, I don't like any better for having finally met. I crossed a line, though, and I shouldn't have. I'm sorry.'

Rachel just nodded her head, not sure what to say to any of this. In a single stroke, Tom had confirmed her theory that the kiss was for Jack's benefit – that it hadn't arisen from some other, deeper desire. At the same time he'd taken full responsibility for it, firmly sidestepping any potential discussion of why Rachel reacted so strongly.

She could only assume this was Tom's characteristically gentle way of making it clear to her that, if she harboured any more-than-friendly feelings for him, it was best for her to extinguish them.

Up until yesterday, it had never occurred to her that such feelings might exist. But when she looked at him now, all spectacles and tousled hair and yesterday's creased clothes, something deep inside her ached. The idea of killing it made her want to cry.

'Please don't apologise,' Rachel finally said. 'Honestly, you've nothing to be sorry for. If anything it should be me apologising – I should never have involved you in my stupid lie in the first place.'

'All right,' Tom said. 'Let's agree that you shouldn't have lied and I should never have kissed you. Deal?'

'Deal.' She nodded – but it felt like a bad bargain.

Tom appeared satisfied, though, and picked up his book again.

*

Tom had known Rachel for a little over four years, and for at least three and a half of them he'd been thinking, with increasing regularity, about kissing her. Last night she'd turned up looking lovelier than ever, and she'd painted her lips with some raspberry-coloured stuff that he'd immediately wished he could taste. It was torturous.

He should have known better than to keep touching her – should have realised that being so close to her all night, hugging her and holding her hand, would make trying to kiss her irresistible in the end.

Now, of course, he felt like a total shit. He was stomping home from Rachel and Anna's flat, cursing his own idiocy. Agreeing to be Rachel's fake date in the first place had been stupid – selfish and exploitative, as well as excruciatingly painful. It was just . . . Some part of him had hoped it might help her see him differently.

Of course, she probably *did* see him differently this morning – just not in the way he'd intended. Most likely, despite her reassurances, she now saw Tom as someone who'd tried to snog her when she'd had a skinful – as if they were fourteen and behind the school bike sheds. As if the #metoo movement hadn't happened.

Tom hated lies. He hated manipulation and mind games. Yet he'd thought that playing along with *this* game might be to his advantage. He'd kidded himself that he could circumvent the rules.

The trouble was that he'd *meant* everything he was supposed to be faking: every touch, every gesture, every word. And then the kiss . . .

He'd put his lips on Rachel's out of wild frustration, mostly with himself. It was as if he wanted to purge himself of the need to do it – as if he thought that kissing her once might fix him; render him disinclined to do it ever again.

It hadn't worked, of course, but the way she'd reacted was devastating. Tom cringed again as he thought of Rachel stepping forward, trying to reach for him a second time. It had been so intense, so *dramatic* – as if she was determined to do this Hollywood-style, in the hope that her ex was watching.

That hurt, and it grossed Tom out a little. It hinted that she had stronger feelings for Jack Harper than he'd ever have believed possible – feelings that were inspiring behaviour he'd never thought Rachel was capable of. Surely she was smarter than this? *Better* than this?

Tom shook his head at himself as he marched past the Hope. He had no business being self-righteous. Yes, this whole thing was grim, but it was his own fault he'd got mixed up in it. That was undeniable.

How many times might he have just *told* Rachel that he liked her as more than a friend? How many opportunities to switch things up – to try to flirt a little more obviously with her – had he squandered?

Too many – especially since the exhibition had thrown them together.

Suddenly, Tom's reasons for staying silent seemed thin and insubstantial: weak, childish and pathetic. It wouldn't have taken a declaration of undying love to work out whether Rachel was interested in him. Maybe just the honest offer of a date would have been enough.

And if she'd said no? Well, they'd have got over it. It might have taken a few weeks – maybe even a few months. But they were good enough friends, Tom now realised, that a mismatch of romantic feeling wouldn't have been the disaster he'd imagined.

If he'd been a little braver, they wouldn't have ended up here – with him feeling like a cad, and Rachel pretending to fancy him for the sake of snaring some total twat from her uni days.

Tom realised he was running. He was still in his jeans, and pounding the pavement in these trainers would probably fuck his knees... But he felt better for it. He wasn't slowing down, and he wasn't going home.

Sprinting until his lungs were screaming – battering his body until he couldn't think about anything apart from breathing – was exactly what he needed.

He kept going: past the flat, through Priory Park and up to Alexandra Palace.

When he finally collapsed on a grass verge, he was exhausted – and still madder with himself than he'd ever been before.

June

~~New Year's~~ Ongoing resolutions

1. Consider exercise an act with actual benefits – both mental and physical – not merely grim punishment for pizzas consumed. ~~Have a proper go at~~ Continue letting Greg drag me to yoga. ~~provided he refrains from making snide comments re Jack/me and Jack.~~ Give up trying to control subject matter discussed over dinner.
2. ~~Also re-download Complete Couch to 5K running app and actually do the programme.~~ Keep running at least twice per week – *always* being careful not to perv on anyone improper.
3. ~~Apply for promotion at work at first chance. Move to bigger account and try to get pay rise. Avoid, if possible, further projects concerning dog biscuits, disinfectant, high-quality printer ink cartridges, 'miracle' grass seed, organic vegetables, etc.~~

    3a. Try to hang on to job (and temper) despite

~~presence of evil ex-boyfriend hideousness~~ control-freakery of certain clients.

3b. Ignore everyone who keeps banging on about how fit ~~he~~ Jack is.

3c. Ignore how fit he is.

3d. Ignore the fact he ~~keeps trying to be friendly/nice/possibly quite flirtatious~~ is openly trying to shag me.

3e. Ignore the fact he is getting divorced.

~~4. DO NOT agree to further dates with Laurence. Remember: it's no use having a boyfriend who is good on paper if you do not actually fancy him.~~

~~4. Forget that Laurence even EXISTS (despite usefulness of overblown 'romantic' gestures for creating illusion of deeply devoted boyfriend. Try not to spin any more tales re 'boyfriend' though — don't want story to get too complicated . . .) — situation is already quite complicated enough.~~

5. Try to remember Mum means well, even during phone calls where she ~~implies I am doomed to a lonely life of penury because I am thirty with no partner, hardly any savings and no mortgage~~ insists on talking about the babies/breasts of people I went to school with.

6. HOWEVER, do not (!!!) speak to Mum when suffering PMT. Set phone alerts for likely spells based on period tracker intel.

7. Try to address 'hardly any savings' situation. ~~(If promoted, set aside extra earnings for future house deposit instead of spaffing it all on ASOS.)~~

(Do not spend entire pay rise on ~~'cheer up' treats to distract from heinous ex-boyfriend mess.~~ hot new outfits for work – see 3c.)
8. Try to eat my five-a-day. (Remember horrid rule that potatoes do not count.)
9. ~~Start using proper night cream with retinol. SERIOUSLY.~~ Regularly apply retinol cream purchased from Boots in pursuit of perfect, Dev-style skin.
10. Do the best possible job helping Tom with exhibition. Be supportive and discreet re Oscar. Avoid arguing with Tom about Jack.
11. Be a good friend (and bridesmaid) to Anna. Help with wedding organisation and keep selfish, sad worries about how much I'll miss her to myself.
12. Find a way to end fake boyfriend pretence before it fucks up entire life.

28

The atmosphere between Anna and Rachel had been strained for several weeks now – ever since the night of Rachel's birthday party.

On the hung-over Sunday that followed her fake date with Tom, Anna had been scathing of Rachel's dishonesty and openly disappointed in her for lying to her work colleagues – especially Greg.

'He isn't just someone you share an office with,' she'd said. 'He's your *friend*. And you've told him a gigantic fib for reasons I'm still struggling to fathom.'

Anna also seemed aware that something had happened between Rachel and Tom, though Rachel hadn't offered any explanation for the tension between them. Whatever she was blaming it on, Anna had certainly noticed Rachel's new and ongoing nervousness around Tom – as well as his reluctance to be left by himself with her, even just while washing up, queuing for drinks or waiting for someone else to come back from the bathroom.

Rachel and Anna had spent barely any time alone together lately. Anna was at Will's a lot, or he – and sometimes Tom – were at their place.

Neither Rachel nor Anna had mentioned the distance between them, but something hostile hung in the space that had suddenly opened up. Disquiet followed them around like a rain cloud: a dark, heavy thing that threatened to burst with no warning.

Rachel was dreading this morning. It was Anna's final wedding dress fitting and she was going along to see her in her gown, as well as look at the selection of bridesmaid dresses Zahra had sourced. It was going to feel weird sitting there, chatting about pretty clothes as though nothing had happened. As if nothing was wrong.

To make matters worse, Rachel knew she was overdue a (probably irate) phone call from her parents. She'd been dodging them for days, trying to avoid talking to them about when she'd be moving – when she'd need their help to shift her boxes, bed frame and the few bits of eBayed furniture she owned.

They wanted to know where she was moving *to*, but she didn't know herself yet. Her mother seemed full of ideas on this front, but Rachel didn't want to hear them. Apparently some Irish cousin was moving to London and needed a roommate, but Rachel hadn't bothered to ask who, when or why.

Dad had sent her a text already, and it was only 8 a.m.

Dad: *For the love of god, call your mother – she's driving me to drink with moaning that she needs to talk to you. (Also we want to know you're all right.) x*

Rachel messaged back:

Rachel: *Sorry Dad – busy Saturday. Wedding dress fitting with Anna and then the final exhibition photo* *shoot with Tom this afternoon. Will call tonight, PROMISE. And don't worry – I'm fine x*

An hour or so later Rachel was showered, dressed and had seen away two Weetabix and a banana.

'Ready to go?' Anna asked her, clipped and businesslike.

'Yep. Just let me grab my bag.'

They made awkward small talk on the way up to Tempo, mostly about wedding stuff: Anna's final choice of flowers, the table plan, the guest list and the annoying handful of friends who *still* hadn't RSVP'd.

Rachel listened more than she talked. After all, what could she say? Anna still didn't know Rachel was working for Lighthouse – she'd never found the right moment to mention it, and the longer she held back the weirder it would seem that she'd kept quiet. Nor did Anna know that Jack had made a play for Rachel . . . Or that Rachel felt like her insides turned to mush every time she remembered kissing Tom.

She told herself she was just being silly – that she'd only ever thought of Tom as a friend and the mushiness meant nothing. Even if she *did* have some sort of crush on him, Rachel reasoned, there was nothing to be done about it. He'd made it painfully clear he wasn't interested, so what was the point in agonising? Better to ignore it – push it down as deep as it would go, then hope it withered away.

If Zahra noticed something was off between Anna and Rachel when they got to her shop, she had the good sense not to acknowledge it. As on the first day they'd met,

Zahra left them to look through the gowns she'd already set aside while she made three cups of tea.

'What do you think, Rach?' Anna asked, running her hand along the rail full of dresses.

'They're all nice,' Rachel answered. 'But it's your wedding. I want you to make the final decision.'

Anna, with barely concealed irritation, said: 'You'd better try them all, then.'

Rachel wasn't sure what Anna was cross about. She was terrible at judging what looked good on herself, and even in normal situations deferred to Anna when she needed help deciding what to wear.

About forty minutes later, and with valuable input from Zahra, they'd narrowed the choices down to a plain green shift dress draped with soft chiffon, and a prom-style gown with a sweetheart neckline in the same shade of peach as the embroidery on Anna's dress.

Either would work with the wedding colour scheme Anna had put together. The flowers – various shades of peach, orange and cream – would 'really pop' against the green gown, Zahra said. Anna could wear a piece of emerald jewellery, or even green shoes, to tie the two looks together.

Privately, Rachel felt happier in the green shift. Peach wasn't a shade she'd ever choose for herself; it robbed her pale skin of warmth and clashed with her red hair. This particular gown made her look bloodless – positively unwell.

'So . . . ?' Anna said. 'What's the verdict?'

'Whichever you're happier with,' Rachel said.

Anna eyed her, frustrated, and didn't bother to try to hold in her answering sigh.

'If you want my view, the green is the one,' Zahra said. 'The style of the dress works better with yours, Anna, and I think it's a better colour on Rachel.'

'*Thank you*,' Anna said. 'I'm glad someone around here is capable of telling the truth. Let's go with it.'

Zahra looked momentarily uncomfortable, then took Anna over to her desk to discuss alterations and payment. Rachel felt desolate.

Then her phone began ringing from the bottom of her handbag. *For fuck's sake*, she thought.

Rachel considered ignoring it, but wondered whether it might be Tom calling about this afternoon's shoot. If there was a problem, or a change of time or location, he'd need to tell her about it.

She finally found her mobile buried beneath a paperback, this week's *Stylist* magazine, her worse-for-wear wallet and several tinted lip balms. *Mum calling*, it said.

'Arrghhhhh,' she groaned out loud, just as Anna reappeared, ready to head back to the bus stop.

'What's up?' Anna asked as they waved goodbye to Zahra and closed the shop door behind them. Her knitted eyebrows betrayed genuine concern, despite her earlier snappiness.

'Nothing,' Rachel said, though she suddenly felt close to tears. 'My mum's harassing me about what I'm doing, living-arrangements-wise, after the wedding. She and Dad keep demanding information: where will I live, who will I live with, blah blah blah. It's driving me mad.'

'Has it ever occurred to you that maybe they just *care*, Rachel?' Anna said, whirling around to face her so fast that Rachel flattened her back against a wall. 'Don't you realise how fucking LUCKY you are that they *give a shit* about whether you're safe, whether you're happy . . . Whether you have some sort of life plan?'

A wave of guilt broke over Rachel's head. She felt sick with contempt for herself – not to mention shocked by Anna's uncharacteristic swearing.

Of course Anna was right. It was the height of insensitivity for Rachel to complain about her parents when Anna's own mother had refused to come to her wedding.

Poor Anna had agonised over whether to contact Nicola – whether to open up and risk feeling, once again, like the dejected teenager whose mum wasn't interested in her. When the wedding response card had come back last week with the *No* box ticked and no personal message or attempt at explanation, Anna had sobbed in Will's arms and eaten a whole pot of Häagen-Dazs.

'Anna, I—'

'*Don't.* I don't know what's going on with you lately, but I think I'm starting to feel the same way your poor mum does: as though you're only giving me half the story, no matter what we talk about. You tell yourself you're sparing other people, stopping them from worrying by holding everything in – but it's just a way for you to hide from how you really feel,' Anna ranted. 'Having said that, there are obviously some feelings you've decided *not* to hide from recently – and I understand entirely why you'd want to keep that quiet. What the hell are you thinking, getting close to Jack again because he's batting his eyelashes at you, buying you birthday champagne and telling you he's changed? It's beyond idiotic. It's desperate.'

Rachel felt like she'd been slapped.

'Hold on a minute,' she said, hurt and suddenly angry. 'I know you're mad with me – but you have no idea what's been happening with Jack.'

'Oh, please,' Anna groaned. 'I know better than *you* do what's been "happening with Jack".' She mimed speech marks, her voice jeering and her face the perfect picture of derision. 'You told yourself you were over him, but he's always had houseroom in your head – he'd been living in your brain, rent-free, for a decade before he ever appeared in your office. Why else would you ever have looked twice at a boring git like Laurence? Since Jack, every man you've been out with has been either a heartless shagger or a total dullard. It's like you need to know up-front that, one way or another, there's no future in any relationship you start. That whoever you're with won't make you care too much, then let you down.'

Tears were rolling down Rachel's cheeks now, and Anna was crying as well.

'I just wish you'd fucking *talk* to me, like you used to!' Anna yelled. 'I'm getting married, I haven't joined a cult or been abducted by aliens. I'm still the same person I've always been. I'm supposed to be your best friend.'

'But you'd never have listened about Jack!' Rachel shouted, finally finding her voice. 'You'd have made me feel stupid – exactly like you're doing now. He's been *there* for me at work. He's been supportive . . .'

Anna took a deep breath and swiped at her tear-soaked cheeks. Her perfect winged eyeliner had run, her lipstick had smudged and her nose was pink and snotty.

'I'd have told you the truth,' she said. 'I'd have reminded you that he never stopped fancying you, even back at uni – he just wanted to have his cake and eat it. So it's no surprise to me that he's after you again. Jack did care about you, he just cared about himself *more* – and I'd bet my entire wedding budget that he still does now. What has he done for you at work that didn't also advantage *him* in some way? Who's been watching every time he's been helpful? It's what people do when no one's looking that tells you who they really are, Rach.'

This made Rachel think of Tom: modest and unassuming, talented but self-effacing. She thought about him singing and playing the piano, and how much he cared about Oscar even though the kid was a total liability. She remembered he'd sent her chocolate dog droppings because he knew it would make her smile on Valentine's Day.

'I don't believe people change, Rach,' Anna went on. 'Not without a shitload of therapy, anyway. You used to think that Jack had a secret softer side, but he's always been precisely what he seems. He doesn't have hidden depths . . . Just moderately well-concealed shallows.'

'I'm not an idiot, Anna, and I am *not* desperate,' Rachel said, her voice heavy with tears.

'But you're *stuck*,' Anna said. 'You're not moving forward or in control of where you're going. Getting sucked back in by Jack is the easy option: he'll chase you and in the end you'll let him win, just like you did before.

But that's not really choosing – it's letting someone else choose for you.

'It's exactly what you did in there with the bridesmaid dresses, even though you knew that peach one made you look like a cadaver.'

'I *am* moving forward!' Rachel protested, sniffing. 'I'm moving out, aren't I? I'm going to live without you for the first time in thirteen years!'

'Only because I'm *making* you!' Anna cried. 'And I feel like a total bitch – like I'm the worst friend in the world! But I can't spend my life looking after you if it means missing out on what *I* need. I can't be responsible for you any more, Rachel!'

Rachel recoiled, as if Anna had fired a gun at her.

'*Responsible* for me?'

As fresh tears flowed down Rachel's face, Anna fell silent. The angry wind had finally gone from her sails and she looked devastated. Stricken.

'Rachel . . . Oh, Rach, I didn't mean that. I'm sorry, I'm so sorry.'

'I think you did mean it,' Rachel said. 'In which case, I'm sorry too.'

She walked away, not caring that she was going in the wrong direction. Anna didn't follow her.

Rachel's eyes were puffy and red-rimmed. She'd cried off most of her make-up and, while she'd stopped weeping for now, she felt as though she was holding herself together with duct tape.

The last thing she wanted to do was spend her afternoon

assisting at a celebrity photo shoot – but what other choice did she have?

She couldn't go home. Anna would probably be there – and right now, seeing her was even less appealing than spending the next few hours with Tom and Sophie French.

Besides, Tom had always been good at spotting when Rachel needed support. However weird things were between them, she knew that he'd sense her distress – that he'd care whether or not she was okay. If she told him what had happened, the likelihood was that Tom would listen calmly and offer her advice if she asked for it – and she trusted him not to take sides or talk down to her.

Anna had tried to call Rachel three times since she'd left her on the street outside Tempo, but Rachel had ignored her phone and, in the end, turned it off altogether. She couldn't face another argument, and she wasn't anywhere near ready to forgive Anna for the things she'd already said.

As Rachel stood in the ladies' toilets of a small cafe near Bounds Green Tube station, she asked herself how on earth they'd ended up here. She and Anna had been friends for almost half their lives and they'd never fought like this. She wasn't ready, yet, to ask herself how much truth there'd been in Anna's angry onslaught.

Instead, she concentrated on damage limitation; de-blotching her face with an emergency concealer stick she'd bought from a pharmacy, removing all traces of this morning's mascara and drinking a takeaway cup of herbal tea in the hope that it would steady her nerves. Once she looked like she could pass for human again, Rachel glanced at her watch. Time to head back into town.

This afternoon's photo shoot was happening at a studio just off Marylebone High Street, and it would take the best part of an hour to get there from here. Rachel tried to read on the Tube, but the effort was wasted. She couldn't concentrate, and in any case her book was about two best friends taking a redemptive, life-changing trip across America. *Pah*.

Rachel got off the Underground at Baker Street, then made the short journey into Marylebone on foot. She looked at the scrap of paper she'd hurriedly scribbled the studio address on, satisfied herself that she was in the right place and then examined the cluster of doorbells next to a four-storey townhouse with a shiny blue front door. She pushed the one labelled *ST*, then heard a cheerful female voice say, 'Hello?'

'Oh. Hi. I hope I've got the right place. This is Rachel. I'm looking for Tom Evans.'

'You've got the right place! He's in the bathroom, I think. Come on up – second floor. This is Sophie, by the way.'

Rachel heard a buzz, then a thump that meant the front door was unlocked. She pushed it open, let it slam behind her and climbed the stairs to the studio.

As she entered the room, Tom emerged from round a corner. His face was ashen, his eyes bright with alarm. What on earth could be wrong?

'Rach,' he said, crossing the sizeable room in two strides. Then, urgently and under his breath: 'I've been trying to call you. I've rung you, like, *a thousand* times. There's a situation – something you need to know.'

'My phone's been off,' she said, frowning up at him.

His eyes swept her face, taking in the telltale signs of her tearful outburst.

'What's going on?' they both said together.

Then the studio door flew open and Dev strolled in. There was a tanned, slender, dark-haired woman on his arm.

Rachel's entire body went cold. She could hear her heart beating in her ears and feel her pulse throbbing somewhere near her tonsils.

As chilly sweat coated her palms and crept down her back, Rachel wondered why she hadn't seen this coming. After all, given the run of luck she'd had lately, it made perfect sense that Jessica Williams should show up, in the flesh, for Tom to take her photograph.

Dev was introducing her to everyone. Sophie – a smiling, genial presence in a simple cotton dress – shook Jessica's hand and said it was lovely to meet her. Then Tom, recovering his professionalism admirably, told her he was happy to have her on board with the show. Only Rachel could tell he didn't mean it.

'This is Rachel, our copywriter,' Dev said.

'Great,' Jessica said, extending her arm.

Rachel took her hand for a moment, noting that Jessica's nails were almost as badly bitten as her own. Where were her perfect French tips?

There was a flash of something like recognition in Jessica's brown eyes, but it fizzled out before it could settle there.

She had lines around them; fine little creases that showed

where her skin furrowed when she smiled. Her forehead was shiny and smooth, implying the presence of Botox.

In 3D, Jessica's face didn't look the same as it appeared on Instagram, nor in the ads that seemed to follow Rachel around London. It was very pretty, but less polished than Rachel might have expected. Jessica had a chickenpox scar below her left eyebrow that was, presumably, airbrushed out of every photo she ever shared. Her chin bore the faded marks of old hormonal breakouts.

Jessica's lips were as abundant as ever, but up close it was clear that they'd been filled. While she'd never judge anyone – even Jessica – for having cosmetic surgery, Rachel couldn't help wincing when she looked at them, wondering if the procedure had been painful.

Unframed by her usual falsies or eyelash extensions, Jessica's real-life eyes were less commanding – less intense – than they were in photographs. She dropped her gaze from Rachel's, looking almost vulnerable as Dev began to explain her last-minute interest in the exhibition.

'This is a vital step towards rebuilding Jessica's reputation,' he was saying. His hand was on her shoulder. 'I think it's fair to say the business with the fat-burner pills has been quite distressing for Jessica personally – but it's done serious damage to her *brand* too.

'She's come to Esteem PR from her previous agency, who gave her some very bad advice. Our first task is to try and reset Jessica's image – strip it back to basics.'

Tom was nodding, but the rigid set of his shoulders betrayed his discomfort. Sophie, who'd taken Jessica's hand, said, 'I did some work with Angeljuice once . . .

Very pushy people. It can be hard to say no to things, and it's tough when you're the face of a campaign that goes down badly.' Jessica said nothing, and continued to stare at the beige loop-pile carpet.

'Right,' Dev interjected. 'Let's have Jessica with Tom first while Sophie chats to Rachel. Then you can swap over.' He seemed keen to avoid further discussion of a topic that Jessica apparently found distressing.

Tom caught Rachel's eye and looked at her in a way that was at once pleading and apologetic. The message was clear: he was sorry she had to do this – that *they* had to do this – but he needed her to keep her cool.

Rachel reminded herself that this exhibition was a huge opportunity for Tom. It was his chance to do more of what he loved – maybe even make a proper living at it. If she had a shit-fit now, she could ruin it for him.

Tom led Jessica over to a stool surrounded by lights and umbrellas. Bile rose in Rachel's throat as she watched him gently position Jessica's head and arms with his hands, then lean over her to take light readings and adjust the angle of a round silver reflector.

In front of the camera, Jessica's quiet apprehension seemed to melt away. She flipped her hair, pouted and tilted her shoulders on cue, somehow managing to look just as alluring as in her poster ads – even in no make-up and a plain grey T-shirt.

As Tom helped Jessica move into a standing pose, she stared up at him through her eyelashes and let her hand linger on his forearm for a few seconds too long. Was she *flirting*? Rachel was incensed.

'We need a shot that looks *apologetic*,' Dev said. 'Something that inspires a bit of sympathy.'

From what Rachel could gather, there'd been some sort of backlash against the diet pill ads Jessica had starred in – a backlash that, to Rachel's mind, wasn't entirely undeserved.

Tom pulled down a white background roll, then placed Jessica towards the back of it, cross-legged on the floor like a primary school kid. He shifted lights downwards and moved the camera up, so it was positioned over her head. This was clever, Rachel thought: Jessica looked plaintive, like a supplicant.

When she lifted up her face, her cheekbones caught the light and she stared wide-eyed into the camera. Rachel told herself not to look any more. She should be concentrating on interviewing Sophie.

To Rachel's relief, Sophie was open and articulate. She spoke in a measured, thoughtful way about her experience of living life online.

'Becoming an influencer is a bit like entering a Faustian pact,' she said. 'You might make a good living – you probably get to do cool stuff you've never even dreamed of – but you can end up feeling like the social platforms, or your followers, own you . . . Like you owe them something. If you're not careful, you begin living life for the sake of creating good content, rather than doing good *things*. That's why I've stepped back from it.'

'That makes sense.' Rachel nodded. 'What do you think of the idea that influencers have a responsibility to the people who follow them? That they shouldn't, for instance, promote products that might be considered harmful?'

'Hm. Not a Jessica fan, I take it?' Sophie whispered. Rachel coloured.

'Off the record,' Sophie said in a low voice, 'I think she's been naive, but also let down by her handlers. I got mixed up with Angeljuice when I was in my early twenties – they pay big money and it's hard to say no when they want a new face. But we're in a different time now . . . Diet pills were never going to go down well in some of the communities she's part of. That doesn't justify what's happened to her, though. She's had death threats, apparently; really awful, graphic stuff. Nobody deserves that, no matter what shit they've been daft enough to advertise.'

Rachel looked across the room to the studio area again. Sophie had a point, but Tom was helping Jessica up from the floor and seeing her touching him made Rachel's palms itch.

She wanted to go and yank him away from her – several miles away, if necessary.

'Looks like it's my turn for photos,' Sophie said. 'Do you have enough ramblings from me to write what you need?'

'Definitely,' Rachel said. 'Thanks. And all the best with acting – I have a feeling you're going to be great.'

As Sophie walked away, Jessica came towards her.

'Can I get you anything to drink before we start?' Rachel asked.

She remembered telling Anna that if she ever saw Jessica again, she'd pour a drink over her head. Now it came to it, she was offering to make her a cuppa.

'Tea would be great,' Jessica said. Her voice sounded

nothing like Rachel had thought it would. Jessica spoke in a high, girlish tone – not the deep, husky murmur that Rachel's mind had seemingly made up. She had a similar accent to Anna's too: spiky, authentic East London, rather than the smooth received pronunciation her image implied.

'Milk? Sugar?'

'Just a bit, and two please.'

Rachel smiled tightly, then walked away in the direction of the kettle.

The interview was forced and uncomfortable, and not merely because Rachel kept wishing she could disappear. Jessica seemed reluctant to say much about herself, her public profile or social media in general.

'Dev'll give you something to put with my picture,' she said.

'You want *Dev* to put words in your mouth?'

'It's probably for the best. He'll know the right thing to say, which I never do. People generally don't believe this, but I've never been all that confident. I'm just good at playing the diva when there's a camera pointed at me.'

'Right,' Rachel muttered. She was shocked, but – based on what she'd seen today – this had the ring of truth.

'Do I know you, by the way?' Jessica asked. 'I feel like we've met before. I'm sorry if we have and you thought I was being rude.'

Damn, damn, damn.

'I think maybe we were at uni together,' Rachel answered, after failing to think of a convincing lie. 'Did you go to York?'

'Yes, that's it.' Jessica nodded, her eyes a little brighter.

'I remember you now. I think we were in the same seminar group once. You were one of the people who always had opinions.' She said this smilingly, without a trace of sarcasm.

Rachel had no memory of ever being in the same room as her. But if Jessica never spoke in class, why would she?

'It's coming back to me now,' Jessica said. 'You used to go around with that good-looking guy – the one who had a different girl on his arm every five minutes.'

She smiled at Rachel as if they were partners in some conspiracy.

'You always seemed so sorted, though – too smart to have your heart broken. I had a thing with him, but only for one night . . . He really wasn't boyfriend material! God, what was his *name*?'

Suddenly Rachel felt as if she'd had a cool glass of something chucked over *her* head. Jessica didn't remember her as Jack's girlfriend . . . She remembered her as too smart to have been Jack's girlfriend. It was an irony that stung.

And there was something else: Jack had always said that Jessica pursued him despite knowing he was taken – flirted with him for months, then talked him into bed when he was drunk and distressed after arguing with Rachel. Based on what Jessica had just said, there was no way that was true. All at once Rachel wasn't sure why she'd ever thought it might be. But hadn't Jack repeated his ten-year-old story when they'd first argued about working on the Lighthouse account?

'Jack Harper,' Rachel said. 'That's who you're thinking of.' Her throat was horribly dry.

'Oh *fuck*,' Jessica said, louder and more animated than

she'd been all afternoon. She was staring at Rachel, giggling anxiously, her lush mouth wide open with worry. 'You didn't end up married to him, did you? Oh God, say you didn't! See – this is why I usually keep my mouth shut.'

As soon as Dev, Sophie and Jessica had left, Tom began apologising.

'I'm so sorry, Rachel. I tried to ring you as soon as I knew she was going to be here . . . Dev and I had already had some discussion about her coming on board – *heated* discussion, I might add – but I never thought he'd bring her today. He only told me an hour before the shoot started.'

'You knew she was getting involved with the exhibition and didn't TELL ME?'

Rachel had the dim sense that she wasn't being fair – that she was about to blow her stack about one thing when really she was upset about something else entirely.

Tom's eyes widened at her overreaction. 'Steady on, Rach. I didn't *know* – it wasn't final. And I didn't see the point in upsetting you by bringing it up until I was sure.'

'You weren't so bothered about upsetting me when you were flirting with her during the shoot!'

'*What?*'

'I'm not blind, Tom! It all looked very touchy-feely, even from the other side of the room. You were on the hook from the second she started pouting and fluffing her hair.'

'Oh my God. Are you serious?'

She wasn't, really, but she was indignant. And – oh fuck – *here* was the realisation she'd been trying to keep at bay all afternoon: she was jealous.

'I couldn't be less interested in Jessica!' Tom ranted. 'Frankly, I felt a bit sorry for her. In any case, I don't know how you can justify having a go at me for being merely polite to her when you're spending half your time cosied up to the bastard who couldn't keep his hands off her. The man who *actually* cheated on you with her. Really, how am I the dickhead here? Do enlighten me.'

Rachel felt around for something to say – something impressive and clever that might obscure the fact that he was totally right.

'I'm not "cosied up" to Jack,' she yelled. 'It's not my fault we ended up working together!'

'No. But, Rachel, *I'm* not blind either – none of your friends are. Don't you think it's a bit ironic, hating Jessica for her Insta-fakery and airbrushed ads, when you've spent the past six months mooning over a man who lives his whole life through some sort of . . . some sort of *charm filter*? Someone unbelievably selfish, but brilliant at playing the hero when it suits him. Someone whose scheming and manipulation has, unfortunately, started rubbing off on you.'

'That's not fair,' Rachel said – though on what basis, she wasn't quite sure.

'Isn't it? Last month I pretended to be your boyfriend in front of a room full of people, most of whom you were lying to, so you could make Harper jealous – intensify this twisted game of cat-and-mouse you've been playing. Yes, you'd been drinking – but you'd have kissed me, *properly* kissed me, just to wind him up. It makes me feel ill, and I wish I'd never been part of it. I wish I could stop *thinking* about it.'

Tom's face was agonised. His blue-grey eyes were wild behind the lenses of his glasses, full of anger, hurt and – even more unbearably – disappointment.

'I wouldn't—That isn't—It wasn't—ARGH.'

Rachel scrubbed her face with the palm of her hand, then decided to try again.

'I'd never have done that. I would never have kissed you just to upset someone else. I couldn't kiss you and be *thinking* about someone else . . . I don't think that's possible.'

Suddenly she knew that it wasn't. For the brief moment Tom's lips had been on hers, she'd forgotten Jack even existed. It had just taken her a while to admit it to herself.

Tom shook his head, still furious – but sad now too. His whole frame seemed to have sagged, weary and defeated, and when he turned his head to look at her the motion was slow and strained.

'Six months ago you would have said you'd never fake a relationship. Six months ago you swore you wouldn't get pulled back into all this Jack drama – yet here we are. I don't think you know what you're capable of any more . . . And it kills me that I don't either.'

Without waiting for her to respond, he turned his back on her. Then, without another word, he picked up his canvas bag of photography equipment and left the studio.

29

Anna didn't come home on Saturday night, or on Sunday. She sent several texts asking Rachel to contact her, but Rachel didn't have the heart.

She didn't call her parents either; she couldn't face more questions about her future living arrangements, and a single kind word from her dad might see her break down entirely. It wasn't fair to distress them when there was nothing they could do about the mess her life was in. They couldn't take away her work troubles, repair her relationship with Anna or fix things with Tom. What was the point in making them worry?

Alone in the flat, Rachel spent the weekend alternately weeping, napping, picking at leftovers and trying to work out how and when she'd developed feelings for someone who, until a month ago, she'd have said was only a friend.

When she arrived at the R/C building on Monday, she was visibly subdued. She plodded across the office to her desk without greeting anyone, ignored Donna's obnoxious smirk, then slumped into her chair and started setting up her laptop.

A moment later Greg was beside her.

'Ray, you look terrible. I take it you've heard?'

'Heard what?'

'Oh God, listen – let me take you out for a coffee. We really need to talk.'

Greg had covered her left hand with his, and his eyes were round with concern.

'Greg, what on earth is going on?'

'Not here,' he muttered, looking around. Rachel's eyes followed his, and with a chill she realised that almost everyone in the office was staring at her.

Greg pulled her up out of her seat, then guided her back the way she'd just come, towards the door. Something was very wrong here, and she had no idea what.

Once they were settled at a corner table in Java Jo's, Greg waved at the barista – a young girl he seemed familiar with – and asked for two flat whites.

'Ray, you're scaring me,' he said. 'You look traumatised and I haven't even *said* anything yet. Or have you heard from him yourself?'

'Heard from who?' Rachel asked, waking up a little.

'Jack, of course, the absolute *bastard*.'

'Greg, you're not making any sense,' she said. 'And what's Jack done to upset you?'

'He's taken advantage of a good friend of mine. Someone I care about a lot.' He sighed. 'He's in Manchester. His wife summoned him back up there yesterday, apparently. She heard rumours that he'd taken up with an old flame and couldn't handle the thought of him with someone else.'

'*Rumours?* What . . . ? I don't understand.'

'Clara – that's his wife – used to work for Mountaintop, so she still has plenty of friends there. Some of your less discreet R/C colleagues appear to have shot their mouths off about you and Jack while they've been up there for meetings, or in emails and IM conversations. You'd think they'd have better things – or perhaps some actual *work* – to do, instead of speculating on who their co-workers might be sleeping with. But apparently not.'

Rachel put her head in her hands and groaned.

'It seems Clara and Jack have a very . . . volatile relationship. Very up and down. Apparently they've split up several times before because one or the other of them's cheated – but this time Clara got serious. Told him to move out because, although they both wanted kids, she didn't trust him to stick around and raise them.'

Rachel remembered Jack's claim in the pub, months ago, that he wanted children but his wife hadn't been keen. She remembered how deftly he'd implied that this time *he'd* been the one who'd been let down.

'I had a long conversation with the Mountaintop MD early this morning. According to him, when they started looking for a London agency to buy out, Jack was the one who helped the exec team research and assess the options. I'm sure there were lots of reasons why R/C ended up at the top of the list – but Jack was well aware you worked here long before the day he and the rest of them came down to announce the merger. Your photo's on the team page of the R/C website.'

Rachel groaned again, the sound ripping painfully from her throat. 'He told me the opposite – that he had no idea I worked at the agency until he saw me in that meeting.'

'I figured. I guess he also told you that he had nothing to do with you getting promoted and ending up on the same team as him. I had to do some digging to confirm this, but it seems that's not entirely true either. He made his boss aware that you two knew one another, so it was suggested to Isaac that you might be well matched. Then, without knowing it, I sealed the deal by singing your praises – saying how great you'd be at charity work.'

This was too much to take in. Fully alert now, Rachel took a large gulp of coffee and tried to digest Greg's revelations.

'I still don't understand where the rumour that Jack and I are an item has come from. We aren't. And I might as well tell you . . .' She sipped at her drink again, deciding the time had come to be honest. '. . . Tom and I aren't together either; we actually never were . . . But, under the circumstances, that's probably a story for another time.'

One of Greg's eyebrows hitched up by a clear inch. 'Okaaaaay, we're going to park the Tom thing – but only because desperate times call for desperate measures. As for why people believe you and Jack are having an affair . . . He's hardly been restrained around you, has he? He's ignored every woman in the office who ever tried it on with him – and believe me, there've been many. Every time you've been out together in a group, he's made sure to be seen leaving with you. Kemi told everyone who would listen that he walked you home after you guys took her back to her flat on the night we went to the speakeasy. There were Manchester people there that night too, and he didn't leave your side the whole evening.'

In fact, Rachel remembered, Jack had been delighted to squire her around, topping her up with drinks and intermittently pressing his hand into the small of her back. He'd introduced her to his old colleagues as his partner – a word so obviously ambiguous she couldn't believe she hadn't noticed it at the time.

'So let me guess: I'm a homewrecker,' Rachel sighed. 'The scarlet woman who's tried and failed to break up his marriage for good. But what about the "old flame" thing? Where has *that* come from? You aside, neither Jack nor I have told anyone we used to go out . . . At least, not that I know of.'

'Clara had heard your name in conversations between Jack and his old college pals, apparently – she knew you were an ex-girlfriend. Then, when you were mentioned as someone he was working with, she supposedly freaked: told her friends there was history between you. It's filtered down through them to people here in London. Unfortunately, the fact that you kept your prior relationship with him quiet . . .'

'. . . makes it seem like I've been dishonest,' Rachel finished. Greg nodded, then reached over the table to pat her arm.

'The rumour is that Clara finally lost it when Jack posted an Instagram photo of you guys from your birthday night out.'

'My birthday was weeks ago,' Rachel said, frowning.

Greg shrugged. 'He's only just put it up.'

Rachel picked up her phone and clicked into his profile – accessible to her since they'd begun following one another – and saw that it was a shot he'd taken of her and Anna just after he arrived at the piano bar. Anna had been completely cropped out.

Rachel was smiling into the camera, a glass of celebratory fizz raised in her hand. He'd captioned it: *Birthday drinks with this one @rach_ryan_1988. So happy we found each other again x*

'Oh my God. *No.*'

She was incensed – not to mention enraged with herself for turning off all her social media notifications. She'd have spotted this earlier otherwise.

Jack was devilishly clever, though, and his post was brilliantly ambiguous. If she'd seen this without knowing all the things Greg had just told her, she had to admit she'd probably have thought nothing of it. Jack was rightly confident that she wouldn't suspect his ulterior motives for tagging her.

'I'm sorry to be the one to tell you all this,' Greg said, stroking her arm again. 'But I wanted you to hear it from a friend – not fucking *Donna* or one of her feeble-minded followers.'

'I'm glad you told me. I'm grateful,' Rachel said. To her surprise, she didn't feel like crying.

She was humiliated, but a cool rage had settled in her stomach – and she found that she didn't care whether Jack's attentions to her had been real or all for show. It was probably some mixture, she thought, but it didn't matter – because it wasn't Jack she wanted. Perhaps it never had been.

And in the end, how much worse was Jack's behaviour than her own? Hadn't she misrepresented things, manipulated people and twisted the truth for her own ends?

Yes, Jack was the sort of master schemer she'd never

be – he'd gone further than she had, been prepared to dredge up long-buried pain and reignite old feelings, probably without a thought for how that might affect her. But what had Anna said on the night of Rachel's birthday? *You're messing with other people's emotions . . . And it seems not to have occurred to you that someone might get hurt*. She'd been right – and it was time Rachel admitted as much.

'Hold on a minute,' she said, snapping back into the now. 'Did you say Jack had gone to Manchester? If so, I presume he's on his way back? We have a huge meeting with Lighthouse this afternoon. Awful Olivia wants to go through the whole content plan again before signing it off.'

Greg made a disgusted face and shook his head. 'I wouldn't bank on him coming back today. Maybe not tomorrow either. Do you think you can lead the meeting if I come with you as back-up?'

Rachel hesitated, then said, 'Yes, I can. I don't need him.'

She felt the truth of her own words as Greg smiled and nodded approvingly.

'Atta girl. Now . . . are you ready to head back?'

'Ready as I'll ever be,' Rachel said.

'Shoulders back, head up and tits out,' Greg told her. 'You've done nothing to be ashamed of. And Jack's boss says he's going to set up a call with you and Florence, in her role as HR director, so they can listen to your side of all this. When that meeting happens, hold absolutely nothing in. Truth will out, Ray – and the truth shall set you free.'

Rachel spent the remainder of the morning ignoring her colleagues' whispers and furtive glances. She put her headphones in and concentrated on preparing for the Lighthouse meeting.

Predictably, Kemi had IM'd her within five minutes of her return from Java Jo's.

Kemi Percival
Is it true about you and HH? What happened to your scientist guy?

Rachel Ryan
No, it isn't true. And Tom is not a scientist <eyeroll emoji> *!!!*

After that, Rachel had set her IM status to *Do Not Disturb*.

The Lighthouse meeting was at their HQ in Bayswater, and Rachel used the journey over there to update Greg on the project's progress.

'Editorially, we've stuck to exactly the brief she gave us back in March.'

'Nothing's changed *at all*?' Greg rolled his eyes.

'She won't hear of it,' Rachel said, 'and Jack was keen for us not to rock the boat by challenging her. Isaac's clearly terrified of her as well – his priority is keeping the account because, in time, it could help us land other things. My view, if you want it, is that we're missing opportunities to reach more readers – and the charity is missing opportunities to do more good – because she won't add in content that even their own research shows they need.'

'Hmm,' Greg said with a frown. 'That seems like the easiest strategy in the short term, but when we're eighteen months in and their visitor numbers are shit it'll be our heads on the chopping block. Isaac has stars in his eyes – he isn't thinking straight. He should have brought me in on this earlier.'

When they got to the Lighthouse office a harried-looking blonde woman greeted them, then ran off to inform Olivia they'd arrived.

They were shown into a meeting room whose walls were covered in posters promoting the charity's work. Forlorn but grateful faces stared down from brightly coloured frames, flanked by statements of thanks. Rachel tried not to look at them, instead concentrating on her laptop.

She connected it up to the overhead protector and screen on the first attempt. *Screw you, Harper*, she thought.

'No Jack today?' Olivia asked, acerbic as ever, when she stalked into the room. 'Is he ill?'

'Yes, he's sick today, unfortunately,' Greg said smoothly. 'It's nice for me to be here in his place, though, Olivia – and not an unwelcome surprise for you, I hope.'

'Not at all,' Olivia said without missing a beat. 'Shall we begin?'

'Good afternoon, Olivia,' Rachel said, determined to be polite even though Olivia seemed typically indifferent to pleasantries. 'Of course. I'll take you through the content plan, though there'll be no surprises there. Then we can chat about further additions and where they should sit.'

Olivia nodded, and Rachel talked through twenty slides on the advice guides and FAQs that had been agreed and drafted, plus her proposals for organising them – all of which were based on Olivia's own sketches.

'Fine,' Olivia said, brushing something microscopic from the sleeve of her navy suit jacket. 'I have a list here of the additional items I'd also like included.' She handed a sheet of A4 to Rachel, and then another to Greg.

'Where were these ideas drawn from, out of interest?' Greg asked. He was smiling and sounded as easy-going as always, but Olivia prickled immediately.

'They're based on my experience – on my priorities for this organisation, which I've worked in for thirty years. Does that satisfy you?'

'It's not a question of whether your content satisfies *me*,' Greg said, calm and unflappable. 'Fortunately I've never experienced anything like the families and individuals up here on your walls – but I know we have access to research that tells us what people in their situations might want. I'm just trying to ensure we make the most of that. Also, it's important we consider the role of search engines in growing your visitor numbers – Google being the main priority. If people are googling for things your website doesn't offer, they'll be directed elsewhere.'

Olivia narrowed her eyes. 'I'm not interested in thinking about *search engines*,' she said, as if they were something Greg had made up. 'This is about creating an orderly, coherent resource that ticks the right boxes – gives a good account of us as an organisation.'

Greg, still smiling, was undeterred. 'Olivia, forgive me – but you're imagining the website as some sort of shop window for Lighthouse, as if it's an interactive ad for your charity. I'd encourage you to think of it as a resource – something that grows and changes to reflect what users need. Something more like a library, perhaps, where the range of books is constantly being refined and updated.'

Olivia scoffed at this and Rachel cringed at her discourtesy. 'If our website is to be a library, *I* shall decide which books it carries. *I* know which books are required.'

'I'm not sure you do,' Rachel said, so softly she wasn't sure that anyone had heard.

'Excuse me?' Olivia demanded.

'I said, I'm not sure you do,' Rachel repeated. Her voice was stronger, clearer now. 'I presented you with a number of ideas for extra content some time ago – all based on the research Lighthouse commissioned at the end of last year. You rejected them and – as an experienced content strategist – I still question that decision.'

Olivia was sneering again. 'I suppose you think reading one report qualifies you to understand what families like these' – she gestured at the walls – 'need to hear from us. You think you know better than I do because you've looked at some *data*.'

'No,' Rachel said, cool and steady despite the hammering of her heart. 'I think I know better because I come from one of those families. I *am* a bereaved sibling. And I know that what's in this content plan' – she pointed at the screen – 'and on this list of yours, barely *scratches the surface* of what someone in my shoes feels when their brother or sister is sick, or slips away forever.'

Silent tears had started spilling from Rachel's eyes. Somehow, she didn't care. Greg's mouth had fallen open, and Olivia had turned an even paler shade of grey than usual.

As Rachel registered their astonishment, she asked herself what she was doing. But no one else spoke, and suddenly she was filling the silence with words she'd held in for too long.

'My sister Lizzy had osteosarcoma,' Rachel said. 'She was first treated for it at fourteen, and we thought she was going to make a good recovery – that she'd been lucky, even. Some kids have to have amputations, as well as chemotherapy, but Lizzy got away with it. She didn't lose her leg. Life while she was in and out of hospital was . . . nothing like life had been before. I'd always been a loud, clumsy, outgoing kid – always clowning around, always the one in trouble. I had to learn to rein that in – be calm in the hospital, gentle with Lizzy at home, and quiet whenever my parents managed to snatch a bit of sleep. But there were days when I didn't *want* to rein it in. Days when I resented it. Days when I'd rather go to the park and play with my gran's dog than visit my sister in hospital. In my rational mind, I know those were natural feelings for an eleven-year-old, but even twenty years later I feel ashamed of them. She was my *sister*, and she had *cancer* – and there were some days I just couldn't be bothered to see her.'

Olivia was staring at Rachel as if she'd never seen her before – as if she'd metamorphosed into an entirely different person. Greg was wide-eyed, not even attempting to catch the tears quietly making tracks down his face.

'You don't stop being a normal kid,' Rachel continued, 'just because you have a sibling who's ill, or who dies. Your range of emotions doesn't shrink to include only grief, loneliness or anger at the universe – which are pretty much the only permitted feelings on your content plan, Olivia.'

Olivia blanched, but said nothing.

'You're not always sorry, and you're not always sad. Sometimes you're bitter, resentful . . . vindictive, even. I feel terrible about it – I've felt terrible about it for the best part of two decades – but I remember one day I saw this boy from school that Lizzy liked, snogging someone else on the bus. I told her about it, even though I knew it would hurt her – revenge for some stupid, big-sister-y thing she'd done to piss me off the day before. Something I can't even remember now. Lizzy was always cleverer, cooler and more beautiful than me,' Rachel said, a sad smile twisting her lips. 'She had the shiniest, loveliest golden-brown hair . . . I idolised her. She was the firstborn, the one who always led the way. My parents adored her. I drove her mad trying to copy her, wanting to do *everything* she did. And I was so, so angry with her for leaving me. I didn't just miss her – I was scared too. Scared that everyone would feel they'd drawn the short straw because Lizzy was gone and I was the one left behind.'

'Oh, Ray . . .' Greg blew his nose noisily, his eyes shining and sad.

Olivia sniffed, then rubbed at her own glistening cheeks. Wait – *what?*

'Please go on, Rachel,' she said, 'if there's more you want to tell us.'

'Lizzy's cancer recurred when she was seventeen,' Rachel continued. 'This time it was in her lungs, and then it spread again. It was unstoppable. But I don't think I or my parents ever really believed she was going to die until she did. I was fifteen then. Awkward. Hormonal. *Ginger*. We lived in a small town and literally everyone suddenly knew me as the gobby girl whose older sister had died of cancer. My parents were broken, so I tried to become more like Lizzy had been – I made it my mission never to add to their load, never to cause them anxiety. And when I went to uni, I found it easier just to say no when people asked if I had brothers and sisters. I got so good at pushing my feelings down I became an emotional pressure cooker – something I've only realised very recently. And when you keep too much in, you get to a point where you don't think clearly. You end up doing rash, self-destructive things . . . Things like *this*. I'm sorry. I didn't mean for this to happen. If you'll excuse me . . .'

Rachel pushed her chair back swiftly and stood up, wiping at her eyes. Greg shook his head and Olivia motioned for her to sit back down, but she was already at the door.

'I'm sorry,' Rachel said again, her voice trembling, tears coursing down her face.

She left the room, found her way out of the building and crossed the road into Kensington Gardens. After finding a secluded spot behind a bush, Rachel slumped down and let herself cry. She sat for what might have been five minutes or fifty – gasping and sobbing until her tears subsided and she could breathe normally again.

Birds were singing. Somewhere nearby there was a bunch of teenagers laughing.

She heard footsteps, the buzzing of a wasp right by her ear and snatches of more conversations than she could count. Someone was mowing the lawns too, riding up and down the park on a motorised vehicle that reminded Rachel of a toy tractor she and Lizzy had had when they were little.

The smell of freshly cut grass tickled her nose, making her want to sneeze. It reminded her she was alive.

'Forgotten something?' Greg asked, looming over Rachel. He had her laptop bag, handbag and jacket hanging from his arm.

'Oh God. Thanks,' Rachel said as he flopped down beside her on the grass. She turned to him and felt her eyes filling up again. 'Greg, I don't know what to say. I'm *so* sorry—'

He gathered her into a hug before she could get properly started with her mea culpa.

'Shut up, shut *alllll* the way up,' he said. 'Don't you *dare* apologise. You have nothing to be sorry for.'

She made a gurgling sound that was half-laugh, half-cry. 'I'm not sure Isaac or Toby would see it that way. And it's my own fault I got so worked up – let Olivia push my buttons for months. I should never have worked on the account. I should have known I couldn't handle it.'

'Why did you work on it? Tell me it wasn't just because Harper was involved.'

'No,' Rachel said. 'It wasn't that. I just couldn't see a way to avoid doing the project without telling someone – probably the whole senior management team – *why*.'

'Would that have been so bad?'

'Yes. Maybe . . . ? I don't know. Talking about Lizzy has . . . unpredictable results. Some people are amazing, like Anna was when I told her, or Will and Tom. For other people, it changes how they look at you. You become a person who's suffered – some sort of victim – or they get upset that you haven't been totally honest with them. Jack said he felt like I'd been lying to him for three years when I finally told him what had happened.'

'Colour me shocked,' Greg said, rolling his eyes. 'I'm guessing that was around the time he cheated on you?'

'Yeah.' Rachel nodded.

'Nothing like a little gaslighting,' he groaned, shaking his head. 'For the record, Jack's decision to put his pencil in some other woman's case had absolutely *nothing* to do with your reluctance to talk about losing your sister. It had everything to do with him being a common or garden shitbag.'

Rachel laughed, but she knew Greg was serious – and that he was right.

'Can I say something?' he asked. 'Something you might find hard to hear?'

'Yes,' Rachel answered. He'd earned the right, and she trusted that whatever awful thing he might come out with, it would be because he cared.

'You keep quiet about Lizzy because you don't want people to think of you as the girl whose sister died. You keep it in because it's more comfortable – because you think it's easier.

'Did you ever think that you *are* the girl whose sister

died, whether you want to be or not? Losing Lizzy is only part of who you are, and anyone worth two minutes of your time will understand that – but it's a part that's real. It's not going to disappear just because you refuse to look at it. And I don't believe denying that part of yourself is comfortable – let alone easy. If anything, I'd guess it takes a tremendous effort. One last point, if I may. You lit up in there while you were taking about her: how smart and lovely she was, how much you wanted to be like her. When you choose not to tell people you lost Lizzy, you cut yourself off from telling them you ever *had* Lizzy. And it sounds to me like she was pretty cool. And maybe more people should know that.'

Rachel cry-laughed again. 'Greg, you could charge by the hour for this.'

'You couldn't afford me. Just promise me you'll think about it.'

Rachel nodded, then pulled up her knees to rest her head on them.

After a few moments of silence, she asked, 'Am I sacked, do you think?'

'Why would you be sacked?'

'For totally fucking up the meeting. For crying in front of the client. For telling her she was wrong about everything. Professionally speaking, I think it's fair to say this has not been my finest hour.'

'Perhaps,' Greg said, 'but you seem to have gotten away with it. Olivia was quite moved by what you said in there. She wants to rejig the website plan and give you free rein to recommend what you think is best.'

'*What?*'

'She *cried*, Rachel. Actual tears. I mean, not many, but it's blown my theory that she's a real-life Cyberman ... Maybe she's just seen so much sadness over the years she's learned to shut it out, unless someone catches her off guard. She and I have also agreed that there's no need to tell anyone else at R/C exactly what inspired the rethink.'

'I don't know what to say.'

'I think the phrase you're looking for is: *Thank God for that.*'

'No,' Rachel said, leaning towards Greg as he wound his arm around her. 'It's just thank you.'

Greg sent Rachel home early with instructions to come back to work tomorrow, head held high. She didn't argue and promised that, when he called, she'd give Jack's boss honest answers to everything he asked her.

When she got back to the flat, Rachel found Anna sitting at the kitchen table with a half-drunk cup of tea and a half-eaten packet of Hobnobs in front of her. Rachel pulled up the chair opposite and flopped into it, and then they both started speaking at once.

'I'm sorry—'

'I've been an idiot—'

'I should never have—'

'—can't believe I've been so *selfish*.'

'Cup of tea?' Anna asked when they finally stopped talking over each other. She sniffed and shoved her seat away from the table.

'Go on, then,' Rachel said, rubbing at her damp eyelashes.

Anna switched the kettle on to boil, then turned to look at Rachel.

'I should never have said I felt responsible for you, or made out like I was tired of it. It's not true. I've been in hell over it, and deservedly so.'

'It's at least a *bit* true,' Rachel said. 'And I don't blame you. You're the best friend I've ever had, but I've leaned on you so much the entire time I've known you. Any normal person would have kicked me into touch years ago . . . Especially because I ignore perfectly sensible, well-intentioned advice every time it's offered.'

'Are you saying I'm not normal?'

'You're superhuman. The *best* human. You were right about the whole fake relationship debacle, and about Jack. It turns out he's the same selfish cesspit of a man he always was.'

Anna handed Rachel a mug, then sat back down – next to her now.

'If I feel in any way responsible for you, it's because I love you. It's because you're my blood. My *family*. The only family I have left – at least until I become the only woman in Will's mob who didn't go to Roedean. Caring about you and carrying some of your troubles isn't a burden to me, it's my privilege. Please, let's never fight again.'

'Never,' Rachel said, pulling her into a hug and then opening the biscuit packet.

'I'm sorry about Jack,' Anna mumbled through a mouthful of Hobnob.

'Don't be,' Rachel groaned. 'I'm far more concerned about Tom.'

'Ah.'

'We had a row and now I think he hates me, which is pretty inconvenient since it turns out I'm totally in love with him.'

'Oh *God.*'

'Yeah.'

'I can't say I'm surprised. And I'm sure he doesn't hate you.'

Rachel slumped and put her head face-down on the table, reappearing a moment later covered in crumbs. 'You *knew* I had feelings for him? How did I miss this?'

'It's been hiding in plain sight, I guess.' Anna licked a finger and wiped a smear of melted chocolate off Rachel's forehead. 'I don't know what's happened between you, but apparently he came home in a mess on Saturday, then announced he was going off to Belfast for three weeks. Some last-minute work secondment or something.'

'When does he leave?' Rachel demanded, half out of her chair before she'd completed the question. She couldn't let him go without talking to him – without telling him she was sorry . . . Without telling him how she'd (finally) realised she felt.

Anna looked up at her sadly.

'He flew out first thing this morning.'

July

~~New Year's~~ Ongoing resolutions

1. Consider exercise an act with actual benefits – both mental and physical – not merely grim punishment for pizzas consumed. ~~Have a proper go at~~ Continue letting Greg drag me to yoga. ~~provided he refrains from making snide comments re Jack/me and Jack. Give up trying to control subject matter discussed over dinner.~~
2. ~~Also re-download~~ ~~Complete Couch to 5K running app and actually do the programme.~~ Keep running at least twice per week. ~~always being careful not to perv on anyone improper.~~
3. ~~Apply for promotion at work at first chance. Move to bigger account and try to get pay rise. Avoid, if possible, further projects concerning dog biscuits, disinfectant, high-quality printer ink cartridges, 'miracle' grass seed, organic vegetables, etc.~~
    3a. Try to hang on to job (and temper) despite

idiocy of gossipy colleagues. ~~presence of evil ex-boyfriend hideousness control-freakery of certain clients.~~

~~3b. Ignore everyone who keeps banging on about how fit he Jack is.~~

~~3c. Ignore how fit he is.~~

~~3d. Ignore the fact he keeps trying to be friendly/nice/possibly quite flirtatious is openly trying to shag me.~~

~~3e. Ignore the fact he is getting divorced.~~

4. ~~DO NOT agree to further dates with Laurence. Remember: it's no use having a boyfriend who is good on paper if you do not actually fancy him.~~

4. ~~Forget that Laurence even EXISTS (despite usefulness of overblown 'romantic' gestures for creating illusion of deeply devoted boyfriend. Try not to spin any more tales re 'boyfriend' though – don't want story to get too complicated . . .) – situation is already quite complicated enough.~~

5. Try to remember Mum means well~~, even during phone calls where she implies I am doomed to a lonely life of penury because I am thirty with no partner, hardly any savings and no mortgage insists on talking about the babies/breasts of people I went to school with.~~

6. HOWEVER, do not (!!!) speak to Mum when suffering PMT. Set phone alerts for likely spells based on period tracker intel.

7. Try to address 'hardly any savings' situation. ~~(If promoted, set aside extra earnings for future~~

~~house deposit instead of spaffing it all on ASOS.) (Do not spend entire pay rise on 'cheer up' treats to distract from heinous ex-boyfriend mess.) hot new outfits for work – see 3c.)~~
8. Try to eat my five-a-day. (Remember horrid rule that potatoes do not count.)
9. ~~Start using proper night cream with retinol. SERIOUSLY.~~ Regularly apply retinol cream purchased from Boots in pursuit of perfect, Dev-style skin.
10. ~~Do the best possible job helping Tom with exhibition. Be supportive and discreet re Oscar. Avoid arguing with Tom about Jack.~~ Sort things out with Tom somehow.
11. Be a good friend (and bridesmaid) to Anna. ~~Help with wedding organisation and keep selfish, sad worries about how much I'll miss her to myself.~~
12. ~~Find a way to end fake boyfriend pretence before it causes any more problems.~~

30

As Greg had predicted, Jack didn't come into work the next day, or the day after that. Rachel knew that stories about them were still swirling around the office; every time she walked into the kitchen it went eerily quiet, and if she was a moment late to a meeting her entrance was typically accompanied by a sudden, uncomfortable hush.

Somehow, though, it had got through to a few of her colleagues that the situation was more complicated than initial reports implied – that Rachel wasn't some formerly scorned woman out to steal back her married ex-lover during a rough patch in his relationship. While she was sure he'd said nothing to break her confidence, Rachel assumed she had Greg to thank for this.

When she arrived at the office early on Thursday, she was shocked – yet not surprised – to see Jack at his desk. She looked at him without flinching, taking in his tousled chestnut hair, razor-sharp bone structure and bright, dancing eyes.

Rachel felt almost as though she were seeing him for the first time. It was as if he were empty: a beautiful shell that she knew was hollow inside. He was a luxury Easter egg.

'I guess you've heard some pretty unflattering things about me over the past few days,' Jack said, eyeing her across the divide between their workstations. No one else from their team was in yet, and he'd apparently decided to seize this opportunity to speak to Rachel alone – to try to countermand the bad press he'd received in his absence.

'I'm not sure that's how I'd describe them,' Rachel said, taking care to sound as detached as possible. '*Unflattering* implies that you've been misrepresented in some way.'

'Clara – my soon-to-be ex-wife – has gone out of her way to make trouble. To make me look like the bad guy who's responsible for our break-up. I'm sorry you got mixed up in that. I didn't intend to start pursuing you, Ryan . . . It was more that I couldn't help myself, especially as we were thrown together so much.' He stared at her through his thick, dark lashes and flashed her a rueful smile worthy of an Emmy Award winner. 'You're a special kind of irresistible, you know. You always were.'

'D'you know what I've realised, Jack?' Rachel asked. 'You're an arch-manipulator partly because you're never *entirely* dishonest. There's always at least a shred of truth in whatever story you spin – you manage to convince even yourself that what you're saying isn't a lie, that what you're doing isn't deceitful. It gives you a very light touch. You're credible even when you're deliberately distorting things, because you feel no guilt.'

'Ryan, look at me. I'm not spinning anything right now. I'm telling you honestly that, in spite of what you may have heard, my feelings for you are genuine.'

'I don't doubt that they are, on some level. But following them was also pretty useful for you, right? Stirring up a little office-romance drama allowed you to keep your hand in at home. You expected that, eventually, Clara would cave in and ask you to go back – or I'd cave in and agree to *have* you back. You were hedging your bets, and you thought you'd win either way. Your big mistake was underestimating Donna, wasn't it? She embellished too much – spread more stories full of out-and-out lies than you ideally wanted. More than you realised. Then you played the Instagram card and your wife totally flipped – but not in the way you expected. She made you go back up there to finalise the split, didn't she? Not to call off the divorce. My guess is that's the only reason you're back here.'

Rachel turned her face away from him and began typing an email.

'It isn't like that,' Jack said – but his teeth were clamped together and his eyes had darkened. He looked uncomfortable. Defensive.

'Oh, I think it is,' Rachel said coolly, still focused on her laptop.

Jack was silent for a few minutes, as if he was trying to regroup – reviewing the situation before he chose his next tack.

The moment she sensed he was ready to launch a new charm offensive she said, 'Do you want to know the one thing that I'll never forgive you for? It isn't that you cheated on me, or tried to convince me it was somehow my own fault. It isn't that you showed up here knowing I worked for the agency, then claimed it was all a big surprise. It's not that you had a hand in us being put on the same team. It's not even that you came so close to making me fall for you again. What I will never forgive you for is lying to me about Lighthouse. I remember you promising me that you didn't "engineer" the situation – that you didn't ask for us to be put on the account, or play any part in how Isaac decided to staff it. But that's not true, is it? Something felt weird about that first day Olivia came in, and it wasn't just that she was early. You were uneasy – and when you first went over to speak with her, you sent me off to fetch Isaac and Greg. I remember seeing you with her and thinking, *How* has he managed to get her chatting so easily? She'd barely said two words to me. Then, when Greg and I met her on Monday, she asked after you. That struck me as pretty odd since she's such a cold fish. I spoke to your boss that evening, you know.'

Jack's lips fell apart at this, and his green eyes flickered with reluctant understanding.

'I told him how things had been between us since January – about how you'd won my trust by being there for me while we worked on a project I found challenging. He let slip that you'd been key to even getting a pitching slot for Lighthouse, not to mention winning the account; something about a family connection. And it fell into place then. My guess is, she's your aunt.'

Jack clenched his jaw, unwittingly emphasising its resemblance to Olivia Mason's. 'Yes, she's my father's sister. I helped to bring her in, but we both wanted to keep things professional – not difficult as she's hardly the touchy-feely type. I didn't know for sure that I – *we* – would end up on the project if we won the pitch, but of course there was a good chance.'

'Congratulations, Jack,' Rachel said, nodding at him in approval that was half-sarcastic, half-sincere. 'That might be the first completely honest thing you've said to me in more than six months.'

Jack's face, usually so inscrutable, betrayed his displeasure. He looked defeated, and Rachel couldn't find it in herself to be sorry.

'Morning, Jack – I didn't know you were coming back today. Morning, *Rachel*,' Donna said, from behind Rachel's chair. 'Isaac's just called the main switch. He's asked you to pop around the corner to Java Jo's, Jack. Soon as you can.'

Jack's eyebrows floated further up into his forehead than Rachel had ever seen them go before. He breathed a loud, exasperated sigh, pushed his chair back with a clatter and stamped away.

'So,' Donna hissed at Rachel once the office door had swung shut, 'not content with trying to get your claws in while he and his wife were on a break, you've gone and got him sacked.'

She looked almost deranged, her eyes tight with contempt.

'I've no idea what Isaac's going to say to him,' Rachel informed her. 'But everything I've told him and Jack's boss is true – and therefore nowhere near as exciting as the version of events you've been sharing with anyone who'll listen. What did I ever *do* to you, Donna? Did I tread on your foot at some point while we were queuing for the printer? Did I accidentally steal your biro during a meeting? Or do you just hate anyone who seems a little less miserable than you are? I've actually had a stupendously shit year so far. But unlike you, I don't delight in making other people feel crap. I could never feel better for making someone else's situation worse. If Jack ends up leaving, I want you to know, you had a far greater hand in losing him his job than I did. In fact – you're going to *love* this – your relentless shit-stirring has actually helped me out enormously. So thanks, Donna. You go and have yourself a lovely day.'

With that, Rachel swung her chair around and resumed work.

It was over a fortnight now since Tom had gone to Belfast, and Rachel had only heard from him once. She'd messaged him to apologise for their fight after the photo shoot and said there was more she wanted to tell him, if he was prepared to listen.

He wasn't.

Tom: *I can't get into this right now . . . Can we talk when I get back?*

She'd sent two texts after that – casual 'how are you getting on' messages that weren't really casual at all. He hadn't responded, which was agonising. He was due back in London in less than a week, and Rachel had no idea what happened then. Giving her the silent treatment would be pretty difficult for Tom if they were sitting opposite one another at the Hope – so would he go out of his way to avoid seeing her, never mind speaking to her, once he was home?

The exhibition press event was scheduled for the night of his return, and Rachel didn't want to ruin it for him by turning up with things still unresolved. She was planning to stay away, but the thought of missing it made her feel sick. Missing *Tom* was making her feel sick.

Since they'd first met four years ago, they'd never gone so long without seeing or speaking to one another. Rachel hadn't realised how much she relied on his calm, steady presence in her life – how much she looked forward to Friday evenings, or how much she valued her certainty that, if she needed him, he'd find a way to be there for her.

She hadn't appreciated how much she enjoyed being with him either – how interesting and clever he was, or how well he understood her, how many times a week she messaged him just to share things she knew they'd both find funny.

Rachel had no idea whether she'd ever been more to Tom than a friend, but she was increasingly certain that – even if he'd harboured deeper feelings at one stage – she'd screwed things up beyond redemption.

As her dad lugged a box full of books towards the flat door, he groaned aloud, 'Where's that nice tall friend of yours with the glasses, Rachel? This is a young man's job.'

'He's in Belfast, Dad. Away for work.'

'You'll have to make do with me, Mr Ryan,' Will put in as he heaved Rachel's chest of drawers along the corridor. 'Though you can rest assured I will berate Tom for not being here for this – as soon as I can.'

'Ach, call me Paddy. *Mr* makes me feel ancient.'

'How much more stuff is there?' Anna called from outside.

'Just the wardrobe,' Rachel yelled.

'Cool, there's a space in the van for it. We're good.'

Ten minutes later, Rachel's room in the Stroud Green flat was bare. There were dark patches of paint on the walls – rectangles of deeper colour where she'd had furniture or hung pictures. In the place where her bed had been, the carpet was an inch deep in dust.

'Rachel Margaret Ryan, that's a *disgrace*,' her mum had said when they took the bed apart to put it in the van. Rachel couldn't disagree.

As she stared around the home she was leaving, Rachel felt as choked with emotion as she'd thought she would. But blended with the pain of going away was the knowledge that this was necessary; this was *right*. Anna and Will needed to move on, and so did she. It was sort of like taking a plaster cast off a long-broken leg, Rachel thought. The skin that had sat beneath it might be pale and the muscles a little withered – but the cast had done its job. The bones it had protected were mended now, and it was time to put them to use again.

Much to her mother's delight, Rachel was moving in with Conor, a second cousin of hers who was coming over from Dublin to take a job at a North London architectural firm. They were the same age, and as children they'd spent many summer holidays together – often ending up in scrapes that Lizzy had had to get them out of. Rachel hadn't seen Conor in person since Christmas a couple of years ago, but they'd stayed in touch online and she had no doubt they'd rub along well as housemates.

Their new place was near Archway, just a few minutes' bus ride from Anna's flat. Rachel's dad drove the van over there, followed by Anna and Will in his Mini, the back seat of which was packed with overstuffed bags of clothes and shoes.

Once both vehicles had been unloaded, Will suggested that he and Anna give Rachel and her parents a little time to start unpacking and get her settled in. Rachel and Anna's goodbye was a strange, dramatic spectacle. They both sobbed, clinging to one another as though one of them were about to go to war. As it was, they were meeting up at a pub near Rachel's new flat for dinner in roughly three hours' time.

'*Tea*,' Rachel's mum said, unboxing the new kettle Rachel had bought and fishing a plastic carton of milk from her gigantic tote bag. Once she, her husband and daughter were settled on the landlord's sofa with mugs in their hands, she said, 'I'm proud of you, Rachel. And while you think I'm a daft old bat who understands nothing, I know how hard today's been for you. The only reason I ever worried about this happening was because I was scared you might not cope with it. But now I can see that you're going to.'

'I don't think you're a daft old bat,' Rachel said. 'Just a bit . . . *Mrs Bennet* about me still being single. But who knows, maybe I'll find my Mr Darcy at Anna and Will's wedding. Weddings are supposed to be good for meeting people, aren't they?'

'Mrs Bennet wasn't the eejit she's made out to be, you know – she had five daughters and no way to take care of them without marrying them off. Sorting them out with husbands wasn't needless meddling, it was responsible parenting. And as for *you* finding a man . . . I don't want you coupled up because I'm keen on the idea of a new hat, or because I think the only valid life choices for a woman are marriage and motherhood. I'm fifty-nine, not a hundred. You're strong and successful, Rachel. I tell everyone how brilliant you are. Mrs O'Shea's sick of hearing about London and advertising and your arty exhibition . . . She talks about nothing but how knackered she is now she's doing two days of free childcare every week for her Helen. But I don't want you to be *alone*, Rachel. When me and your dad are gone, I worry about who you'll have . . .'

Bloody hell. Jean Ryan was crying.

'It wasn't supposed to be this way,' she said. 'You weren't meant to be an only child, and I'm so sorry you are.'

'Oh, Mum,' Rachel murmured, pulling her closer. She was tiny and slight – only a little taller than Anna. Not for the first time, Rachel marvelled that a person this small had given birth to her.

'It's okay, Mum. *I'm* okay. We all miss her. And I promise you, I'm not going to end up alone and miserable.'

'Sure you won't,' Rachel's dad said. 'Not when you've inherited my stunning good looks. Now come on, the pair of you, and stop your crying. We need to rebuild Rachel's bed – and based on the amount of nuts and bolts that came out of it this morning, we'd better get started if she's going to want any sleep before next Thursday.'

Rachel arrived at the Hope on Friday night to find Anna and Will fighting over what remained of a packet of cheese and onion crisps.

'Er. What the heck are you doing here?' Anna asked her, bug-eyed.

'Charming,' Rachel said, throwing herself into a vacant chair and slinging her bags under the table.

'I mean it,' Anna said fiercely. 'Why aren't you on your way to the exhibition press night? You worked on it for months – your words are on display in a trendy gallery that, in about an hour's time, is going to be stuffed full of journalists and celebrities. Not to mention shitloads of free snacks and drinks.'

'I can't go, Anna. You know why. We talked about this.'

Will took a gulp of Guinness – he'd developed a taste for it since Conor had started hanging out with them – then shook his head. 'Have you and Tom still not sorted things?' he asked. 'Someone needs to bang your bloody heads together.'

'What. Are. You. *Talking. About?*' Anna demanded. Rachel had sworn her to secrecy about the fight she'd had with Tom, and Anna hadn't breathed a word.

'The fact that he loves her and, apparently, she's now realised she loves him. Facts that nobody – apart from me, now – has actually stated out loud.'

'How long have you known about this? And why in *holy hell* didn't you tell me?' Anna yelled.

'Not my secret to tell,' Will said with a shrug. 'And . . . I dunno. A couple of years, maybe? Three years tops.'

Anna's jaw had dropped. Rachel was staring, not quite able to believe she was hearing this.

'I mean, he's never actually made a *confession* of love or anything,' Will was saying. 'I just know.'

'This gets better and better,' Anna said, looking at Will

in a way that made Rachel fear for his safety. 'How do you "just know"?'

Will rolled his eyes at her. Under the circumstances, Rachel considered this semi-suicidal.

'I've known him since we were twelve, Anna. He's my brother from another mother. And look at the evidence: when was the last time he had a proper girlfriend? How much has he hated everyone Rachel's ever dated? How close did he come to laying one on Loser Laurence the night he turned up in here? He was prepared to fake a relationship for a night so she could save face. He helped to organise her birthday party. And he *always* remembers to buy her prawn cocktail crisps.'

It was in rare moments like this that Rachel understood how Will had ended up becoming a lawyer.

'I mean, Tom's my best mate and everything – but I think the question here is less how did I know than how the hell did you girls *not* know?'

This was too much for Anna and she poked him in the ribs. He yelped and laughed, 'Calm down, Scrappy-Doo. You don't get to be right about everything. Just, like, ninety per cent of things.'

'Are you sure about this, Will?' Rachel asked. 'I've thought he might be seeing someone. There was . . . well. There was what seemed like a mystery date, plus this rose-smelling stuff in your bathroom.'

'Rach, I've never been surer,' Will said. 'The only dates he's been on lately are with his rather unexpected little brother . . . Trips to Camden Market and other such places. You met him, didn't you? Oscar? Tom told me he vommed on you, as well as on the sitting room rug. And if you mean that glass jar of gubbins on the window ledge, it was Alice's – my sister's. She left it last time she stayed on the futon after a weekend of West End shopping. Come on Rach,' Will went on. 'He looks at you like . . .'

Like you're the sun coming up . . .

In a flash, Rachel remembered Jack's words, spoken with scorn on the night of her birthday. She finally believed them. She just hoped they hadn't come back to her too late.

'Okay, but what do I *do*?' Rachel said, not waiting for Will to finish. She already knew the answer.

'You get your arse to Soho, of course!' Anna screeched, confirming it. '*NOW!* WHY AREN'T YOU MOVING ALREADY?'

Rachel nodded, then jumped up and ran for the door.

It was only when Rachel arrived at the gallery on Greek Street that she realised she was hideously underdressed. The event wasn't black-tie or anything, but everywhere she looked there were women in tiny designer dresses and men in jeans that probably cost a week's rent. There were actual *bouncers* on the door.

Bollocks. Her tea-dress-and-Doc-Martens combo was fine for the office, but entirely inappropriate for cool events full of photographers, journalists and famous people. Also, the majority of her make-up had melted off on the Tube and her hair had gone past the textured, sexy stage, crossing the border into 'eighties tribute act' territory.

Dev – looking sharp as ever in a grey double-breasted suit – raised his eyebrows at her as one of the bouncers got ready to stop her from going in. 'She's okay, Mike. I *think* . . .'

His eyes followed her as she pushed into the first room of the exhibition. Tom's photographs, blown up in black and white and carefully hung on the clean walls, sat next to her biographies of each participant. The quotations she'd been asked to pull out were printed larger and dotted around the walls and up the stairs. They brought everything together, telling the story of the show and what it meant in just the way she'd hoped.

The photographs were incredible. As Rachel wandered through the room, then up to the next floor, she briefly forgot she was looking for Tom; she was transfixed by what he – *they* – had put together, and she was glad she wasn't missing it.

Here was Zack, vivacious and smiling in his YSL suit. Here was an MP whose campaign to end the use of airbrushed images in advertising for children had recently made the news. Here was a body positivity campaigner: an Instagram influencer whose photographs of her tummy rolls, cellulite and body hair had garnered her more than a million followers.

And here was Jessica: slender, pretty and wide-eyed in the childlike pose Rachel remembered from the shoot. It was odd, seeing her and feeling unmoved by envy or anger – but where bitterness used to be, Rachel found something approaching understanding. Jessica was just a person, not the femme fatale of Rachel's worst imaginings, nor a standard she had to be measured against. She smiled.

By the time she reached the third floor, she'd begun

sweating. What was she going to say when she saw Tom? What was *he* going to say when she found the words to tell him how she felt?

And where the hell *was* he?

She went all the way up to the fifth floor and still couldn't find him. Rachel felt herself starting to panic. This wasn't the sort of place where he could have slunk past without her seeing him. Perhaps *he'd* decided not to come to the press night in case she turned up. Maybe he was missing his own exhibition simply for the sake of avoiding her . . . In which case, it seemed to Rachel, there was surely no chance of convincing him they could be happy together.

Despair welled in Rachel's stomach and pushed up into her throat, forming a thick lump that she couldn't swallow away. She wandered down the gallery's spiralling staircases, willing herself not to cry.

She was tired of crying. She wondered how, after the past few weeks, she could possibly have any tears left.

When she reached the ground floor, her last hope of finding Tom was extinguished. He wasn't here. Feeling bereft, she left the gallery and stood on the pavement outside.

Press night guests were wafting in and out, some leaving the event for cigarette breaks, others clustering near the entrance to pose for pictures. Rachel tore her eyes away from an influencer couple hugging and kissing for a tabloid paparazzo. That was it, she decided. She couldn't take any more.

She turned in the direction of Leicester Square station, then stopped before she took a single step. Tom was standing in front of her, dressed in his usual jeans, trainers and well-worn T-shirt. And he was carrying a huge, thin, rectangular thing. A last-minute addition for the exhibition? Maybe he'd had some printing emergency, and that was why he wasn't all dressed up.

Rachel's heart swelled at the sight of him – grew so big inside her chest she was scared it might crush her lungs. How could she ever have thought he was just her friend?

His grey-blue eyes were wide and wary.

'Are you leaving?' he asked.

'I was. You weren't there,' Rachel said. 'I'm glad I saw the show – it's brilliant. You should be proud of it. *I'm* proud of it. But . . . I didn't come to look at the photographs. I came to see you.'

'You did?'

'Yes. I came to see you because . . . because I've been too *stupid* to see you. *So* stupid, for so bloody long.'

Her eyes had filled with tears and her voice was wobbling in her throat. But if she didn't say this now, she'd never forgive herself.

'I love you, and not just as a friend. I think that, in some quiet corner of my head – no, my *heart* – you've been more than a friend to me for a really long time. I just couldn't let myself admit it. I'd got so good at shoving my feelings away that I pushed this away too. Maybe I was scared – maybe I thought I'd lose you forever if you didn't feel the same. But I can't believe how blind I've been.'

Rachel looked at Tom, her eyes travelling from his blondish curls to his tightly folded arms, then back up to those thousand-coloured eyes and NHS-style specs. Her heart flip-flopped in her chest as she suddenly understood.

'It's like Clark Kent and Superman,' she said.

Tom made a quizzical face.

'They can't occupy the same space,' Rachel went on. 'And I think . . . you being such an important friend to me, and me being in love with you – I couldn't reconcile those things. Clark and Superman are never seen in a room together, are they?' she said. 'And yet it turns out . . .'

Tears spilled from her eyes as she said it out loud: 'It turns out that they are, and always have been, one and the same person.'

'Are you trying to tell me I'm your Superman?' Tom asked. But he was smiling. Soft and gentle and smiling, with his kind eyes and his crooked smile and his dimpled bottom lip that, suddenly, *powerfully*, she wanted to kiss.

'I think that's stretching the metaphor a bit far, but I suppose so,' Rachel said.

'What about Jack?'

'Ugh. Who? From the moment you fake-kissed me on my birthday, Jack may as well have disappeared . . . He's back in Manchester now, thank God. For reasons I'll bore you with another time, the senior management at R/C – and Mountaintop – thought it better that he return to his old job.'

'I didn't fake-kiss you,' Tom said. Bright-pink blotches had appeared on his cheeks. 'I kissed you because I was so incredibly exhausted with the effort of *not* kissing you. But the situation was all wrong, and I thought *you* were fake-kissing me.'

'I wasn't,' Rachel said, shaking her head. 'There was

nothing fake about me trying to get you in a headlock after you stepped away from me . . . Much to my own surprise, I just really, *really* wanted to snog you.'

Tom laughed and Rachel moved forward a couple of paces.

'Do you still want to?' he asked, raising an eyebrow.

She took his hand in hers and looked up at him with an answering grin. '*Obviously.*'

Then his arms were around her and they were crushed together, but his lips were so gentle on hers that it made her want to weep. She kissed him harder, pushing his mouth open with her lips.

She loved him, she loved him, she loved him. Of *course* she did.

'You're going to give me a heart attack and I haven't even said my bit yet,' Tom whispered when they broke apart. His head was still bent down, his forehead resting on hers.

'Your bit?'

'Yes. *My* bit. I went to the Hope tonight, to find you. I figured you wouldn't come here after I'd ignored you for three weeks – that I needed to make some sort of . . . *gesture*. To apologise for freezing you out when you'd tried to open up to me. Anna looked like she might actually murder me when she said they'd sent you here.'

Rachel laughed, then asked, 'What sort of gesture?'

Tom bent down to pick up the huge rectangular thing that he'd rested against the wall of the building they were next to. He pulled off the tape that was holding its brown paper wrapping in place, then turned it to face her.

It was a photograph of her.

'It's one of the test shots I did from the shoot with Zack,' Tom explained. 'You refused to look at them, remember? This one is my favourite . . . You're so beautiful in it, because you look natural, real . . . Like who you really are.'

In the A3 image, her big brown eyes were gleeful and alive – full of wit, as if she was about to make a joke. Her skin was smooth and creamy, and her lips were parted in a half-smile. Her hair tumbled over one shoulder, an unruly mass of shining auburn waves.

'I don't know what to say,' Rachel said.

Tom grinned. 'Say I'm your Superman again.'

'Oh, shut up,' Rachel said, shoving him, then raised herself onto her tiptoes to smile up at his face.

'Gladly,' he whispered, and bent down to kiss her again.

August

~~New Year's~~ Ongoing resolutions

1. Consider exercise an act with actual benefits – both mental and physical – not merely grim punishment for pizzas consumed. ~~Have a proper go at~~ Continue letting Greg drag me to yoga. ~~provided he refrains from making snide comments re Jack/me and Jack. Give up trying to control subject matter discussed over dinner.~~
2. ~~Also re-download Complete Couch to 5K running app and actually do the programme.~~ Keep running at least twice per week, sometimes with hot boyfriend who it's totally fine to ogle. ~~= always being careful not to perv on anyone improper.~~
3. ~~Apply for promotion at work at first chance. Move to bigger account and try to get pay rise. Avoid, if possible, further projects concerning dog biscuits, disinfectant, high-quality printer ink cartridges, 'miracle' grass seed, organic vegetables, etc.~~

3~~a.~~ Try to enjoy job without stressing about it so much. ~~(and temper) despite idiocy of gossipy colleagues. presence of evil ex-boyfriend hideousness control-freakery of certain clients.~~

~~3b. Ignore everyone who keeps banging on about how fit he Jack is.~~

~~3c. Ignore how fit he is.~~

~~3d. Ignore the fact he keeps trying to be friendly/nice/possibly quite flirtatious is openly trying to shag me.~~

~~3e. Ignore the fact he is getting divorced.~~

~~4. DO NOT agree to further dates with Laurence. Remember: it's no use having a boyfriend who is good on paper if you do not actually fancy him.~~

~~4. Forget that Laurence even EXISTS (despite usefulness of overblown 'romantic' gestures for creating illusion of deeply devoted boyfriend. Try not to spin any more tales re 'boyfriend' though – don't want story to get too complicated . . .) – situation is already quite complicated enough.~~

5. Try to remember Mum means well – she just wants me to be happy~~, even during phone calls where she implies I am doomed to a lonely life of penury because I am thirty with no partner, hardly any savings and no mortgage insists on talking about the babies/breasts of people I went to school with.~~

6. HOWEVER, do not (!!!) speak to Mum when suffering PMT. Set phone alerts for likely spells based on period tracker intel.

7. Try to address 'hardly any savings' situation. ~~(If promoted, set aside extra earnings for future house deposit instead of spaffing it all on ASOS.) (Do not spend entire pay rise on 'cheer up' treats to distract from heinous ex-boyfriend mess.) hot new outfits for work – see 3c.)~~
8. Try to eat my five-a-day. (Remember horrid rule that potatoes do not count.)
9. ~~Start using proper night cream with retinol. SERIOUSLY.~~ Regularly apply retinol cream purchased from Boots in pursuit of perfect, Dev-style skin.
10. ~~Do the best possible job helping Tom with exhibition. Be supportive and discreet re Oscar. Avoid arguing with Tom about Jack. Sort things out with Tom somehow.~~ Kiss Tom as often as is humanly possible.
11. Be a good friend (and bridesmaid) to Anna. ~~Help with wedding organisation and keep selfish, sad worries about how much I'll miss her to myself.~~
12. ~~Find a way to end fake boyfriend pretence before it causes any more problems.~~

Epilogue

It was a beautiful wedding. Will's grandfather's estate was lush, gorgeous and green in the late-August sunshine. Champagne had been flowing endlessly for hours, and the band was playing what Will had charmingly termed 'the erection section': a series of romantic songs for slow-dancing.

Anna and Will were happier than Rachel had ever seen them. Anna was glowing: a tiny, almost fluorescent ball of joy ricocheting around the gardens and kissing everyone she met. Will was as laid-back as ever, but happiness seemed to be seeping out of him – rolling off him in gentle waves.

'It's been a lovely day,' Rachel said into Tom's shoulder.

'It has,' he said, pulling her closer as they danced. 'And *you* are lovely too. I'll have to make sure Oscar never sees you in this dress – he'd probably offer to duel me in the street for you. He still isn't over his crush.'

'Ah, this old thing?' Rachel shrugged, gesturing at the green chiffon shift that – even she had to admit – was giving her major Joan Holloway vibes. 'I'm lucky Anna picked me such a stunning outfit. You should have seen me in the peach death-shroud I almost ended up with . . . You'd have had nightmares for a week.'

'Like you did with *The Blair Witch Project*?' he snickered.

'I think that might have been a fortnight, actually.'

Tom looked stupidly handsome in his navy-blue suit. His eyes were more bright and beautiful than ever – almost flamboyantly so, since he'd started wearing his new contacts.

He caught her peering at him. 'Are you checking me out?'

'Absolutely.'

'Superman mode's working for me, then?' He pointed at his lack of spectacles and smiled wolfishly.

'I kind of miss your glasses, actually. I always thought they were cute.'

'Come on, pick a side: sexy or specs-y?'

He whirled her around the parquet floor of the marquee. The band had moved on to a Motown set and was playing Marvin Gaye's 'Let's Get It On'.

'Am I the glasses-wearing pal you call in a jam,' Tom asked, 'or the planet-saving hottie you're madly in love with? You have to decide.'

'The thing is . . .' Rachel replied, reaching up to kiss his face. She would *never* get tired of kissing this face.

'The thing is that, with you, I really don't.'

Acknowledgements

I always hoped that one day I'd get to write a list of people I'd like to thank at the end of my first published novel. Now I have the opportunity, of course, I'm bricking it. What if I do it all wrong?

I will wade in and begin, though, by thanking the whole Embla team. Endless gratitude to everyone who has worked with me on *Rachel Ryan's Resolutions*, especially my super-smart and talented editor Jane Snelgrove. You've made my first experience of authoring so enjoyable and exciting, and I couldn't have asked for better support.

To Kate Hordern, my unflappable agent: thank you for keeping your head while all about you (i.e. me) were losing theirs. Your experience and insight have been invaluable, as was your insistence that this book COULD be finished despite a global pandemic, a national lockdown and the horrors of home schooling. Your enthusiasm for this story powered me through many early mornings and late nights of writing. Were it not for your regular emails demanding more of the manuscript, I'm not entirely convinced I'd have finished it.

Thanks to Tom Bromley, my tutor at the Faber Academy, and to all of my classmates. You were the first people I allowed to read my ramblings after around 15 years of procrastination, and your kind and thoughtful comments meant the world to me.

I'm lucky enough to have a gaggle of wonderful friends who've always believed I could do this. Eleanor, Emily, Hayley, Vanessa, Jess, Darren and Charlee – I love and thank you all.

To my first draft reader and dear pal, Sarah: thank you for your time, your encouragement and for always asking 'But what happens NEXT?!' when I sent you bits of this book via email. Your next Blue WKD is on me.

To Liz, my BFF: thank you for always being there for me, for having faith in me and for being proud of me. Without our friendship, there would be no Rachel and Anna. Without our shared London flat (which I seem to recall we lost the security deposit on?) these two best friends would never have had a home. Here's to many more Wagamama lunches, skincare obsessions and big weekenders.

Thank you to my parents, my sister, my extended family and my in-laws. Your unshakable certainty that I would one day write a novel convinced even me in the end. You are all incredible, and I couldn't have done it without you.

To my beautiful children: you amaze me in countless ways every day. I hope that when you're old enough to read it, this story doesn't embarrass you too much. I love and treasure you both.

And Dan. Eternal blessings on you for putting up with me over the past 18 years. I'm sure that when we met on that Tube platform, you'd never have thought you'd end up married to me – let alone jointly responsible for a houseful of dependent humans and animals. This just goes to show how careful you have to be when chatting up random women on public transport. Thank you for never doubting me, for listening to me rant on about my characters and their fictional world without complaint and for letting me soak up your sunny calm whenever I'm stressed. You're the best partner I ever could have wished for. Thank you for being on our team. This book simply wouldn't exist without you – and I can't imagine how I would either.

About Laura Starkey

Laura was born in Warwickshire in 1982. She studied English & Related Literature at the University of York, then spent several years as a secondary school teacher before going on to work as a digital copywriter, editor and content designer. Despite her disbelief in real life 'meet cutes', Laura first encountered her husband on a Tube platform in London, in a plot twist worthy of any romcom (and she has read and watched a lot). She now lives in a small village in the West Midlands with her family, her book collection and a mini menagerie of pets. Laura is a graduate of the Faber Academy. *Rachel Ryan's Resolutions* is her first novel.

About Embla Books

Embla Books is a digital-first publisher of standout commercial adult fiction. Passionate about storytelling, the team at Embla publish books that will make you 'laugh, love, look over your shoulder and lose sleep'. Launched by Bonnier Books UK in 2021, the imprint is named after the first woman from the creation myth in Norse mythology, who was carved by the gods from a tree trunk found on the seashore – an image of the kind of creative work and crafting that writers do, and a symbol of how stories shape our lives.

Find out about some of our other books and stay in touch:

Twitter, Facebook, Instagram: @emblabooks
Newsletter: https://bit.ly/emblanewsletter

Milton Keynes UK
Ingram Content Group UK Ltd.
UKHW031311090824
1219UKWH00022B/43